A SILENCE AT ARLINGTON

A Novel of the Civil War

By

Richard L. Busenkell

To [redacted],
Many happy hours reading about
Abraham Lincoln, Robert E. Lee,
and all the fascinating characters
of the early Civil War. But--
beware of the killer from the past!!

Rick Busenkell
Oct. 17, 2004

This book is a work of fiction. Aside from the historical characters, any resemblance to actual persons, living or dead, is coincidental.

ISBN: 1-4107-8873-3 (e-book)
ISBN: 1-4107-8874-1 (Paperback)
ISBN: 1-4107-8875-X (Dust Jacket)

Libarary of Congres Control Number: 2003096457

This book is printed on acid free paper.

Printed in the United States of America
Bloomington, IN

Cover photograph by the author.

1stBooks - rev. 11/14/03

BOOKS BY RICHARD L. BUSENKELL

Fiction

Wolf Valley
A Silence At Arlington

Non-fiction

BMW Since 1945
Jaguar Since 1945
Pontiac Since 1945
These Hallowed Grounds
(with Deborah L. Busenkell)

DEDICATION

To my mother, Mary Kathleen Lloyd Busenkell, who loved history and instilled a deep appreciation of it in me.
In 1820, her ancestors helped build a small church in southeastern Pennsylvania in what is now part of the Hopewell Village National Historic Park. By special permission of the National Park Service, for which I am profoundly grateful, she now lies at rest among her ancestors in the churchyard of that church.

To my father, Capt. Charles Clement Busenkell, United States Navy, who also loved history and made some of it himself with his services to his country. He now lies amid thousands of his fellow officers of the United States military in Arlington National Cemetery.

ACKNOWLEDGMENTS

Barbara Bahney and Susie Fisher of the Willard Intercontinental Hotel in Washington, the modern successor to Willard's, the greatest and most famous hotel in Washington's history; Karen Byrne, Historian of Arlington House, National Park Service, and Colleen Curry, Curator of Arlington House, National Park Service, for their information concerning the Arlington estate, Arlington House, and the other Lee family-owned estates; Richard Hanks of the Smiley Library of Redlands, California, the best repository of information about Abraham Lincoln west of the Mississippi River; Jim Mackay of The Lyceum, Alexandria's History Museum, for his information concerning the city of Alexandria and the Orange & Alexandria Railroad; Maj. Gen. George Mayo, Jr., USA (Ret.), for his detailed knowledge of Christ Church in Alexandria; Don Sutton, for his knowledge of military formations; Donald L. Wilson of the Prince William Public Library System in Virginia, who was a fountain of information about the area around Manasses and the Manasses Gap Railroad; and my many friends who have encouraged me to write this book.

My thanks to all of you. This book could never have happened without the generous assistance and immense historical knowledge you supplied about specialized areas in this novel.

FOREWORD

A Silence At Arlington is set in the opening days of the Civil War, covering the period from April 10 to April 23, 1861. In this short span of two weeks, just five weeks after Abraham Lincoln was inaugurated as the 16th President of the United States, occurred a series of tumultuous events which rocked the United States and the new self-proclaimed Confederacy, which had adopted a provisional constitution at Montgomery, Alabama, on February 8. The tense confrontation between the Union and the seven seceded states of the Confederacy came to a flash point at Fort Sumter, a Federal fort in Charleston harbor, which Confederate artillery started bombarding on the morning of April 12. By this action Lincoln, who had stated emphatically in his inaugural address that the Union would not initiate war, considered that the Confederacy had done so. The long-dreaded Civil War began.

The fate of Fort Sumter was decided in just two days. Running low on food and ammunition, it surrendered on April 14, to wild jubilation in the South, anger and frustration in the North. How would Lincoln respond? He delivered his answer the following day, April 15: a call for 75,000 volunteers to bolster and enormously expand the U.S. Army. Such a huge army could have only one purpose: to invade the South and conquer the Confederacy by military force.

Lincoln's action had huge repercussions in the South. Led by influential Virginia, four previously-loyal states of the "Upper South"—Virginia, North Carolina, Tennessee, and Arkansas—made plans to secede from the Union and join the Confederacy. Only strong military pressure prevented three other states—Missouri, Kentucky, even Maryland—from joining them.

A Silence At Arlington is set amid the actual swirl of historical events which accompanied the onset of the Civil War. It is centered around an astonishing but historical fact which seems little known to anyone today except deep-dyed Civil War buffs: President Lincoln, acting through a trusted but unofficial adviser, offered field command of the huge new Federal army to Robert E. Lee. An officer with a distinguished 30-year career in the army, including a three-year stint as Superintendent of the United States Military Academy at West Point, the 53-year-old Lee was socially prominent but still only a colonel; he was offered the command by Lincoln because he was recommended for the position by Major General Winfield Scott, the heroic but aging General-in-chief who was the nation's greatest military figure since George Washington. (The position of "General-in-chief" has long vanished from American military ranks, at least in name; it was somewhat analogous to today's Chairman of the Joint Chiefs of Staff.) Scott had been the commanding general of the U.S. Army in the Mexican War, and Lee was his chief of artillery there. Scott developed a lasting appreciation of Lee's abilities, and glowingly recommended Lee to Lincoln for field command of the Union army. He even went so far as to say to the president that Lee was "the finest officer I have ever seen in the field with troops," and that Lee "would be worth 50,000 troops to the Union cause." Though he had never met Lee, Lincoln could not ignore such a recommendation from the nation's highest and most respected military figure, a man who had twice been voted a gold medal by Congress.

The public mind today naturally associates Robert E. Lee with the Confederacy. Indeed, he became the very symbol of the Confederacy, overshadowing its president, Jefferson Davis. That he was once offered command of the *Union* army—by Abraham Lincoln, no less, acting through an intermediary—almost seems impossible. Yet it is true. It has been recounted any number of times in reputable books; Lee himself confirmed it after the war in 1868; the intermediary, Francis Preston Blair, and his son, Montgomery Blair, later confirmed it; and it was confirmed by the only person who was present at the meeting between Scott and Lee on April 18, 1861, immediately after Lee met with Blair. The news inevitably leaked out, as the novel states; when Lee arrived in Richmond in the evening of April 22, he was wildly cheered by a large crowd when he stepped out on the balcony of his hotel room, because even the people of Richmond knew by then that he had been offered command of the Union Army and had turned it down. There is even a metal sign today, on the lawn in front of Blair House in Washington, which recounts this fact.

A Silence At Arlington is built around that offer, its refusal and its consequences.

This novel combines the stories of Lincoln and Lee, the two greatest figures of the Civil War, yet remains true to the historical record by never having them meet. To my knowledge, no other novel ever written has focused on this fascinating offer to Lee, nor has any novel ever successfully combined Lincoln and Lee, as major historical characters, into the same story.

There are a number of historical locales connected with the Civil War in this novel: the Kansas Territory as it was in 1856, Harpers Ferry in 1859, and Montgomery, Washington, Richmond, Alexandria, and Arlington in 1861. I have visited most of these places and lived for seven years in Richmond. I hope that the combination of personally-observed detail and exhaustive historical research has resulted in accurate and interesting portraits of these places, and the people who lived in them, as they were at the time of the novel's setting.

Some readers may mildly object to the spelling of the town of Harpers Ferry without a possessive case, and might prefer that it be spelled "Harper's Ferry." The town received its name from a ferry service operated in the mid-18th century by Robert Harper, the owner of the land upon which the town now sits. Although there is precedent for spelling the name of the town both ways, it is generally agreed that the modern way does *not* employ the possessive case. The non-possessive form is the way in which it appears on modern maps, for example. Most historical books, such as Douglas Southall Freeman's monumental 4-volume biography of Robert E. Lee, also use the non-possessive form. Although it is quite possible that the possessive form was commonly used in 1859, the time of John Brown's raid, I have chosen to use the modern form in this book.

Harpers Ferry was located in Virginia in 1859. When the western part of Virginia seceded from that state in 1863 and then joined the Union as the new state of West Virginia, Harpers Ferry was included as part of West Virginia. That is where it is now, although it is very close to the state line with Virginia.

Christ Church in Alexandria is one of the most famous churches in the United States. It was the church at which both George

Washington and Robert E. Lee worshipped. As described in this novel, its white-painted pews do have the unusual feature of little doors with black numbers on them. The Washington family pew was No. 60, and the Lee family pew was No. 46; I have briefly sat in both of them. This was the church in which Washington's funeral service was held on December 18, 1799, four days after he died; a plaque listing the names of the pallbearers at that service is today on the outside wall to the right side of the entrance.

Willard's Hotel, at the corner of Pennsylvania Avenue and 14th Street, was the greatest and grandest hotel in Washington in Lincoln's time; he himself stayed there for more than a week before his first inauguration in 1861. Refurbished several times since the Civil War, the modern Willard Intercontinental Hotel maintains that grand tradition. One of the hotel services upon which the Willard brothers were insistent was the provision of generous amounts of great food; the lavish dishes described in this book as available there in 1861 were taken from a hotel menu of the time.

The National Hotel, which once stood at the corner of Pennsylvania Avenue and 6th Street, is accurately described in this book. It was the favorite gathering place for Southern-leaning people in Washington, who had to be more and more careful about expressing their sympathies as the war went on. Unlike its rival, Willard's, the National Hotel no longer exists, having been torn down in the 1930's.

The interior of the White House is described accurately as it was when occupied by Lincoln. The White House had no wings then—they were not added until the early 20th century—so today's famous Oval Office, located in the west wing, did not exist. The residential areas for the president's family were located on the west side of the second floor, while the east side of the second floor was reserved for offices, including the president's office. As the novel states, there was a short staircase of several steps on the east side of the second-floor hallway, as several of the offices were located above the high-ceilinged East Room on the first floor.

During the middle of the 19th century the term "White House" started to become popular as the name for the presidential residence, replacing the earlier names "Executive Mansion" and "President's

House." During Lincoln's time all three names were used, and all three are used in this novel.

"White House" was a familiar name used by the Lee family to describe a family plantation along the Pamunkey River in Virginia, so named because the plantation house was painted white. Before, during, and after the Civil War it was owned and operated by William Henry Fitzhugh "Rooney" Lee, the second-oldest son of Robert E. Lee. The plantation house was burned by Union troops during the Civil War, but rebuilt after the war. Because of the obvious confusion that could have arisen, I have avoided referring to that plantation by its Lee family name in this book.

Carter Cosby, Meagan O'Connor, Benjamin Tilton, and Rufus Sloan/Joshua Cutler are the major fictional characters in this story. There are several minor fictional characters, such as Amos Grinell, Oswell Apperson, Ephraim Tanner, Andrew Kirby, Donnie Wilson, Lester Ebert, and the two agents who accompanied Allan Pinkerton. All the people described in this book as being at the luncheon at the National Hotel on April 20, 1861, are fictional with the exception of Rose Greenhow. Any resemblance of any of these fictional characters to any real person, living or dead, is entirely coincidental.

All other characters are actual historical personages. These include President Abraham Lincoln and the members of his cabinet, Robert E. Lee and the members of his family, Mary Todd Lincoln, Thomas "Tad" Lincoln, Jefferson Davis, Winfield Scott, Robert Anderson, John Letcher, John Robertson, Francis Preston Blair, John Brown and members of his family, Rose O'Neal Greenhow, John and Anne Lloyd, Allan Pinkerton, Pierre G. T. Beauregard, and Ward Hill Lamon. All of them are described as accurately as possible. Moreover, in this book they do what they actually did in history, or something very close to it. Even certain minor characters, such as Captain Rowan of the Charles Town militia, the Rev. Cornelius B. Walker of Christ Church, Winfield Scott's secretary E.D. Townsend, little Rose Greenhow, and Daniel—Lee's black butler/coachman—were real people.

I have taken some liberties with the activities of those great adversaries, Rose O'Neal Greenhow and Allan Pinkerton, but not many. Greenhow *was* a prominent Washington socialite and a daring

Confederate spy; detailed information she smuggled out about Union troop movements under the command of Gen. Irvin McDowell (who used Lee's captured home of Arlington House as his headquarters) is credited with being one of the principal reasons for the stunning Confederate victory at the battle of First Manasses, the first engagement between the two great armies of the Civil War, the Army of the Potomac and the Army of Northern Virginia.

Greenhow was arrested by Pinkerton at the front door of her house on August 23, 1861, and kept under house arrest until January, 1862. She and her youngest daughter were then transferred to Old Capitol Prison. In May, 1862, she and her daughter were officially escorted through the military battle lines and released to the Confederacy, on the condition that she never appear in the Union again for the duration of the war. Although the military prosecutors had been unable to prove the charges of espionage against her, the Union had had enough of her.

Allan Pinkerton *did* discover and foil a plot in Baltimore against President-elect Lincoln, who *did* give him a commission in the army under the fictitious name of "Major E. J. Allen," and placed him in charge of all counter-espionage activities in and around the city of Washington, in effect creating the forerunner of our modern Secret Service.

The title *A Silence At Arlington* comes from the fact that when eleven regiments of Union troops poured across the Potomac River during the early morning hours of May 24, 1861, and seized the Virginia Heights overlooking Washington, they found no one home at Arlington, the Lee home. All the Lees had left, and the house was silent. They would never return. Now owned by the government and operated by the National Park Service, that house is now a museum and is staffed by museum members, many dressed in Civil War costume. It is at the center of what is now the famous Arlington National Cemetery, the nation's final resting place for its honored dead.

CHAPTER 1

Wednesday, April 10, 1861
Montgomery, Alabama
10:05 AM

"The president will see you now, Mr. Cosby."

Carter Cosby rose and followed the male secretary, conscious of the eyes of the other three people in the waiting room. He went through a doorway and down a short corridor lined with white wood paneling. The secretary paused before a white door, then opened it and stepped inside. "Mr. Cosby, Mr. President," he announced with crisp ceremony.

Cosby stepped inside and found himself in the presidential office. The secretary stepped outside and closed the door behind him.

The ascetic, patrician president stood up, walked around his desk, and extended his hand in greeting. "Welcome, Mr. Cosby," Jefferson Davis said warmly, indicating a chair. It was the only chair in front of the desk. "Thank you for being so prompt in answering my request to see you." When his guest was comfortably seated, Davis walked around the desk and seated himself.

"I believe we've met a few times before, Mr. Cosby," Davis began, "but nothing serious."

"That's right, Mr. President. Social occasions. Before the Confederacy was formed."

"Yes, I remember. Your dear wife, too. Letitia. A beautiful and charming lady." Davis shook his head sadly. "Such a waste. It's been what—two years now?"

"Yes, sir. She died of consumption two years ago last February. Thank you for your condolences. You were a Senator from Mississippi at the time, and you sent a letter, a very nice one. I was honored to receive it."

Davis waved his hand deprecatingly. "It was the least I could do. How long were you married before she became ill?"

"A little more than four years, sir. She died only a few months after we first noticed the symptoms."

"And everything I've heard indicates that it was a happy marriage."

"Yes, sir. The happiest. There isn't a day that goes by that I don't think of her. I miss her very much."

"Quite understandable, Carter. May I call you Carter?"

"Of course, Mr. President," Cosby smiled. "Everyone else does."

"No children?"

"No, sir. We were not blessed."

Davis nodded sympathetically; he had six children. "Tell me about this plantation that your wife inherited and that you now own. How do you pronounce its name again?"

"Cymru, sir." Cosby pronounced it *Kimru.* "It's Welsh for 'Wales.' Letitia's ancestors were mostly Welsh. Some of mine are, too, though my name is Scottish. The national symbol for Wales, a red dragon, is also the symbol of our estate. Her father, Colonel Jones, selected it."

"Well, you're certainly making it known, Carter. You're growing some experimental crops, and have written three papers about them. You also, I understand, have some unconventional views about how to run a plantation."

"Actually I wrote four papers, sir. One on fruits, one on rice, and two on cotton."

Davis smiled. "I must have missed one on cotton. I liked the ones I read. Is it correct that you have no servants at Cymru?"

"Yes, sir, that's correct. No slaves." Davis had used the common euphemism for slaves. Cosby was used to it, as he frequently had to explain his position. "I employ only free blacks, and pay them a decent wage. I find it works much better for me. They work harder, and I don't have a large investment tied up in them."

"So your position regarding servitude is an economic one, rather than a moral one?"

"Both, sir, if I may say so. I personally dislike slavery, but I'm no abolitionist. If the laws permit it and other people want it, that's up to them. The point I've been trying to make with Cymru and my papers and lectures is that the investment cost of slaves is simply too high. It absorbs money that could better be used elsewhere."

"This situation started more than fifty years ago, Mr. President," Cosby went on earnestly, "when the importation of slaves was forbidden. That had the effect of raising the value of existing slaves. Now, half a century later, the value of a prime field hand is more than a thousand dollars. I think that's bad, Mr. President. Not just bad for the slave, but bad for the slaveowner, bad for the economy, bad for the country. You can buy a lot of land for that much money. Anybody who pays that kind of money for a slave naturally has a vested interest in slavery, and cannot abide any talk about its ending. When I hire a worker, I'm only interested in paying for his work. I don't want to own him. What he does with his life outside his job should be his responsibility, not mine. I find it's much more efficient that way."

"You certainly believe strongly in your convictions."

"Yes, sir, I do. But there's more at stake here than just my convictions. If we could adopt a hiring system like this across the South, it would not only free up millions of dollars for real investment, but it would remove the thorniest problem between North and South. Then there would be no need for war."

President Davis leaned back in his chair and smiled at Cosby with a hint of indulgence. "You *are* an idealist, aren't you, Carter? The end of slavery by natural means, not abolition. What an idea! It's a bit late for that, I'm afraid." He leaned forward, rested his elbows on the large desk, and rubbed his eyes with the backs of his hands. "The thorniest problem, as you put it, now facing the North is not slavery. Not any longer. It's me. It's *us.* The Confederacy. What is the North going to do about us? Most specifically, what is *Mr. Lincoln* going to do about us?"

"He hasn't done much yet," Cosby commented.

"Give him time," the Confederate president grinned, lighting up his thin face. "He's only been in office five weeks. That's even less time than I've been in office."

Carter Cosby regarded the aristocratic person before him and thought how perfectly suited Jefferson Davis was to be the president of a country. He had the necessary government experience, having been a long-time senator from Mississippi, and the Secretary of War during the Pierce administration. He was a genuine hero of the Mexican War, the organizer and leader of a splendid volunteer group, the Mississippi Rifles. Moreover, he *looked* like a president. Even though he had weak sight in one eye, he was tall and graceful. His wavy gray hair was properly distinguished, accented by his narrow goatee. He appeared to be careful in thought, gracious in manners, temperate in appetites, and forthright in nature, all of which he was. The Confederacy could have chosen no better person.

"Mr. President, will there be a war?" Cosby asked quietly.

"Dear God, I hope not," Davis replied. "If I could have my way, the Confederacy would live in peace side by side with the United States, two separate nations that were partners and allies in almost everything. We could, theoretically, have somewhat the same relationship with the United States that it has with Canada. However, I have grave doubts that it will turn out that way. We must be prepared for the worst." He regarded Cosby keenly. "Let me tell you what I think may happen. This has some relationship to why I asked you here, in case you were wondering."

Davis got up and slowly began to pace the room. "Mr. Lincoln has a dilemma, Carter. He has said many times that he considers secession unconstitutional and the Confederacy an illegal assembly. 'The Union is a marriage, not free love,' he once said. A nice metaphor. However, the Confederacy is now a fact. He cannot disband it merely by fulminating against it in Washington. He cannot wish it away or will it away. In order to get rid of the Confederacy he must conquer it militarily. That means invading it. And *that* means a big army. A *very* big army."

Davis stopped his pacing near Cosby's chair. "When I was Secretary of War, several years after the Mexican War, our troop strength was down to 20,000. It's even less now—about 15,000. That's all, Carter; 15,000 troops in the entire U.S. Army. They exist primarily to control the frontier; many of them were in Texas before that state seceded two months ago. That isn't enough troops to even begin to think of invading the South. Yet Mr. Lincoln has made no move at all to increase the size of his army—not yet, anyway. Why not? Partly because he wants *us* to make the first move. He doesn't want history to say that he was inaugurated President of the United States and immediately began planning for an invasion of the Confederacy."

"A bigger reason, however, is a practical one. I cannot imagine states like Virginia and North Carolina lying down supinely while a massive Federal army marches across their territory to invade the Confederacy. They would *never* permit it! Long before such an army was ready to march they would have seceded from the Union and joined us. Even the knowledge that such an army was being raised would trigger that action. The whole upper South would pull away from the Union and join the Confederacy—Virginia, North Carolina, Tennessee, Kentucky, Arkansas, and Missouri. We would then have thirteen states. The same number," Davis smiled grimly, "as the colonies at the time of the Revolution eighty years ago. That is my dream, Carter—a Confederacy of thirteen states, not seven. At such a size we would be well-nigh unconquerable. War, then, might well never come, since the Union would recognize the futility of trying to subdue such a huge area."

"My dream is also Lincoln's dilemma, Carter. Any action on his part to invade the South would therefore trigger a ripple effect which would double the Confederacy in size and population. So what is he going to do? Sit back, do nothing provocative, and allow a seven-state Confederacy to exist unmolested? Or take action and see the Confederacy double in size, coming right up to the banks of the Potomac?"

"That is a nasty choice, Mr. President. Thank you for sharing your thoughts with me. Perhaps I am a little dense, but I'm not sure what all that has to do with me."

"Patience, my dear Carter." Davis walked over to his desk and tapped the topmost of several file folders that were on it. "It says in here that you served in the Mexican War."

"Yes, sir, I did. Only as a private, however."

"Not so modest, my friend. You were promoted later. It also says you were present at the storming of Chapultepec Hill and its castle."

Cosby shrugged.

"And that you were decorated for bravery. Tell me about that."

Cosby shrugged again. "My sergeant took a ball in the foot. He fell over, screaming. There was a lot of smoke. A Mexican infantryman appeared out of the smoke and ran toward the sergeant, ready to bayonet him. I was able to intercept him. We fought. I won. That's all, really."

"That's all?" Davis stopped and raised his eyebrows. "You make it sound so simple." He sat back down in his chair and gravely eyed the plantation owner. "I've been around fighting men long enough to know that much bravery is instinctive, not the product of cold logic. But a man has to have the right instincts. And you do, Carter. You do. And you have considerable military experience. Now then—suppose war should come. What does your military experience, and your knowledge of the South, tell you about how such a war would be conducted?"

Cosby looked at the president, who was gazing keenly at him. The Confederate president had been a Secretary of War, a senator, and a military leader in combat, and was now asking *him* about the approach of war? "I'm not sure what you mean, sir," Cosby answered cautiously.

Davis put his elbows on the desk and steepled his fingers. "I mean this, Carter. Mr. Lincoln is not a military man. He's been a lawyer and a politician almost all his adult life, though he did serve briefly as a volunteer. His Secretary of War, Simon Cameron, is a former governor of Pennsylvania—also not a military man. These two nonmilitary men are contemplating a massive invasion of the South. From whom, then, are they getting their military advice? Who would plan and implement such a huge campaign?"

Cosby thought a moment. "I suppose General Scott, sir."

Davis gently slapped the top of his desk with his right palm. "Right you are, Carter. Of course. Winfield Scott, General-in-chief of the Army. Twice voted a gold medal by Congress for service to his country. Victorious commander of the army in Mexico; I served under him there, as you did. Whig candidate for president in 1852. The most decorated man in American military history with the exception of George Washington himself. The man is a national icon. To whom else would Lincoln and Cameron be talking about military affairs?"

"He's the best, sir."

"Do you know how old General Scott is, Carter?"

Cosby reflected a moment. "No, sir, I don't," he finally replied. "I remember, however, that he was not a young man in Mexico, and that was thirteen years ago."

"He's seventy-four," Davis said. "He's quite a tall man—six feet five, as I recall—and has become quite stout. He must now weigh all of three hundred pounds. I'm not even sure he can still mount a horse. And if he could, I pity the horse." The president smiled thinly. "I'm surprised he hasn't retired yet. One thing is certain: if war comes, Scott may sit around in his office at the War Department and pore over maps, but he will not take the field. The field command of the Union Army must go to someone else, someone younger and fitter. Lincoln and Cameron know this. They will not, of course, simply pull a name out of a hat. Inevitably they will ask Scott—delicately, I'm sure—whom he would recommend for the field command. And," Davis added slowly, "I think I know whom Scott will recommend." Davis was a somber man, but his eyes came close to twinkling. "And that, my dear Carter, is where you come in."

"Me, sir?" Cosby asked in astonishment.

"If you wish. Have you ever heard of Robert E. Lee? Colonel Robert E. Lee?"

"Lee." Cosby thought for a moment, then shook his head. "The name rings a bell, but I can't place him. Should I know him?"

"He was General Scott's chief of artillery during the Mexican War. I thought perhaps you had heard the name there."

Cosby snapped his fingers. "Yes, I remember now. I did hear his name mentioned there. Just in passing, though. I never met him. I was just a foot soldier."

"He is a remarkable man," Davis said. "Fifty-four years old. West Point graduate, class of '29. A year behind my class," the president smiled. "I remember him. He has been in the army ever since, more than thirty years. He was most recently at San Antonio. I had good reason to remember Colonel Lee when I was Secretary of War, because he was the Superintendent of the United States Military Academy at West Point at the time. We corresponded regularly, and on most friendly terms."

"Is this the man you think Scott will recommend for field command of the Union army?"

"Yes," Davis nodded.

"May I ask why you think so, sir?"

"There is something between those two," Davis replied slowly. "I sensed it several times when Scott talked of Lee. I could say that Scott considers Lee his protege and Lee considers Scott his mentor, but I think it's actually closer than that. I think it's almost a father-son relationship. No one has said anything like that, but it is definitely a relationship that extends beyond mere professionalism. Lee became Superintendent at West Point because Scott recommended him for it."

"So this is the man the Confederacy will have to face if war comes. He must be very good if Scott says he is."

"He *is* very good," Davis nodded. "As to whether we would have to face him or not, well, that depends on some things. Maybe we would, maybe we wouldn't."

"What things, Mr. President?"

"Mr. Lincoln is going to have trouble with Scott's recommendation," Davis replied. "Lee is a socially prominent Virginian. He comes from one of the finest families in the country."

"Virginia?" Cosby interrupted. "He's one of the Lees of Virginia? I've heard of them. Everybody has."

"Exactly," Davis went on. "He has a large estate on the Potomac heights overlooking Washington. It's so close to the capital city that he could fire a cannon from his front porch and put the ball through a window of the Executive Mansion. One could say that he's the most northern of southern gentlemen, though certain Marylanders might take exception to that." Davis smiled at his own joke.

"Why should that give Lincoln pause, Mr. President? There's lots of southerners in the army. Besides, you said this Lee has faithfully served in the army for thirty years."

"Because this would be a *civil* war, Carter. A civil war that would have started over the constitutional questions of secession and states' rights and Federal property in the seceded states, but which could well turn into a crusade against slavery. That's the way most northerners are going to see it. Certainly the abolitionists are. On his estate Lee has servants. Slaves, if you will. Dozens of them. Is a prominent slave-owning Virginian the man Lincoln wants in charge of an army to invade the South and end slavery? I sincerely doubt it. But who is Lincoln to turn a deaf ear to Scott, the national hero who was in the army before Lincoln was born? So I think Lincoln will approach Lee, perhaps indirectly. Yet that raises another problem."

"Will Lee accept?"

"Very good, Carter," Davis beamed. "Will Lee accept, indeed? We are postulating a condition where a huge Federal army will be raised. Virginia will secede if that happens. Virginia is the first state south of Washington, the first state that would be invaded. Inevitably Virginia will become a major battleground if civil war comes. If Lee is the head of that Federal army, he will be invading his own state, making war on his own people. How can he do that?"

"He would be caught in a very nasty squeeze," Cosby admitted. "He would either be considered a traitor to his country or a traitor to his state. Not a pretty choice."

"Precisely. Now tell me this, Carter. Suppose Lee does refuse to accept command of such an army. What do you think would happen?"

Cosby shrugged. "Well, Lincoln would have to find somebody else. I have no idea who that would be. I'm sure Scott can recommend someone."

Davis waved a hand deprecatingly. "Yes, yes, of course. I mean what would happen to *Lee*? Remember, this man would have turned down a request from his president, a request that would have resulted in the highest honor that president could bestow. Could an officer who did such a thing even remain in the army? Would not his fellow officers scorn and spurn him for turning down an offer that all of them would give their eyeteeth for? Above all, what would Gen. Scott say about such a refusal, the very man who recommended him to Lincoln in the first place? And Scott is his superior officer."

Cosby nodded his head in understanding. "I see what you mean, Mr. President. Scott would be embarrassed, even angry. Lee might very well have to resign his commission."

"Bravo, Carter!" Davis tapped the top of his desk again with the palm of his hand. "So Col. Lee becomes a private citizen. He is a resident of Virginia, a state which, in our scenario, has seceded, or shortly will secede. Then what? Does he think he will live comfortably in his mansion and sit out a massive civil war? Suppose Virginia asks for his services? Then what? Will he answer that call?"

"He might, sir."

"He might very well, Carter. Do you see where all this is heading?"

"Um, I'm not sure, sir."

"Think, Carter, think!" Davis was becoming animated. "We know Virginia will secede if an army is raised. Does anyone think Virginia will then stay a sovereign state, a nation unto itself? Of course not! It will join *us*! It will become part of the *Confederacy*! If Col. Lee joins his state in its secession, what will he do when it joins the Confederacy? Do you see the staggering possibility?"

The light dawned for Cosby. "*Lee* would become a part of the Confederacy!"

"Exactly!" Davis stood straight up. "The very man whom Scott and Lincoln picked to invade the South would become the *defender* of the South! Can you imagine the effect on the morale of our people when such a thing is learned?

"It is dazzling, Mr. President," Cosby agreed. He was more restrained in his enthusiasm than the elegant Mississippian. "Yet it all depends on a series of decisions, doesn't it? We can't be sure all these decisions will come out just the way you envision."

"No, we can't," said Davis, seating himself again. "Yet all of those decisions seem reasonable, do they not?" He gazed quietly at Cosby. "Wouldn't it be wonderful if we had someone right there with Lee, gently nudging him at just the right times, helping him take the path which we would like him to take?"

Cosby caught the look. "Someone *with* Lee, Mr. President?"

Davis paused significantly. "How would you like to be that person, Carter?" he asked softly.

Cosby was genuinely astonished. "Me? With *Lee*? Mr. President, how could I be? I don't know him. I never met the man. How could I even get close to him, let alone *be* with him?"

"Of course you don't know him," Davis agreed imperturbably. "More importantly, he doesn't know *you.* We wouldn't want that, would we? The connection between you and me must be a secret. Don't sell yourself short, Carter. You are a genuine agricultural expert who also happens to be a decorated veteran of the Mexican War. Suppose the governor of Virginia should contact Lee and tell him that, in view of his estimable services to the state, an agricultural expert will be sent to Lee's estate to advise him about plants and procedures. Lee is no farmer; he would appreciate such advice. The state, of course, would pay for it."

"The governor of Virginia?" Cosby raised his eyebrows. "There's somebody else I don't know."

Davis opened the topmost file on his desk and silently perused its contents for a few moments. "You've lived in a number of places and a number of states could claim you," he finally said. "You're now a resident of Alabama, but according to this, you were born in Danville, Virginia, in 1825. June 17." He glanced up at Cosby. "Is that correct?"

Cosby nodded.

Davis looked back to the folder. "You have also attended a number of schools, but it says here that for a year and a half you were enrolled at the University of Virginia in Charlottesville. Is that also true?"

"Yes, Mr. President."

"The very school founded by none other than Thomas Jefferson," Davis mused. "The author of the Declaration of Independence, the first Secretary of State, third President of the United States, and one of the greatest names in American history, let alone Virginia's history."

"That's true, Mr. President."

"And, I might add, the very person for whom my parents named me."

"A wise choice, sir."

"Well," Davis said with an air of finality, closing the folder. "It certainly seems to me that the governor of Virginia would have no trouble recommending a native son of the Old Dominion to someone like Col. Lee for a mission of importance to the state." A wisp of a smile played on the face of the president. "Don't you agree, Carter?"

Carter Cosby could not suppress a small laugh. "Something tells me, Mr. President, that you've already been in touch with the governor."

"Indeed I have," Davis said, his smile broadening. "John Letcher is a fine man. He thinks the way I do, which is, of course, my definition of right thinking. He also thinks Lee will follow his state if it secedes, and therefore he concurs in my plan to have someone keep an eye on Lee." Davis turned serious. "I have not, however, revealed to the governor my belief that Lee will be offered command of the Union army. That is something I have discussed only with you, my dear Carter. Keep that in mind when you talk with the governor."

"When I *talk* with the governor? Mr. President, when would I do *that*?"

"At your meeting with him, of course," Davis said coolly. "That's when he will give you the letter of introduction to Lee. You are scheduled to meet with him at nine o'clock this Sunday evening."

Cosby's astonishment grew not only at the boldness and detail of Davis' plan, but also at the obvious assumption of the Confederate president that he, Cosby, would accede to it. A part of him was irritated at the arrogance of that assumption, but he had to admire it. "In Richmond?" he asked, knowing the answer.

"That's where they keep the governor of Virginia these days," Davis smiled. "We made the appointment for a Sunday evening so that you could meet privately at his residence rather than at his office. So much more discreet. It will also be dark. Few people will see you, and no one will recognize you. Even so, the governor insisted on a password you should use with any sentries on duty at the residence, and also with the butler. For his purposes, you will be known as 'John Rolfe.' That's with an 'e.'"

"John Rolfe?"

Davis shrugged. "That's what he wants." He noticed a small smile on Cosby's face. "Does that name have any significance? I must admit it puzzled me."

"I think the governor was having a small joke, sir. John Rolfe is a name that would be known to farmers, especially in Virginia; he was the Virginia pioneer who first cultivated tobacco. It may also be a way for the governor to identify me, as my own name would mean nothing to him."

"I see."

"Exactly where is the governor's residence, sir?"

"Virginia has an official residence for its governor, adjacent to the state capitol building. A nice mansion, so I'm told. The governor has sent a small map of Richmond, which will be included with your other papers."

"Sunday evening," Cosby mused. "That's only four days, not counting today. Then I can't go by ship. Even a fast boat could not get me to Richmond in only four days."

"Correct," Davis agreed. "A ship would be simplest, but too slow. You'll go by train." He opened another file folder. "Maybe someday we'll have a unified rail system when one simply gets on and then off at a destination hundreds of miles away, but we don't have it yet. Here are the schedules for the various railroads between here and Richmond. I could have arranged a rail pass for you—at least in Confederate territory—but it would have taken too much time and called too much attention to you. You'll buy your tickets." He passed over a thick envelope. "Here's $500 in U.S. currency, in various denominations." He dropped a small leather bag on the desk. "And here is another $300, in gold coins. U.S. money. We're working on the design of our own money now, but this is better for you anyway—it will be accepted anywhere."

The president was quiet for a time as Cosby opened the envelope and counted the bills, then did the same with the gold coins. "I would suggest a money-belt to carry that around with you," he finally said. "No point in putting any of it in a bank and drawing attention to yourself."

"This Col. Lee must mean a great deal to you, sir," Cosby said quietly as he put the envelope and the bag on the desk.

"Indeed he does," Davis rejoined. "It would be sufficient if somehow we could prevent him from leading the invasion of the South after Lincoln and Scott have determined that he is the best officer for the job. To actually have him change sides, however, and *resist* such an invasion—well," he beamed, "that possibility simply cannot be overlooked. It would be an astounding feather in our cap, and conceivably might even turn out to be the very salvation of the Confederacy itself. This mission is that important." He looked across the desk at Cosby's lithe figure, at his intelligent face topped by close-cropped curly brown hair. "Well, there you have it, Carter—my little plan to obstruct the invasion of the South and snatch the chosen invasion leader for ourselves. Do you accept?"

Cosby met the president's direct gaze and shifted slightly in his chair. "Your plan is admirable, sir. You have obviously spent much time on it, and I am certainly flattered that you thought of me as the instrument for carrying it out." He paused. "I have two questions."

Davis raised his eyebrows. "Only two?" he smiled. "I expected more."

"The first is Cymru. Who will run my plantation in my absence? I have an overseer, who is quite trustworthy and can handle the day-to-day details, but he should have some supervision. I have no wife nor any blood relative to step into my place."

"No problem. I will arrange for you to meet a member of our Agricultural Department, to whom you can give detailed instructions about your plantation. We will run it while you are away, because you would be, after all, on the Confederacy's business. What else?"

Cosby shifted in the chair again. "Lee, sir. Suppose I do make contact with him, and he accepts me on his estate. Then suppose something in this plan goes astray, and it looks as if he is going to head the Union army on its great invasion of the South. What do you propose I should do?"

Jefferson Davis looked at his guest a long moment. His eyes, never strong, seemed to cloud over, as if he were gazing into a far distance. "If Lee does not lead the invasion of the South," he said slowly, "then someone else will. That person, however, will not be as good as Lee. If we are to be deprived of his services, it would not be a good idea to let the North have them." He let his gaze linger on Cosby. "The Confederacy is more important than any one man, Carter. Should the case go against us, I will leave it to your discretion as to what is to be done."

Cosby's chest tightened. Was this courtly leader of the Confederacy making a veiled suggestion to cripple Lee, or eliminate him in some manner? Possibly even *kill* him? Whatever happened, Davis could deny responsibility, for he never mentioned violence of any kind.

"My discretion, sir?" Cosby asked carefully.

"Your discretion, in which I have the greatest trust."

"Then I accept."

Davis smiled brightly. "Good. Now, I would suggest you settle up your affairs today and leave tomorrow morning. By the way, you'll need to sign this. It's a receipt for the $800. That's far more money than you should need, but I wanted you to be prepared for unforeseen circumstances. Naturally, I will expect the return of any money not spent, as well as an accounting of all that was spent."

"Naturally."

"One more thing." Davis held up a folded sheet of paper and passed it to Cosby. "Take a look at this."

Cosby unfolded the sheet. It was a note written on letterhead stationery of the Office of the President of the Confederate States of America. Its contents were brief.

> To whom it may concern,
>
> This will serve to identify Carter Cosby, a friend of the Confederacy. Any service which you can render to him will be greatly appreciated by me personally and by our nation.
>
> Jefferson Davis, President

"You may keep that," Davis said. "In certain circumstances it may be very useful to you. However, I will understand if you choose not to take it with you. In certain other circumstances it could be dangerous for you if it were found on your person."

Cosby looked at the note and considered if for a moment. "I'll take it, Mr. President, with my thanks to you." He handed the note back. Davis' words of caution were well-founded. However, he could always get rid of the note.

Davis placed the note in one of the folders. "There are several files I will give you, Carter. One of them—this one—you should read on your trip north. It is a report on Col. Lee, his background, family, and estate. You should know as much as possible about him before you meet him. Now, take this material with you, and my secretary will introduce you to a member of our Agricultural Department." He glanced at a clock on the wall. "I must be off to a meeting at a hotel, where I believe the decision will be made to test Mr. Lincoln's mettle." He rose and walked Cosby to the door. "Good luck, Carter, and a safe journey. Report back to me when you return."

"Thank you, Mr. President. I shall."

The two men shook hands, Davis opened the door, and Cosby walked out. The door was shut behind him.

CHAPTER 2

Thursday, April 11
Alabama
9:37 AM

The train rolled smoothly across Alabama under lowering skies, pulled by the *John C. Calhoun*, a Baldwin-built 4-4-0 woodburner. Like many locomotives of the time, the *Calhoun* was brightly colored: her wheels were painted red, her boiler was gray-green, her bell, steam dome, and cylinders were polished brass, and her cab was resplendent in varnish and gilt. Behind her tender was a mail/baggage car, followed by three coaches, all painted pale yellow. Carter Cosby sat in the forward part on the right hand-side of the last coach, gazing out the window at the storm the train was approaching.

Cosby liked rain, so long as there wasn't too much of it. Rain made crops grow, rivers run, and grass greener. It cooled the earth, washed dust from houses, and made scents sweeter. Land without rain would be a desert. The best way to experience rain, he had decided long ago, was from the deep verandah of a Southern home. He had done this any number of times at his own home, sitting with Letitia on a porch bench, the two of them wrapped in blankets with their feet propped up on stools, watching with deep satisfaction the stately advance of curtains of rain across the woods and fields of Cymru, feeling in their faces the rush of wet wind containing the heady mingled scents of multitudinous growing things, experiencing that deep primeval sense of well-being that comes to those who live close to the earth at the appearance of the earth's great benefactor.

The days of rain at Cymru were wonderful, but the nights of rain were spectacular. Then he and Letitia would huddle together under the same blanket, after dousing all the lights, and revel in the power of nature in the magical darkness. That natural power had sometimes transformed itself into sexual power, and they had made passionate love on the bench in the darkness, with the pouring rain all about them and raising a din on the verandah roof. Now he sometimes sat alone on that bench in the darkness, missing her with an ache that was a physical pain. When it rained, the sense of loss was unbearable.

The clouds darkened the day, making it seem like dusk. The tracks curved to the right, and Cosby could see the gaudy locomotive pulling the train straight toward the darkest mass of clouds. He leaned back in the brown velvet seat and marveled once again at the way the coming of the railroad was transforming the country and its life. Watching rain approach from a moving train was not quite so fine as from his verandah at Cymru, but it was no bad thing indeed.

The comforting vibration and gentle jostling of the train, combined with the sight of the locomotive and the mesmerizing motion of its drivers, brought Cosby to the ideas which gladdened him the most: the ways that the onrush of human knowledge was changing men's lives. It was happening almost unbelievably quickly, yet few seemed to grasp that stunning fact. At the time of his birth, just 35 years ago, there were no locomotives, no trains, no railroads. Cargo was transported on land by horse-drawn wagons, as it had been for centuries. *The way the Romans did,* he thought, *although their roads were better than ours.* A few years after he was born, the first crude locomotives were invented in England, and they revolutionized transportation as soon as enough track was laid to make them useful. Several locomotives were brought to America, and then a few built here, where they pulled small cargoes around at a few miles per hour. Just three decades later there were now *thirty thousand* miles of railroad track in the United States, almost all east of the Mississippi

River. The first railroad bridge across the Mississippi, between Rock Island, Illinois, and Davenport, Iowa, had been completed only five years ago. With the "Father of Waters" conquered, railroad men were now planning the most spectacular and daunting task of all: reaching California. That state was already part of the Union, having been admitted as the 31st state in 1850. However, California was an isolated part of the Union stuck out on the west coast of the continent, with no other state contiguous with it or even near it. To reach it would require crossing more than a thousand miles of prarie, inhospitable deserts, and two mountain ranges with 14,000-foot peaks, the Rockies and the Sierra Nevada. Such a stupendous engineering task would obviously be done sometime in the future; the only question was when.

Cosby wryly noted that both new rival presidents had been heavily involved in railroad affairs before being elected president. While Secretary of War during the Pierce administration, Jefferson Davis had been in charge of exploring four alternative routes across the West for a proposed transcontinental railroad. Abraham Lincoln, in the most noteworthy case of his legal career, had been the lawyer for the railroad which built that bridge across the Mississippi, when it was sued for damages caused by an errant steamboat packet ramming one of the bridge's piers.

Locomotives could now pull trains faster than the speed of a racehorse, covering hundreds of miles a day, and would obviously become bigger, faster, and more powerful. It was a staggering change, unparalleled in human history. This rapid transport had lowered the price of goods, making things much cheaper, some things many people had never even *seen* before.

The steam engine was also revolutionizing ocean travel, being fitted in ships with iron hulls. Wooden ships propelled by the wind were as old as recorded history; all that had happened in several thousand years was that they had become bigger, faster, and more complex. Now all that was changing, so fast it was but an eyeblink in historical time. It was clear as crystal to Cosby that iron steamships would obsolete wooden sailing ships within his lifetime, making ocean commerce faster, cheaper, safer, and more reliable.

And then there was the telegraph, a wonder that few people understood since it involved that new elemental force, electricity. It took longer to tap out a message than it did for that message to travel a hundred miles through the wires. Hundreds of miles in *seconds!* Cosby shook his head at such incomprehensible speeds.

All these changes had come about in Cosby's lifetime. *Some sort of cosmic ball has been set rolling,* he thought, *and it will roll even faster in the future.*

He was proud of his contribution to this onrushing future. He subscribed to several scientific journals, had an Earnshaw chronometer in his house because it was the most accurate timekeeper he could obtain, and had developed hybrid plants which significantly increased crop yield per acre. He was developing a strain of cotton which he believed would have smooth seeds, rather than the usual prickly seeds, making it far easier for cotton gins to clean the cotton. With a stream on his property he was experimenting with a water wheel to drive a large gin. He was thinking of a small steam engine to drive a gin, or even a series of them. Perhaps a cooperative could be formed with other plantations to spread the cost…

As he watched the approaching storm, Cosby thought it a too-perfect symbolism of the approaching national crisis. Everyone said they didn't want war, but nobody was willing to back away from the precipice. They would rather fight than compromise on their cherished principles. Their notion of honor would drive them to the very catastrophe they all said they didn't want. And that included Jefferson Davis, his protestations to the contrary.

Cosby thought of what Davis had said to him, and especially what Davis had *not* said. The Confederate president had not asked him, for example, what he thought of the Confederacy, apparently assuming he approved of it. Cosby did not approve. He was very careful about voicing his opinion, however, for almost all his neighbors and acquaintances *did* approve, most exuberantly so. He thought the whole notion of a breakaway nation from the United States, very similar to it in form and structure, was nonsense. *How can a viable nation be formed,* he thought, *from states which have already seceded from one union and claim secession from any union to be an inherent and fundamental right of states?* South Carolina had been the first state to secede from the Union, four months ago. It was now part of the Confederacy. Suppose, for some reason, South Carolina should decide some day that it wanted to secede from the *Confederacy*. What Confederate politician could possibly say that it had no right to do so? The notion of secession as a fundamental right was a principal common thread running through all seven Confederate states. They could not possibly deny it without simultaneously denying that they had a right to secede from the Union in the first place. The practical result of such an insistence was that every single bill passed by the Confederate Congress in Montgomery would have to be ratified by every state legislature, with the implicit threat of secession if a state didn't get its way. That was a recipe for total chaos. Cosby knew little about Lincoln and neither liked nor disliked him, but thought he was absolutely right in his statement that Davis had mocked: "the Union is a marriage, not free love." The Confederacy was an illogical joke.

Yet what could he do? *Nobody asked me if I thought the Southern states should pull away from the Union and form their own rump nation, and nobody would have paid the slightest attention to me no matter what I said.* It was done. Signed, sealed, and delivered. He was now a citizen of the Confederacy, like it or not. He did not enthusiastically endorse it, but he would obey it. And the president of the Confederacy had personally asked him to undertake a mission of importance, one which conceivably might save lives and prevent a war. He didn't see how he could honorably, or even reasonably, refuse.

When the first raindrops smacked into his window and were blown backwards by the speed of the train, Cosby opened the file on Lee.

CHAPTER 3

Thursday
Alabama
10:14 AM

Robert Edward Lee had been born on January 19, 1807, at Stratford Hall, a family mansion near the Potomac in Virginia. Even by the snobbiest of standards in Virginia society, his lineage was extraordinary. Two ancestral cousins, Richard Henry Lee and Francis Lightfoot Lee, had been signers of the Declaration of Independence. His father was Henry "Light Horse Harry" Lee, a renowned soldier in the Revolution, and later a three-time governor of Virginia. His mother, Henry Lee's second wife, was Ann Hill Carter, a member of the Carter family which owned Shirley Plantation, founded in 1619 and the oldest plantation in America. He was the fifth oldest of six children born to his parents, the oldest of whom had died in infancy; there was also a half-brother, Henry, a child by his father's first wife, who inherited Stratford Hall. Lee's family left Stratford Hall while he was still quite young, and he lived most of his life before college in a rented house in Alexandria.

Though Lee's family was illustrious, it was poor, due to bad investments made by his father. After his father's death in 1818, Lee entered the Military Academy at West Point in 1825. He graduated in 1829, second in his class, with the rank of brevet second lieutenant in the Corps of Engineers. His mother, to whom Lee was devoted, had been in poor health for some time, confined to a wheelchair for several years; she died later that year, with Lee at her side.

If there was any bluer blood in Virginia than Lee's, it flowed in the veins of his wife. She was Mary Anna Randolph Custis, whom Lee married on June 30, 1831. She was the only child who survived to adulthood of George Washington Parke Custis, who was the youngest child of John Parke Custis, who was the only son who survived to adulthood from the union of Daniel Parke Custis, a British army officer, and Martha Dandridge, of Fredericksburg, Virginia. When Daniel Parke Custis died his widow married another British army officer, George Washington, thereby becoming Martha Washington. John Parke Custis died suddenly in 1781 at Yorktown, Virginia; he had four children, the youngest of whom was a son only six months old. This baby boy—named George Washington Parke Custis after his illustrious step-grandfather—the Washingtons took and reared at Mount Vernon. They even adopted him, since they had no children. Mary Anna Custis was therefore the great-granddaughter of Martha Washington by her first husband, and the daughter of George Washington's adopted son.

When G.W.P. Custis reached manhood he acquired a large estate on the Virginia heights above the Potomac River overlooking the Federal capital, the new city named for his adoptive father, the first president. It comprised 1100 acres, and was named Arlington. On it he built, over a period of fifteen years, a magnificent mansion which he called Arlington House, which he openly admitted was an attempt to recapture the graciousness and charm he had known as a child at Mount Vernon. It was here that Robert E. Lee met, courted, and married Mary Anna Custis.

The Lees had seven children: George Washington Custis, born in 1832; Mary, 1835; William Henry Fitzhugh, 1837; Anne Carter, 1839; Agnes, 1841; Robert Edward, 1843; and Mildred, 1846.

Lee was appointed to a number of military posts for the next fifteen years, but his military career began to move rapidly during the Mexican War. He was Gen. Scott's chief of artillery in Mexico. He was twice wounded, and came out of the war with a promotion to lieutenant colonel and the admiration of Gen. Scott, who specifically mentioned him in several dispatches.

From 1852 to 1855 Lee was the Superintendent of the U.S. Military Academy, becoming the ninth superintendent in West Point's history. Almost certainly the proudest event in Lee's life must have been being the Superintendent at West Point at the time his oldest son, Custis Lee, graduated at the head of his class in 1854.

In 1855 Lee left West Point and the Engineers and joined the newly-formed 2nd Cavalry Regiment in Texas. In 1857 his father-in-law, G.W.P. Custis, died at Arlington, leaving the estate to his only child, Mary Anna, and her husband. Lee was granted an extended leave of absence to tend to the affairs of the estate.

A provision of the will specified that all the slaves at Arlington—sixty-three of them—were to be manumitted in five years from the death of Mr. Custis. Lee had agreed to this provision.

That made Cosby sit up and take notice. Lee was going to free his slaves, no later than next year!

The next entry really caught his attention. When John Brown made his notorious raid on Harpers Ferry in northern Virginia in October, 1859, it was none other than Lt. Col. Robert E. Lee whom the U.S. Army sent to take command of the situation. Lee, who happened to be home at the time, immediately took a train to Harpers Ferry, and was in command of the ninety U.S. Marines who captured Brown and most of the raiders.

The next entry concerning Lee's military career was also noteworthy. On February 6, 1860, he was placed in temporary command of the Department of Texas in San Antonio and held that position for ten months, until relieved on December 14 by Gen. Daniel E. Twiggs. He thereupon left San Antonio for Fort Mason, where he reassumed command of the 2nd Cavalry Regiment. On Feb. 4, 1861, he received an unexpected order from the War Department relieving him of duty with the 2nd Cavalry and ordering him to report in person to the general-in-chief of the Army, Maj. Gen. Winfield Scott, in Washington by April 1. By the time of that order seven Southern states had seceded, the most recent being Texas itself on Feb. 1. Lee relinquished command of his regiment on Feb. 13 and proceeded to San Antonio, on his way to the coast and then home to Virginia. When he reached San Antonio on the afternoon of Feb. 16, he found that on that very morning, a band of Texas secessionists had seized the headquarters of the Department of Texas and all its buildings and stores. They were not resisted by Gen. Twiggs, a noted advocate of states' rights. Lee himself was detained and informed that he could leave, but his personal effects would be impounded unless he, then and there, resigned his commission in the United States Army and joined the Confederacy. Lee indignantly refused. After making arrangements about his luggage with a friend, he left San Antonio several days later and arrived home in Arlington on March 1.

The chronicler of the report stated that, in his opinion, had Lee, not Twiggs, still been in command of the Department of Texas, he would never have surrendered it without explicit orders from Washington, and the Civil War might then have begun in San Antonio on Feb. 16. On March 1 Gen. Twiggs was dismissed from the army for his actions in Texas.

The report did not state why Gen. Scott had wanted to meet with Lee so urgently.

The Confederate Secretary of War, Leroy P. Walker, had written a letter to Lee dated March 15, directly offering a commission as a brigadier general in the Confederacy. No reply to this letter was ever received.

The last entry in the dossier stated that on March 28, Lee was promoted to full colonel and placed in command of the 1st Cavalry Regiment. He was still at Arlington, waiting to move.

There was no photograph. Cosby was not surprised. Perhaps no photograph existed of Lee, but Cosby thought one might have been taken of him during the national excitement over the Harpers Ferry raid a year and a half ago. The reason was undoubtedly the newness of the Confederate government. The Confederacy was little more than a month old, and its files were still being organized. Its officials simply didn't have such things as photographs of officers in the United States Army. They probably didn't yet have file photos of their own officers.

Cosby closed the file, leaned back in his seat, and looked out the window. The sky was darker and the rain was heavier, a steady drumming on the glass. The coach suddenly seemed stuffy, and he had to think. He opened his window just a tiny crack at the bottom, and was gratified by the thin draft of cool moist air which rushed in and relieved the stuffiness.

So this was Col. Robert E. Lee, the man Jefferson Davis believed—well, *suspected*—would be offered field command of the Union army. To Cosby, that seemed more like an educated guess than a shrewd deduction. Lee had an excellent record and an unmatched family background, but was still only a colonel—and a recently-promoted one, at that. Is that why Scott relieved Lee of his command and brought him back to Washington? To groom him for the top field command? Maybe even Scott's *own* position when he retired, which could not be far in the future? How could Lee leave an army in which he was on such cordial, even intimate, terms with its highest-ranking officer? And then join the *Confederacy*?

On the face of it, that seemed preposterous. It was certainly true that many West Pointers had followed their native states into the Confederacy—Jefferson Davis himself was such a one—but Lee had been the *Superintendent at West Point*. How much attraction could the Confederacy have for a man who, for three years, had been the final authority at the heart of the nation's future officer corps, the ruler of the gray buildings overlooking the Hudson?

What about Harpers Ferry? Cosby had not realized that Lee had been the commander of the military detachment which had captured John Brown. It must have been reported in the newspapers at the time, but like everyone else he had been so mesmerized by Brown's audacity and abolitionist violence that he had not paid much attention to such details as the identity of Brown's captors. Could anyone possibly read into Lee's actions there that he was an anti-abolitionist, and therefore sympathetic to the South's position on slavery? No. Brown's raiders had attacked and occupied a Federal arsenal, and it was the government's obvious duty to suppress an attack on its own property. Lee was home at Arlington on leave at the time, and just happened to be the highest-ranking field officer close at hand whom the War Department could send up the Potomac to take charge of the situation at Harpers Ferry. The raid, which had so polarized the country, seemed to be of little interest to Lee after he completed his duty. He testified only briefly at Brown's trial, and was not present at his execution.

Of particular interest to Cosby was Lee's action at San Antonio. He had strongly objected to the surrender of the Department of Texas to the secessionists. If the decision had been Lee's to make, Cosby realized that the Civil War might now have already started, and that Lee would either be dead or a prisoner in some Texan jail.

As for the letter from Walker dangling a generalship in the Confederacy, Lee had not even bothered to answer it.

This was the man Davis thought might be induced to become a defender of the Confederacy, a hero of the South?

Cosby sighed and looked out at the dim landscape between streaks of rain on the coach window. How could such a thing be done? And how could anyone possibly expect *him*, a man whose only military experience had been as a foot soldier in a war fifteen years ago, to influence a man who had been in the United States Army for more than thirty years—and a Superintendent of West Point—to, in effect, betray his country? On top of that, it was a man whom he had never met. How could *anyone* do such a thing? The more he thought about it, the more unrealistic and hopeless—fantastic, even—Davis' optimism and enthusiasm seemed to be. He felt like a man just awaking from a dream in which strange and superhuman acts were commonplace, but which were impossible in the cold light of reality.

He closed his eyes and fantasized Letitia beside him at this very moment. How she would have enjoyed this train ride! How he missed her high intelligence, bright smile, and teasing ways! She would have told him to open the window wider. He did, and the draught of cool air increased.

How did he really feel about this mission, and about the war which loomed so near? One thing seemed certain: Lee would not join the Confederacy, nor even leave the army, if his native state did not secede. For Davis' plan to have any chance of working, therefore, Virginia must first secede. But Virginia, still in the Union, would not secede unless a massive Federal army were raised to invade the Confederacy. Therefore, even if Davis' improbable plan worked, there would still be an invasion. Lee might not be at the head of it, but somebody else would be. In any event, it still meant war.

What would he, himself, do in the event of war? Cosby despaired. He had military experience, and was the right age to become an officer, but he did not want to. It was not fear. He thought all wars were wasteful, and a civil war was the worst of all. How many nations had been ruined, and lives lost, in civil wars? He thought of the Peloponnesian War, in which the ancient Greeks had so exhausted themselves in their long civil war that they not only ruined the splendor of their own civilization but were unable to defend themselves against the Macedonian army when Alexander invaded Greece. And what would be the point of it, anyway? The states-righters could thunder away all they liked, but at the root of it all was slavery. The people who talked about a state's right to secede would not want to secede if it were not for the question of slavery. And fighting a massive war over slavery was about as stupid a reason as anything Cosby could think of. If he was certain of anything, it was that slavery was a dying institution. Every other civilized nation in the world had long since outlawed it. Even the Spanish, whom the English once habitually accused of being barbarically cruel to their slaves, had outlawed slavery throughout the Spanish Empire in 1775, a year before the American Declaration of Independence and long before the British themselves had outlawed it. There was practically no other country in the world, however backward, which officially recognized slavery. That the United States of America, founded on such Enlightenment documents as the Declaration of Independence and the Constitution, full of noble phrases such as "all men are created equal" and "life, liberty, and the pursuit of happiness," should continue to countenance slavery while claiming to be some special force of morality in the world, was absurd.

Suppose war should come? And suppose Jeff Davis' dream of a much larger Confederacy came to pass? And suppose that Confederacy could hold off the Union and maintain its independence as a separate nation? How would that affect slavery?

Cosby thought that the Union would then pass a national abolition law, while the Confederacy would continue to allow it, possibly passing a national law specifically stating so. Then what? Cosby believed that slavery was a dying institution; not just for moral reasons, but also economic ones. The day would eventually come when slavery would be dead, even in a victorious Confederacy. What then? The only major philosophical point separating the two nations would be the Confederacy's insistence on the right of state secession. Was that enough to justify a separate nation? And what about trade? The Union might well impose an embargo, but suppose it didn't. The only product the Confederacy had which other nations wanted was cotton. Suppose the Union started growing cotton, especially in the new lands to the West? The South couldn't compete in any other field. It didn't even have a single textile mill to process any of its own cotton, because it had no ready source of energy to drive power looms. So all the cotton was exported to Britain, where coal-fired steam engines ran looms, or to New England, where small fast-flowing rivers spun water wheels to drive the looms. The South then had to buy back its own cotton, just to get clothing.

The whole thing is ridiculous, thought Cosby. *The very locomotive pulling this train, even though named for a prominent Southerner, was built in Philadelphia—a Baldwin locomotive. In the Confederacy as presently constituted, there wasn't a major locomotive factory, hardly even a decent ironworks.* The Confederacy was not viable morally, philosophically, or economically. *So why am I doing this?* Because Jefferson Davis asked me, and made it seem like a patriotic challenge. *So I do something I'm not really equipped to do, and don't really believe in anyway, just because a high-ranking politician asked me.*

Maybe patriotism really is the last refuge of scoundrels. Including me.

He sighed again. *Maybe that's what's wrong with the South.*

He pulled out his pocket watch and glanced at it. The train was making good time. He would be in Birmingham well before sunset, rain or no rain.

CHAPTER 4

Thursday
Washington, D.C.
12:21 PM

"Well, Rufus, suppose I made a dress out of *this*?"

Meagan O'Connor gracefully held a swatch of purple fabric between her neck and her waist, artfully outlining her breasts, and blinked her blue eyes coquettishly. "How would I look?"

Rufus Sloan thought it looked ghastly. "Very pretty, Miss O'Connor," he said smoothly. "Perhaps I might suggest something a little lighter. Something to match your eyes. I must say, though, I don't think I've ever seen a fabric quite that color. I'm not sure it could be made."

O'Connor's face lit up as she smiled widely, showing perfect teeth. "Oh, Rufus, you do say the *sweetest* things." She put down the piece of fabric and glided across the floor to him until only the store counter was between them. "And if I made a dress out of this unobtainable fabric, do you think I'd look pretty?"

Sloan caught a whiff of her lilac water, knowing that she knew he did. "Oh, yes, ma'am."

"Just...*pretty*?"

"*Very* pretty, Miss O'Connor."

"Humph. You said I was very pretty in the purple, and you didn't even like that. I could tell." Her merry blue eyes were laughing at him.

"Um, what I meant was, in light blue you'd be...*beautiful*, Miss O'Connor. One might even say...*ravishing.*" *And you'd be even more ravishing with absolutely nothing on at all,* he mentally added.

Almost as if she had read his mind, her dancing eyes turned serious, just for the briefest moment. She reached a gloved hand across the counter and rested it lightly on his forearm. "You *are* sweet, Rufus," she said quietly. Then she withdrew her hand, the casual flirt once more. "Now—show me the latest combs. I have to get back soon."

Sloan enjoyed her obvious flirtations; she could do it all afternoon, so far as he was concerned. She *was* beautiful and exciting, a breath of fresh air. Her trim figure was graceful, and her blonde hair made her look more Scandinavian than Irish. It was her dancing blue eyes, quick smile, and light chatter, however, which made her presence such a pleasure. She was bright and inquisitive, but very self-centered. She was one of six seamstresses employed at Apperson's Apparel, half a block up 11th St. from Amos Grinell's general store, "Grinell's Goods," where Sloan worked as a clerk.

Sloan knew that O'Connor flirted with other men; she was a natural flirt. He didn't mind, even if he was becoming semi-serious about her. Several times he had cautiously used her first name, calling her "Meagan" rather than "Miss O'Connor," but every time she had withdrawn slightly. He was conscious he had stepped over an invisible line; he was "Rufus" to her, but she was still "Miss O'Connor" to him. He had twice asked her out for a simple social engagement—an evening walk—but she had politely declined both times. So he was grateful that she came into the store every so often, like today, and shared her lunch break with him, sitting on a chair and eating an apple or a sandwich while chatting and flirting with him. On occasion she actually bought a few notions, which especially pleased him since he knew she didn't have much money.

She had once revealed that she was 23 years old, which meant she was two years younger than he was. He knew he was not a particularly handsome man, barely two inches taller than her medium height; his sharp features and lank, dark hair contrasted with her regular features and shimmering golden tresses. He knew he had a good smile, however, and something of a gift for minor repartee, both of which were useful in his job; he tried to use them liberally on her. However, she clearly had her eye on making a good catch, and he was smart enough to know he wasn't one; that explained her distance, despite her flirts. He knew he was a man of convenience to her. The only man in her shop was the owner, that fuss-budget Oswell Apperson, sixty years old and the father of five. O'Connor craved the companionship of men, especially complimentary ones, so she came here when she could. He accepted that, and was grateful for her propinquity.

O'Connor seemed fascinated by politics, the usual topic of conversation in the nation's capital, though she knew little about it. Politics was something Sloan could talk about endlessly. He was careful, however, not to take sides on political matters, but to always appear nonpartisan. That intrigued her. "Well, what do *you* think ought to be done, Rufus?" she would often ask. He would deftly turn aside such questions, just as he would turn aside questions about his past. Other than a few vague references to Pennsylvania, which were true enough, he spoke little about his youth.

He was especially quiet about the major political topic of the time: slavery. O'Connor, however, evinced little interest in it, rarely asking him about it. He had, for once, taken a stand, but made it sound almost neutral; he said the slavery question would have to be settled sooner or later, and agreed with Lincoln that the nation could not indefinitely continue to exist "half slave and half free."

"That means war, then?"

He had shrugged. "It might."

That was much more on her mind than an abstract question like slavery. She had never met a slave.

The possibility of war was much on her mind again today. "Do you think there will be a war, Rufus?" she asked plaintively as he showed her some combs.

"That depends, Miss O'Connor," he replied in his surprisingly deep voice. "I don't think the government is going to give up any more of its forts to this new Confederacy just because it asks for them. That happened in Texas and a number of other places, but Abe Lincoln wasn't president then. The government's done giving. The major sticking points are now Fort Pickens and Fort Sumter. The rebels can't do much about Pickens, off the coast of Florida, but they can about Sumter."

"That's in North Carolina, isn't it?"

"*South* Carolina, ma'am. On an island in Charleston harbor. The fort's strong, but there's batteries all around it. And the entrance to the harbor from the sea isn't all that wide. That's one reason it's a good harbor. The South Carolinians turned back a relief ship in January. They want that fort. I hear they'll even *buy* it, but Lincoln isn't selling. I don't think either side's going to budge."

"Then what?"

Sloan led her along to the pins. "When the South Carolinians fired on that relief ship in January, they were alone. Now there's a Confederacy, with seven states. So decisions about Fort Sumter are now being made in Montgomery, not Charleston. That fort is not threatening Charleston. Is the Confederacy willing to risk war by attacking it?" He shrugged. "I don't know. But it seems to me that there *will* be war if they *do* attack it."

"Oh, sweet Lord. War." She wrung her hands. "What will we do?"

"You're safe enough here, ma'am. Nobody's going to attack Washington."

"What will *you* do, Rufus?"

He averted her searching eyes and held his breath. She had unwittingly touched the core of his being, the seat of his deepest-held convictions. He knew what he would do if war came, but he wasn't going to tell her. Not now, anyway. That would get a little too close to his deepest secret.

"Whatever I have to, ma'am," he replied quietly.

She bought a black comb, which he wrapped carefully. "Thank you, Miss O'Connor. Hope to see you soon again."

"You will, Rufus," she smiled brightly as she left. "You will."

CHAPTER 5

Friday, April 12
Charleston, South Carolina
3:58 AM

Pierre Gustave Toutant Beauregard, his arms folded across his chest, looked across the moonlit water of Charleston harbor to Fort Sumter, sitting on its little artificial island. There were no lights showing in the fort, but the moonlight illuminated it brightly, softening its grim contours. By the light of the moon, the fort appeared clean and new, which is exactly what it was. Even at the distance of three and a half miles, the 50-foot height of the walls looked formidable. With its big guns, high walls, and nonexistent beaches, the fort could not be taken by assault.

Beauregard was not planning an assault. The fort had been designed to protect Charleston from a seaborne invasion; now the situation was exactly opposite, and the fort had to protect itself from Charleston. Normally it would have been resupplied by the city; now the city had cut it off from all supplies. It could be resupplied by the Union only by ships, and those ships would have to run the gauntlet of gun batteries ringing the harbor and lining the entrance. It was a

Federal fort sitting right in the harbor of the capital of the first state to secede, a bone in the throat of the Confederacy.

The handsome Creole general thought about all the factors which had led up to this point. There were two other fortified positions in the harbor, Fort Moultrie and Castle Pinckney. They had been occupied by Federal troops commanded by Major Robert Anderson, a Kentucky-born West Pointer generally sympathetic to the South. On the evening of December 26, 1860—six days after the secession of South Carolina—with no advance notification, Maj. Anderson quietly moved his entire force of 85 men across the harbor to Fort Sumter, a newly-built and far stronger fort in a far more defensible location. Later that evening they were joined by 45 dependents.

This action outraged the South Carolinians, for on Dec. 10 President Buchanan had privately assured several South Carolina congressmen that there would be no change in the military status at Charleston. The president then refused to order Anderson to evacuate Fort Sumter, and Anderson refused to leave without a direct order from his superiors.

The most outraged South Carolinian of all was the governor, fiery Francis Pickens. After the state convention's passage of the Ordinance of Secession on December 20, 1860, he urged that Fort Sumter, then unoccupied although almost completely finished, be immediately seized by the state militia. For various reasons, it wasn't. A week later, Anderson beat him to the punch. Almost apoplectic with fury, Pickens immediately ordered the seizure and occupation of every piece of Federal property in the Charleston area: Fort Moultrie, Castle Pinckney, the post office, the custom house, the treasury, and even the arsenal.

These actions might have ignited a war with a sterner president, but Buchanan—a lame duck with only a few months left in office—was desperate not to have the long-threatened civil war break out during his term. He did everything possible to mollify the South Carolinians. *Almost* everything—he never ordered Anderson to leave Sumter. And Anderson busied himself mounting the fort's cannons, the one task remaining to turn Sumter into a truly formidable fortress.

More followed. On January 9, 1861, an unarmed paddlewheel steamer, the *Star of the West*, attempted to bring supplies and reinforcing troops to Sumter; it was turned back by cannon fire from batteries along the channel entrance to the harbor. Maj. Anderson did not know this relief ship was coming, but the South Carolinians did—they had intercepted the War Department's letter to Anderson, which had been sent by ordinary mail.

On February 9 the Confederacy was proclaimed at Montgomery, Alabama, and Jefferson Davis was inaugurated as president nine days later. Now the decisions regarding Fort Sumter would be made in Montgomery, and Davis was inclined to talk peace while preparing for war. The Confederate officer he placed in charge of Charleston was Brig. Gen. P.G.T. Beauregard, the darkly handsome Creole from Louisiana.

Political machinations had now risen to a boiling point. Jeff Davis had sent three commissioners to Washington with the principal purpose of persuading the government to evacuate Sumter. They had no luck with the new president, Lincoln, but received sugary assurances from the new secretary of state, William Seward. Now the Confederates learned that a new naval relief effort had already set out from New York. They did not know the full details, but they did know it contained several warships—no more unarmed steamers like the *Star of the West.* This time the Federal government, with that ape-like Abe Lincoln, was playing for keeps.

This was unforgivable treachery. Sumter must be attacked at once, before the relief force arrived.

Late the previous afternoon, Beauregard had sent three officers to the fort to demand immediate surrender. Anderson had refused, but revealed he was low on food. After a telegram to Montgomery, Beauregard had received authorization to attack. A last warning at 3:20 AM had notified the Federals that bombardment would commence shortly. At last—this morning, *now*—the Confederacy would finally do something about this damned fort. It would be yielded, come hell or high water.

Beauregard looked behind him. Fort Sumter may have been dark, but the city wasn't. The word had spread about the imminent bombardment. Half the population was up, and lights were everywhere.

Turning back to the water, Beauregard felt a huge surge of personal satisfaction. Last year he had been appointed Superintendent at West Point, but had been unceremoniously removed after only five days when he had incautiously stated that he would follow his native state of Louisiana if it seceded. *Five days!* The pain of that searing ignominy and peremptory rejection still burned in his proud soul. He had indeed resigned his commission on January 20, 1861; six days later Louisiana seceded. He and his state joined the Confederacy, and now here he was in Charleston, a brigadier general in the service of the South. In a few minutes he would make history, and all those haughty stuffed uniforms in the War Department in Washington would be powerless to prevent it. *He would show them!*

The range to Fort Sumter was 6,000 yards, within the capability of the 30 cannons and 17 mortars in the Charleston battery. However, there were other batteries considerably closer to the fort. Fort Johnson, on James Island to the west of Sumter, was 2,400 yards distant; Fort Moultrie, to the northeast, 1,800 yards; and an iron-protected battery on Cumming's Point, to the south, was a scant 1,450 yards distant, almost point-blank range. All their guns were trained on Sumter, and could hit it even in the dark.

An aide approached Beauregard. "Almost time, General." He spoke quietly, yet his voice sounded loud in the stillness of the night.

"Thank you, Lieutenant." Beauregard was surprised to find his voice husky with emotion. "Where is Mr. Ruffin?" he managed to ask. Edmund Ruffin was a fire-eating secessionist from Virginia, a confessed Yankee-hater, who had come down to South Carolina specifically to be in the action over Fort Sumter. He wanted to fire the first shot; although he was a civilian, the amused Beauregard said that he could.

"I don't know, sir," the aide replied. "Let me find out." He returned a half-minute later and reported that Ruffin was at the Iron Battery on Cumming's Point. "He has the closest shot," the aide commented.

Beauregard smiled wryly. "He wants to be sure he hits it."

A white arc sailed skyward out of the dark to the southeast, followed a few seconds later by the unmistakable rumble of a cannon shot. "Fort Johnson, sir," the aide cried excitedly. "The signal to commence firing."

"Indeed it is." The rumbling sound increased and became constant as all the batteries began firing. Beauregard raised his voice. "You may inform our battery to open fire."

The Civil War had begun.

CHAPTER 6

Friday
Washington
12:04 AM

Meagan O'Connor dashed into Grinell's Goods. "Oh, Rufus, I got here as fast as I could," she exclaimed breathlessly. "Ran all the way from Apperson's. Have you heard the news? Of course you have," she added, eyeing the several newspapers on the countertop.

She seated herself in her favorite chair and began unwrapping her light lunch. There were several other customers in the store, but she paid no attention to them. "Fort Sumter!" she said, eating a grape. "How did you know? You *predicted* it!"

"Not really, Miss O'Connor," Sloan smiled indulgently. It was very satisfying to hear flattery from a beautiful young woman, something Sloan had precious little of in his life. "It's been known for weeks now that Fort Sumter might well turn out to be the flash point, especially since the election. Now it's happened."

"How long can it hold out?"

"I don't know. Weeks, maybe. Perhaps only days. If it could somehow be reinforced and resupplied, it could probably hold out indefinitely. But unless the navy sends down some serious warships, which could knock out the shore batteries as well as provide more men and supplies, I don't see how it can hold out very long."

"You think it will surrender?"

Sloan shrugged. "If they're out of food, they'll have to."

"Then what? Will Congress declare war?"

"That depends, ma'am. We don't really *have* to go to war. After all, it's just one fort. Even if it surrenders, it's only a small loss. Having it doesn't really make the Confederacy more powerful. It's the principle of the thing. However, I can almost guarantee you Congress won't declare war."

"It won't?" O'Connor's hand, holding half a bun, paused halfway to her mouth. "Why not?"

"Well, for one thing," Sloan smiled, "Congress isn't in session. It won't be for several more months, unless President Lincoln calls an emergency session. For another thing, the official government position is that it doesn't recognize secession, therefore doesn't recognize the Confederacy. How can Congress declare war on an organization it doesn't recognize? That would be an implicit act of recognition, something Lincoln seems determined to avoid."

"So what will Mr. Lincoln do?"

"You have me there, Miss O'Connor. The president hasn't spoken to me lately." They both grinned. "However, you must remember his inaugural address, just a few weeks ago." O'Connor's frown showed her puzzlement; she wasn't in the habit of remembering inaugural addresses. "He said the question of war was in the hands of the Southerners. The general interpretation of that statement was that he was saying the Union wouldn't fire the first shot. If there was going to be war, the Confederacy was going to have to start it. Well, now it has. Nobody can now say that a war-crazy South-hating president commenced hostilities. The South did."

"So what will he do?" O'Connor asked again.

"The gauntlet has been thrown. I think the president will pick it up. He'll make preparations for war. Big preparations. He certainly won't wait around several months for Congress to convene. I think he'll do it on his own, acting as commander-in-chief, although he may call a special session of Congress."

"So it's going to be war."

Sloan turned his palms upward. “Something may happen in the next week or so to stop it, but I’d say the chances are slim. I think it *is* going to be war.”

O’Connor looked down at the half-finished lunch in her lap, her golden curls falling on her cheeks. “War.” She started sniffling. “War. And for what? Pride. That’s what it is! Stupid, stiff-necked pride! What is the matter with everybody?”

Sloan looked at the crying girl a few moments. “You know what, Miss O’Connor?” he asked softly. “I’m glad it happened.”

“What?” She looked up at him, tears in her eyes.

“I’m glad it happened,” he repeated, a bit stubbornly.

“For heaven’s sake, *why*?”

Sloan sighed lightly and looked away. “Washington is the first city I’ve lived in,” he said slowly. “Most of my life I’ve lived in the country. New York, Pennsylvania, out West—farms, small towns. Places like that, especially out West, you can see storms coming a long way off. Miles and miles—tens of miles. The dark clouds get bigger, it gets dark, the air becomes moist and heavy. Sometimes there’s a wind, sometimes not. It gets tense. Tight. You get fidgety. Everything stops. Everybody’s *waiting.* Sometimes it’s almost unbearable. Then comes that first bolt of lightning, followed by thunder. Then rain. Lots of rain. And you know what, Miss O’Connor?” He looked back at her, but seemed to be looking through her. “The rain—it was a *relief.* You knew it was coming, and the waiting was worse than the rain itself. Well, we’ve waited a long time, watching the clouds get bigger and bigger. Now the lightning has hit. Soon there will be thunder. Then rain.”

She followed his analogy. “Lots of rain?”

“Yes, ma’am. Lots of rain.”

“And you *like* that?”

His eyes focused on her. “You know what I often did in a rainstorm? Ran around in it. Stuck my tongue out, let the rain fall on it. Nothing sweeter than fresh rain.”

O’Connor looked at Sloan a long moment, her face expressionless. He had never revealed so much of himself before. Not even close. She was both fascinated and appalled.

“New York and Pennsylvania? That’s where you’re from?”

Sloan nodded.

"The West. Where were you in the West?"

Sloan did not answer for a moment. "Missouri, Kansas," he finally said quietly.

"Kansas? You've been to Kansas?

Sloan nodded again.

"I've never even been to the Alleghenies," O'Connor said wistfully. "Someday I'd like to see the Mississippi. But Kansas—that's *past* the Mississippi, isn't it?"

"Yes, ma'am, it is."

"What is it like?"

Sloan shrugged. "It's prarie. That's almost all you see. Goes to the horizon, in every direction. Not many hills, not many trees. If you want a place to be alone, that's it."

"Is that why you went there, Rufus? To be alone?" Sloan didn't answer. "Did you have a farm there?" she persisted.

"Helped out some," he finally said.

O'Connor's finely honed sense of inquisitiveness was aroused as Sloan became his usual close-mouthed self regarding his personal life. "What did you do there?" she asked quietly but bluntly.

Sloan gave her a lingering look, then turned and glanced at the large wall clock. Its ornate hands and Roman numerals indicated 12:27. "It's getting late, Miss O'Connor. We wouldn't want Mr. Apperson to come down here looking for you."

"Goodness, so it is." O'Connor rewrapped the remains of her lunch and stood up. "Thank you, Rufus. I'll see you again."

At the door she turned to give a little wave; Sloan was already talking to another customer.

CHAPTER 7

Friday
The Executive Mansion
2:00 PM

Abraham Lincoln rapped on the table. "Order, gentlemen," he said quietly. The murmur ceased and eight faces turned toward him expectantly. "We all know why we're here," the president continued. "Just for the record, however, and just so Mr. Hay knows, this is an emergency meeting of the Cabinet, called by me." Without turning around, Lincoln waved a hand over his shoulder. John Hay, the recording secretary, was seated in a chair against the wall, and waved back. Several of the Cabinet members smiled at him.

"We are here to discuss the situation at Fort Sumter, and what our response should be. We have had this discussion before, but now the fort has been attacked. The situation is now changed. Before we proceed further, we should have a review of the current situation, for which the Secretary of War is eminently qualified. Mr. Cameron, if you please."

Simon Cameron, the former governor of Pennsylvania, cleared his throat. He was the most impressive-looking member of the administration, including the president. Tall and handsome, he had a leonine head of silver-gray hair, neatly parted on the left side. Though he was the most presidential-looking person present, he had the reputation for being just a bit slow-witted.

"Fort Sumter was attacked," he began in his ponderous way, "at approximately four o'clock this morning by several batteries of artillery on the coastline ringing Charleston harbor. Artillery pieces in the fort are firing back. We have no report of the damage yet."

"The garrison consists of 85 men—nine officers and 76 enlisted men. The commander is Maj. Robert Anderson, who was appointed last November."

"He was actually appointed to Fort Moultrie, wasn't he?" Gideon Welles interrupted.

"Yes, Mr. Welles, thank you," Cameron continued, glancing at the bushy-whiskered Secretary of the Navy. "He was indeed appointed to Fort Moultrie, which also lies in Charleston harbor. Fort Sumter was unoccupied at the time, since it was not quite finished. Without specific orders, Anderson secretly moved the garrison to Sumter on the night of December 26 and the following day. Sumter is a much stronger position, so this was militarily a wise move on the major's part, but it violated an apparent understanding between the previous administration and the government of South Carolina that the Federal forces would not be moved. The South Carolinians were infuriated by this move, and the Charleston militia immediately occupied Fort Moultrie and Castle Pinckney, both of which were unoccupied."

"And that's why they fired on the *Star of the West*," Welles pursued.

"Yes," Cameron continued. "On January 9 a relief ship, the *Star of the West*, entered Charleston harbor and attempted to reach Fort Sumter. She had 200 soldiers on board, as well as supplies. Although unarmed, she was fired upon by several shore batteries and turned back before reaching Sumter. After this administration took over, we found that the previous administration had attempted to alert Maj. Anderson that the ship was coming, and what was in it, by sending a letter by ordinary mail to him. They didn't use a military courier, an obvious precaution. Naturally the South Carolinians intercepted it. The result was that Anderson didn't know the ship was coming, but the rebels did, and were waiting for it."

Cameron smiled indulgently at the snorts and caustic comments from the table. The ineptitude of the previous administration, beginning with President Buchanan himself, was a frequent source for derision from the current Cabinet.

"How high are the walls?" asked Montgomery Blair. "Could the fort withstand a direct assault?"

Cameron turned toward the Postmaster-General. Some might think it easy to dismiss Blair as a lightweight, though he was an able lawyer and had been one of Dred Scott's lawyers in that explosively controversial 1857 decision by the Supreme Court. Everyone knew that Blair was in this Cabinet because Lincoln was paying a political debt to his father, 71-year-old Francis Preston Blair, who had been a major player in the Jackson administration and was an influential publisher. *The Jackson administration,* thought Cameron. *An age ago! Everyone remembers that administration, however, because Jackson was the last two-term president.* Montgomery Blair's brother, Francis P. Jr., was a congressman from Missouri. Together the Blairs were the most politically influential family in politics. The elder Blair even lived diagonally across from the Executive Mansion, right next to Lafayette Square. Cameron liked Montgomery Blair.

"No fear there, Mr. Blair," he replied easily. "The walls are fifty feet high, solid masonry twelve feet thick. The fort sits on a small artificial island. Assault forces attempting to land would be under the fort's guns long before they landed, and after they landed would have no place to hide. If adequately garrisoned, that fort simply cannot be taken by assault."

"How big is it?" Blair pursued.

Cameron looked at the ceiling, trying to remember. "Several hundred feet on a side. I don't remember exactly. It's quite large."

"It's built in the shape of a pentagon," volunteered Welles, who did remember exactly. "Three hundred feet on its longest side, two hundred and fifty feet from that side to the apex. It *is* large. I agree with Mr. Cameron—it cannot be taken by assault. I'm not sure it can even be taken by bombardment. That's not the problem."

"What *is* the problem, Gideon?" Lincoln asked quietly, knowing the answer.

"Food, Mr. President," Welles answered briskly. "The garrison used to buy its food directly from Charleston. After secession, the rebels started to become increasingly selective about the victuals they sold. For example, they would sell bread, which has to be eaten quickly or it will spoil, but not flour, which can be stored for long periods. Even that stopped two weeks ago. Now the garrison is living off its own internal supplies. They can't last long."

"How long *can* they last?" the Secretary of the Interior wanted to know.

"I estimate less than a week, Mr. Smith," Welles replied. His curling white hair and full white beard made him resemble the caricature of the Christmas St. Nicholas which had appeared in several news magazines the last few years.

There was momentary silence. "So the rebels didn't really have to attack, is that it, Mr. Welles?" Caleb Smith asked. "They could have waited and starved the garrison out? Just a few days? So why did they attack?"

"Maybe they didn't know the supplies were so low," Edward Bates volunteered.

"They knew, Mr. Bates," Lincoln said unexpectedly in his quiet voice. "They wanted a military victory. Shot and shell, crashing guns, thunder and lightning. A big show. Something glorious, something to brag about. They didn't want to accept the surrender of a starving garrison. No glory in that. No heroism. No *stories.* Nothing makes a Southerner happier than telling a good story." The trace of a smile played around his craggy face. "You gentlemen should know that. I've told a few of them myself."

Laughter arose from most of the men at the table. "One thing I am sure of, gentlemen," Lincoln went on, his smile widening. "Regardless of what lies ahead of us, there will never be any such thing in the Confederacy as a small victory. They will all be great victories, *grand* victories, *magnificent* victories. There may not even be any defeats. We must all be on guard to prevent the Union from being washed away in a sea of Southern stories." More laughter.

Salmon P. Chase, the Secretary of the Treasury, spoke up. "How is our relief expedition doing, Mr. President? Didn't we send some warships several days ago? Have they arrived yet? I've read nothing in the press about them."

The president looked at his Secretary of the Navy. "Care to reply, Mr. Welles?"

"Yes, Mr. Chase," Welles answered immediately. "There is a relief expedition. It consists of several warships, a supply ship, and three tugs. In addition to food and munitions, the supply ship, the *Baltic*, has 200 troops on board. That ship and the tugs left New York on Monday, April 8, just four days ago. They are expected to rendezvous with the warships off Charleston harbor."

"The plan was this. The president will officially notify—*has* notified, I believe—the governor of South Carolina that an attempt will be made to resupply Sumter. The *Baltic*, an unarmed ship, will attempt to enter the harbor first, alone and unescorted. If it is not fired upon, the resupply will be provisions only—no troops. If it is fired upon, the *Baltic* will turn about, the troops and supplies will be transferred to the tugs out of sight of land, and then run into the harbor at night. Being much smaller, the tugs have a much better change of slipping past the batteries. If all else fails, the warships can open fire on the batteries."

"The expedition is commanded by Gustavus Fox, a former naval officer who is now in the textile business in Massachusetts. This daring plan was his."

"You all will recall that a month ago, the president asked each of us to provide a written reply to the question of whether we should attempt to reprovision Fort Sumter, assuming it were possible to do so. The reason the president asked us was that the day before, Mr. Fox had explained his plan to the president. Without yet knowing the details of the plan, five of us—including myself—voted in the negative. The president decided otherwise, and so the plan was put into effect. The president confided in me because it was my duty to arrange these naval matters. The soldiers and supplies were provided by General Scott."

This was the first time several of the Cabinet officials had heard the details of this plan, although they knew of its bare outline.

"Mr. President, did you indeed notify the governor of South Carolina that a relief ship was on the way?" asked Bates quickly.

"I did," Lincoln admitted calmly. "And to make sure there would be no mistake, I sent a note by military courier directly to Gov. Pickens in Charleston. On Monday. The courier should have arrived on Wednesday."

"May I ask why, sir?" the Attorney General pursued, his voice tinged with the slightest hint of incredulity.

"For this reason, Mr. Bates." Lincoln leaned forward and rested his forearms on the table, an action which made his coat sleeves look too short for his lanky arms. "As I understand it, the reason the South Carolinians were so outraged by the *Star of the West* attempting to reach Fort Sumter in January is that they thought it violated some understanding they had with the Buchanan administration. Moreover, the supply attempt was made in secret; the only way the Carolinians discovered it was, as Mr. Cameron pointed out, that they intercepted the mail. To them, it was a sneak attempt to circumvent an agreement."

"Now, I do not condone their firing on that ship. Fort Sumter is a Federal fort, and the Federal government has every right to supply its own forts, regardless of what hotheaded secessionists may claim. But I will not sneak about it; I will be open. This is a new administration, and we are not bound by any back-room unwritten understanding that the Carolinians thought they had with the previous administration. I want to resupply that fort, I have every right to do it, and I want the government of South Carolina to *know* about it. So I tell the governor openly. And I offer him a deal: no firing, no troops. There will be no mistake this time, no claim of misunderstanding. Either they will let this ship pass, or they will fire on it. If they let it pass, well and good; the fort will be resupplied, provisions only, and a precedent would have been established to have it supplied at regular intervals in the future. If they fire on it, they do so knowing full well they are opening hostilities in a major war."

Lincoln looked down at his hands on the table. Not for the first time at a Cabinet meeting, he wished he had something to whittle. He thought better when his hands were busy. It seemed unnatural to simply rest his hands on a table, and not have them holding a book, writing a letter, fixing or examining something, or even whittling. "In my inaugural address," he continued slowly, "I promised I would not fire the first shot. If war was to come, they would have to start it. I meant to keep that promise. But I would not, *will* not, keep it by running away from every confrontation. I *will not* give up military installations to the Confederacy or various states just because they demand them. We are not the only ones who have to weigh what war will mean; they do, too."

"Until this morning I thought the real test would be the attempt by the *Baltic* to reach Sumter. It turns out now that the rebels have fired on the fort itself. No matter; they have fired the first shot. I have kept my promise, but on my terms. That is very important to me. I want the whole country to know it. I want the *world* to know it."

There was silence at the table following this forceful declaration from the president. Montgomery Blair, seated at the far end of the table, was one Cabinet member who did not have to ask for details of the relief expedition. He already knew them; Gustavus Fox, the expedition commander, was his brother-in-law. Knowing of Fox's naval experience and intrepid nature, he had invited Fox to come down from the textile mills in Lowell and arranged for him to speak privately to the president.

Blair noted that Lincoln had said nothing about Blair's involvement in the expedition, and he now knew enough about the president to know why: Lincoln was waiting to see how the expedition turned out. If it proved to be a success, Lincoln would praise Blair in a subsequent Cabinet meeting; if it proved a failure, Lincoln would take the blame without mentioning Blair. There were not many politicians, especially presidents, who would do something like that.

Blair noted something else. That business that Lincoln said about the rebels attacking Fort Sumter because they wanted glory, a big show, something to tell a story about—it wasn't really true. Well, maybe a little bit, which was why Lincoln's exaggeration of it was amusing. It was really *Lincoln's* story, a story on himself. The real reason the fort was being bombarded, right this very minute, was that the rebels knew a relief ship was coming. Deal or no deal about troops, they had decided they would attack the fort itself *before* the relief ship tried to get in. And how did they know the relief ship was coming? Lincoln himself had told them. By courier to the very governor of South Carolina, no less.

Blair marveled at the breathless audacity of it all. The normal reaction of almost anyone in Lincoln's position would have been to *conceal* the fact that the relief ship was coming, just as Buchanan had done. Lincoln was smart enough to know that would have led to a repetition of the *Star of the West* incident, and even a charge by the rebels that he had broken his inaugural pledge. By his openness, Lincoln was not only acting honorably, he was forcing the Confederacy's hand. It would have to let the ship pass or fire on it. Either way, Lincoln would have achieved a major objective.

There was more. Lincoln deliberately left unsaid something he surely knew. By notifying Gov. Pickens directly Lincoln put him in an impossible bind. How could the governor of the most rabidly secessionist state in the Confederacy, the first state to secede, ever tell anybody that he had received advance notice of the relief ship—from the *president*, the hated Abe Lincoln himself—and then ordered his military forces *not* to do anything about it? It was unthinkable. Pickens would have been hung in effigy from every lamp post in Charleston, if not in actuality. Regardless of anything Jeff Davis might order, Pickens *had* to order the attack, and Lincoln knew it. The attack turned out to be on the fort itself rather than the ship, but, as Lincoln said, it didn't matter. If Davis himself, rather than Pickens, had ordered the attack, then so much the better. No matter how you looked at it, wily Abe Lincoln had used the South's bellicosity against itself and had successfully maneuvered the Confederates into firing the first shot.

He would not let them forget it.

Blair gazed idly but appreciatively down the table at Lincoln, who was listening to Salmon Chase. Gangly, awkward, rough-hewn, homespun, slow-speaking Abraham Lincoln, who looked like the world's tallest chimney-sweep when he put on his stovepipe hat, was a ridiculously easy target for the criticism of editors and the caricatures of cartoonists. He had been a compromise candidate for the Republican Party, but benefited from massive vote division in the four-candidate election. He won less than 40% of the popular vote, the lowest in history, but a clear majority in the electoral college. His erstwhile debating opponent, Stephen Douglas, who had beaten Lincoln in the 1858 senatorial race in Illinois, was also a candidate for president in 1860; he had finished dead last in the college, with only twelve electoral votes. So Lincoln was president, fair and square, and Southern states started seceding the month after the election.

The amazing thing was, Blair realized, that this controversial figure was showing unexpected and enormous capacities for sensitivity, intellect, diplomacy, clear-headedness, determination, humor, and even that old-fashioned and much misused word, honor. He even had a special quality almost impossible to find in any politician: self-deprecation. From his close vantage point, Blair could see that Lincoln was much better, infinitely better, as president than any of the other candidates would have been, better than any president he had ever known. His father had been absolutely right to back Lincoln early and often.

"Then these relief ships might already be off Charleston harbor, isn't that so?" Chase was saying. "Since the Confederates are already firing on Fort Sumter, they will assuredly fire on the relief ship if it approaches. The possibly peaceful option of slipping that ship in unopposed is now gone. What then about using the tugs at night? Can we still do that?"

"I don't know," Welles answered. "We don't know if the supply ship and the tugs are in position yet. We also don't know if they have met with the warships. The principal problem with the garrison was, and still is, food. However, now that its guns are firing, it will also soon run out of powder."

Lincoln broke in. "I think we will simply have to leave the wisdom of the attempt up to Commander Fox." Welles and Cameron nodded. "I must admit, however, that the prospects are not sanguine."

Secretary of State William Seward leaned forward. Fifty-nine years old, short and energetic, he had been senator and governor of New York State and the leading presidential candidate at the Republican convention in 1860. He thought he should have been the Republican nominee, and if he had been he would now be president. Lincoln surprised many people by selecting his convention opponent for the most important position in the Cabinet. Seward tended to treat the actual president, who had been neither a senator nor a governor but a simple one-term congressman, like a professor lecturing a slow-witted student.

"Mr. President, now that Fort Sumter is under bombardment, surely the most important thing we should be discussing is the disposition of the fort and its garrison. If the relief supplies do not get through, then the fort will have to surrender in just a few days. We are all agreed on that, are we not?" Seward glanced around the table, reading assent in the glum faces. "Even if supplies and troops *do* reach the fort, it will only have to be resupplied some time soon again. More troops will mean more mouths to feed. The Confederates will bring up more and more cannon, and they have no problem with resupply. A few weeks from now, even the whole United States Navy would not be able to break through to Sumter. The fort's surrender, therefore, is only a matter of time. Why, then, cause the deaths of many good men by continuing to hold out in a hopeless cause? The point has been made. The Confederacy, as you say, has fired first. Why not simply surrender the fort now? No one would blame you. The garrison might not even have to be incarcerated. We could negotiate their evacuation to the supply ship, and they could be returned to the North. As *heroes*," Seward added.

Everyone looked at the president. This was a challenge, but it sounded so reasonable, humane, and pragmatic that no one thought ill of it.

"Let the Confederates have Sumter, Mr. President," echoed Bates. "We can't threaten Charleston with it, even if we keep it. Having it doesn't really make the Confederacy stronger. South Carolina is not going to invade the United States, with or without Sumter."

Abraham Lincoln looked around at his Cabinet. He was not going to argue points of view with them; they were here to advise him, not he them. "Thank you for your input, gentlemen. Mr. Seward raises a worthwhile point. Should we surrender the fort now? I would like to have a vote on that single issue. All those in favor of immediate surrender please say *aye*."

There were five *ayes*: Seward, Smith, Welles, Bates, and Cameron. Blair and Chase voted *nay.* It was exactly the same split as the voting on the resupply of Fort Sumter a month before.

"Did you get that vote, Mr. Hay?" Lincoln asked. "Five *ayes*, two *nays* on the surrender of Fort Sumter?" He would make sure the record showed just who was in favor of giving up government property.

"Yes, sir, I did."

"You didn't vote, Mr. President," Caleb Smith observed.

"No, I didn't," Lincoln affirmed. "I will decide. And my decision is that the question of surrendering Fort Sumter will be postponed until Monday. I would like all of you back in this room at 10:30 AM. By that time we will have more information on the condition of the fort and the situation with the relief ships. Good day to you all."

The president arose and left the room. The Cabinet members all arose, waited until Lincoln left, and then filed out. The thought occurred to more than one of them that the reason Lincoln postponed the surrender decision was that by Monday morning, Fort Sumter may have surrendered on its own, relieving the president of that onerous decision. Abraham Lincoln hated to surrender *anything.*

CHAPTER 8

Saturday, April 13
Washington
4:12 AM

We struck on the night of May 24, 1856. It had been three days since the sack of Lawrence by a large band of Border Ruffians. We had waited long enough. John Brown, leading a group of nine other men, all settlers near Osawatomie Creek in southeastern Kansas, set out to "regulate matters," as the Old Man put it, on Pottawatomie Creek. It was a few miles distant, and had a number of proslavery settlers. The Old Man distributed cutlasses and sabers to all of us; Brown himself and another were the only ones with guns. We would do the Lord's work in quiet that night.

We called ourselves the "Army of the North," the Old Man's idea. He, of course, was "Captain," a rank he had actually held in a militia. As he passed out the swords we each had to repeat an oath, even the three of his sons who were with us that night: Owen, Frederick, and Salmon.

"Mr. Cutler, dost thou believe that slavery is a sin, accursed by God?" he asked me.

"Yes, sir." John Brown always spoke in Biblical "thees" and "thous" when he was serious, and half the time even in casual conversation.

"Dost thou believe that anyone who defends this abominable sin deserves to be judged by God?"

"Yes, sir, Cap'n." The dark straw hat looked quite incongruous on John Brown's head, but it hid his hawklike face, and in the uncertain moonlight made him appear much taller than his actual height of five feet, nine inches. Nothing, however, could dim those blazing eyes or soften his iron soul.

"Judgment will be delivered this night, as we will instill a restraining fear among the proslavers. Dost thou swear to obey my orders, without hesitation, without equivocation?"

"Yes, sir."

"So help thee God?"

"So help me God."

"Choose thy weapon."

"Thank'ee, Cap'n."

I chose a saber rather than a cutlass, as it was longer yet easier to maneuver and much better for stabbing; cutlasses were for hacking.

We climbed aboard the wagon in silence. The road to Pottawattomie was bumpy, and our keenly-honed swords chinked softly in the darkness. A cool wind moved across the great Kansas prarie; it felt cold to my clammy skin. I shivered. The Old Man must have felt it too, for he turned to us. "The Lord's work will warm us this night," he said quietly.

All of us were part of the huge rush of settlers, proslavers and abolitionists, who had been pouring into the Kansas Territory ever since the passage of the Kansas-Nebraska Act two years earlier, which decreed that these territories would enter the Union as free states or slave states depending upon the vote of the inhabitants. There was constant warfare, resulting in "Bleeding Kansas." The sack of Lawrence, center of the Free State movement, was the latest and greatest outrage. Tonight we would make amends. John Brown of Osawatomie and the Army of the North were coming to call on their neighbors. It would not be a friendly call.

The first house we visited that night was that of John Mentzig, a frequent juror in the local court, who always voted the proslavery line. He warded us off by sticking a rifle through a hole in his house wall.

We left after a short time. We had bigger fish to fry.

We then visited the home of James Doyle, a loudmouth braggart who recently had ridden into Osawatomie, on a day when he knew we were all away, and threatened our women. Doyle unbolted his door after the Old Man tricked him into thinking we were proslavers. We rushed the house, marched out Doyle and his two oldest sons—all members of the proslavery Law and Order Party—and hacked them to death. We spared his wife, his daughter, and his 14-year-old son.

Allen Wilkenson was next. He was a member of the proslavery territorial legislature which had ejected its Free State members and made any violation of the Fugitive Slave Act a capital offense in Kansas. We dragged him out of the house and hacked him to death, leaving behind a widow and two orphaned children.

The natural gathering place for proslavers in the Pottawatomie area was Dutch Henry's tavern, and it was there we went next. "Dutch" Henry Sherman was the worst proslaver in a twenty-mile radius; he sold bottled courage to scum like Doyle. We looked forward to ventilating his rum-soaked gut with some abolitionist steel. For some reason the Lord decided to spare him; he was not there. Six others were, including his younger brother. We took Dutch Bill outside, killed him, and left his body in the creek. We spared the others, only because the Old Man said so.

The predawn darkness was showing the palest tint of gray when we finished at the tavern. We knew we had left a trail of witnesses and that there would be trouble later, but we didn't mind at the time. We had actually done something about slavery, something not soon forgotten. It was exhilaration beyond description.

It was especially sweet for me. I had taken part in three of the executions. "Good work, Josh," they told me. Even the Old Man had a kind word for me. I was a man.

It was Salmon Brown who gave me the nickname that night of "Cutter" because of my saber work. That is how Rufus Sloan, a refugee from a Pennsylvania farm, who used the name Joshua Cutler when I entered Brown's circle, became Cutter Cutler, a feared member of John Brown's band of avenging angels.

It was the finest night of my life.

* * * * *

Rufus Sloan awoke in a cold sweat. He was awake in an instant, shivering despite a pile of blankets. Kansas! He had dreamed the Kansas dream again!

He turned over on his back and willed himself to gradually stop the shivering, to gradually slow his racing heart. In his conscious mind he relived that humid, chilly night under the vast starry vault of the open Kansas sky—the anticipation, the wrenching fear, the trembling excitement, the soaring ecstasy. There was nothing so sweet, so totally fulfilling, so worthwhile, so dearer than life itself, as an all-out fight for a grand cause, and the abolition of slavery was the grandest cause in the world.

Sloan could not go back to sleep. He knew that some night soon, he would dream of Kansas again. And he would also dream of Harpers Ferry.

CHAPTER 9

Saturday
Washington
8:16 AM

Rose O'Neal Greenhow walked along the rows of the Central Market, ignoring the drab frame shed-like buildings on either side of it. The market, on Seventh St., was a bit of a walk from her home in the fashionable district just north of Lafayette Square, but it was along the best and most entertaining street in the entire city, Pennsylvania Avenue. The large market was always lively, if not downright rowdy, and had easily the best selection of food in the city. She enjoyed it.

There were a lot of shoppers, even at this early hour. Most of them were men. Even if her late husband were still alive, she would never have let him do the shopping, for he knew nothing about food. Poor Robert! Place him in front of a book, even if in Latin or Greek, and he was perfectly at home. Ask him about food, and all he knew was how to eat it. And he would usually rather read than eat, no matter what the food.

It was too early in the year for some of her favorite fruits and vegetables. In July there would be magnificent tomatoes, huge watermelons; a bit later there would be crisp apples. Maybe somehow, someday, by some miracle there might show up in this market that most exotic and heavenly of all fruits, oranges, which she had tasted and marveled at during the time she had lived in California.

While waiting for the far-off oranges, there were plenty of other things here to tempt the palate. The Central Market was famous for its delicacies, especially seafood. Thank heaven for the Chesapeake Bay! There were fish of all kinds, Maryland crabs, terrapins, oysters…her guests this evening might really like oysters. She reached out her hand to examine one.

"One of these terrapins would make a delicious soup for your party, Mrs. Greenhow."

Rose's hand stopped in midair. The voice was low, well-modulated, and polite. Definitely masculine, definitely unfamiliar. She was not afraid. She could not remember ever fearing a man in her life. Especially an intriguing one.

Greenhow turned slightly to her right. A handsome and well-dressed man in his mid-thirties was standing close to her, speculatively holding a small melon and carefully not looking at her. He was a total stranger. She had a sharp memory for faces and names, and knew she had never met this man. She also knew instinctively that she would like to meet him.

"Perhaps you are right, sir," she said smoothly, keeping her voice low. "Terrapin soup is a delicacy greatly savored by persons of discrimination and sophistication. Might you be at the party this evening? A guest of someone?" She picked up an oyster, examining its brown mottled shell as if it offered some hidden clue about the quality of its contents, discernible only to shellfish experts.

"Alas, no, Mrs. Greenhow. It is most regrettable. Your parties are the talk of the city."

She looked up from the oyster. "An invitation could easily be arranged from the hostess," she smiled, meeting his clear gray eyes.

"Thank you, Mrs. Greenhow." The man returned the smile, making him one of the most charming-looking men Rose Greenhow thought she had ever met. "You are most gracious. Unfortunately I must decline, for reasons I trust will soon become apparent."

Greenhow replaced the oyster. "Oh? You seem to know a great deal about me, Mr.—ah—"

The man looked carefully about him, hefting the melon. There was scant chance of being overheard. The bustle of shoppers and marketeers was everywhere, and voices of every description filled the air. "Thomas, ma'am. You may call me Mr. Thomas. Yes, I do know a great deal about you. You are one of the most prominent socialites in Washington, but everyone knows that. As a young woman you were one of the principal reasons why Mrs. Hill's boarding-house, the old capitol building, was the most popular boarding-house in Washington. Your dark eyes, dark hair, magnificent figure, gracious manners, and keen intelligence captivated everyone, as they still do. You were a great companion to Senator Calhoun, who cared for you very much; you were his nurse at his death. You were in Dolley Madison's social circle during her later years. Your late husband, Dr. Robert Greenhow, was a distinguished scholar, lawyer, and cartographer, who rendered great service to the government by mapping western territories and serving as an emissary to various Indian tribes. You lived for a time in San Francisco. Dr. Greenhow was unfortunately killed there in 1854 when he fell into an unmarked excavation pit. You sued the city for negligence, were awarded a handsome settlement, and moved back to Washington. You currently live with your four daughters in a three-story house near the corner of Sixteenth and H Streets, just north of Lafayette Square and across the street from St. John's Church."

Rose Greenhow had never heard her life expressed so succinctly. "You do indeed know much about me, Mr. Thomas," she said, moving slowly over to several large trays full of crabs. "You politely haven't mentioned my age, although you know that too, of course."

"Of course," Thomas replied easily. "It is not important. Two things *are* important. One is that you are still the most beautiful woman in Washington, as you have been ever since you came here. The second is that you are in a unique position to help our cause."

Greenhow ignored the heaping tablespoons of flattery, welcome though they were, to focus on the last words of this Mr. Thomas. *Our cause!* Her fantasies of a titillating social relationship with this man were instantly erased by the huge import behind those words. Thomas must be a Confederate agent! That was indeed a cause to which she would give anything.

"I am at your service, Mr. Thomas," she said, her voice even lower.

Thomas outlined a plan by which Greenhow would glean items of social, economic, and especially military interest to the Confederacy from her extensive social circle. If she could, she was to recruit new informants, especially attractive young women, who could obtain information from powerful and influential men. Information was the currency of Washington, and the Confederacy needed all it could get.

Thomas suggested they meet again next Friday morning at this market, an excellent rendezvous where they could not be overheard.

Greenhow was more than willing, but she was wary. This could be some kind of a trap. "Mr. Thomas, you are a most charming and intriguing person, but I do not know you. No one has introduced us. I do not even know if Thomas is your real name. I do not care if it isn't, but, to speak frankly, I need to know you are what you represent yourself to be. Is there some proof you can offer me to reassure me that I would be aiding our cause, and not simply putting myself, and others, into prison?"

"Well taken, Mrs. Greenhow. I appreciate and understand your circumspection. I will provide proof for you when we meet again." He replaced the melon and walked off without a backward glance.

That satisfied Rose Greenhow. She couldn't wait to get started. She started thinking of pliable and attractive young women she knew.

CHAPTER 10

Saturday
Washington
11:23 AM

Oswell Apperson was helping one of his seamstresses measure some cloth when Rose Greenhow stepped through the front door of Apperson's Apparel, the door bell tinkling merrily.

Apperson almost dropped his spectacles. Mrs. Greenhow was almost—make that *certainly*—the most important single customer he had. It was not that she bought a huge amount—her buying habits were actually rather modest, though she bought the best quality—but that her influence was so great. Many of his best customers bought at Apperson's simply because she did.

"My *dear* Mrs. Greenhow." The rotund little man dropped the cloth and rushed to meet her, almost tripping in the process. "How *are* you?"

Rose Greenhow looked quite fashionable in a cloak of dark blue, with a matching bonnet that hid only the upper part of her lustrous dark hair. "Very well, thank you, Oswell." She gave him her hand to kiss, which he gallantly did. She knew it gave him an even greater thrill to kiss her hand that it did to have her call him by his first name. "Your cloak is holding up remarkably well, as you can see."

"Oh, yes, one of our finest works. You remember I designed it especially for you." Out of the corner of his eye Apperson could see that all six of his seamstresses had stopped work and were ogling the notorious *grande dame* of Washington society. "Would you like to see some of our newest fabrics?" Apperson guided Greenhow toward a wall full of dozens of samples, while behind her back he gestured furiously at the seamstresses to get back to work.

"Actually, Oswell, I had something else on my mind. I wonder if I might see you in your office for a moment."

"Of course, dear lady. Right this way." He led her into the elegantly furnished office, which he also used as a consulting room with his clients. Shutting the door, he seated her, then himself. "There we are. Now, how can I help you? I do hope nothing's wrong." He stood back up. "Oh, may I get you something? I forget myself. A glass of water? Some tea, perhaps? Or—"

"No, no," Greenhow interrupted with a reassuring smile. "I assure you nothing's wrong, Oswell, though I thank you for inquiring. Please do sit down." She smiled again as he did so. "Actually, I came to ask a small favor."

"Oh. A favor?" Apperson smiled in relief. "Certainly. Why, I would be honored. What can I do?" He almost mopped his brow, but thought the better of it.

Greenhow gazed at this balding little man, so skillful in clothing design yet so lacking in serenity. "You have a remarkable group of seamstresses, Oswell," she said after a few moments. "Did you pick them yourself?"

"My seamstresses?" Apperson scratched his balding forehead. "Yes, I picked them myself. Quite a job. Not easy. Good seamstresses are hard to find, you know. And harder to keep, I might add."

"I think you have the best in the city. You are to be congratulated on your diligence and taste, Oswell."

Apperson smiled widely at this unexpected compliment from someone so noted for her taste. "Why, yes, yes, I think so, too," he beamed. "They are the best I've ever had. They could make *anything*.

Is there perhaps something you had in mind for us to make? Something special? I do assure you, Mrs. Greenhow, that we could—"

"Actually, I was thinking of one in particular. Miss O'Connor."

"O'Connor. *Meagan* O'Connor? The blonde one? With the blue eyes?" Apperson had two blonde seamstresses.

"Yes. She's very pretty. Tell me a little bit about her. How long has she worked here?"

"Mm, about a year. No, wait, more like a year and a half. Yes, yes, I remember now. I took her on just before Christmas, two years ago. That's it."

"So you've had her for a year and a half. She must be very good for one so young."

"Oh, she *is* good, I assure you. Very good."

"I'm sure she is. She is the one who fitted me for this cloak, as I'm sure you recall."

Apperson snapped his fingers. "Oh, yes, that's right. She was your fitter. Would you like her assigned to you as your regular fitter?"

"I would greatly appreciate that, Oswell. Yes. Thank you." Greenhow paused. "Where does Miss O'Connor live?"

"Somewhere is the northeastern part of the city. I forget exactly where. I can look it up in the records here, if you like."

"That won't be necessary. Does she live with her parents, do you know?"

Apperson considered. "I think so. Her father's in the leather business, I think I once heard her say. I never met them. Never been to her house, either, of course."

Greenhow regarded Apperson with her dark eyes. She could see that he was becoming concerned, not knowing the direction of her questions, yet wanting to please an important customer. "You are very patient, Oswell," she smiled warmly. "Just one more question. Would you consider Miss O'Connor to be—*reliable*?"

"Reliable? Oh, my, yes. She's here on time every day. She's rarely late even when it's snowing. And she's as healthy as a horse. I cannot remember a day she missed because of illness, but I *can* remember several days she worked when she wasn't feeling well. Yes, she's very reliable." Apperson paused and frowned, wrinkling his bald forehead. "Is there perhaps something special she could make for you? Or for someone else?"

A report on O'Connor's health was not quite what Greenhow had in mind, but she let it pass. "I'm sure that can be arranged, and I would be delighted. I have a different purpose today, however. There *is* something Miss O'Connor could do for me. Your shop closes at four on Saturdays, doesn't it, Oswell?"

"Yes, madam. Nine to four."

"Then here is my special request. I would like you to release Miss O'Connor at noon today. Give her the afternoon off. She will not be alone; she will be with me. There is something I have for her. It does not involve sewing, but it does involve meeting people. People who could become your customers, Oswell." Greenhow reached out and took Apperson's hand. "I would count it a very special favor."

Apperson melted, while visions of one of his employees entering the highest social circles in the city danced in his head. "Of *course* you can have her, dear lady. It would give me the greatest of pleasure."

"I knew I could count on you." Greenhow withdrew her hand. "Perhaps you would be kind enough to bring Miss O'Connor in here, so that the two of us can converse a few moments alone." As Apperson started for the door, Greenhow added, "And, Oswell, please do not mention to the other girls why Miss O'Connor will not be returning after her lunch. I know I can trust your discretion."

"Of course, madam. Thank you for your confidence."

Meagan O'Connor appeared at the doorway a few moments later. Apperson gave her a slight push inside, then closed the door behind her.

"Please do come in, my dear," Greenhow invited warmly, indicating the chair Apperson had vacated. "I'm Rose Greenhow. You remember me."

O'Connor gave a little curtsey before seating herself. "Yes, ma'am, I do. You've been here several times. I helped make your cloak, then I fitted you. Is there anything wrong?" Her face was pale with controlled apprehension.

"Not at all," Greenhow assured warmly. "In fact, it is my favorite cloak. It served me very well in the bitter cold of last January.

You are to be commended on your skill. My good friend Mr. Apperson is lucky to have you."

"Oh." This praise, so different from what O'Connor had expected, put her at ease and brought a tinge of color to her cheeks, but she kept her eyes politely downcast. "Thank you." She didn't know what else to say.

"Oswell and I have been talking. In view of your excellent service, he has agreed that you should have a free afternoon. Today. So when you leave for your lunch at noon, you will not have to return. He is a kind man."

Meagan O'Connor looked up quickly, her eyes widening. "A free afternoon?" She could scarcely believe it.

"Well, perhaps I exaggerated. Not *quite* free." Greenhow leaned back in her chair, speculatively eyeing the young woman. "I assured Mr. Apperson that I would be responsible for you. He is most concerned for your well-being. So I would appreciate it, Meagan, if you would have tea with me this afternoon."

O'Connor's head started to swim. *Me*? Have tea with *Mrs. Rose Greenhow*? And she called me *Meagan*!

"Two o'clock. At my house."

At her house?

"Do you know where I live, Meagan?"

O'Connor tried to control the soaring thrill rising within her. She forced herself to smile. "I…I'm not sure, ma'am."

"It's 398 16th Street, just north of H Street. A three-story house. Sixteenth Street stops at H Street, at Lafayette Square. If it continued across the park it would intersect Pennsylvania Avenue at the Executive Mansion. So I'm just north of the square, across from St. John's Church."

O'Connor's head was awhirl. *Sixteenth Street! Pennsylvania Avenue! St. John's Church! Lafayette Square! The Executive Mansion!* Mrs. Greenhow was offhandedly describing the most exclusive area in the entire city of Washington. "I'll be there, ma'am. Thank you. Thank you very much."

Greenhow arose to leave and walked toward the door. "Meagan," she said, turning, "if I were you I wouldn't mention this to the other girls. Just tell them I thanked you for the cloak," she smiled conspiratorially. "It's now almost noon. See you at two."

CHAPTER 11

Saturday
Washington
1:55 PM

Meagan O'Connor stopped at the northeast corner of 16th and H Streets and admired the view. Across the block-wide expanse of Lafayette Square to the south, with Pennsylvania Avenue beyond it, the stately mass of the Executive Mansion arose amid its extensive grounds. She had walked in this area several times and thought this view of the mansion to be the best, framed by the beauty of the parklike square, now budding in the vigor of spring. People were now commonly calling the Executive Mansion the White House, which was less pretentious and easier to say. The nickname certainly fit today, she thought, as the springtime sun made the building gleam like a fantasy atop a wedding cake.

O'Connor looked about her with a sense of pride. In her previous visits she was an outsider, simply admiring this exclusive area, feeling privileged just to be allowed in it. Now she was here with a purpose. Somebody had *asked* her to visit here, almost as if she *belonged* here. She felt again a rising thrill as she crossed 16th Street and then walked north.

She stopped before an elegant three-story brick house with black shutters, almost directly across the street from the distinctive pillar-fronted church she knew was St. John's. She went up the white steps to the front door and timidly operated the brass knocker.

The door was opened after a few seconds by Rose Greenhow herself. "Come in, Meagan," she smiled brightly. "It is brisk out, isn't it?"

"Yes, ma'am," O'Connor answered as she entered. "A wonderful day. I like the breezes."

"Here, let me take your cloak. Oh, it is handsome. You must have made it yourself."

"Yes, ma'am. Mr. Apperson let me buy the material, and I made it at home."

The famous society woman hung up the cloak in a coat closet, then led her guest into the parlor and sat beside her on a plush settee, in front of which a silver tea service gleamed on a low table of dark mahogany. She was wearing a simple green dress with a white collar and puffed sleeves, which complemented her dark eyes and the faint olive tint of her skin. Her glossy black hair, parted in the middle, was pulled back into a bun, tightly framing her handsome head.

"You have a beautiful house, ma'am." Meagan's eyes took in the Chinese fan in front of the fireplace, the brocaded chairs, and the fine carpet, worlds removed from the simple row house she lived in with her parents.

"Thank you."

A door slammed somewhere in the back of the house, and two young girls dashed giggling into the room, then stopped as they saw the visitor. "These are my two youngest daughters, Leila and Rose," Mrs. Greenhow said. "Girls, please greet Miss Meagan O'Connor."

The girls curtsied and shyly said hello. "Now run along to your rooms." The girls scampered up the stairs, starting to giggle again.

"Do you have any other children?" Meagan asked. She had barely spoken to Mrs. Greenhow at Apperson's Apparel when she had made and fitted the society lady's cloak, and knew little about her except for gossip.

"My, yes. I have two older daughters. They are presently with friends. Would you excuse me a moment?" Greenhow disappeared into the back of the house, returning a minute later with a plate of delicacies, and placed them on the low table. "I expected that you would be prompt," she smiled, "so I made the tea and let it steep."

It was not until Greenhow poured her a cup of tea that Meagan realized this affair was not what she had expected. She thought there would be a group of people, to whom she would be introduced, and had worried about what she would say and how she would fit in with a group of distinguished older strangers. She now realized this would be a *private* tea with Mrs. Greenhow, and was thrilled again that such a person would take an interest in her.

"Four children, ma'am?" Meagan had not known about the daughters. She had the notion that society women were somehow free of the normal cares of ordinary people. She held the cup and saucer in one hand, trying to act as if she did this sort of thing regularly. "They must be very trying at times."

"Indeed they are," Greenhow agreed, taking a sip of tea and imbuing that simple act with regal grace. Her voice was pleasant, low and measured. "Lovely, but difficult now and then. Especially with Robert gone. He couldn't help much, always busy with his books, but the children loved him so."

"Robert? That was your husband, ma'am?"

"Yes. He worked for the government as a lawyer, surveyor and mapmaker. He was very well educated, fluent in several languages. He died seven years ago, in an accident in San Francisco."

"Oh. I'm sorry."

"Thank you. I wasn't there at the time," Greenhow went on quietly, her eyes gazing into a far-off distance. "I had accompanied him out, but I was here in Washington when it happened. When I received the news by post, I simply couldn't believe it. It seemed impossible. I took a ship to Panama, crossed the isthmus, and took another ship to San Francisco. After settling the affairs there, I came back here. The girls were never there."

A silence followed. "I've never met anyone who has been to California," Meagan finally observed wistfully. It sounded as far-off and romantically mysterious as the Orient. "What was San Francisco like?"

"Very different. Warmer winters than here, and drier. Cooler summers, with much fog. I found the fog delightful at first, but it soon became a bother. Spectacular views, exotic plants. What I remember most, however, was the immense raw energy of the city. Robert and I arrived only a few weeks after California had been admitted as a state, and the people were still celebrating. The gold fever was still high, and fortune seekers were pouring in. The streets were dirty and there was little society, but the sense of destiny was overpowering, like a great ocean wave. It was a frontier on the sea. However, it was very self-contained, with little identification with the rest of the nation. Had Robert lived, I would have shared it with him, even brought the girls there. But without him, there was nothing there for me. This is the center of the country, this is where my friends are, this is where I want to be." She smiled graciously at Meagan. "I trust you do not find my recitation boring."

"Oh, no, ma'am. It's fascinating. I would like to do something like it some day."

"And so you shall, my dear." Greenhow patted Meagan's knee. "Enough of me. Now how about you? I've had the love of a wonderful man. Is there a man in your life?"

Meagan could feel herself blush at this directness. "No, ma'am. I'm afraid I don't know many men. I don't have a brother to introduce me to his friends, and all the people I work with are women."

"Perhaps I could do something about that," Greenhow smiled. "You're a very beautiful young woman, Meagan. You should mingle with men. It is a law of nature. It would be better for you. And certainly better for the men," she added with a smile. "Here, taste this." She pointed to bite-size delicacies on the plate; they had a toasted-brown coating. "It's a Maryland crab cake I have cut into small pieces."

Meagan did, and a mingling of delightful flavors exploded on her tongue. "Oh, ma'am, it's *delicious.*" She reached for a second morsel.

"Of course it is. Meagan, do you know there are men who would provide you with crab cakes—and a great deal more—every day in the week, just for the honor of your occasional companionship? And that is all I mean. Just your companionship."

"That is not a small matter." Greenhow eyed the younger woman speculatively. "In my experience, few women really make good companions for men. It helps if a woman is beautiful, even more if she is young and beautiful, but what a man really looks for is a woman with whom he can share himself. That means his mind, his interests, something that is really important to him. Most women don't care about the things that interest a man, and they make no effort to cultivate such interests. They rely on the natural attraction of their sex. When that fades, they have nothing left but male courtesy and female demands." She took a sip of tea. "Do you have such thoughts, Meagan?"

"Now and then, ma'am." Meagan said perfunctorily. She bit into another morsel of crab cake.

"This is Washington," Greenhow continued. "The capital city of the country. Men here care about politics, about power. I have found that as a man rises in prominence here he tends to value an interesting woman more and more, because almost all of his associates are men. A politically astute woman is rare. I am a confidante of former President Buchanan, for example, simply because we find each other interesting. We corresponded in lengthy letters long before he was president, before he was the ambassador to Britain. He has told me things I doubt he has told to anyone else, certainly not to another woman, just because I shared his intellectual passions. Do such things interest you?"

Meagan brightened. "Oh, yes, ma'am, they do. The other girls at the shop never talk about politics. They're boring. I often have lunch with a young man who works a short distance from Apperson's. He loves politics. That's what we talk about."

"Good for you. Was this young man in the army? Does he have an office?"

"No, ma'am. He's a clerk in a general store. But he's very well informed. Why, he even predicted the attack on Fort Sumter the day before it happened."

"Indeed." Rose Greenhow raised her eyebrows. "How prophetic. Are you romantically involved with this gentleman?"

"Oh, no, ma'am." Meagan colored again before Greenhow's directness. She had never met anyone so casual and open about affairs of the heart. "We're friends. He has asked me out several times, but I've never done it. I just like talking with him." She paused. "I sense he actually knows more than he tells me. He will talk freely if we stick to events of the day. If I ask about his personal background, he becomes very quiet. I know he's been out West. Not as far as California, like you," she added quickly. "Kansas. He was in Kansas."

"How interesting." Rose Greenhow smiled enigmatically. "Well, Meagan, I have a task for you. A pleasant one, I trust. As part of your expanded relationships with men, why not accept the request for companionship from your friend? You say he wants to go out with you. Accommodate him. Do something innocent, like walking. Young men like to walk with young ladies. Explore some part of the city together. Find out what pleases him. He sounds intelligent, so compliment his mind. Learn about something he likes to talk about, and then bring it up yourself. He'll be flattered. Be a companion, a friend. Then he will confide in you. See if you can discover why he was in Kansas and what he was doing there. Probably nothing, but there must be some reason why he is reticent with you. Kansas was a very busy place a few years ago."

"Go out with Rufus Sloan?" Meagan sounded dubious. Going out with a clerk she had already refused several times was the last piece of advice she would have expected from Mrs. Greenhow. She had hoped to meet exciting *new* people.

"Of course. Your friend is the perfect person with whom to sharpen your social skills, my dear. You already know him, you trust him, you know his proclivities. Practice your womanly wiles with him. It would be more than mere empty flirtation. You will be learning things about him. More importantly, you will learn things about yourself and your abilities. With your beauty and your sweet nature, you can go far, Meagan. I expect great things of you. Someday soon I would like to introduce you to accomplished and influential men, whose company I'm sure you will enjoy. You don't want to appear awkward and tongue-tied with them. You want to be friendly and warm, sociable and sweet, a woman they cannot forget and want to see again as soon as possible. They just don't know about you yet. I will see that they do." Greenhow's dark eyes rested appreciatively on Meagan's trim figure and blond curls, as her modulated voice seductively described the girl's dreams. "The world can be your oyster, my dear, and you can be the pearl in it."

That's more like it, Meagan thought, as the dazzling society world reopened again in her imagination. "I would be so grateful, ma'am."

"Why don't you make an arrangement with your Mr. Sloan for the coming week? Perhaps more than one. Don't tell him I suggested it, of course. It's your idea. Then come here again for tea at two o'clock next Sunday, a week from tomorrow, and we'll discuss our plan." Rose Greenhow stood up, and gave Meagan a light hug when the younger woman did likewise. "Won't it be fun? Remember, Meagan," she said at the door, "you can be the pearl."

Meagan O'Connor's head was in the springtime clouds as she descended the steps to Sixteenth Street. She did not walk towards home.

She knew exactly where she wanted to go.

CHAPTER 12

Saturday
Washington
3:58 PM

Rufus Sloan had just glanced at the big Excelsior wall clock, which showed two minutes until closing time, when he was astonished to see Meagan O'Connor walk through the double front door of Grinell's Goods. She made straight for him.

"Afternoon, Miss O'Connor. Missed you at lunch today."

"Thank you, Rufus. I was engaged."

"Mr. Apperson let you girls out a little early today?"

"Well, he let *me* out a little early. That's why I'm here."

"You wanted to buy something before the store closed? What would you like?"

Meagan looked casually around the store, took a step nearer, and lowered her voice. "I would like *you*, Rufus." She smiled up at him invitingly. "Would you like to escort me home after the store is closed?"

Sloan wasn't sure he had heard correctly. How many times had he dreamed of walking with this sparkling-eyed, golden-haired beauty? He had asked several times, but been quietly rebuffed. Now *she* was asking *him*! "I would be honored, Miss O'Connor," he finally said.

"I'll wait."

The clock chimed the hour. "Not for long," Sloan grinned. He came from behind the counter and locked the front door, pulling down shades over the inset glass panels. "There's two customers still in the store, and we'll have to wait until they leave. I'll settle accounts with Mr. Grinell and the other clerk. It should only take a few minutes."

It did. Four minutes after four o'clock Sloan and O'Connor stood outside Grinell's Goods, at 11th St. near G. "Which way?" Sloan asked. "I don't know where you live, Miss O'Connor."

"This way," Meagan replied, gesturing south on 11th St. "About twelve blocks."

Sloan dutifully took up position on O'Connor's outside. He had never before publicly escorted a young woman through the streets of Washington, let alone one as stunning as Meagan O'Connor, and it gave him a heady sense of power.

They were silent for two blocks, enjoying the bustle of the city and the satisfied feeling of having completed a week's work. "A beautiful day, isn't it," Sloan volunteered.

"Oh, yes. A wonderful day. I enjoy the breezes so," O'Connor replied. They had reached E Street. "We turn left here." They did so, and started walking east on E. "Rufus, what's the latest about Fort Sumter? I've heard nothing since this morning."

"The afternoon papers say a heavy bombardment is still going on. No surrender yet. We have had customers during the day who have received telegrams, or know people who have, and they all say the same thing."

"Has anyone been hurt or…or killed, yet?"

"No reports of casualties, ma'am. I don't know."

"The Confederates—could they invade the fort? With troops?"

Sloan smiled. "The word is *assault*, ma'am. No, they couldn't. The fort, which is new, is built on an island in Charleston harbor. Its guns control the site. But the Confederates don't have to assault it. They can simply wait until the garrison runs out of food or ammunition. You see, the fort was not built to fight against

Charleston. It was built to defend it. It cannot hold out if the city it was built to defend turns against it and withholds supplies."

"But that could take weeks, couldn't it?"

"Yes, ma'am. It depends on the provisions the fort has, and whether or not it can be reprovisioned. But, yes, it could take weeks." He glanced over at his companion. "If I may say so, Miss O'Connor, you take a lively interest in national affairs. I've never met a woman who had much interest in such matters."

"And I've never met a man who had such a knowledge of them as you do," Meagan smiled, her eyes sparkling. *Mrs. Greenhow's ideas are working!* "I find it hard to believe you were never in the army. You must have been, Rufus."

"Well, not the regular army, Miss O'Connor."

"I knew it! You *did* have some army training! How exciting! Oh, Rufus, you mustn't be ashamed of it. I *admire* you for it. Tell me about it."

"I'm not ashamed of it, Miss. I'm *proud* of it."

"So tell me, Rufus. It's sounds so exciting. And so mysterious. I didn't know there was such a thing as an *irregular* army."

Sloan realized he had said too much. "It's very private, Miss O'Connor. Please don't be offended. It has nothing to do with you."

They walked on in silence a few moments. "Is that what you did in Kansas, Rufus?"

Sloan slowed down, almost stopping. "I'm sorry," Meagan said, matching his pace. "That was thoughtless of me." She gave his arm a little squeeze. "Please forgive me. It's just that I like you so much, I'd like to know more about you." She injected a note of gaiety into her voice. "Would you like to know more about me?"

"Whatever you'd like to tell me, Miss O'Connor."

"I'd like to tell you my father's in the leather business. Wholesale. He has a warehouse in the southeastern part of the city, not far from the Navy Yard. We used to live in Maryland, where I was born. Two years ago we moved here. My father wanted to be closer to government offices, for the army is one of his largest customers. I tried to help my father for a time, but it really isn't an occupation for a woman. I've always liked sewing, so I got a job with Mr. Apperson as a seamstress."

"Do you like your job?"

"Oh, yes. Mr. Apperson is the designer, but he lets us help him if he thinks we show some design talent. Lately he's been letting me take more responsibility. He trusts me. I'm grateful to him." They had to walk out in the street to avoid some scaffolding being used in remodeling the front of a building. "How about you? Do you like your job at Grinell's?"

"It's all right."

"You'd like more excitement, wouldn't you?"

"You're very perceptive, ma'am. Yes, I would like more excitement."

They were silent for half a block. "Rufus, if you could do anything you'd like, what would it be? Something in the army?"

"No. In the army you have to take orders. I'd like to *give* orders. A politician, maybe. But that's not likely, so maybe it would be the army. But I'd only join if there was really something to fight for. I'd never join just to have something to do."

"Do you still think a war's coming?"

"Yes. I do."

"If it does, would you join the army?"

"I don't know, Miss O'Connor. I want to see *how* it comes. I don't want to be backed into it." Sloan looked around. "By the way, exactly where do you live?"

"Not far now. We turn right on Second Street. I live near the intersection of Second and E Streets."

They were nearing a section close to the northeastern limit of the city, an area colloquially called "Swampoodle." It was not the most attractive or safest part of Washington. Meagan eventually stopped before a two-story house with the unusual feature of two front doors.

"We rent half the house," Meagan explained. She reached for Sloan's right hand and held it in both of her own. "Thank you, Rufus, for walking me home. It was very good of you."

"My pleasure, Miss O'Connor. Really."

"Rufus," Meagan said, "please call me Meagan." She was still holding his hand.

"Meagan. Yes. Yes, I'd like that very much."

"Good. Are you free tomorrow?"

"Tomorrow?"

"Yes, Rufus. Tomorrow. Sunday. If you're not engaged, I'd like to walk with you again. Perhaps we could walk down by the new capitol building. See how they're getting along."

"I'd be honored, Miss—Meagan. Yes. I'm free."

"I could make us a little lunch, and you could find us something to drink. We can have a picnic."

"That would be wonderful."

"Can you be here at noon?"

"Indeed I can."

"See you then." Meagan gave Sloan's hand a final squeeze, and, with a gay wave, disappeared inside the house. Sloan stood wondering on the sidewalk, feeling as if he had been struck by sweet lightning.

CHAPTER 13

Sunday, April 14
Fort Sumter, South Carolina
12:43 PM

Major Robert Anderson saluted the flag of the United States flying over Fort Sumter. It was then taken down and reverently folded.

Ever since the bombardment by the Confederate batteries all along the shore of Charleston Harbor had begun during the early morning hours of April 12, Anderson knew it was only a matter of time—a short time—before he would have to surrender. He had delayed responding to the Confederate cannon fire until 7 AM on the morning of the 12th, when it was light enough to see the rebel batteries. He had only 700 bags of powder, and he could not waste any shots. He also decided to use only casemate guns, which were protected, rather than the guns mounted on the parapet, where the crews would be exposed. Unfortunately, all of the fort's largest guns were mounted on the parapet, except for a few set on the parade ground which were used as mortars, since they had to be aimed high to clear the fort's walls.

Worse, Anderson could fire only solid shot, since the fort had no fuses for its supply of exploding shells. That was not due to negligence on the Army's part. Anderson and his men had seized the brand-new and not-quite-completed fort in a surprise move last December 26, and it had not yet received a supply of artillery fuses. It could not receive any later, for the South Carolinians had fired on and turned back the only supply ship which had attempted to reach the fort.

The demands on the garrison's limited manpower of operating and supplying the guns soon meant that only six guns, all 32-pounders, were being used regularly. Their lightweight solid-shot balls did little damage, and not one of the targets at which the garrison had aimed those guns was put out of action.

Perhaps the most frustrating aspect of the situation was that some sort of a naval relief expedition had unexpectedly appeared on the afternoon of the 12th, lying off the harbor entrance outside the range of shore batteries. Everybody in the fort could see it; so could everybody in Charleston. Using a spyglass, Anderson could see that at least one of the small fleet was a serious warship. Was it, or perhaps the whole fleet, going to attempt a dash into the harbor, running the gauntlet of Confederate batteries to resupply the fort? Cut off from all communication with the Union, Anderson did not know the plans of this expedition, but it was clear that the U.S. Navy was up to something.

As comforting as the realization was that the garrison at Fort Sumter had not simply been abandoned to its fate, Anderson knew that unless that something happened successfully and quickly, he would have to surrender.

The fleet made no attempt to sail in on the 12th, nor the next day, Saturday the 13th. The fort kept up desultory return fire to the much heavier Confederate bombardment.

Shortly after noon on the 13th, a Confederate cannon ball severed the fort's flagstaff, causing the flag to fall. A sergeant, assisted by several others, managed to have the stars and stripes fly again by replacing the staff and nailing the flag to it. However, the disappearance of the flag, however temporary, caused many of the Confederates to believe the fort was surrendering, and the bombardment tapered off. During the lull a small boat approached the fort, waving a white flag. In it was Col. Louis T. Wigfall, a native South Carolinian who had been a senator from Texas before that state seceded from the Union. While the boat's crew kept it from banging against the walls, Wigfall had conferred with Anderson through an embrasure and demanded the fort's surrender. Down to his last few bags of powder and with several fires raging, Anderson had agreed to surrender Fort Sumter the following day.

A final indignity had occurred Sunday morning. Although not one member of the garrison had been killed during the two-day bombardment, a gun had exploded while saluting the flag during the surrender ceremony, killing one man instantly and severely wounding five others.

Now Anderson ordered his men to march out. Part of the surrender agreement was that none of the defenders would be interned or even charged with a crime. The Confederates had agreed to provide a ship to take all of them out to the Union fleet and, under a flag of truce, transfer them peacefully. They were allowed to take their flag.

CHAPTER 14

Sunday
Richmond, Virginia
12:51 PM

The train slid smoothly to a stop with a squealing of brakes and a hissing of steam. Carter Cosby descended from the second coach, blinked in the bright noonday sun before putting on his hat, and located a porter to help with his three pieces of luggage from the baggage car. The two larger ones he entrusted to the baggage master at the Richmond & Petersburg depot and pocketed the claim checks for them; the smallest he carried to the end of the building where cabbies were loudly hawking their hacks to the newly arrived passengers. He chose a modified surrey, which had a weatherproof top and rolled-up side curtains, and was surprised when a Negro approached him.

"Yes, suh, you lookin' for a good hotel? We got some fine ones in town. St. Charles, Union, American, Ballard House, Powhatan House, Exchange, Spotswood—"

"Spotswood," Cosby replied. He had been there before. "Are you the cab owner?"

"Yes, suh. Ephraim Tanner, at your service." The middle-aged man swept off his hat and bowed slightly, but did not offer to shake hands. "The Spotswood, that'd be twenty-five cents. If I get another passenger, that is. Otherwise, thirty-five cents."

"I'll take it, Ephraim."

"Yes, *suh,*" the black man grinned, showing some yellowed teeth. He picked up the suitcase and strapped it onto the platform behind the seats. "Now you jus' take a seat an' wait a bit, an' we'll see if we can get us some company."

Cosby swung up into the rear seat, musing that he had never ridden in a cab—maybe not any vehicle—owned by a free black before. Why didn't Ephraim Tanner simply move to the North, if he were free? The answer was that he must *like* the South, as many blacks did; they just didn't like slavery. That fitted in with Cosby's own views about the economic nonsense of slavery.

Tanner returned with two more people, a husband and wife visiting from Baltimore; Cosby moved into the front seat so that they could share the rear seat. Their destination was the Ballard House, so Tanner headed his horse from the depot to Franklin Street, then northwestward up Franklin. Cosby remembered that the center of Richmond was a hilly area. He had been here twice before, but the last time was four years ago.

As they approached 14th Street, they spied a curious structure spanning Franklin. It was an enclosed passageway connecting two buildings at the second-story level. What made it even more arresting were its windows, large lancet-shaped openings which looked as though they belonged in a church.

"What's that?" asked the woman.

Tanner chuckled. "That's where you're goin', ma'am. The buildin' on the right is the Ballard House. The one on the left is the Exchange Hotel. The story goes that Mr. Ballard built his hotel because he got such poor service at the Exchange. Did so well that he ended up buyin' the Exchange, so then he built that passageway to connect his two hotels. Now you can move back an' forth, have dinner in both hotels, even if it's pourin' rain. Sure looks different, don't it?"

"Sure does," Cosby agreed. He had never seen anything like it. It looked...*modern.* Surely such things would eventually connect many new buildings, would they not?

After dropping off the couple from Baltimore, Tanner dropped down one block to Main Street, then continued uphill six more blocks to 8th St. The Spotswood Hotel, named for a former governor of Virgina, was five stories of grand stone whuch dominated the southeast corner of 8th and Main. Cosby generously tipped Tanner after the Negro had carried in his bag, and five minutes later was comfortably ensconced in a room on the third floor.

After more than three days of train travel, Cosby wanted to stretch his legs, and Richmond was the perfect city for it. He walked to the Shockoe Slip area and the tobacco warehouses, near the James River waterfront. Tobacco was Virginia's chief agricultural export, as important as cotton was to the states of the Deep South, and Richmond was the place where this cash crop was stored, processed, and shipped. There were more than fifty tobacco warehouses. The city was the state capital and was centrally located; more importantly from a commercial standpoint, the reason for such a concentration was that it was positioned at the highest navigable part of the James River. Just upstream were the Falls of the James, a mile-long stretch of rocks, whirlpools, and rapids unnavigable even by a rowboat; downstream the James was an ever-broadening highway to the Chesapeake Bay, thence through the Virginia Capes to the Atlantic and Europe, where Virginia tobacco was recognized as the world's finest. Close behind tobacco surprisingly came flour, as Richmond had a dozen large mills.

Cosby was not a smoker and did not raise tobacco, but the use of any agricultural product fascinated him. Though it was a Sunday, several of the tobacco warehouses were open, and he could see stacks of the fragrant cured golden-brown leaves ready to be put into hogsheads for shipping. There were few cigar makers in Richmond, but several tobacco companies did cut and shred the leaves for use in pipes and that new "little cigars" product, cigarettes.

Wandering around the Shockoe area, Cosby came upon a cobblestoned street he remembered from a previous visit. It had a number of auction houses on it, and these houses regularly held auctions of slaves. He had attended a number of slave auctions, but never one as far north as Richmond. Yet he knew there were slave auctions even in Washington. "What a waste," he sighed.

There was another place he wished to visit this afternoon, something infinitely more edifying than auction houses where slaves were sold. He walked back in the direction of the Spotswood, the land rising gently. Two blocks from the hotel he turned north and entered Capitol Square, the very heart of the city.

Two blocks long and three blocks wide, most of the square was built on a rather steep slope, with only the upper part level. Cosby started at the lowest part, at Bank Street on the southern edge, and walked up the center path. Well-trimmed trees and manicured lawns surrounded him, for most of the square was a park. From that direction was the best way to approach the crowning glory of Richmond, and one of the greatest in the country: the Virginia state capitol. Its white Greek shape stood like a cloud of classical purity at the top of the hill, with a huge columned portico gazing majestically out over the city. It inspired pride, devotion, even reverence, a touch of the gods come to earth.

Ancient Greeks could scarcely have had greater feeling as they approached the Parthenon, which this building greatly resembled, than Cosby did approaching this civic citadel. He was proud that men could construct such monuments of utility and grandeur to grace their cities. Above its classical appearance and exquisite location, however, this building had something which made it compelling to anyone with a sense of history: an association with the two greatest names in American history, George Washington and Thomas Jefferson.

Several years after the capital of Virginia was moved from Williamsburg to Richmond in 1780, Jefferson, then minister to France, was asked to recommend a suitable architect for the new capitol. He complied, naming a famous French architect, and also selected a building on which he thought the Virginia capitol should be based: it was the Maison Carree, a 1st-century Roman temple in Nimes, France, and which itself was built in the Greek style. Though Jefferson was not the architect, the building incorporated a most unusual feature which might easily have come straight from his fertile mind—an interior dome, underneath the Greek roof, which allowed a rotunda in the center.

The association with Washington involved a remarkable statue inside that rotunda. However, another association with Washington had been added since Cosby was last here, and it was this he now wished to see. He rounded the western edge of the capitol, and there it was.

Fifty feet high, a bronze equestrian statue of Washington stood on a stone pedestal, surrounded by six more bronze statues of Virginia pioneers. All the statues were larger than life. The complex arrangement was unveiled just three years ago, and even now, Cosby noted, there were still minor parts of it yet unfinished. It was every bit as grand as he had imagined, one of the finest monuments he had ever seen.

Walking past the north side of the capitol, Cosby reached the east side and the entrance to the Governor's Mansion. He paid close attention, for this was where he would visit the governor this evening. The official residence was a handsome Georgian two-story house, painted gray, with a hipped roof and two chimneys. The railing of a widow's walk extended between the chimneys, while a substantial portico over the front door was supported by four white pillars.

Handsome as the house was, the most unusual feature was the entrance road. A mixture of dirt and gravel, it was easily forty feet wide, and Cosby estimated its length as nearly two hundred feet. Large trees, greening in the spring, flanked both sides. The width, Cosby surmised, was to allow carriages to turn around in front of the house, while the length allowed many of them to park whenever the governor held a social function.

The openness of the approach could create problems. If he walked right down the middle, he would attract attention from anyone who happened to be nearby, even if it was dark. If he tried to keep to the deep shadow of the trees, he might be mistaken for an intruder.

Was there a security detail? Cosby walked about, admiring the eastern side of the capitol, the lawns, the flowers, keeping an eye on the mansion. He was soon rewarded by the appearance of a uniformed man who came around the edge of the house, walked up the several steps to the porch, and sat down in a chair beside the front door. In the deep shade of the portico Cosby could not be sure of the uniform, but the guard looked more like a policeman than an army trooper.

A police guard, then, and probably only one. If there was one here in the early afternoon, there would almost certainly be one here tonight.

Cosby walked into the capitol.

There were none of the usual weekday employees. A few security guards kept bored but watchful eyes, while a number of docents took groups of tourists from room to room. Cosby ignored them and went straight for the rotunda.

Just as Richmond was the heart of Virginia, Capitol Square the heart of Richmond, and the capitol the heart of the square, so the rotunda was the heart of the capitol. Carter entered the holiest of holies of Virginia.

The room was rectangular, about thirty feet square, and two stories high. Its floor was a checkerboard pattern of white and black limestone, while its ceiling was a richly-ornamented dome with a skylight in the center. In the center of the floor, directly below the skylight, was a life-size statue of George Washington. It stood on a pedestal five feet high and was surrounded by an iron picket fence. Cosby was spellbound by its sublime beauty, as he had been before.

A docent was explaining the statue's details to an admiring group. It was made of white Carrara marble, was commissioned by the General Assembly at about the same time as the capitol building itself, and was made by the Frenchman Jean Antoine Houdon, the foremost sculptor of his day. "It is the only statue of Washington made from life," the docent went on. Her voice was animated, despite the fact she must have made this speech hundreds of times. "Houdon traveled across the Atlantic and personally measured Washington, making many sketches of him during a two-week stay at Mount Vernon."

The docent invited the group to draw closer to the statue and examine it closely. They did, surrounding Cosby. "Look at Washington's right hand, grasping the cane. He's wearing a glove, yet so fine is the workmanship that you can see the musculature of his hand inside the glove. Look at the wrinkling of his clothing, his boots.

There's even a button missing from his coat, Houdon's sense of humor."

Murmurs of admiring astonishment floated from the group. "Amazing," said the man on Cosby's right, his face rapt. They all agreed with the docent when she gave her opinion that this was the finest and most valuable statue in the entire United States. Cosby thought so, too.

Far-off noises of a crowd intruded upon the quiet group. Somewhere down a long corridor a man shouted something unintelligible. The scuffling sound of fast-moving feet was heard, while animated voices grew louder.

A disheveled man burst into the rotunda, closely pursued by a security guard. "Fort Sumter has fallen!" he shouted gleefully at the startled group. "Sumter has fallen!" A second security guard joined the first and they bundled the man away, but they could not silence him. "O great day!" he bubbled. "Sumter has fallen!"

Crowd voices could be heard outside the building, muted but growing in volume. Members of the group looked at each other, their own animation growing. "Amazing," the man beside Cosby repeated, his face lighting up. "Sumter! At last!"

"It only took three days," another man chimed in brightly.

"Sumter," an older woman in a blue bonnet said dubiously. "What is that?"

"It's a Federal fort in Charleston harbor," the second man replied, speaking rapidly. He was well-dressed and sported a cane, though he was not past middle age. "Confederate artillery opened fire on it last Friday. Now it has fallen."

"What does that mean?" the woman pursued.

"War, ma'am," Cosby answered quietly. "It means war. Perhaps a very long and costly war."

"That cannot be, sir," the cane-sporter said, turning to Cosby. "Surely the government would not go to war over a mere fort, when seven whole states have already seceded without hostilities."

"Let them come!" said the first man, his voice rising in indignation. He was about fifty years old, with a thin face, full mustache, goatee, and a gold tooth. "The Yankees will have to come to the South if they want to save their precious Union, and we'll whip 'em when they do!"

"Your pardon," Cosby said with forced courtesy. "Do you identify with the Confederacy, even though Virginia is in the Union?"

"I do," came the quick and flat reply. "We have more in common with Georgia than New York. We should join the Confederacy. Then the Yankees would never dare invade."

"I see." Cosby turned to the second man. "And you, sir?"

"I'm for the Union," the man with the cane cautiously answered, "but only if it does not use force against the Confederacy. If it did, my sympathies would lie with the South. What about you?"

"I'm against war," Cosby said slowly. "I fought in one war, and that was enough for one lifetime. Being against war, however, isn't always enough to avoid one. I sense a war coming, but I hope we can avoid it."

"Amen to that," said the woman.

"I ask you all this," Cosby went on. "We are standing here before a representation of the greatest American of all. He was a Virginian, but he was the first president of the United States. He was inaugurated in New York, and served his terms in Philadelphia. I have never read that he used the term 'Yankee' with scorn. He was a unifier, not a divider. What do you think he would have done in this current situation?"

No one in the circle around Cosby spoke, although the hubbub was rising both inside and outside the capitol. "I don't know," the woman finally said. "Times were different then."

"I don't know either," Cosby smiled, "but I like to think it would not have been war."

Without a word, the woman walked over to Cosby and gave him a hug. Cosby caught a scent of lilac. She then walked out of the room, not looking back.

The three men stood silently, all slightly abashed. The other two men then quietly murmured perfunctory farewells to Cosby and also walked out, joining the exodus of the group. In less than half a minute Cosby was alone, quietly contemplating the magnificent statue of the "Father of His Country," now radiantly glowing from the afternoon sun shining through the skylight.

What, indeed, would he have done? Cosby wondered.

CHAPTER 15

Sunday
Washington
2:23 PM

"Someday I'm sure it will be quite grand, but right now it's a mess."

Meagan O'Connor and Rufus Sloan were seated on a bench on the west side of First Street, facing the west side of the capitol. Most of the lower portion of the great building was completed, but the huge dome was not. Naked iron beams jutted high into the air like the skeleton of some giant sea monster washed up on some far-off beach. "When do you think it will be done, Rufus?"

"I don't know, Meagan. Six months. A year, maybe. The important thing is that it will someday be done. It's certainly better than the old building."

"Think it will be done before the Washington Monument?"

They both laughed. The monument was a joke to Washingtonians. Begun with much fanfare thirteen years before, mismanagement and a shortage of funds had brought it to a halt. The imposing but unfinished stump was 156 feet high. No one knew when it would be finished, if at all.

"Why does it have to be so large?' Meagan asked, gesturing toward the unfinished capitol.

Sloan shrugged. "The senators and congressmen have to have some place to meet. We are a growing nation. We cannot build for the present. We have to build for the future, when there will be many more states than there are now. That is, we *were* a growing nation," he corrected himself bitterly. "Now the Confederacy's taken away seven states. And it wants more."

Meagan wrapped up the remains of the lunch which had been spread out on the bench between them. "You know, Rufus, in all the time I've known you, I've never heard you express an opinion for or against the Confederacy. You have been very neutral. Am I hearing that you don't *like* the Confederacy?"

Sloan shrugged. "I have to be very careful, Miss O'Connor." He still found it difficult to call her *Meagan*. "All kinds of customers come into Grinell's. Many are highly opinionated, and they like to talk about their opinions. I want to be informed, but not sound opinionated. I must be neutral. The store is no place for a debate. Besides, no one really asks for my opinions. I'm just a clerk."

"But you do have them?"

"Yes, ma'am. I do."

"Well, *I* think your opinions are worthwhile. And I'd like to hear them."

"You are very sweet, Miss—Meagan."

A strong breeze blew across the area, bringing with it the heady scent of a thousand growing things. "Goodness," Meagan said. "I almost feel as if I'll fly away." She picked up the pink bonnet she had removed and put it back on, tying a wide bow under her chin. "There." She smiled at Sloan as she tucked wisps of her golden hair under the bonnet. She knew he could scarcely take his eyes away from her, and that knowledge glowed like a warm fire in the pit of her stomach, at the very core of her being.

"So. What is your opinion of the Confederacy?"

Sloan looked steadily into Meagan's eyes, as if weighing how much he should reveal to her. "The Confederacy is a disaster," he finally said. "A disaster for everybody. That those states should have pulled out of the Union, and then threaten war, is unbelievable. Is there no one of common sense in them? They're like spoiled children at a party. They go home because they can't get everybody else to play their games. All this, and for what? For the worst—"

Meagan reached out and put her hand on Sloan's arm. She was looking past him, into the grounds of the capitol. "Something's happening, Rufus."

Sloan turned around. There was a large group of people near the north end of the building, more than a hundred yards away, with more people joining it. A few were even running. The wind carried the faint noise of some shouting. An accident? Had a carriage overturned? It didn't seem so. A number of the people were standing in small knots, each looking intently at something.

"What are they doing?"

Sloan shaded his eyes with his hand. What were the people in the small knots looking at? *Newspapers.* "They're looking at newspapers."

"Let's go see."

Meagan tucked away the leftovers from the lunch into the small basket she had brought, and they walked quickly over to the crowd. Excited murmurs from the crowd as they approached told them the news: Fort Sumter had surrendered. The newspaper was a special edition of the *Post-Intelligencer.* The supply was sold out, but people did not have to buy a copy; owners were holding them up so others could read over their shoulders, and reading aloud so everyone could learn the details.

The crowd grew larger and noisier. When readers started repeating the story, Meagan tugged Sloan's coat sleeve. "We've heard enough, Rufus. I'm frightened. Can we walk?"

They walked northwest along Pennsylvania Avenue. There was an unusual bustle and stir along the city's main thoroughfare, with groups reading newspapers and other groups talking animatedly. The news was spreading throughout Washington.

"I don't want to go home," Meagan said dispiritedly. "I couldn't stand to be cooped up in the house with this awful news. I want to walk and walk until I drop from sheer exhaustion, as if walking will somehow make the news go away."

Meagan glanced at her companion, walking wordlessly beside her. "When we talked of this on Friday, you said a war might be better than endlessly waiting for it. Like a storm clearing the air. Are you now sure there will be a war?"

Sloan did not answer immediately. They walked on for a few moments, skirting yet another small group of people talking animatedly on the city's main street. "Yes, I think so," he finally said. He walked with long strides, his shoulders hunched and his thin face thrust slightly forward. "It all depends on what Mr. Lincoln will do now. If he does nothing, the southern states will think there is no penalty for secession, and it may encourage more states to secede. The president will be scorned in both the North and the South as a weakling. If he responds with military force, more southern states will certainly secede. The president will be damned if he does and damned if he doesn't. Beggin' your pardon, Miss Meagan."

Meagan pretended to be slightly shocked. "Really, Rufus." She tucked a curl inside her bonnet. "But you think he will do something?"

"Yes, ma'am, I do."

"And you think that something will bring on the war?"

Sloan nodded. "And you still think that would be a good thing?" Meagan persisted, her voice incredulous. "Rufus, we're talking about people, not rain."

"Yes, we are talking about people. But to me, that includes slaves. Have you ever seen slaves, Meagan?"

"Well, I—yes, I suppose I have. I mean, I've seen Negroes. I know some were free blacks, but I suppose some were slaves. I don't know. I never asked."

"Ever been to a slave auction? You don't have to go to the deep South to see them, you know. You don't even have to go to Richmond. There are some right here in Washington."

Meagan shook her head, making her bright curls dance in the sunlight. "No. Never."

"Think you'd *like* to attend a slave auction?"

"Rufus, really. Of course not."

"Why not?" Sloan pressed.

"It's—well, it's none of my business."

"It is now, Miss O'Connor. It's everybody's business. The Confederacy has started a shooting war, we're all in it, and it's all about slavery. I don't like war, but if there must be one, then let it be about slavery. That is an evil that must die, and it will." Sloan's lean face was set and determined. A forelock of his lank dark hair fell over the right side of his face. O'Connor thought it added a touch of animal intensity to Sloan, and was half thrilled, half frightened.

"So you would go to war, even kill people, to banish slavery?"

I already have, Sloan thought. "Yes, ma'am, I would," he said aloud. "Gladly. If an army is raised to invade the South, I'll be the first to join."

O'Connor slowed her pace of walking, forcing Sloan to match her speed. "You're an abolitionist, aren't you, Rufus." Her tone was flat, declarative.

"Yes, ma'am, I am. But I'd appreciate it if you'd keep that to yourself."

To O'Connor, abolitionists were wild-eyed radicals with no sense of proportion, who would rather smash something than fix it. That's what her father said, and held up that crazy John Brown as a perfect example. "I don't think I've ever met a real abolitionist before." There was an undercurrent of danger here, and O'Connor was surprised to find that it made Sloan more attractive to her.

"There's plenty of us around. A lot more to the North."

They walked on in silence for a time. As they approached O'Connor's house, Sloan asked her again to refrain from revealing his political beliefs to anyone. "It's not that I'm ashamed of my feelings regarding slavery, Meagan. Not in the least. But I don't think Mr. Grinell would understand. To him, I'm just a nonpolitical clerk. I'd like to keep it that way."

Meagan smiled graciously. She now had that thing which women prize so highly—*power* over a man. It was a heady feeling, almost as great as the thrill she had when Mrs. Greenhow invited her to tea. "Of course, Rufus. It will be our little secret." She extended her hand at her door. "See you tomorrow?"

"Yes, Miss Meagan," Sloan replied as he briefly took her hand. "I look forward to it."

Neither made any attempt to kiss the other. *That can wait*, Meagan thought as she waved goodbye.

CHAPTER 16

Sunday
Richmond
8:58 PM

Carter Cosby walked slowly down the right side of the wide entrance road to the Governor's Mansion. He made no effort to blend with the nearby trees, yet avoided the open center of the road. Only a few gas lamps lit this wide driveway with small pools of light, so he had no trouble remaining obscure. He saw no one.

As he expected, there was a policeman on duty under the overhang of the portico, which was faintly illuminated by a small flickering gas lamp beside the door. He identified himself as "John Rolfe" and stated that he was expected. He also showed his empty hands.

"Yes, sir," the burly policeman said respectfully. "I've been told to expect you." He knocked on the door, said "John Rolfe" to the butler when the door opened, and stood aside to let Cosby pass.

"Right this way, suh," the butler said in the obsequious way of all butlers. He led the way down a hallway, past a sitting room and an elaborate dining room, to a closed door in the rear of the house. He knocked three times, eliciting a faint "Enter." Opening the door, he said, “Mr. Rolfe is here, Governor.” He let Cosby enter, then closed the door.

Cosby found himself in a medium-sized and well-equipped study. A man of average height with a large, open face arose, took off his spectacles, and extended his hand. “Welcome to Virginia, Mr. Cosby. I’m John Letcher. Please sit down,” he said, indicating a wooden armchair with a thin red pillow. “We can dispense with your assumed name now,” he grinned. “However, the few staff people who are aware of your presence know you as ‘Mr. Rolfe,’ so do not be surprised if I address you in that manner before them.”

“I understand, sir. Thank you.” Cosby shook hands and sat down.

Letcher turned around the caneback desk chair in which he had been sitting and faced his guest. He had a prematurely balding head and a figure that ran to fat unless exercised, but his gray eyes were intelligent and cheerful behind his spectacles. Despite the lateness of the hour, he was still dressed in a business suit, complete with vest.

“So,” the governor said. “Have you found comfortable lodgings?”

“Yes, sir. At the Spotswood Hotel. I’ve stayed there before.”

“A fine choice. Would you care to join me in a small libation? A little port or sherry, perhaps? We also have some excellent rye and corn whiskey.”

Cosby rarely drank, but to refuse a cordial with the governor of the state was unthinkable. “Some sherry would be nice, thank you.”

“I think so, too.” Letcher pulled a cord hanging on the wall. “How was your trip?”

“Too slow,” Cosby replied. “Quite comfortable, but too slow.”

“Too slow?” Letcher showed his surprise. “My dear Mr. Cosby, Montgomery is more than five hundred miles away. You made the trip in less than four days. Why, only a bird could have made the trip faster, and I’m not even sure of that. I myself have never even been to Montgomery. What do you mean, too slow?”

The door opened and the butler stuck in his grizzled head. “You rang, suh?”

“Yes, Walter. Two sherries, please.”

"Right away, suh." The door closed.

"So the trains are too slow?" the governor continued.

"No, Governor, the trains are fine. Once you're on board and the train is moving, it is indeed a modern miracle. It is travel at its finest, swift, smooth, and comfortable. It is the scheduling that is the problem. There are a great many railroads, and they are all rather small. Many of them connect only two cities, and that's it. A number even have different gauges for the rails. Long-distance passengers are therefore always changing trains, which is especially cumbersome if one is carrying baggage, which must be transferred. Each railroad has its own depot in a city, and usually they are at some distance from one another, which necessitates a carriage ride. Then one spends much time simply waiting in depots, for the schedule of the new railroad is not in harmony with the previous one. Consider this, Governor: if I could have boarded a train in Montgomery and stayed on it, and it averaged only twenty-five miles per hour, I could have been here in two days. And if it didn't have to stop at night, the trip would have taken but a single day."

"Didn't have to stop at night?" John Letcher smiled indulgently. "Of course trains have to stop at night. Where would people sleep? Or eat, for that matter?"

"I'm not sure," Cosby said slowly. "Perhaps on the train itself in some manner. Based on my experiences on this trip, however, there is one strong suggestion I would make to you, Governor. Like most major cities, Richmond has several train depots. Commerce and convenience would be much aided if all its depots were made into one. I urge you to consider it."

A quiet knock on the door announced the butler. He entered carrying a silver tray with two glasses of sherry, and set it down on a small side table.

"Thank you, Walter," the governor said. "That will be all for this evening."

"Very good, suh."

Cosby realized this servant must have stayed up specifically waiting for him. He added his thanks as the butler withdrew.

"Well, I was informed that you had a scientific turn of mind, Mr. Cosby, and it certainly seems so. I will indeed take your suggestion under consideration." The governor handed a sherry to his guest. "Your health, sir."

"And yours."

Letcher picked up a document from his desk and handed it to Cosby, silently sipping his drink while Cosby read it. "Does it meet with your satisfaction?" he asked when Cosby looked up.

"Indeed it does, sir." It was a letter of introduction to Robert E. Lee of Arlington, Virginia, introducing Carter Cosby and informing Lee that Cosby's services as an agricultural advisor, for a period of several weeks, were being provided by the state as a recognition for Lee's outstanding record of service to his native state. It was written on official state stationery, and signed by the governor. "Thank you."

"Let us put it in this envelope, then," the governor said. He took the letter, folded it, and inserted it into a white envelope, then sealed it and handed it back to Cosby. It was addressed simply to "Robert E. Lee," with no address or military rank. Cosby put it in an inner pocket of his jacket.

The two men sat and silently regarded each other for ten seconds, quietly sipping their drinks. "Governor," Cosby said suddenly, "do you mind if I ask you a sharp question or two? I'm curious about certain things. You needn't answer if you don't wish to."

"Ask away," Letcher said amiably. "I may not answer, but you're on an important mission. You certainly have the right to ask."

Cosby adjusted himself in his chair. "You are the governor of an influential state in the Union, yet you are in correspondence with the president of the Confederacy. You are even cooperating with him on a plan in which I, a resident of the Confederacy, am involved. Do you not find that position a bit…*odd*?"

"Oh, my," the governor smiled. "It is a bit sharp. You make it sound almost as if you think I am involved in some nefarious plot with the head of a foreign government." He raised his eyebrows quizzically.

Cosby waved a hand deprecatingly, but said nothing. "You live in the Confederacy, Mr. Cosby," the governor said. "Do you believe it is a separate nation from the United States?"

"Its leaders say it is."

"Ah. Precisely the point. They *say* it is. But who else says so? Does the government of the United States say so? No. Does any other nation? No. Quite the opposite. President Lincoln has said repeatedly that secession from the Union is illegal, and that he cannot and will not recognize any combination of seceded states as a legal government. The Confederacy therefore exists in some sort of legal and international limbo, claiming to be an independent nation but finding no one to recognize that claim. From the standpoint of the United States government, the Confederacy is a legal fiction. It is most certainly not a foreign nation. Since Virginia is part of the United States, I must accept the government's view. Therefore when I correspond with someone in the Confederacy—any one, even its self-proclaimed president—I am not dealing with a foreign national living in a foreign nation. I am dealing with a fellow American living in the United States. There cannot be treason if there is no foreign nation involved, and the president of my country has repeatedly said that there isn't."

Cosby grinned. "You must have been a great lawyer, Governor."

Letcher laughed. "I still am, I hope. By law, Virginia's governors cannot succeed themselves. In a few years I expect to find myself back out in the legal market, seeking clients with solid cases." He became serious. "President Davis wrote to me about Lee, a prominent Virginia citizen, which *is* my business. He proposed a plan which might prevent this state from becoming a vast battlefield, which *certainly* is my business. I would be derelict in my duty if I did *not* do something to avert a potential great tragedy."

"What do you think will happen, Governor, now that Fort Sumter has fallen?"

Letcher sighed and shook his head. "A very big question, Mr. Cosby. I really don't know. President Lincoln will do what he will do, and no amount of suggestions from me is going to make any difference." He stared down at the remaining sherry in his glass, slowly twisting the stem between his fingers. "I'm much more concerned about what is going to happen here."

"What will happen here?"

"A vote, that's what. You're staying at the Spotswood. A block north of that hotel you may have noticed a large building, Mechanic's Hall. Since February a convention has been meeting regularly there, considering solely the question of Virginia's secession from the Union. So far, it has not voted. The delegates have simply discussed matters, often quite vigorously. My information is that sentiment is strongly in favor of staying in the Union. However, Fort Sumter has now been attacked and has fallen. President Lincoln is going to have to do *something* about that fact. I have no idea what that will be. However, every political instinct I have tells me that the president's response is going to prompt a vote from that convention. And that same instinct says that the vote will be for secession if the president's response is warlike."

"You must understand, Mr. Cosby, that I cannot oppose a vote from that convention, regardless of my personal feelings. Technically, its vote is only advisory; the final decision rests with the state legislature, the Senate and the General Assembly. However, members of the legislature feel as I do. They are not going to oppose any vote from the convention, whose delegates were elected specifically to consider that one issue. We will consider a vote by that convention to be the will of the people regarding secession, and we were elected to implement the will of the people. So Virginia will go the way the convention votes, and I think its vote is going to come soon."

Cosby sat silently, regarding his own sherry glass, and remembering some of the things Jefferson Davis had said to him. "This is merely technical, but a vote of the convention for secession is not necessarily a vote for the Confederacy, is it?"

"Technically, that is correct. A vote for secession, if confirmed by the legislature, would make Virginia an independent state. A small nation, if you will. To join the Confederacy would require a separate act of the legislature. However, I have no doubt that is what the legislature would do, regardless of Mr. Lincoln's wishes or lack of recognition. The very possibility that this might happen is why Virginia sent two official observers to the convention in Montgomery several months ago which proclaimed the birth of the Confederacy."

"So you see my dilemma, Mr. Cosby. So long as the convention does not vote for secession, I will be—I must be—the governor of a dutiful state of the Union. But that situation could change in a day, and I am personally powerless to influence it."

"And that is why you are supporting my mission?"

"Yes. If Virginia secedes and then joins the Confederacy, then my objective would coincide with that of Davis. We don't want an invasion, because it would be invading *us.* If Virginia stays in the Union, we still would not want Virginia used as a highway for armies marching south to invade *them.* But perhaps there will be no invasion. Lincoln has been absolutely silent on this matter. I've not even heard rumors that he plans to invade. In that case your mission would be superfluous. However, we simply don't know, and that makes it important." Letcher drained his glass and placed it on the tray. "Lord, how I wish I had the gift of prophecy right now."

"Don't we all. These are indeed unsettled times."

"The worst since the Revolution. And we have no great figure around whom we can rally, as we did then."

"Troubled times have a way of raising heroes. Perhaps you might even be one of them," Cosby added with a smile.

Letcher laughed, an act which seemed to come easily to him. "Thank you, but I think troubled times make heroes of presidents and generals, especially if there's a war involved. Governors raise taxes and build roads. Not the stuff of history. Do you remember who the governor of Pennsylvania was during the Revolution? I don't."

Cosby grinned. "I don't, either."

"There. You see? My epitaph." Letcher ran a hand over his bald forehead. "Ah, well. Now. Do you have enough money?"

"President Davis was generous."

"Good. Now, about reporting. Unless you have set up some special way of corresponding with Davis, I would suggest you do so with me. I can pass on anything you require. You do trust me?"

"Implicitly, Governor. Do you want me to use the Rolfe name?"

"No. Use your own. That's perfectly innocent. You are, after all, my appointee. That name was just a precaution against anyone who might have seen you here tonight, on the remote chance they might have placed you from the Confederacy. So long as your name is a signature on a private letter posted a hundred miles from here, no one will make any inquiry."

"How often would you like a report?"

"Well, that depends on the length of your stay. If it is only a few weeks, you may not have to send a letter at all. Simply stop by here on your way home and see me personally. In many ways, that would be safest. If you write, send it to me here, at this residence, not to my office. A secretary handles official mail at my office in the capitol, but I open all my own mail here." The governor stood up. "Well, I can't think of anything else. You will see Colonel Lee tomorrow. Please give my best regards to him, his wife, and his wonderful family."

Cosby put down his empty glass and stood up. "I will, sir. It has been a pleasure and a privilege."

"Thank you. Godspeed to you, sir. I will show you to the door."

CHAPTER 17

Monday, April 15
Washington
10:31 AM

Major Thomas Eckert looked down the first-floor hallway of the War Department just in time to see the Secretary of War, Simon Cameron, open the front door, and follow the lanky figure of Abraham Lincoln into the building. Cameron, Eckert knew, was returning from a Cabinet meeting, but the new president had apparently told no one he was also coming, so the various officers and adjutants were a bit surprised to see him. They were becoming used to it, however; in the few weeks he had been in office Lincoln had unexpectedly dropped into the War Department several times, and would undoubtedly do so many times again.

Eckert was pleased at the new president's personal interest in the War Department. He knew one reason why: the military Telegraph Office, of which he was the head, had later and more accurate information than was available in the Executive Mansion.

Lincoln's attitude was a refreshing change from that of the previous president, Old Buck, who was infinitely more interested in State Department information, protocols, and diplomatic gossip than military intelligence. Staff officers could hardly recall a time when Buchanan had personally visited the War Department, despite the fact that it was located just to the west of the Executive Mansion.

Cameron caught Eckert's eye and waved him over.

"Good morning, Mr. President, Mr. Secretary. May I help you?"

"Is General Scott in, Major?" Cameron asked brusquely.

"Yes, sir. In his office."

"Good. You will please accompany us, Major. I have here a copy of the president's remarks he said to the press concerning the recruitment of new troops. General Scott should see this before you send the news out to the units in the field."

"I thought the general might be able to make them sound a little more military," Lincoln winked. "Nice to see you again, Thomas."

"Thank you, sir." Eckert felt pleasure at the president's remembrance of, and use of, his first name. It may have been a personal trait, or even a politician's deliberate tactic, but he thought it was a good one.

The party went up the steps to Scott's second-floor office, and was shown in by an aide. Winfield Scott, his uniform jacket neatly hung up on a wall, stood up to greet his visitors. He was an inch taller than the president and a hundred pounds heavier, an outsized human being. His white hair was not neatly arranged, like Cameron's, but followed the contour of his head in an unruly manner. Except for long sideburns, he was clean-shaven. In a toga, he would have been the very personification of an elderly distinguished Roman senator, except for his countenance. Naturally gruff mannerisms had been overlaid by years of high command, and he simply looked grim, whatever the occasion. He also looked as if he were suffering from perpetual dyspepsia. His fanatical insistence on proper appearance and presentation, even in the lowliest recruit, had long ago earned him the sobriquet "Old Fuss and Feathers," which he didn't seem to mind at all. Administration after administration put up with him—*valued* him—because of his truly expert military advice, his unswerving loyalty, unquestioned honesty, and rock-solid incorruptibility. He was also the only person in Washington of whom Lincoln was slightly in awe. "Welcome, Mr. President, Mr. Secretary. Please be seated. Did the Cabinet meeting go well?"

Lincoln smiled. Scott was always bluntly direct, even abrupt, an attribute the president admired in a military man. "If gaining unanimous backing for a call for 75,000 volunteers for the army can be called a good thing, then it went well, General. After the meeting I made some remarks to the press, amplifying the official call I issued this morning. You already have a copy of the official announcement. Mr. Cameron here has a copy of the additional remarks. You may edit them as you see fit for transmission to the various military units."

Scott read through the piece of paper Cameron handed him, then gave it to Eckert. "Repeat that the president issued a call for 75,000 volunteers today. Fill in the details about length of service and pay. Add some of these presidential remarks. Prepare the dispatch, but hold it until I see it."

"Yes, sir." Eckert saluted, left the room, and closed the door behind him.

"Now, then, General," Lincoln said, "I have asked for the number of volunteers you suggested. I have no doubt the nation will respond, and respond quickly. The South now knows we are raising a huge army, which can have only one purpose: to invade the Confederacy and subdue it by force. I know this is a course of action favored by you. Now that we have taken the first step to produce your army, I and the secretary would like to hear again your general plan for the conquest of the Confederacy."

Scott rose and walked over to a large map of the southeastern part of the United States. "When those volunteers arrive," he began, "they will be stationed here, in Washington. They will simultaneously be trained and serve as defence for the capital city. I do not expect that anyone will attempt to attack Washington soon, but we cannot be too careful. I intend to build a ring of forts around the city, even on the north. I'm not a politician, Mr. President, but even I know that Maryland is full of secessionist sentiment."

Lincoln smiled at the venerable general's characterization of himself as "not a politician." He had been the Whig candidate for president in 1852, but had been soundly defeated by Franklin Pierce.

"If you're going to build protective forts to the south of Washington, then they will have to be built in Virginia, will they not, General?"

"Indeed they will, Mr. President. There's room enough in the District for some forts, but we really must deny the Virginia heights above the Potomac to any hostile force. It could easily bombard the city from there. The best way to prevent such a situation is to build our own forts there. Those forts could also serve as bases for the invasion army when it moves south."

"Virginia may not be in the Union when the army is ready," Lincoln observed mildly.

"Yes, sir, I'm aware of that. However, that shouldn't matter, so far as the forts are concerned. If Virginia is still in the Union, well and good; we build the forts, because we have the authority. If Virginia is not in the Union, we build the forts anyway, because we have the power. The Confederacy will have no power, even if Virginia joins it, to control those heights. We do."

"Good," the president said. "When do you think the army will be ready to march south?"

"Gentlemen, if there is anything I must caution you against, it is precipitate moves." The general eased himself into his chair with a gracefulness which belied his bulk. "We must bring the recruits here, they must be properly trained, then equipped with the best weapons and gear we can afford. The two of you are going to have to approve of the ordering of vast amounts of military materiel, from tents and blankets to cannons and ships. It will take time, but the worst thing we could do is to rush ill-trained and ill-equipped troops into battle and have them lose. The effect on the army would be devastating. It would hurt our future recruiting efforts more than anything else imaginable."

"Indeed so," the president agreed. "So when might the army be ready to move south?" he pressed.

Scott hesitated. "If everything goes right, perhaps by July," he finally said.

"July?" Cameron said acidly. "General, that's three months from now. These recruits will be signing up for only three months. Are you saying you cannot put them into action before their service time is over?"

"If we take proper care of them, we can induce the great majority to reenlist. And we can issue more recruitments, for larger numbers and longer periods of service. The population of the North is more than twenty million. Half that population is male, so a mere two percent of the male population would be 200,000 troops, a number almost three times as large as the call the president made earlier this morning. But I repeat my warning: we cannot throw them into battle without proper training and equipment. That would be our worst possible mistake. If I may say so, we must make haste deliberately."

"Senator Douglas came to see me last evening," Lincoln said slowly, "to pledge me his support. I cannot tell you how much I appreciated his action. We talked about a number of things. He agreed with me about issuing the call for recruits, but said he would have asked for 200,000 men—exactly the same number you just mentioned, General. So, yes, I agree that the army can be greatly expanded. There is, however, another matter to consider. Congress will be in session in two months. It will want some action. I cannot risk alienating Congress by endlessly pleading the need for more training and equipment, however justifiable that need may be. I would say that we must prepare for our first engagement, even if it is a minor one, some time during the summer."

Scott nodded. "I'll do my best, Mr. President. There is something we could do right now, however, which could hurt the Confederacy yet not cost any lives."

"Now *that* sounds like something the secretary and I could surely support," the president grinned. "What is it?"

General Scott leaned back in his chair and reflectively rubbed his chin. "The South is the greatest cotton-growing area in the world, gentlemen," he began. "There is enormous demand for cotton in New England, where textile mills weave it into the cloth which is supplied to the rest of the United States. There is also a great demand for it in Europe, especially France, and most especially Britain. Yet it cannot grow in any of those places. Egypt is the only other place in the world which can supply cotton in any appreciable quantity and quality. So the South exports almost all of its cotton. Fully 90% of the total value of the South's exports is cotton. There is really nothing else the South produces which has any exportable value, except tobacco. And the

South *must* export its cotton, for there are no textile mills in the South. There lies its extreme vulnerability. And *that* is where we should attack." Scott leaned back with an attitude of satisfaction.

Lincoln and Cameron glanced at each other. "*What* should we attack, General?" the Secretary of War asked with a slight air of puzzlement.

"How does the South get its cotton to market, Mr. Cameron?"

The former governor of Pennsylvania thought a moment; Pennsylvania did not export cotton. "By ship, I suppose."

"Exactly," Scott agreed. "By *ship.* And the Confederacy has no navy, but *we* do. A good one."

"Blockade. You're suggesting a blockade," Lincoln said.

"Indeed I am, Mr. President. We have enough warships to blockade every port in the Confederacy. Take Charleston, for example. We were unable to resupply Fort Sumter because that harbor has a long entrance and multiple batteries. There's only one entrance, but it's also the only way *out.* Several of our warships, standing offshore just out of range of the coastal batteries, could seal it as effectively as if we had pushed a giant cork in the channel. We could do the same with every Confederate port, even New Orleans. *Especially* New Orleans. The Confederates could do nothing about it, except try to run the blockade with some fast merchantmen. Perhaps a few might get through now and then, but we have the better and faster ships. They don't even have any warships at all. We can *strangle* the Confederacy. That is an ace we have, gentlemen, and I urge you to play it as soon as possible."

"I like it," Cameron said quickly. "The South's economy is overwhelmingly agricultural, not industrial. We could stop the Confederacy from exporting its cotton, and also stop it from importing the manufactured goods it needs but does not manufacture itself. And as the general says, we can do it right away, and without risking a major engagement. The blockade can be fully in place by the time Congress meets, so we can truthfully say we are already putting heavy pressure on the rebels." He looked expectantly at the president.

Lincoln thought a few moments. "Yes, we can do it, and we will," he finally said slowly. "Thank you, General, for your plan, which has obvious merit." He gently tugged at his lower lip. "I have several reservations about this anaconda strategy. The first is that the effects of a blockade, no matter how tight, will take time to transpire. During that time the Confederate armed forces will grow stronger, at least for a considerable time. The second is that the common people suffer first, suffer the most, and suffer the longest from a blockade. I would expect that the very last person to really feel its effects would be Jeff Davis himself, precisely the person we would prefer to feel its consequences *first*. The combination of these factors is that a blockade will have little effect on the fighting qualities of Confederate armies, not for a long time."

"The Confederacy will not surrender because of strangulation. To defeat it we must invade it, beat its army, literally take the guns out of the hands of its soldiers, and occupy it. We must dictate the terms of the peace from a position of absolute control. There cannot be any armistice which recognizes the legitimacy of the Confederacy. And to beat the rebel armies we must defeat them face-to-face on the field of battle. There is no other way. A blockade will help, but it will not be decisive. There is no simple, bloodless way to subdue the Confederacy at long distance."

Lincoln paused. "I foresee a long and deadly war, gentlemen. I hope to God I am wrong, but I do not see how this war will be a short one. You are right, General; our troops must be well trained and well equipped, and that will take time. They must also be well led. That brings up another problem. Many of our best officers were from the South, and have resigned their commissions and joined the Confederacy. The army is being expanded enormously at precisely the time of this shortage of officers. Where will we get our officers?"

"We have a good officer corps," Scott stoutly stated. "In any peacetime army, the ratio of officers to troops is high, because the officers are in the army for a career while almost all the troops are there for a short time. Wartime expansion brings that ratio into proper balance. For additional officers, particularly non-commissioned ones, we can promote from within. I do not think this will be a great problem, sir."

"That's very good news, General. You have relieved my mind." Lincoln paused momentarily. "May I ask how you see your role in the coming conflict? You personally led the army in Mexico to its great victory. I might respectfully suggest that you are too valuable to do such a thing now. We need you here. No one has your strategic skill, and this will be the biggest job of strategy and coordination that ever faced any general in American history. So you plan to stay right here in the War Department, do you not?"

Winfield Scott smiled widely. "Thank you, Mr. President. I see your reputation for persuasion is well earned. What you are politely suggesting is that I'm too old for field command. No, no, don't protest. I happen to agree with you. These old bones have seen their last field campaign. Frankly, I prefer an office to a tent, where it always seems to be freezing, boiling, or dripping rain. I also understand the situation much better here, for it has much better and more comprehensive information than any field headquarters. You'll need someone else for field command. And," he added with a nod, "I have just the person for you."

"Indeed," Lincoln murmured, his face expressionless.

"He is Colonel Robert E. Lee, sir. Recently promoted to commanding officer, Ist Cavalry. Do you know him, by any chance?"

"Lee," Lincoln ruminated. "I'm afraid not, General. My familiarity with military officers is not what it could be. He must be very good if you recommend him. What is his record?"

"He was previously second-in-command of the 2nd Cavalry in San Antonio," Scott answered. "Fifty-four years old. He has been in the army more than thirty years. For three years he was the Superintendent at West Point. He was with the engineers in Mexico, my chief of artillery, and his placement of guns in every battle was flawless. He has an exemplary record, but that alone isn't why I'm recommending him."

"Oh? What more is there?"

"Let me tell you a story," Scott began. "It happened in the Mexican War. After a string of battles from our landing in Vera Cruz, we were approaching Mexico City in September of '47. If we could capture it, the war would be over. I could see that conquering the capital would not be an easy task, and I needed some hard intelligence about the approaches to the city. Gathering such intelligence was not easy, because on one side of the city is a huge expanse of solidified lava, three miles across. It is very hard and rough, like a frozen storm-tossed sea. It is also extremely sharp, and can even cut boots to ribbons. As if that weren't enough, it is also full of crevasses. The local Mexicans call it the *pedregal*, and no one ventures onto it."

Scott saw that he had the president's and the secretary's rapt attention. Everyone loves a story. "Lee ventured onto it with a small party, avoiding Mexican patrols. He wanted to see if a road could be built across it. He then wanted to report to me, since I had specifically requested the information. So he led his group to San Augustin, where he thought I was. A powerful storm came up. It was as dark as night, with heavy rain and high wind. The group was caught out on the *pedregal*, and could see their way only by occasional flashes of lightning. Somehow Lee brought the group in safely, only to learn that I had left for Zacatepec. Leaving his group at San Augustin, he went out on the *pedregal* again, this time alone. It was still stormy, still dark, still raining. He finally reached Zacatepec, and then learned that I had returned to San Augustin! So he crossed the *pedregal* a third time, found me, and made his report. He was exhausted, thoroughly soaked, and bloody, yet I have no doubt he would have gone out again had it been necessary."

"To put that feat into perspective, at the same time I was trying to reach General Persifor Smith. I sent seven messengers out onto the *pedregal.* All returned unsuccessfully; not a single one was able to cross it once. Yet Lee did it *three times*! It was the most astonishing feat of physical and moral courage performed by any individual, to my knowledge, in the entire war."

"There's more. During the assault on Chapultepec, I ordered Lee to assist at a certain point in the battle line. He received a bullet would, but considered it so slight he did not bother to have it dressed. After we had scaled the height and taken the citadel, I ordered him to survey a line of march to Mexico City. When he returned and pulled his horse alongside mine, he literally fell out of the saddle from fatigue and blood loss. I later found out he had spent fifty hours in the saddle without sleep *before* he received his wound."

"I should add that the troops under his command loved him, which is a situation so highly unusual it is worth noting in any military recording. All in all, gentlemen, Colonel Lee is the finest officer with troops I have ever seen in the field. I unhesitatingly recommend him for field command of the army of invasion." Scott leaned back with an air of finality.

"Well, General, your enthusiasm for this Colonel Lee is certainly understandable," Lincoln said cautiously. "Thank you for your recommendation. He sounds like the right man for the job."

"I will go further, Mr. President. As the head of the army, I believe Lee would be worth fifty thousand troops to the Union cause."

"Fifty thousand troops!" Cameron exclaimed incredulously. "General, that's larger than the entire size of the army! How could one man be worth so much?"

"It's larger than the army is *now*, Mr. Secretary. Thanks to the president, the army will become much larger. And I think we all know that the army is soon going to become even larger. Very much larger, if I may say so. The leadership of all those troops will become one of the key factors in its success. Without good leadership, an army is just a huge disorganized mob. With good leadership, it becomes a mighty force, capable of determining the destiny of nations. One good leader, at the right place and the right time, is worth thousands of troops with no direction. Lee is such a leader."

"If he is worth so much, I would hesitate to estimate what *you* are worth, General," Lincoln said with a grin. "Whatever it might be, I am very grateful you are on our side." Scott smiled. "I have several questions about this Colonel Lee. What state is he from?"

"Virginia, Mr. President." the general answered. "The same as I."

"Ah. Perhaps that explains a tiny bit of your enthusiasm. And exactly where is he now?"

"At home, sir. He has an estate not far from Alexandria, just across the river."

"Conveniently close," Cameron observed drily. Scott ignored the comment.

Lincoln was picking again at his lower lip. "By any chance, General, have you communicated with Colonel Lee the fact that you were going to recommend him for this position?"

"Indeed not, Mr. President." Scott seemed irritated that the president would even think such a thing. "The decision as to who will command the army is entirely up to you. It is not my place to speak to anyone concerning my recommendations. The two of you are now the only ones who know it. No one on my staff does, and certainly not Colonel Lee himself."

"Good," the president responded. "The secretary and I will keep it that way, I assure you. We would like to see the colonel's file as soon as possible. Simon, as soon as you are finished with it, please send it over to my office, with your recommendation." He stood up. "Thank you, General. Your insight, as always, bolsters your great reputation." He left Scott's office, exited the War Department, and walked across the landscaped grounds back to the White House.

Back in his office, Lincoln immediately sent for Ward Hill Lamon. The Virginia-born Lamon, almost a decade younger than the president, had been a former law partner of his and was his closest friend in Washington. Tall and heavy-chested, Lamon was an imposing-looking man with wavy brown hair. Lincoln had brought him to Washington and made him the Marshal of the District of Columbia, giving him police powers which exceeded even those of the Chief of the Metropolitan Police. The president, who affectionately called Lamon by his middle name, appreciated his former partner's advice and companionship, even though he deprecated Lamon's constant carping about presidential security as so much exaggeration.

"Hello, Hill," he said as Lamon entered. "Please be seated." Long ago, Lincoln had found that his great height tended to intimidate people, so he habitually conducted business sitting down. Ever since his election, and especially since the inauguration, he noticed people would respectfully remain standing unless specifically invited to sit, so he automatically issued such invitations even for old friends.

"Hill, I need some special help, and I thought you would be just the person who could help me."

"Of course, Mr. President. What is it?'

"There is an Army officer, a colonel, about whom I need some information. His name is Lee—Robert E. Lee. He lives in Virginia, but close by; I am informed he has an estate near Alexandria. He is the commanding officer of the 1st Cavalry Regiment, but at the moment he is not in the field; he's at home. Here, I've written it all down for you." Lincoln passed over a sheet of paper; Lamon glanced at it. "By any chance, do you know this officer, Hill?"

"No, sir. I'm sorry, but I can't keep track of all our military officers."

"That's all right, Hill," the president smiled. "That's what the War Department is for. I never heard of him myself until just this morning."

"So what information about him would you like?"

Lincoln leaned back in his chair. "General Scott is sending over his military file, so you needn't bother with military records or any military information. What I want is more personal information, like his family background. Does he drink or gamble? What is his reputation among those who know him? Perhaps you can find some neighbors, or merchants in Alexandria with whom he does business."

"Yes, sir. That should be no problem."

"There is something in particular I need to know, Hill." The president spoke cautiously as he regarded his friend directly. "Although this Colonel Lee lives only a few miles from here, it's in another state—a state where slavery is legal. He apparently lives on an estate, and I would not be surprised to learn that the estate is large. A large estate in Virginia could very well have slaves. I need to know about that, Hill. Are there any slaves there, and if so, how many? Can you find that out?"

"Yes, sir, I can. Is there anything else?"

"Yes, one more thing. I need this information soon. I want your report here by tomorrow morning. Eleven o'clock at the latest. Put all the men you need on it. Top priority."

Lamon grinned. "Sounds as if this colonel is being considered for something important."

"Sounds that way, doesn't it?" Lincoln grinned back. "Hill, I know you well enough to know that you will keep this under your hat. And that you will not ask me exactly why I want this information. That's all. You'd better get started right away, my friend."

"Yes, sir." Lamon stood up. "I would just like to add, sir, that you did the right thing today. I know it must have been the hardest decision you ever made, but calling for the recruits was the right thing to do."

“Thank you, Hill,” Lincoln smiled appreciatively. “I think so, too.”

“Eleven o’clock tomorrow, Mr. President.” Lamon left and closed the door behind him.

Abraham Lincoln remained seated for a while after Lamon left. He leaned back and gazed at the ceiling, thinking back on his meeting with the legendary general. Anyone watching might have seen him momentarily close his eyes, and might have mistakenly thought he had fallen asleep. He hadn’t. *“Fifty thousand troops,”* he said quietly to himself.

CHAPTER 18

Monday
Alexandria, Virginia
2:35 PM

The train pulled into the Alexandria depot of the Orange and Alexandria Railroad with a hissing of steam and a jolting of the coaches. Carter Cosby alighted from the third car, carrying a grip in his right hand and a jacket on his left arm. A narrow ribbon tie adorned his white shirt, and his wide plantation hat shielded his face from the mild spring sun.

This depot had more hacks that the usual one. Cosby hired one and stood by it waiting for the baggage to be unloaded, and looked around. It had been four years since he had been here.

Alexandria was unusual in that it was serviced by several railroads. Their depots were near each other because the town was rather small. The railroads were there because Alexandria was the closest Virginia town to Washington, directly across the Potomac from the national capital. There were two bridges, both of timber, spanning the river: the Long Bridge, connecting Washington and Alexandria almost directly, and the shorter Key Bridge farther upstream. The Long Bridge carried the tracks of the Washington & Alexandria Railroad, only five miles long.

Cosby reflected again on the marvel of train travel but the inefficiency of connections. Richmond, from which he had just come, was only a hundred miles from Washington, yet there was no through railroad service between the national capital and Virginia's capital. To reach Alexandria he had been forced to take the Virginia Central Railroad to Gordonsville, northwest of Richmond, then change to the Orange and Alexandria Railroad. If he wanted to actually reach Washington itself he would have to cross the Long Bridge on the short Washington & Alexandria Railroad, or by walking or riding a horse across that bridge. But he wasn't going to the national capital.

He retrieved his luggage and had the hack driver load it. "Where to, sir?" The hackie had a noticeable Irish brogue.

"The Arlington estate." Cosby donned his jacket and climbed into the open carriage. "Do you know where it is?"

"Oh, yes, sir. About six miles. Everybody around here knows it." The Irishman took the hack out into the town and headed north. "You a relative of the Lees? They have many, so I hear."

"No, not a relative." Cosby did not care to get into a conversation with this hack driver, knowing everything he said would be repeated. "I'm here on business."

"Oh? What sort of business, might I ask?"

My, aren't you the nosy one, Cosby thought. "Private business," he said, emphasizing the adjective.

The hackie asked no more questions, but couldn't help pointing out objects of interest in the town as they rode past. Cosby let him go on without comment, and indeed learned some new things about Alexandria.

Leaving the town, the road wended its way through open fields, the river visible on his right at intervals. The land rose gently, Cosby noted, as the river seemed slightly lower and farther away each time he saw it.

After half an hour, Cosby saw a building ahead which had to be the Lee mansion. Though he had been given only a vague description of it, he knew it had to be impressive. It was. Situated on the top of a hill, the mansion's dominant feature was the eight stone columns supporting a portico roof two stories high. The columns were almost pure white, with goldish-brown veins running through the stone, topped by dark Doric capitals. Cosby thought they were probably the most magnificent columns he had ever seen on any building. Yet to his eye they seemed a bit too massive, more suited to temples of antiquity than a private residence. In his own state the pillars would have been slimmer, farther apart, fluted, and made of white-painted wood.

The house itself was handsomely executed in similar stone, two stories high. It was, Cosby noted wryly, far larger and more impressive that the governor's official mansion in Richmond.

The loquacious hack driver retrieved Cosby's luggage, thanking him for the fare and tip. As the hack left, the front door of the mansion opened, and a well-dressed black man in his sixties approached.

"Carter Cosby," the Alabaman smiled. "I'm expected."

"Indeed you are, suh. Welcome to Arlington." The black man smiled back, revealing a set of surprisingly even teeth. "I'm Daniel, the butler. Please come in. Leave your bags. I'll get them later."

This Daniel had a perfect combination of deference and authority, Cosby thought as he followed the butler into the house. "Let me take your hat and coat, suh." Cosby obediently handed over his wide hat, which Daniel placed on a nearby hat rack, but kept his jacket. "Please follow me." Daniel led Cosby into a parlor on the right side of the hallway and indicated a chair. "Wait here a moment, suh. I'll tell the colonel you're here."

Cosby admired the room while the butler disappeared across the hallway. A few moments later a tall handsome man entered the room and greeted Cosby affably. "I'm Robert E. Lee," he said warmly, shaking his visitor's hand. "We were expecting you, but we didn't know precisely when you'd arrive. Did you have a pleasant trip?"

"Yes, I did, sir." Cosby seated himself again in the chair. "The countryside is quite beautiful."

"We are indeed having a wonderful spring. Would you care to join me in a glass of wine? Your trip may have left you dry."

"A little red wine would be appreciated, sir. Thank you."

Lee opened a liquor cabinet. “Port? Claret?”

“Claret.”

Cosby studied his host while Lee poured the drinks. The colonel was six feet tall, with a trim and muscular figure which spoke of an active life and belied his fifty-four years. Even dressed in casual clothes, he radiated energy and authority. His handsome face and high forehead were framed in graying hair. His most striking feature, however, were his eyes. The pupils were dark, almost black, and gave the impression that they missed nothing, though his gaze was steady. In the few minutes since Cosby had met Lee, those eyes had been friendly and welcoming, yet Cosby could easily visualize them cold and commanding. It was easy to believe this man had spent thirty years in the army and had been the Superintendent of West Point. He was a born leader. Jeff Davis—and apparently General Scott—were right: this Robert E. Lee, though only a colonel, could and should command an army. The only question was *which* army.

“Here you are.” Lee handed a wine glass of red wine to Cosby. “To your health, sir.”

“And yours, Colonel.” Cosby sipped the claret, then reached inside his jacket and pulled out the letter of introduction from the Virginia governor. “You might want to read this, sir. It’s from Governor Letcher.”

“Yes, I would.” Lee took the letter and sat down in an armchair next to a window. He read the letter in a few moments, then rose, went to a desk, pulled open a drawer, extracted a large envelope, and returned to his chair. He withdrew several sheets of paper and began reading them.

Sipping his wine, Cosby again contemplated Lee, silhouetted against the window. Although he had read and reread the file on Lee, Cosby was not prepared for the enormity of Lee’s physical presence. Cosby felt it powerfully. It wasn’t just the authority of an experienced military officer. There was a strong personal magnetism about this man, something that transcended mere position. Cosby had met important people in his life, including two in the last several days. Curiously, most had not impressed him that much. Indeed, many had seemed rather ordinary people who, for one reason or another, had risen to high position. Even President Davis, impressive as he was, had a cool and clinical nature which inspired respect but not affection. Lee had something more. Cosby surmised that part of it was due to Lee's magnificent appearance—he was the absolute personification of a distinguished Southern gentleman. Yet more: his mannerisms, gestures, deportment, even his speech patterns, spoke of the purest aristocracy. He was an aristocrat to his fingertips, yet without the slightest hint of effeteness. He was even regal. Yet it was all natural. Cosby marveled at this unexpected aspect. He did not think he was being unduly influenced by sitting in this man's grand mansion on a grand estate, for he had been on many great estates. He even owned a very good one himself. He wondered if Jeff Davis was aware of Lee's magnetic qualities, for the Confederate president had not mentioned them. Yet Davis had said that he remembered Lee when both were cadets at West Point.

Robert E. Lee put the papers he had been reading back into the envelope. "I've just been rereading the information about you which the governor was kind enough to send me several days ago," he explained, facing Cosby. "Most impressive. So you were with General Scott's army in Mexico?"

"Yes, sir. All the way from Vera Cruz to Mexico City."

"So was I."

"Yes, sir, I know. You were the chief of artillery."

"It seems we never met. At least I do not recollect it."

"No, sir, we didn't. I was a private in a volunteer group."

"What did you think of that war?" Lee asked quietly.

The question took Cosby by surprise. "I'm not sure what you mean, sir."

"The war started fifteen years ago and ended thirteen years ago, Carter. May I call you Carter?"

"Please do."

"Well, Carter, fourteen years ago you were a young man in your early twenties. Young men join armies for different reasons. Did you join out of a sense of adventure? Patriotism? Glory?"

Cosby thought a moment. "Adventure and patriotism, I'd say, sir. Not glory. I didn't expect to find that, and didn't. The campaign was months of drudgery and routine punctuated by hours of deadly and frantic activity."

"Well put," Lee smiled. "You were decorated for bravery for your part in the assault on Chapultepec Castle, I understand."

"Yes, sir."

"That was a nasty piece of work—or heroic, depending on your point of view. Scaling that steep hill, then the walls—my congratulations."

"Thank you. The Mexicans were fierce fighters."

"Indeed they were. Did you happen to see any of the young cadets that the Mexicans made into heroes?"

Cosby looked carefully at Lee, but the Virginian showed no change of expression. Was this some kind of a test? Everyone in the war knew about Chapultepec Castle; it was a fortress, a palace, and a military training center situated atop a steep hill a short distance outside Mexico City. It had to be captured in order for the siege of the capital city to be effective. The American assault on Chapultepec was brutal and bloody, but ultimately successful. During the last part of the battle several dozen Mexican cadets, some as young as thirteen, threw themselves into combat. Most were killed. They became "Los Niños," the children, heroes to the Mexicans and the perfect symbol of American brutality and outrageousness. The siege and occupation of Mexico City eventually resulted in the Treaty of Guadalupe Hidalgo which ended the war. The Americans withdrew peacefully, but it would be a very long time before the memory of Los Niños faded from the Mexican national consciousness, if ever.

"I never saw any of them during the battle," Cosby replied. "I saw several of them afterward. Some dead, some alive."

"A tragic thing."

"Yes, sir. It was."

"So now, Carter, more than a decade after the war—a war which you experienced at the most difficult level—would you say the result was worth it?"

Again Cosby searched Lee for the slightest lightness. He could find none. Perhaps professional soldiers were incapable of regarding war with anything but the utmost seriousness. "When I volunteered," he said, "I was under the impression that the war was about Texas and the location of the international boundary. I thought that Texans should be allowed to declare independence and join the United States, if that's what they wished. I never thought about California and the lands of the West, all that territory which Mexico ceded in the treaty. I'm glad the Texas question is settled, and California with its gold and ports is certainly valuable, but the rest of the land is mostly desert, I understand. I don't know how useful it will ever be, even if some day we build a railroad across it. If I had believed that a vast seizure of western Mexican territory was the real object of the war, I would never have volunteered."

"Wars have a way of changing as they are fought," Lee observed quietly. "Once you were in the army, you obeyed orders, as any soldier must. So did I. I knew nothing of President Polk's western objectives, and frankly would not have cared. I had a job to do, and did it."

"Yes, sir. I understand."

"Carter, forgive me if I seem a bit too inquisitive about your part in the war and your motives in it. I don't mean to pry, or even just reminisce about a war that both of us were in. It's the current situation today. We are facing a potential war far greater, and certainly more divisive, then the Mexican War. I am interested in informed opinions about the country's position. I hear enough opinions in the War Department from fellow officers, but I rarely hear from someone who has had military experience, but who is not now in the military or in politics. That is why you interest me. I know your primary interest is agriculture, and I will certainly be grateful for any professional advice you can give about the estate, but I would also be happy to hear your thoughts about the current political situation."

Cosby carefully composed his thoughts; he had several rehearsed answers to questions about his own views, but he hadn't expected to be drawn into a political discussion so quickly. While thinking, he became aware of the drumming of hoofbeats coming through a front window, which was open slightly to let in the spring air. It was a single horse, drawing nearer. A few seconds later he saw the horse and uniformed rider pull up in front of the great columns, the rider dismounting. So did Lee, who had risen from his chair and faced out the window.

"A military courier," the master of Arlington said. "Your pardon, sir." He left the house and talked briefly with the courier, who handed him an envelope. Lee opened the envelope, quickly scanned the contents, then spoke to the courier. Cosby could read his lips: "No reply." The courier saluted, remounted, and rode off.

Lee lingered over the dispatch, reading it again, then slowly walked back into the house. He entered the parlor, paced the floor for a full minute, then finally sat down, his face grave. "This," he said, indicating the envelope, "is a dispatch from the War Department. A courtesy notice—they wanted me to know what just happened." He paused, lost in thought again.

"What did happen, Colonel?" Cosby prompted.

"We now have the president's response to the attack upon Fort Sumter. He has just issued a call for 75,000 volunteers to join the army."

Carter Cosby felt a faint sense of unreality, as if the floor underneath his chair had suddenly started sinking. *Seventy-five thousand volunteers!* Cosby recalled the estimates of Jefferson Davis about the troop strength of the U.S. Army.

"Seventy-five thousand troops? That's a large number, isn't it, Colonel?"

"A very large number," Lee agreed quietly.

"What is the current size of the army?"

"About 15,000 troops," Lee said. "Much of the army was in Texas before that state seceded. I myself was in San Antonio. Now they have been withdrawn to various camps in the Union."

Lee's estimate of the size of the army coincided with Davis' number. "So if all those volunteers actually sign up, the size of the army would become 90,000 troops?" Cosby asked.

"Yes."

"Has the United States Army ever been that large?"

"No," Lee replied. "Even though most of them would be volunteers, not regular army, that would be far larger than the army has ever been." He looked at Cosby. "Do you remember the size of General Scott's army in Mexico, where we both served?"

"I'm not sure, Colonel."

"We landed 8,500 troops at Vera Cruz, without losing a single man. Some more came in later. There were troops in some of Mexico's northern states, but the army that conquered Mexico had about 10,000 troops. That's all. Now Mr. Lincoln is raising an army that will be *nine times* as large."

Cosby felt that sense of unreality again, a sense of being swept up in events he could not control. Abraham Lincoln had finally responded to the Confederacy, decisively and massively. The Union was indeed raising a huge army of unprecedented size. There would be no turning back now. That list of possible interlinked events that Davis had speculated about no longer seemed quite so improbable, for the first and most critical of them all had just come to pass.

Cosby looked at Lee, the very man Davis believed was going to be offered command of that huge army. "What will you do, Colonel?" he asked softly.

"Do?" Lee's dark eyes sharpened. "I'll do what I've done for thirty years—my duty." His intent gaze softened as he stood up. "Come, Carter. I forget myself as your host. Let me show you to your room. I wouldn't think of having you stay at a hotel in Washington, as we have several guest rooms here. You'll meet the rest of the family later today, and dine with us tonight."

Cosby followed Lee out of the room, but he could not quickly readjust his thinking to something which now seemed so prosaic as land management. Unbidden, the thought entered his mind: *just what will your duty be, Colonel?*

CHAPTER 19

Monday
Arlington House, Virginia
6:37 PM

Robert E. Lee tapped his water glass with a teaspoon. His family members, gathered at the dinner table, ceased their sibling chatter and turned toward him.

"Dear Lord, we thank you for the food which we are about to eat. We thank you especially for the safety of all here present. Grant us the wisdom to know and obey your divine will, so that we may continue in your blessings. Through Christ our Lord." All at the table finished, "Amen."

"You can see that we have a guest here tonight." Lee gestured toward Cosby, seated on Lee's right at the head of the table. "Some of you have already met him informally, but now we can properly meet since we are all together. May I present Mr. Carter Cosby."

Cosby arose, smiling, bowed slightly, and sat down.

"Mr. Cosby, I would like to introduce the family members. My wife, Mary, is at the other end of the table; I believe she has already met you. I believe you have also met my eldest son. His full and august name is George Washington Custis, but I am sure that he has already informed you that everyone simply calls him Custis."

"I have, father," Custis said, echoing the grins around the table.

"Then there is Mary, our eldest daughter. And here are Annie, then Agnes, Robert, and Mildred. We have one more son, William Henry Fitzhugh, who is not here."

"We call him Rooney," Mary volunteered.

"Thank you, Mary. Rooney married several years ago; he and his wife, Charlotte, live on family property in New Kent County."

"I am honored to meet you all," said Cosby.

Mrs. Lee motioned for the servants to bring in the food. While the family was being served, Lee continued to expound about his guest. "Mr. Cosby is here because of the generosity of our beloved state of Virginia. In fact, he is a personal representative of the governor. Is that not so, Mr. Cosby?"

"It is indeed," Cosby agreed. "In fact, I met with Governor Letcher in Richmond only yesterday. I found him to be a charming person. He sends his regards to all of you."

"Are you a military person, Mr. Cosby?" asked Mrs. Lee. "We often have military officers as guests at Arlington."

Cosby had already learned of Mrs. Lee's arthritic condition, which appeared to be degenerative. She was not confined to a wheelchair, but moved about with difficulty. "No, ma'am. I regret to say that I do not have a long and distinguished military career like your husband. However, I did serve with the army in Mexico. Although the two of us never met at that time, the colonel was kind enough this afternoon to indulge in some reminiscing with me about that campaign."

"Indulge?" Robert E. Lee laughed mildly, a melodious rippling sound. "Our guest is a bit too modest. He was wounded during that war. And at that nasty charge up the steep hill at Chapultepec, the final assault which sealed our victory. He was even awarded a medal for bravery. In a conversation with such a soldier, I was the one honored."

"Really? How interesting, Mr. Cosby," observed Mary, the oldest daughter. She was an attractive young woman, brown-haired and dark-eyed, comfortable and intelligent; Cosby had noted that she was the most talkative of the Lee children. "I should tell you that our father rarely professes himself to be honored by the presence of someone not in the army." She smiled impishly.

The food was served and the family ate with polite relish. During the meal Cosby was peppered with questions, during which he revealed that he was a native Virginian, had attended the University of Virginia at Charlottesville, and was now running a large plantation. He had achieved some fame in the field of agriculture because of several techniques he had pioneered, and had written articles about them which had been printed in agricultural journals. He was at Arlington at the specific request of Governor Letcher, who wished him to offer agricultural advice to Colonel Lee, in view of Lee's long service to the state.

"Remarkable," said Custis. "Most unexpected, but most welcome. You will note, Mr. Cosby, that not only is our father in the army, but I am too, and so is Rooney. Soon, I expect, Robert will join us. Therefore we are not often at home to supervise the farming. We would really appreciate advice from a noted agricultural expert."

"That was exactly the governor's reasoning, Mr. Custis." Cosby said.

"And we don't have to pay for it?" asked Agnes.

"No, ma'am. As I understand it, the governor is using discretionary funds that are part of his office."

"We must thank the governor," opined Mary, to a chorus of assent.

"I shall indeed send him a letter," said Lee. "He, I am sure, will be most interested to learn exactly what it is that Mr. Cosby will propose."

"Are you married, Mr. Cosby?" Mrs. Lee interjected quietly. The daughters, none of whom were married, abruptly became very attentive.

"Not now, Mrs. Lee," Cosby said into the silence. "I am a widower. I had a lovely wife named Letitia. She died of consumption two years ago."

"I am so sorry. I am sure you were very much in love."

"Yes, ma'am, we were. Not a day goes by that I do not miss her. She was extraordinary."

"Do you have any children?"

"No, Mrs. Lee. We were not blessed." Cosby remembered using the same phrase with Jefferson Davis. Was that only six days ago? "You have been abundantly blessed. I envy you."

There was a small silence around the table. Lee finally said, "How soon do you think you can start on your mission, Mr. Cosby?"

"There is no reason I cannot start tomorrow, Colonel."

"Very good. I think the first thing to do would be to have someone show you around our property. Perhaps Custis or Robert—"

"I would be happy to do that, father," Annie interrupted quietly. It was the first time she had spoken at the dinner.

Lee looked at Annie, then around the table to see how his two sons would react to this mild usurpation of their familial authority. Neither said anything. "Perhaps that would be best," he assented. He turned to his guest. "Annie is very good with plants."

CHAPTER 20

Tuesday, April 16
Arlington
7:27 AM

Carter Cosby arose early. His series of train rides had tired him more than had realized, and he had slept soundly. He had arisen early not only because he was refreshed, but because he wanted to explore the grounds around the house. A peek into the dining room showed no one at breakfast, and a servant informed him that family members would not be arriving for at least another twenty minutes. Apparently breakfasts at Arlington House were not the tightly-scheduled affairs as dinners.

The guest room was on the first floor in the right wing, with a window facing the front of the house. Cosby walked out the front door and across the elevated stone floor, admiring again the great columns of light gray stone, two stories high and topped with Doric capitals, that held up the Greek-styled roof of the portico. He slowly paced off the stone floor: it was approximately 60 feet wide by 25 feet deep. He noted that this massive structure was not a true porte cochere, where carriages could stop under the roof in inclement weather and pick up or discharge passengers in safety; here they were prevented from doing so by the raised floor, which had several stone steps down to the ground. This structure was therefore a glorified porch, a usage emphasized by several wooden outdoor chairs placed with their backs against the front wall of the house. This grandiose and oversized entrance gave Arlington House an appearance more akin to a public building than a private residence.

Cosby left the house entrance and walked across the front lawn. It extended for little more than a hundred feet in front of the house before dropping abruptly. Though not quite a cliff, the slope for the next hundred feet was so steep as to be almost impossible to walk upon, with an imminent danger of falling and then rolling helplessly down the hill. The slope then leveled out and fell in wide graceful sweeps to the Potomac River, three hundred feet below and almost a mile distant.

Standing a few respectful yards back from the edge, Cosby beheld a breathtaking view. The city of Washington lay at his feet. He could see the Potomac, the Long Bridge across it, and a tributary river he knew was the Anacostia. A few of the major streets and boulevards could be discerned, but at such a distance as to be touched with a faint sense of unreality. Wisps of light gray smoke from breakfast fires wafted upward from a thousand chimneys. He could even see the grand new capitol building, still under construction, seemingly a toy abandoned by its child architect. The rising sun bathed the entire prospect in a rosy glow punctuated with occasional golden tints, a fairyland dawn.

"There you are, Mr. Cosby. Please do be careful." Annie Lee came up and stood beside Cosby. "It would be most inopportune for the governor's own agricultural expert to fall and tumble down our hill."

"Never fear, Miss Annie," Cosby laughed. "I am transfixed by the majesty of this view and cannot be moved."

"Often I cannot tear my eyes from it myself," Annie agreed. "There is a story in our family that when the Marquis de Lafayette visited here in 1824, he described this view as the finest in the world."

"The celebrated Marquis de Lafayette himself said that? Hmm. I can well believe it, for I am certainly inclined to say so myself. However, the opinion of so distinguished and well-traveled a gentleman—and a Frenchman, at that—carries infinitely more weight."

"Even if you aren't French, I'm glad you like it."

"So who built the house?"

"My grandfather," Annie replied. She had the regular features, trim figure, and long light brown hair of her older sister Mary, but seemed quieter and more introspective. "Mother's father, Mr. Custis. He died several years ago."

"When was it built?"

"It took quite a time. Fifteen years. He started in 1802, and did not finish until 1817. And he built it the opposite way from what I understand is the usual manner by which large houses are constructed." Annie turned to face the imposing house, and Cosby followed suit. "He did not have enough money to build the house all at once, so he built the two wings first, then built the center section, with the portico, years later."

"Hmm. You're right, that is unusual. Most people build the center section first, then add wings as their families become larger and their income increases." Cosby paused. "Do you know if your grandfather had any children, or was even married, at the time he started building this house?"

"Goodness, what an interesting question! No, he wasn't married in 1802; he married my grandmother two years later. Why do you ask?"

Cosby grinned. "If he built the wings of the house before he built the center, and built them before he was married, he was planning the full size of the house long before he needed that size. He was thinking ahead. Far ahead. That's a rare trait. Most people, if they plan ahead at all, cannot seem to plan a year ahead, let alone fifteen years ahead. He must have been a remarkable man."

"Oh, he was. He was quite well educated, and knowledgeable in agriculture as well as architecture. You would have liked him."

"I'm sure I would have."

"What he liked to do most of all was paint. A number of pictures in the house were painted by him."

"I noticed them. Very good. I think the term for someone like your grandfather is 'renaissance man.' Have you perhaps inherited your grandfather's talent for painting?"

"I'm afraid not," Annie smiled ruefully. "I often watched him, though. It seemed like magic to watch a beautiful picture slowly emerge from his canvas. That took a long time, however; many weeks, sometimes. I liked listening to him even more."

"Listening to him?"

"He was the best storyteller I ever met, Mr. Cosby. He could create pictures with words as well as with paint. I think the favorite times of my childhood were listening to the wonderful stories he told in the evenings. After supper we often would gather in the parlor, turn the lamps low, and he would relate his stories by the flickering flames of the fire. Many times I would be in my night clothes, with a blanket around me, and sometimes I would fall asleep in mother's arms." Annie looked at Cosby, and her eyes were bright. "Forgive me, Mr. Cosby. It's just that I miss him so. And those wonderful times. But I'm much too old to be crying about the past."

Cosby put his arm on her shoulder, resisting the urge to hug her. "How old are you, Annie?" he asked gently.

"Twenty-one," Annie replied, dabbing at her eyes. "Twenty-two in June."

"That's not too old to miss your grandfather. I read somewhere that there's scientific evidence to prove it." Annie giggled. "I miss my own grandfather. And he didn't even know how to paint." She giggled again. "What sort of stories did your grandfather tell?"

"Oh, many," Annie replied, brightening. "He rarely told a fairy tale, or any kind of fictional story. They were almost always about times past, the way things were. Family members. Interesting people he had met. Diplomats, government people, generals, even presidents. My favorite stories were the ones about George Washington."

"George Washington? He personally remembered George Washington?" Something tugged at the back of Cosby's mind.

"Of course. Oh—I forgot. You are not familiar with our family history, while I hear it almost every day. Forgive me. I thought that the governor or someone may have told you a bit of it. Mr. Custis was the adopted son of George Washington. He grew up at Mount Vernon. In fact, he was probably spoiled a bit, since the Washingtons had no children of their own."

Then it came back to Cosby: the file he had been given on Lee. He had focused so much on Lee's background, his military record, and its relationship to the brewing sectional crisis, that he had glossed over the information on Lee's wife, a member of the Custis family. Now he remembered much of it. The grandfather of whom Annie Lee was now speaking so fondly was the baby boy whose father had died at Yorktown, and who was then adopted by George and Martha Washington and did indeed grow up at Mount Vernon. Moreover, he was there during the heady days when George Washington was the commander of the victorious Continental Army in the Revolution, the president of the Constitutional Convention, and the first president of the United States. Naturally he would have had many memories of the Washingtons and Mount Vernon, memories unduplicatable by anyone else.

"Mr. Custis was named after George Washington," Annie continued. "My brother Custis, who also carries that name, was named for our grandfather, not President Washington."

Cosby, long an admirer of George Washington, marveled at all the historic connections in which he now found himself. He was talking, right now, to a young woman who was a granddaughter of George Washington's adopted son and a lineal descendant of Martha Washington, the original first lady of the United States. Since she had listened so often and so raptly to a man who had actually grown up at Mount Vernon while it was the home of the most famous person in American history, Annie Lee had perhaps the best store of knowledge of the private life of George Washington of anyone now living.

Cosby looked at her with heightened interest. He felt he could talk to her for weeks on that one subject alone.

"So here we are," Cosby said, glancing around, "on a hill overlooking the capital city of the country, a city named for the first president, the same man for whom your grandfather was named. And since he started building this house shortly after leaving Mount

Vernon, your grandfather must have built it in an attempt to recreate the gracious life he had known there, perhaps even improve upon it."

"Indeed so," Annie agreed. "Many of the interior furnishings are actually from Mount Vernon. Martha Washington left them to my grandfather in her will."

Carter Cosby shook his head. In this very spot he somehow seemed to be closer to the aura of the first president than if he were at Mount Vernon itself. "Your family has a marvelous history."

"Do you know you might be a part of that history?"

"Me? What do you mean, Annie?" She was grinning broadly.

"Your first name. Carter. That was my paternal grandmother's maiden name. My father's mother; her name was Ann Carter. No one mentioned that to you?"

"No."

"Well, it was. And as I was named after her, it is also my middle name: Ann Carter Lee. I know that your name is a first name, and does not necessarily denote a connection to a family name, but perhaps it does. We might even be distant cousins. Wouldn't that be fun?"

"Yes," Cosby grinned. "It would. I'll have to do a little family research. In the meantime, I'd like to see some artifacts from Mount Vernon, especially any in the dining room." He offered his arm. "May I escort you in for breakfast, *madamoiselle*?"

"*Oui, certainment*," Annie replied gaily, taking his arm. "*J'ai gros faim*."

Cosby grinned again. "I'm hungry, too."

After breakfast Cosby and Annie took two horses from the stable and set out to explore the estate. They rode to the west, behind the house. Annie rode sidesaddle comfortably; almost as well as Letitia had, Cosby thought. She did not wear a hat. Neither had Letitia.

Holding the horses to a walk, they rode in silence for a few minutes, enjoying the morning. Spring clouds were flying, plants were blooming, the sun was rising, and a gentle breeze from the west blew lightly on their faces.

"What an absolutely beautiful day," Cosby finally commented. It reminded him of riding around Cymru, but was somewhat cooler.

"A perfect day for riding," Annie agreed.

"So how big is the estate, Annie?"

"Eleven hundred acres," she replied. "Mr. Custis did not buy it; he inherited it from his father."

The land near the house was open grassland with a scattering of trees. The farther they rode from the house, the larger and denser the trees became. Cosby saw several large areas of tilled land, with a number of Negroes working on them.

"How much land is under cultivation here, Annie?"

"About two hundred and fifty acres. About a quarter of the property."

"What do you grow here?"

"Mostly corn and wheat. The gardens behind the house provide extra vegetables which are sold in the city markets. We grow some different crops at our other lands."

"Your other lands?"

"Yes. We have two other estates. They were also inherited from my great-grandfather. I don't believe my grandfather bought any land at all. He inherited everything."

"Where are these estates?"

"There are two of them, both in Virginia. They are down near the Pamunkey River. One of them is the one Rooney is living on. They total about 10,000 acres."

Cosby almost stopped his horse short. "Ten thousand acres? That's a great deal of land."

"Yes. It is. However, none of them are as attractive as Arlington. Incidentally, that name is not original to this estate. It came from one of the first Custis holdings on the Eastern Shore." Annie looked over at Cosby quizzically. "You didn't know we had other properties?"

"No. I didn't." It wasn't in the file.

"How odd. I would have thought the governor would have known. He didn't mention it?"

"No, he didn't. I'm sure he must know it. He probably just forgot. He is a very busy person right now, as you might imagine. Richmond is full of political talk. I encountered much of it myself, and I was there less than a day."

"Oh. What sort of political talk?"

Cosby sensed danger. His pretty companion was someone who had listened to many important people talk about many important things. "We can talk about that later, Annie. Right now I would like to focus on agriculture. Are there any other agricultural activities you do here at Arlington? For example, I see a lot of trees. Is there any lumber activity here?"

"No. That sounds like a good idea, though. Washington is growing and could use lumber. You can see we have a lot of meadowland. Although we don't raise cattle, we often let cattle from neighboring estates graze here, and charge a grazing fee."

"Good idea. Do you raise any animals here at all?"

"No. My grandfather related how he once raised sheep here, but that was many years ago. We do raise hogs on one of of our other properties, but none here. No animals."

Cosby looked around him, the saddle creaking slightly. "Arlington is truly a beautiful estate, Annie," he said with admiration. "It strikes me as already being very well managed. You have an excellent balance between farming land, grazing land, gardens, and house grounds. You grow several different crops, so you do not have the problems of a monoculture, and they are familiar and useful staples. And if you wanted to expand the farming activity, you have enough land to do so."

"Thank you. My father has worked hard the last several years to put Arlington on an even keel. Mr. Custis was a wonderful and artistic man, but he was not a practical farmer."

"You do practice crop rotation, don't you? Not planting the same crop in the same field each year?"

"Yes, we do. Father may not be a full-time farmer, but he knows enough to insist on that."

"I may have trouble suggesting improvements."

"Oh, I am sure you will think of something," Annie retorted gaily. "Now I have something to show you." She set her horse to a brisk canter. "Follow me."

A few minutes later they entered a glade, shade from the many trees dappled with patches of sunlight. Birds chirped in the trees. A tiny brook wended its way through the trees, fed by a small bubbling spring. They were about a mile from Arlington House.

"Our family spring," Annie announced, reining in her horse to a stop. "The first house on this property, a small one, was built near here in the late 1700's. I often come here for privacy. It is such a beautiful spot. I can sit under a tree, listen to the brook, and be by myself."

Cosby gazed around. It was indeed a beautiful and idyllic spot. "Do you like to be by yourself, Annie?"

"Often." Annie dismounted from her horse. "Not always, but…often." She led her horse to a nearby open space where there was fresh spring grass, and let it graze. "Much of it probably has to do with our living arrangements. My older sister Mary has her own room in the house, but I have to share a room with my two younger sisters. When we were much younger it was fun, but now that we're grown it's rather cramped. I should be thankful we have such a splendid house—and I am—but there are still times when I feel hemmed in. That's when I come out here. I can be by myself, yet I know the house is not far away. And I can dream my dreams."

Cosby had also dismounted and let his horse graze. He leaned back against the trunk of a venerable oak tree. "What do you dream about, Annie?"

"Oh, girlish things." She laughed quietly. "A loving husband. Children. A home like Arlington House. Gardens. Kitchens. Fireplaces. And books. Lots of books."

"Such dreams are not so girlish. And certainly not foolish. I dream of such things myself."

"Thank you, Mr. Cosby." Annie looked about her with a mixture of delight and regret. "Perhaps after I marry and move away someplace else, I can come back here from time to time. Relive my youth in my dream spot." She sighed. "That would be wonderful." She looked slightly away from him, up at the trees. "I must tell you that I do not dream dreams so much now. I have fears. They seem to get bigger every day. And they won't go away." She had seated herself on the ground, and looked up at Cosby with eyes once again bright with unshed tears.

Cosby made to speak, but Annie held up her hand. "Not now, Mr. Cosby. I'm supposed to be helping you, not burdening you. I brought you here because I wanted to show you the spring. If more crops are planted here, might they not need this water?"

"Thank you for showing it to me." Cosby moved away from the tree, walked over to the edge of the brook, and squatted down. He dipped a hand into the brook and scooped up a handful of water. He looked carefully at the water in his hand, sloshing it a bit with the index finger of his other hand. He sniffed the water carefully. He licked his index finger, then drank from the handful of water. "This is very good water, Annie." He looked back at the way they had come. "We would not need this water unless we planned to use it for irrigation. And we would not need to irrigate unless very thirsty plants were planted. Look at these big trees, and your meadows back there. Your rainfall here should be quite adequate for almost any crops. In places like Texas, or the new lands to the West, irrigation is necessary, but not here."

"Then my dream spring is safe?"

"It is indeed safe. Of course, there is the remote possibility of a drought. Then it might well be useful. In the meantime it is good insurance. A spring is always a good thing to have. Now," Cosby said, "I would like to see the rest of the estate. Would you mind showing me the land that lies in front of the house?" He started walking toward the horses.

"*Mais oui, monsieur*." Annie jumped up and followed him. "And I promise not to lead you over our cliff."

CHAPTER 21

Tuesday
The Executive Mansion
2:02 PM

Francis Preston Blair was escorted into the presidential office on the second floor of the White House. Blair took several steps up in the hallway, for this room was directly above the high-ceilinged East Room. It was not the room which had been used as the presidential office when he had been a member of Andrew Jackson's Cabinet; that had been a smaller room nearer the center of the second floor.

President Lincoln was already standing in front of his desk and greeted the older man warmly. "Good afternoon, Francis. Thank you for coming so quickly." He indicated a chair in front of the desk. "It's a nice day out, isn't it?"

"A bit brisk for me, Mr. President," Blair replied, settling comfortably into the chair. A small fire blazed cheerfully in the fireplace behind the president's desk. Blair found the yellow wallpaper hideous, even if it brightened the room. "I don't mind, though. Good to get out and about. Besides, it isn't far to come here."

Both men smiled. Blair lived in a townhouse at 1651 Pennsylvania Avenue, just diagonally across the street from the

Executive Mansion, adjacent to Lafayette Square. He was practically the president's next-door neighbor.

Lincoln gestured at the silver tea service on a tray sitting on the desk. "I was just about to have some tea, Francis. Would you care to join me?"

Blair knew the tea service must have been brought in just before his scheduled arrival. It was really for him, not the president, who was not known to be the greatest of tea drinkers. He could hardly refuse. "I would be honored, Mr. President."

"Here, let me," Lincoln said as Blair started to rise. He poured out the steaming amber liquid into a china cup decorated with intertwined red roses and a gold rim. "Milk and sugar?"

"Both, please, thank you."

Lincoln carefully added a teaspoon of sugar and a little milk to the cup. Placing a small spoon on the saucer, he presented it to Blair.

"Thank you, Mr. President." This man had once been "Abraham" or "Mr. Lincoln," even "Abe" to Blair, who had vigorously and publicly supported him during the campaign. Ever since the inauguration, however, that certain respectful distance between a president and even his closest followers had inevitably opened. Now the chief executive was "Mr. President" to everyone except his family, the form of address originally decided upon by George Washington himself. Lincoln's only recognition of their new status was the regular use of the name "Francis," rather than the "Frank" he had often used before. Blair missed the intimacy of "Frank."

Blair leaned back in the chair with a deep satisfaction and watched as Lincoln prepared his own cup. *There aren't many people who are personally served tea by the president of the United States,* he mused. *Even Jackson never did that for me.* He had no idea why Lincoln had asked to see him, but the president was buttering him up royally. It must be important.

Lincoln sat down behind his desk and sipped slowly from his own cup. It almost disappeared in his great hands.

"How is my son doing in your Cabinet?" Blair asked by way of opening. "He's not been a disappointment yet, I hope."

"Not yet," Lincoln grinned, "but give him time. Montgomery may yet turn out to be a disappointment, but I don't think so. Not with your stock. You were a great Cabinet officer."

"That was a long time ago. I think you have assembled a very fine Cabinet."

"Thank you. I think so, too. We are about to find out, aren't we?"

"Fort Sumter has fallen, Mr. President. Yesterday you issued a call for 75,000 volunteers for the army. What are you going to do next?"

The president took a long sip of tea. "What do you think I should do, Francis?"

Blair carefully placed his cup and saucer in his lap. *This,* he thought, *is the reason I was asked here. He wants my advice, on precisely this point.* "As I see it, you have only two basic choices, Mr. President. Either let the Confederacy exist in peace, or subdue it by military power and force it to return to the Union at the point of a sword. The first way seems much easier, simply because the second way will obviously be bloody and costly. I know you must have received much advice about the first choice, but I think the greatest danger lies that way."

Lincoln placed his cup and saucer on the desk and folded his hands underneath his chin, resting on his elbows. "Why so?"

"If you let the Confederacy continue to exist," Blair expanded, "it will become entrenched. Even if the United States refuses to officially recognize it, other nations eventually might, especially Britain. Right now Britain doesn't need much cotton, as it has a surplus from previous trading. Someday, someday rather soon, it will. If we are not at war with the South, claiming it to be a rebellious section in a civil war in which no outside interference is welcome, what is to prevent Britain from recognizing the Confederacy and trading with it? What would we do then? Claim that Britain has no right to trade with a nation that we do not recognize? That is nonsense. We might end up in a war with Britain rather than the Confederacy. This is not a minor matter, Mr. President. You might remember that the War of 1812 was fought over similar principles, only that time it was the British attempting to interfere with *our* right of trade."

"Thank you, Francis. I have heard similar arguments before, but never put so simply and so well. There is much to be said for it."

"There is more, Mr. President." Blair held his saucer while he adjusted his position. "This does not involve foreign involvement, but I believe it is even more powerful. The hope behind letting the Confederacy alone is that someday it will want to return to the Union, after it learns that it would be better off in the Union than outside it. The prodigal son will return; just give it time. Above all, don't threaten it, which would only harden its position."

"Yes, that is the argument," Lincoln agreed. "Many find it persuasive. You don't, though?"

"No, sir, I do not. In all the states which seceded, the decisions were made by representative bodies, either legislatures or conventions. Those representatives were put there by popular vote. They believed they were doing the will of the people, which may be an accurate belief. How would those states ever vote to come back into the Union? Would the representatives publicly vote to reverse the most important decision they ever made? Would the people ever vote for a new slate of representatives, ones publicly opposed to the continuation of the Confederacy?"

"I put it to you, Mr. President, that it would never happen. It is some dream. Absent military pressure, the very existence of the Confederacy would become its own sacred cause. People would vote to continue it just to continue it, regardless of any benefits or catastrophes involved. How could they turn their backs on their honorable forbears who underwent such sacrifices to make and keep the Confederacy independent? I tell you, sir, the Confederacy will never become a returning prodigal son. It is a myth."

Lincoln grinned broadly and gently rapped his knuckles on the desk. "I think I should have *two* Blairs in my Cabinet, Francis."

"My Cabinet days are long over, Mr. President. Now I am content to simply give what wisdom I can when it is asked for. Yet there is still one more point I might make, if you would allow me."

"*More,* Francis?"

"Yes, sir. It is this: the Confederate states make a big point about the right of secession. Indeed, it is their most pivotal point, around which all their other points rotate. Suppose we leave the Confederacy alone, and suppose at some future time one of its states tries to secede from *it.* Georgia, say. The Confederate national government explicitly recognizes the right of a state to secede. It *has* to, otherwise it would be admitting that the states of the Confederacy had no right to secede from the Union in the first place. Would it therefore let Georgia secede peacefully? To, in effect, form its own little independent nation? That way lies anarchy and the eventual Balkanization of this great country, rendering it impotent in national and international affairs as well as causing endless internal strife. Secession is a selfish, corrosive concept. It is the exact opposite of the sentiments and actions of our founding fathers, who sought to *unify* a group of squabbling Balkanized colonies. Recognizing a looming disaster, might not the government in Montgomery reverse its position on secession and say that no state may secede from the *Confederacy*? And use military force to hold it in? If the Confederacy used the very thing against one of its own states that we forswore against it, what becomes of our philosophic point that force against secession is wrong? And then what? Would we go to war against the Confederacy to uphold Georgia's right to secede from it and rejoin the Union? A war *supporting* secession? This is impossible, Mr. President. Absolutely impossible." Blair picked up his cup and sipped from it.

Lincoln was enjoying Blair's logical expositions. "So you think military force is the only answer, Francis?"

Blair nodded. "I am sorry to say so, sir, but yes, I do. It worked for us in 1832 when South Carolina passed its Nullification Act, and it will work again."

"That was only one state. And it didn't even secede."

"Yes, it was only one state, but it could have been more. Suppose President Jackson had not mobilized troops and threatened South Carolina. Suppose he had let the Nullification Act stand. Why, we would have had other nullification acts popping up all over, willy-nilly, in every state legislature. The national Congress would have become a mockery. He had to act as he did. The principle was the same as it is today. Either the Union is one nation or a mere temporary assemblage of sovereign states, subject to change with every bill that blows through Congress. It is either a marriage or free love," Blair added mischievously.

Lincoln rapped on the table again. "Bravo, Francis," he chuckled. "A ringing phrase if ever I heard one. I might have known you would use my own words to advise me."

"You flatter me, Mr. President. You are the one looked upon as the great popular advocate of the Union, not I. And I don't think you need much persuasion to invade the South. Yesterday you issued a call for 75,000 troops. What else are you going to use such an army for?"

"'To invade the South,'" Lincoln repeated, leaning back in his chair. "What a phrase. Yet it is an accurate one. Horrifying, but accurate. Our nation rent by a massive civil war, one section invading another. It is the saddest imaginable prospect for any citizen. Yet I see no real alternative, as you have just pointed out better than anyone I have yet heard. So invasion it will have to be."

"If I may ask, Mr. President, when do you think we will be ready to move?"

"Patience, my friend. As the farmer said to his horse, we cannot eat the corn until we first grow it, we cannot grow it until we plant it, and we cannot plant it until you pull the plow. The South has an advantage: it is easier to prepare for defense than it is for attack. We will need a far larger army than theirs, and a far better-equipped one. That will take time. The Confederacy will be ready for us sooner than we are ready for them. There lies great trouble, which brings me to the point why I asked to meet with you."

"Oh?" Blair's cup paused halfway to his lips. He thought the point had just been discussed.

"This army to invade the South," Lincoln explained, carefully watching his guest, "must have a commander. It will be the biggest job in American military history. The number of troops he must lead will dwarf anything General Washington ever commanded. In many ways it will be the worst job in our history, for he will be invading a part of his own country." Lincoln paused. "Have you given any thought, Francis, as to who this commander might be?"

Blair did not immediately answer. He knew he could talk at length on political and philosophical issues, but this was a straight military question. He was not a military man, as the president well knew. The president had access to many fine military men, one in particular. So why was he being asked this question? "No, sir, I have not," he finally answered.

"No one at all? Not even a favorite general?" Lincoln almost sounded teasing.

Blair felt belittled. How could this possibly be the point the president asked to see him about? "Mr. President," he said, controlling his irritation, "you have as your General-in-chief Winfield Scott, in my opinion the greatest military commander in our history since George Washington himself. Even if I had someone to recommend, it would count for nothing against General Scott's recommendation. Surely he is the person to ask such a question, is he not?"

Lincoln gently deflected the pointed question. "You and General Scott go back a long ways, don't you, Francis."

"Yes, sir, we do," Blair replied, his irritation easing. "We are almost the same age. He served gallantly under Andy Jackson in the War of 1812, for which he was awarded a gold medal by Congress, as you know. During my time in government he was a trusted advisor. He led our army in the war with Mexico, which ended up bringing California and the West into our nation, and for which Congress awarded him another gold medal. I have always found General Scott to be the absolute ideal of all that is good and noble in our military service. He is a paragon."

"High praise indeed," Lincoln smiled. "Your opinion coincides with that of everyone else, so it must be true. You would, then, trust any recommendation Scott might make?"

Blair sensed that he was being led somewhere, something he knew Lincoln was very good at doing. It was too late, however; he had already committed himself. "Yes, sir. Implicitly and absolutely." A light dawned. "He *has* recommended someone, Mr. President?"

"Yes," Lincoln affirmed quietly. "He has."

"Who, may I ask?"

"A colonel with a long and distinguished record. Robert E. Lee. Do you know him?"

A colonel? Scott recommended a mere colonel? Blair could not place Lee, although the name seemed to ring a faint bell in his mind. "No, sir. I can't place him, though I have the feeling I should."

"He's been in the army more than thirty years, most of them in the engineers. He was the Superintendent of West Point for three years. Scott knows him from the Mexican War, where he was the chief of artillery. He was recently given command of the 1st Cavalry Regiment." Lincoln quietly gazed at Blair. "I'm surprised you don't know him, Francis. He's socially prominent. One of the Lees of Virginia. He lives in a mansion in the Virginia heights just across the river, overlooking Washington."

Blair snapped his fingers. "Oh, yes, yes, of course. The *Custis* estate."

"Pardon?"

"Custis, Mr. President. I've lived in Washington so long, that's how I remember it. Mr. Custis, who built it, was the adopted son of George Washington, and an actual descendant of Martha Washington by her first husband. He was even named after Washington. He died several years ago, leaving the estate to his only child, a daughter, and her husband. That husband is this Col. Lee. I suppose everyone now calls it the Lee mansion, but I remember Mr. Custis, so to me it will always be the Custis mansion. Beautiful place. I was there once."

"You were?" Lincoln leaned back in his chair. "Tell me about it, Francis. What was it like?"

"I went to pay a courtesy call on Mr. Custis—we had met at some function or other. He was not very active in politics, so he was rarely seen in the city. He liked to paint. I met his daughter, Mrs. Lee, and several of her children."

"Did you meet Lee?" Lincoln asked quickly.

"No, Mr. President. He wasn't home. I gathered he was rarely home, always at some army post somewhere. He must have been homesick, for the estate was magnificent. 'Arlington,' I believe Mr. Custis called it. The house has a large portico supported by great stone pillars. What I remember most, however, was the view. It looked east across the river, across the city, all from exactly the right height. It seemed to go on forever. I think it was the grandest view I have ever beheld, even to this day. No wonder Mr. Custis liked to paint."

Lincoln mentally compared this great estate with his own humble beginnings. No city at his feet, but warm spring mud between his toes as he guided the plow. No porticoes with stone pillars, but a log cabin. No separate bedrooms, hardly separate bunks. The greatest companions of his youth were books and a warm hearth to read them by. He wondered how differently he might have turned out had he been raised as a lineal descendant of the sainted George Washington himself. Or at least his wife.

"Did you ever meet Lee at a later time?"

"No, Mr. President. I never met him. That's why it took a few moments to make the connection."

"That's unfortunate. I'd like to meet someone who knows him well. Someone besides General Scott, I mean, who obviously thinks the world of him. I wish *I* knew him well."

Francis Blair placed his saucer, spoon, and empty cup on the desk, settled back and folded his hands in his lap. "I take it you're having some trouble with this recommendation. Is it possibly Col. Lee's rank? If you give him field command of the army, you'll have to jump him several levels. Not impossible, of course, but highly unusual."

Lincoln waved his hand. "No, no, that's not it. He's just the right age for such a command. Older than I am, in fact." He hesitated. "I have two points that trouble me." He arose from his chair and slowly began to pace behind the desk. "Francis, when you were at the Arlington estate, did you see any slaves?"

"Slaves, Mr. President?"

"Yes. Slaves. Did you see any slaves?"

Blair furrowed his brow. "I don't really recall, sir. The estate is large, and there must have been a number on it, but I don't recall seeing any. There were some servants—Negroes—in the house, but I don't know whether they were slaves or not. They may have been. May I ask why you want to know?"

The president resumed his pacing. "After Scott recommended Lee yesterday, I requested an investigative report about him. It was delivered late this morning. It states that Lee owns sixty-three slaves at that estate. *Sixty-three*, Francis. Now I know there are plantations in the deep South which have hundreds of slaves, but sixty-three is a very considerable number to me, especially considering that the overwhelming majority of Southerners don't own any slaves at all. And there may be more. The report stated that the Lee family owns several other properties, at which there may be more slaves."

"Now this war is beginning over secession, as you pointed out, but we both know that slavery is at the root of it. We know how we feel about it, and the way most Northerners feel about it. We may have to seize the moral high ground about it, if only to keep Britain out. This war can become a war about slavery, something the abolitionists desperately want. In such a case, how can I possibly have as my army commander a man who owns at least *sixty-three* slaves himself? It's preposterous!"

"It is preposterous," Blair agreed, "but perhaps something can be done about it." He tugged at his lower lip. "Let me think a moment, Mr. President." Lincoln resumed his stately pacing while Blair stared sightlessly at the desk, still gently tugging at his lip.

Twenty seconds elapsed. It was so quiet Lincoln could hear the clock on the mantelpiece ticking. He was about to go over to the clock and adjust it when Blair muttered softly. "Ah. I think I have it. Something, anyway."

Lincoln sat down. "I'd love to hear it, Francis."

"That report you said you had on Lee, sir—did it mention how big the Arlington estate is?"

"I don't recall. I can get the report, if it's important."

"The exact size isn't; I'm sure it quite large. My point is this: we are now embarked on a large war with the Confederacy. You issued a call for 75,000 troops yesterday. This is the capital city. Many of those troops, if not most, will find their way here. General Scott, I am sure, will want a series of forts ringing Washington. There will be camps, troops, training grounds, supply depots everywhere. Washington will eventually become a giant army camp. There will be a lot of money spent on all this military preparation."

"That may well be so," Lincoln agreed. "Pardon my denseness, but what has all of that to do with Lee?"

"Just this, Mr. President: suppose one of those forts or camps should be built on his property? Perhaps a large one; fifty acres, say, or a hundred. His property is very strategically located. It's on the heights overlooking Washington, a perfect place to build a defensive army position. An arrangement could be quietly reached with Lee. In return for a lease agreement on that land for the duration of the war, for which he would be very handsomely recompensed, he would manumit his slaves. Most of them would probably stay on the estate, but now they would be free people working for a wage, which Lee could easily pay them from the proceeds of the lease agreement. Probably from the interest alone on it, if it were invested wisely. And at the end of the war he could have his land back. Or perhaps, if the government wanted to keep it, he could sell it, and the government would pay him another handsome price. This could work out very well for everyone, Mr. President. Lee could have his command and financial security, the army could have a strategic base, the slaves would be freed, and you would not be embarrassed."

Lincoln threw back his head and laughed. "Frank, you are a genius." He rapped the table again. "No wonder President Jackson thought so much of you."

Blair's smile had a touch of smugness. He especially enjoyed the return, however fleeting, of the president's use of the name *Frank*. "Are we agreed, then, sir?"

Lincoln's eyes twinkled. "We are certainly agreed that I will take it under advisement, and we are agreed that your plan could certainly solve the problem, if it arises." The president turned serious. "It may not arise, because of the second part of the problem."

Blair waited expectantly. *Now what?*

"I will tell you my gravest fear, Francis. It is that Virginia will secede. If it does, the whole Upper South will follow it. The Confederacy will double in size. I will be able to look out the western and southern windows of this very building and *see* the Confederacy, or at least land that it claims. I do not see how anyone can think of a short war if that happens. It will be a tragedy of tragedies."

"Virginia may not secede, Mr. President."

"No, Francis, it may not, but it *may.* Do you see how this affects my decision concerning Lee? I do not know the man. Except for Scott, I do not know anybody who does. I was hoping you might, and give me some clue about his political inclinations. Many Southern-born officers have gone South with their seceded states, while many others have remained true to the Union. There is no pattern. Where does Lee's ultimate loyalty lie? If I offer him the command, and he accepts, and we make a big noise about it, and then Virginia secedes, would he resign his commission? That would be humiliating in the extreme. Suppose Virginia secedes first, and then I offer him the command? Would he accept? Suppose he refuses? That would also be humiliating."

"I have a suggestion, sir. Why not ask Scott for another recommendation, someone whose loyalty to the Union is absolutely unquestionable? Someone from a Northern state?"

"I thought about that," Lincoln replied. "Scott, however, said some things about Lee I cannot put out of my mind. He said that Lee was the finest officer he had ever seen with troops in the field. He even said Lee would be worth fifty thousand troops to the Union cause. Think of that, Francis. *Fifty thousand troops!* Do you realize that's more troops than there were in either the Revolution or the War of 1812, on both sides, *combined*? It sounds like obvious hyperbole to me, but that's what he said. If I cannot trust Scott's judgment on military matters, whose can I trust?"

"You see my dilemma, Francis. I *must* consider Lee for this position, but I also *must* know how he will react if Virginia secedes. I cannot do this by myself. And that is why, my friend, I asked to see you."

Blair finally understood. "You want me to examine him."

"Yes, Francis. Would you?" Lincoln's dark eyes kindly regarded his guest. "I cannot think of anyone better suited for such a delicate task. You have experience, diplomacy, and tact. You are also not an official of the government, but a private citizen, yet you have known ties to the government. Arrange a private meeting with him. Your own home would be ideal, not a government office. Sound him out. Make sure he knows he is being considered for the highest military position it is within our power to give. I have decided that if I can be assured of his loyalty, I will definitely offer him the position. I can then talk to him about your clever plan concerning his slaves. If you sense that he will waver, then we will have to look elsewhere. Either way, you and I will keep quiet about our little arrangement. Even if, by some chance, word of it should somehow surface, I can always truthfully state that the offer was never made officially, and that he and I have never even met."

Blair smiled broadly, lighting up his thin face. "I would be honored, Mr. President. And if I may say so, Andy By God Jackson would be proud of you."

"The highest of praise," Lincoln laughed, standing up. He walked around the desk and offered his arm to the older man, who stood up on his own. "You'll report back to me?"

"As soon as possible," Blair replied as the two men walked to the door. "I'll try to set the meeting up for tomorrow or the day after, and report back immediately."

"Thank you, Francis." Lincoln opened the door. "It has been the greatest of pleasures, as always."

"Thank *you*, Mr. President."

CHAPTER 22

Wednesday, April 17
Arlington
9:23 AM

"Right about here would be a good place." Carter Cosby shaded his eyes and looked toward the east, toward the sun now climbing the sky on a beautiful spring morning. He and Annie Lee were on part of the broad sweeping area of the front part of the Arlington estate. They were a bit more than a hundred feet below the level of Arlington House, below the steep slope in front of the house, and a bit more than that above the Potomac River, shimmering in the near distance. They had left their horses in the shade of a nearby tree. The grassy land on which they were standing was not level, gently sloping down to the river, but was not difficult to walk upon.

"I'm on pins and needles, Mr. Cosby. Yesterday when I showed you this area you said you might have an idea about it. Yet you wouldn't say a word about it to anyone, either at dinner last night or at breakfast this morning. I don't mind telling you that my brothers and sisters are putting the pressure on me to find out what you have in mind."

"Ah, the impatience of youth. Never fear, Annie, all will be explained to you in due time. You will observe this advanced scientific instrument I hold in my hand." Cosby held up a trowel.

"Yes. An ordinary garden trowel you borrowed from the garden shed. How big a hole can you dig with that?"

"Not a large one, my dear young lady. But then I don't want to dig a large one." Cosby knelt down and plunged the trowel into the ground, bringing up a clump of earth with stalks of grass attached to it. He held the clump up and carefully looked at it from all sides, then gently broke off small pieces of dirt from it and speculatively rolled them between his fingers. He smelled the dirt on his fingers, then smelled the clump directly.

Annie knelt down beside him. "Mr. Cosby, what in the world are you doing?"

"Investigating, Annie. Investigating."

Annie watched in silence as Cosby used the trowel to dig a small hole six inches deep. He brought up dirt from the bottom of the hole and then went through the same routine, looking, rolling and sniffing. He placed the dirt next to the original clump. He then proceeded to dig the hole down to a depth of about a foot, brought up dirt from the bottom, and went through the examination routine again. He placed the third clump of dirt next to the first two. He proceeded to look at the three clumps of dirt for a time, not saying a word.

Finally Cosby sat on the ground and wiped off his hands. "Annie, I'd like to ask you a question."

"You would like to ask *me* a question?" she laughed. "I can think of a dozen questions I would like to ask *you*."

Cosby smiled. "You have lived here all your life. You have looked at the splendid view here more times than you can remember. And you are a very observant and intelligent person. Tell me, have you ever seen fog on the river? I don't mean fog everywhere, just on the river and perhaps its banks and nearby areas."

"Fog? On the river?" Annie looked keenly at Cosby, who nodded. "Why, yes, any number of times. It followed the course of the river. Just as you say, it usually covered the banks and spilled out onto the adjacent areas."

"Often?"

"Well, no. Not often. But it is not uncommon. I have seen it many times."

"Even in summer?"

"Let me think a moment. Yes. Yes, I believe so. I have seen it at all seasons. Even in summer."

"Hmm. Good."

"But I have also seen fog that *did* cover everything. The river, the city, as far as the eye could see, but not up to the level of the house."

"You did? Tell me about that."

"It was as if the ocean had somehow rolled in, Mr. Cosby. The line of separation between the fog and the clear air above it was surprisingly sharp. Sunlight sparkled off the gray and white top layers of the fog, making them look like waves. It was as if you were on a gigantic ship crossing the Atlantic, or perhaps riding a great bird soaring above the clouds of heaven." Annie beamed at the man gazing at her. "Does that sound impossibly romantic?"

"Of course," Cosby grinned. "But it sounds so much better than saying a cool ground layer condensed tiny droplets of water out of humid air. *Very* much better."

Annie seated herself on the ground. "Why do you want to know about fog?"

Cosby did not answer immediately. He plucked a long stalk of grass and speculatively chewed on the end, looking out over the grand view. "Let me tell you a little story, Annie. It's about Thomas Jefferson, a great Virginian and a great American. Jefferson was one of those wonderfully gifted people who seem to come along once every century or so. He was interested in everything, and he was a genius at everything. Everyone knows about his political career, but he did so much more."

"One of the things he was interested in was agriculture. He kept detailed notebooks about every place he visited: temperatures, humidity, rainfall, soil conditions, winds, things like that. He was always open to new ideas. He was the first one to cultivate the tomato. During his time the tomato was regarded as some strange plant with no food value, though possibly with some medicinal value. Jefferson, however, deliberately grew tomatoes at Monticello. He regularly would pluck a tomato there, cut it into slices, sprinkle the slices with salt, and eat them, pronouncing them delicious to anyone who would listen. His guests and neighbors thought that was crazy. Now look at the tomato. It makes a hearty soup, many sauces, and is a wonderful ingredient of stews. Tomato wedges enliven a salad. Tomato slices can be fried, or can be eaten raw, as Jefferson did. And the tomato plant is one of the easiest plants in the world to grow. Although it is a New World plant, Europeans have taken strongly to it, especially Italians. Thought worthless not so long ago, the tomato is now well on its way to becoming a staple in world cuisine, thanks to Mr. Jefferson. I believe if he had done absolutely nothing else in life except foster the cultivation of the tomato, he would still be regarded as one of the great benefactors of the human race."

Annie Lee laughed merrily. "Mr. Cosby, how you do go on! The author of the Declaration of Independence, the third president of the United States, valued more for growing tomatoes? And you speak riddles in riddles! What do dirt, fog, and Thomas Jefferson have in common?"

Cosby took his eyes away from the vista of Washington and looked at Annie. "I think you could grow a crop here that Jefferson believed would grow well in parts of Virginia, but very few have tried."

"Not tomatoes, surely? We already have many tomato plants in our garden."

"No, not tomatoes. Grapes."

"Grapes?"

"Yes. Grapes. They are very particular about growing conditions, but you appear to have the right conditions here. Drainage, for example. Grapevines want well-drained soils, so they do best on slopes rather than level ground. You have several hundred acres of sloping land here. The vines also prefer certain types of soil. That's why I dug the hole; to examine the soil, and at different depths. For grapevines I think a more granitic soil would be slightly better, but your soil is very good. Your water supply is also very good, both in quantity and quality; there is even a spring of sweet water on the property, the one you showed me yesterday."

"Does the fog have something to do with it?"

"Yes. Grapes don't like hot muggy weather. They want warm days, cool nights. Washington can be muggy in the summer. Your land faces east, so it is more exposed to the cooler morning sun rather than the hotter afternoon sun. Moreover, it is next to a major river, which can moderate the temperature on land near its banks. You say that even fog is regularly produced, which has a powerful cooling effect. Some of the best wines in Europe come from river valleys, such as the Rhine and Moselle in Germany. The Bordeaux region of France, which produces the best French wines, is really a very large valley of several rivers. Jefferson was interested in all this because he liked wines very much, and was irritated that he had to buy French wines to get good ones. He always wanted someone in the United States to produce a great American wine. I think such wines could be produced right here." Cosby stopped as Annie jumped up. "Is something wrong?"

Annie's eyes were sparkling and her face was shining. "No, no, nothing's wrong," she exclaimed. "Everything's *right*!" She clapped her hands. "I'm so *excited*! When you first mentioned grapes, Mr. Cosby, I thought you meant *table* grapes. I thought that was mildly interesting, but then started thinking of all the problems in getting such a perishable product to market. But you didn't! You mean *wine* grapes!" The words tumbled out of her. "*Wine*! Oh, how *exciting*! Do you really think we could *do* it? Make *wine* right here?"

"Goodness, such enthusiasm! Yes, I see no reason why you couldn't. After choosing the right vines, the hardest part of making good wine is finding the right climatic and soil conditions, and you already have them here. Now comes the human effort."

Annie dropped down on her knees beside Cosby. "What would we have to do?"

"The first thing would be to select what varieties of grapes you want to grow. That is a big decision. You must pick grapes that do well in this climate. Merely planting varieties that do well in Europe is not enough. Jefferson himself found that out. He brought an Italian friend over, experienced in winemaking, who supervised the planting of European varietals at Monticello. They did not do well. We now know the reason was that the European vines were not resistant enough to certain American diseases. So you must plant grapes that do well in American conditions, or graft choice European varietals onto American rootstock."

"Could you advise us about which varieties to plant?"

"I would be happy to do so. I could also place you in contact with successful wine-grape growers, who would be happy to help you."

"All right, so now we have planted lots of grapevines. How long do we have to wait before they bear fruit which can be harvested?"

"Most grapevines will produce grapes which can be harvested in in the autumn of the same year in which they were planted in the spring."

"Really? You mean you don't have to wait several years for the first harvest, as with fruit trees?"

"As grapevines mature they will produce better grapes, but they can be harvested in the first year."

"How wonderful! So the grapes are harvested and then crushed, which makes a lot of grape juice. How does grape juice become wine?"

"By natural fermentation, Annie. The grape juice is stored in wooden barrels. The naturally-occurring yeast then changes the sugar in the juice to alcohol, producing wine. The fermentation process takes a few months. Then the wine is withdrawn from the casks and bottled. The bottles are then stored until they are sold. All this is done in a winery."

"Would we have to build this winery?"

"The grapes are grown in a vineyard, but not all vineyards have their own wineries. However, the grapes have to be processed at somebody's winery somewhere. For a fee, wineries will usually process grapes from vineyards other than their own. Do you know of any wineries in this area?"

"No."

"Then you would have to build your own. Wineries are usually made of stone, in order to keep the temperatures cool inside. The actual processing equipment does not take up much room. However, some wineries are large buildings because of the room required to store the casks and bottles. You have lots of room here.

You might even consider something often done in Europe: the casks and bottles are stored in man-made caves, which keep them constantly cool. To do that requires a hill. You have a hill here."

"I am still marveling at the concept, Mr. Cosby. You make it sound so…*manageable*. It does not sound so difficult. Laborious, but not difficult. Would that be correct?"

"Laborious, yes. Difficult? That depends on how you define the word. The key points about wine-making are knowledge and delicacy. More than most crops, wine grapes are sensitive to the weather. Too much rain and the grapes will rot. Too little rain and they will not mature properly. Too much heat and they will shrivel. Too little heat and they will not develop their full sugar content. The fermentation process generates heat, which subsides as the fermentation approaches completion, so the temperature of the wine in the barrels indicates the proper time for bottling. You will have to have a very good wine-master."

"That does sound complicated. You're throwing water on my enthusiasm."

"I don't want to dampen your enthusiasm, Annie. I just want you to know that growing wine grapes, and then making wine from them, is a much more intricate process than growing corn."

"But much more interesting."

"Yes indeed. Much more interesting."

"How do you know so much about making wine?"

"I'm the world-famous agricultural expert, remember?"

"Do you have a winery on your own estate?"

"No, unfortunately. The climate is not right."

"Where is your property, Mr. Cosby?"

Cosby went back to chewing on the stalk of grass. "Annie," he said finally, "the decision as to whether to establish a vineyard and winery here is entirely up to your family. If they choose to do so, however, I think there would be something in it which could be of special benefit to you personally, if you wanted it."

"What might that be?"

"You have a natural interest and enthusiasm for this idea. You could be involved in the operations from the very beginning. You could be part of the selection of the grapes, the planting of the vineyard, the construction of the winery, the gathering of the first harvest, the first pressing, the first bottling. No one could know the operations here, or the history of them, better than you. You could make yourself the chief apprentice to the wine-master. Over a period of several years, you could learn everything he knows. You could become the business manager of this enterprise. And then, some day, you could even become the wine-master yourself."

Annie's eyes grew large. "Me? A business manager? A *wine-master*?"

"Why not? Nobody is born a wine-master. They have to learn it and earn it. You could do it."

Annie placed her hands on her cheeks. "A *wine-master*! How incredible! Still, it isn't very lady-like, is it?"

"Bosh. I believe there are several women wine-masters in Europe right now. Would you rather go to some women's college and learn more French? While someone else runs your family winery? For the rest of your life?"

"No. No, I wouldn't. You're right, Mr. Cosby. I would like to try. At least I think I would. You have opened up so many wonderful new ideas in the last few minutes that I am both delighted and dazzled. But I have an idea of my own. Wouldn't this winery require a name?"

"Yes, it would. It would have to appear on the bottle label. Do you have one?"

"How about *Arlington Acres*?"

"Hmm. Sounds like a dairy farm. Not bad, though," Cosby added as Annie's grin turned to a frown. "You're right about including the name 'Arlington.' That's a name that would mean something, especially in Washington. How about…mmm…*Arlington Heights*?"

"*Arlington Heights*?" Annie clapped her hands with glee. "I love it! Maybe even…*Arlington Crest*?"

"Oho! Even better! And on the label would appear the words, 'Estate Bottled at Virginia's Finest Vineyard.'"

"Oh, how *wonderful*! Mr. Cosby, I could *kiss* you!"

She did. She leaned over, threw her arms around Cosby's neck, and planted a big kiss on his cheek. For a brief moment he felt the indescribable thrill of a beautiful and vibrant woman in his arms.

"Annie," Cosby said as she withdrew, "don't you think it's about time you started calling me Carter?"

* * * * *

Early that afternoon, John Lee came to visit. He was a Lee relative who lived in Washington. Acting as a personal courier for Mr. Francis P. Blair of Washington, he delivered a sealed note from Blair to Robert E. Lee. The note requested a personal and private meeting with Lee at Blair's residence, 1651 Pennsylvania Avenue, at nine o'clock in the mornng the following day. The reason for the meeting was not specified. Lee agreed to the meeting, and John Lee left after a short visit.

Two hours later a military courier arrived from the War Department, bearing a message from Gen. Scott: Col. Lee was ordered to present himself to Scott at the general's office in the War Department the following morning. Since the meeting time was unspecified, Lee decided to visit Blair first, then go to the War Department, which was only a short distance from the Blair house.

CHAPTER 23

Wednesday
Richmond
4:03 PM

The scene inside Mechanic's Hall, at the southwest corner of Capitol Square on 9th Street opposite the entrance to Bank Street, was chaotic. The Virginia Convention, convened in February solely to consider the question of Virginia's secession from the United States, had been meeting here at irregular intervals. Hot debate had been frequent during those meetings, but no official votes had been taken. Informal polls of the delegates revealed that a majority were in favor of staying in the Union.

Sentiment for staying in the Union was strong. Virginia had been one of the original 13 colonies, and had contributed perhaps more than any other colony to the formation of the United States. The climactic battle of the Revolution, in which the British were finally defeated decisively and which resulted in the Treaty of Paris, which formally recognized the independence of the United States, had been at Yorktown. The commander of the victorious Continental Army had been the Virginian George Washington; he had been the president of the Constitutional Convention and the first President of the United

States. Indeed, four of the first five presidents had been Virginians; the state was known as the "mother of presidents." Such a bond could not be easily broken.

However, this convention had first met in February because that was the month during which the Confederacy had been declared in Montgomery, Alabama. Seven seceded states were now in the Confederacy. It was clear to everyone that this convention was deliberately delaying its vote until the formal reaction of the government of the United States to the appearance of the Confederacy was clear.

Today was different. Spurred into action by President Lincoln's call for 75,000 volunteers for the army on Monday, the delegates had formally voted that a vote on secession be taken today. That motion had carried; today the secession vote would be taken at last.

There were ramifications. Informal polls of the delegates showed that the sentiment had turned, and that the formal vote would surely be for secession. The delegates then did several unusual things. The first was that the formal vote on secession would be made in closed session. Mechanic's Hall was therefore cleared of all unauthorized personnel. This was a lengthy procedure which resulted in a good deal of grumbling from citizens who wanted to be present at the historic vote, and especially from newspaper reporters who considered it their duty to record and report on the proceedings. They were finally persuaded to leave by several delegates who pointed out that seventy years before, during the summer of 1787, the constitution of the United States had been hammered out in closed sessions in Philadelphia, and that process had taken three whole months.

The delegates then voted to keep the secession vote itself, and any other matter on which they might vote, secret. Not only would the voting process be done away from the prying eyes of the public, but even the *results* of the voting were not to be divulged.

The reasons for doing this were freely discussed among the delegates, once they knew that the formal vote for secession was inevitable. Once the convention vote was publicly known, the Federal government would almost certainly rush reinforcements to Federal properties in the state, such as Fort Monroe, and especially the big

Gosport navy base in the Chesapeake. All the seven states in the Confederacy had seceded while James Buchanan was president, and he was not inclined to fight for Federal properties in those states when they seceded. Abraham Lincoln was now president, and it was now clear he would not give up Federal properties without a fight. The Virginia military installations were much closer to Washington than Fort Sumter, and much more accessible to Federal land and sea power.

There was no point in asking or demanding those properties from Lincoln. If the Virginians wanted them, they were going to have to seize them with the state militia. And that meant attacking before the Federal government learned of the secession vote.

After all the speeches and fulminations, the long-delayed formal vote was almost anticlimactic; it was 88 to 55, in favor of secession. A committee voted to establish a military post with command over all the military and naval forces of Virginia, to be filled by appointment by the governor; a subcommittee recommended that Colonel Robert E. Lee, United States Army, be offered this position.

CHAPTER 24

Wednesday
Richmond
7:42 PM

"Good of you to come, John. Some wine?"

"My pleasure, Governor. No, thank you. I had plenty at dinner." John Robertson seated himself in a comfortable chair in the governor's office, on the top floor of the capitol. The most unusual feature of the office—actually a number of rooms—was not anything inside it, but something just outside. One door opened to an upper-level walkway around the inside of the building's unusual interior dome, from which one could gaze down into the rotunda at the marble statue of George Washington and the busts of the other six Virginia-born presidents. It was an exhilarating overview of Virginia's unmatched presidential array, a vantage point from which it was easy to make the facile assumption that American history was somehow simply an extension of Virginia's history. Robertson, who had enjoyed the scene a number of times, tried hard not to make that assumption.

"Have a good dinner?"

"Griffin's. Steak. I thought I deserved the best after what we did today," Robertson laughed. "Apparently others did, too. The place was packed with convention delegates."

John Letcher leaned back in his chair and regarded his old friend. Robertson was as distinguished-looking as Letcher was not. Tall with dark wavy hair, he had a handsome open face and the easy gracious manner of a born aristocrat. From a distinguished family, he was a popular and efficient local judge. He had a strong interest in politics but little desire for elective office, and preferred being an inner-circle advisor, especially in legal matters. He worked well with Letcher, who had appointed him as half of a two-man official state observing team at the convention in Montgomery in February which had established the Confederacy.

"So you think we did the right thing today, John?"

Robertson shrugged elegantly. "The convention has been meeting for two months solely to consider secession. Today it finally voted, and secession it will be. My opinion really doesn't matter."

"Frankly, I would have preferred to stay in the Union," Letcher volunteered, "but not at the point of a gun. The secession will not really become official until the legislature votes for it, but—"

"But you can't wait that long."

"Right. I can't. The Federals will have heavily reinforced everything by that time. This won't be like Texas, John, where the Federals handed over everything just because the Texans asked for them. Lincoln is president now. We're going to have to fight for everything, just like Fort Sumter."

"Have you alerted the militia?"

"The orders have already gone out. We're going to try and seize everything all at once, in a day or two. Probably Friday. If not, Saturday. I don't see how we can keep the convention proceedings secret any longer than that."

"I agree. And surely the principal target will be the Gosport Navy Yard in Nolfolk, will it not?" Letcher nodded. "Will the militia be able to take it? That's mightily important to the Union."

"I think so," the governor responded. "I'm told our militia has been swamped with volunteers ever since Lincoln's proclamation Monday morning."

"Then it will be interesting."

"Indeed it will." Letcher adjusted his spectacles. "Now then, John, to business, as if you didn't know why I asked you to come here. Today the convention, in addition to its major vote for secession, also voted to establish a position which is in command of all the military and naval forces of Virginia. This position is to be filled by appointment by the governor. A subcommittee of the convention recommended that Col. Robert E. Lee be the person to fill that position." Letcher glanced over the top of his spectacles. "You are, of course, familiar with all this."

"Of course."

"Well, then, I have decided to follow the subcommittee's recommendation. I really cannot do otherwise; I would ignore that recommendation at my political peril. Besides, I happen to agree with it. However, the subcommittee did not address the delicate question of exactly *how* the estimable Col. Lee might be induced to fill that position. He is an officer in the United States Army. I am not, and have absolutely no power to *order* him to do anything. And I certainly cannot merely *appoint* an officer of the U.S. Army to a position in a state which has just *seceded* from the U.S. Such an appointment would mean nothing, even be laughable. In order to get Lee into that position, he is going to have to be *persuaded* to accept it. And to do that, he must first be *persuaded* to resign his commission as an officer in the U.S. Army. And he has been an officer in that army ever since he graduated from West Point more than thirty years ago. Now then—exactly who is going to be this grand persuader?"

Robertson laughed. "Don't look at me, Governor."

Letcher smiled. "Of course not, John. It has to be me." His smile vanished. "I cannot delegate this job to anyone else. I surely wish I could. The offer has to come directly from me. And it has to be personal. I cannot simply send a telegram to Alexandria and have it delivered to Lee by some nameless courier. He would probably just throw it away, and I wouldn't blame him. A letter might be somewhat better, but much slower. It *has* to be personal. Face to face. That means it has to be done *here*, in Richmond. And *that* means someone is going to have to persuade Lee to come here." The smile returned as he looked directly at Robertson. "*Now* do you see where you come in, John?"

Robertson nodded. "You are the grand persuader, and I am the lesser persuader."

"Precisely," Letcher grinned. "John, I am appointing you as my personal representative to go north and contact Lee in person. Tell him that I wish to see him here as soon as possible. Do *not*, however, tell him exactly *why* I want to see him. That is my business. If you wish, you can intimate that you do not know exactly why I wish to see him. He may not believe you, but that is better than getting into a complicated discussion about his potential role. Leave that to me."

"As you wish, Governor. And I am happy to accept your appointment."

"Good. As to where you should meet with him, I leave that to you. I suppose on his estate would be best. Lee goes back and forth to Washington, as it is just across the Potomac from his estate. An obvious precaution is that you *not* meet with him in Washington. You are the personal representative of the governor of Virginia, and your meeting with him must take place in Virginia."

"Agreed."

Letcher leaned back in his chair. "You know, John, your mission is doubly important. I have a state to run, so obviously I cannot take the time to go to Lee's estate and attempt to persuade him to do something he may reject out of hand. Your mission, to persuade him to come here to meet with me, makes sense from that standpoint alone. However, there is much more. Although he is a Virginian born and bred, he lives right at the northern edge of the state. Moreover, he lives directly opposite the capital city of the United States. Although I have never been to his estate, I understand there is an unparalleled view of Washington from his front lawn. While there, he may be held in thrall to the United States government simply by his proximity to its center of power. If we can get him *here*, away from the capital of the United States and into the capital of his native state, he may be much more amenable to accepting our position. I will tell you frankly that I do not think we have any hope of success unless you *do* manage to bring him here. Your mission is that important."

"Thank you, Governor. My only reservation is that I do not really know Lee. There is no mutual friendship to ease my mission. However, I will do my best."

"That is all I could ask of anybody, my friend. Godspeed."

After Robertson left, Letcher pondered his emissary's mission. He wondered if he had done the right thing by not mentioning Carter Cosby to Robertson. Cosby should be at Lee's estate by now. He was on a mission for the Confederacy, while Robertson was on a mission for the state of Virginia, but their missions were complementary. However, although he could have told Robertson about Cosby, there was no way he could tell Cosby about Robertson. A letter was too slow, and if he sent a telegram, the telegraph operator might learn enough to expose Cosby. *Best to leave well enough alone.*

CHAPTER 25

Thursday, April 18
Washington
4:19 AM

We came down out of the mountains of Maryland on the night of Sunday, October 16. It was 1859, three years after our group regulated matters along Pottawatomie Creek in Kansas. This time we would do more than kill a few loud-mouthed proslavers. Now we would seize an entire government arsenal, ready to equip the horde of slaves which John Brown assured us would rise up when they heard the news, flee their plantations, and join us. Most daring and delicious of all was the fact that the arsenal was located in the most prominent of all the slave states: Virginia.

Our size had grown. Counting the old man, but not his daughter or daughter-in-law, there were 22 of us. Five were Negroes.

We also had a new and grander name. Instead of "Liberty Guards" or "Army of the North," names we had used in Kansas, we were now "The Provisional Army of the United States." This was not mere whimsy on the old man's part. In May of the previous year he had called together a "constitutional convention" in the town of Chatham in Ontario, Canada. There a "Provisional Constitution and

Ordinances for the People of the United States" was drawn up and unanimously adopted by all the "delegates" present. This was nothing less than the laws for some sort of government Brown intended to establish somewhere in the United States. Naturally it had to have an army, and naturally Brown was appointed to head it, with the title "Commander-in-Chief." One thing about John Brown—he sure thought big. Perhaps because of my previous service with him, he allowed me to continue to address him as "Captain" rather than his new grandiose title.

Brown's appearance had changed. In Kansas he had been clean-shaven, which made his tanned and wrinkled skin look like a piece of worn leather. Since then he had grown a bushy gray-white beard that gave him an aura of Biblical authority, a great asset when lecturing audiences of rapt abolitionists about doing the Lord's work. For this operation he had trimmed the beard back so that he resembled a Midwestern farmer, an effective disguise.

We were also better armed. Brown had become famous since Kansas and was a celebrity in abolitionist circles. He had made many fund-raising speeches and now counted influential abolitionists among his supporters and financial backers. As a consequence we all had modern firearms. And they were the best carbines available: the Sharps, with its lever action and breech-loaded cartridge.

I was issued a Sharps, but I also requested, and was issued, a saber, my Kansas weapon. Cutter Cutler could not be without a sword.

Brown expected Negroes by the hundreds, even thousands, to join us. Since most of them would not be familiar with firearms, he had a thousand pikes made, with a two-edged iron head attached to a 6-foot wooden shaft.

We were more than ready. I had been there two months, but the old man had been there even longer—three and and a half months, since early July. He had scouted around for a base, which clearly could not be in the small town of Harpers Ferry itself. He finally discovered a farm for rent about five miles from the town, in the hills on the Maryland side. He rented it under a false name, notified us by mail, and we slowly began to assemble there, one by one.

The old man's greatest fear was that our plans, even our mere presence, would be discovered. Since we didn't actually work the farm, the presence of almost two dozen men, apparently doing nothing, would have been difficult to explain. We therefore kept to a strict daytime schedule, with only a few men allowed outside at any time. The farmhouse was large enough to roam around in, with two stories, a spacious attic, and even a porch which ran the full length of the house on the second story. The neighboring farmers generally kept to themselves. If anyone came into the lane, those of us inside the house went into the attic, kept quiet, and stayed there until the visitor left.

A clever ruse to allay any suspicions was the obvious presence of two women in the farmhouse, who were always on display to any visitors. They were one of Brown's daughters, Annie, and one of his daughters-in-law, Martha, the wife of his son Oliver. The old man persuaded them to come to the farmhouse and help care for our group; Martha did the cooking and Annie did the household chores.

Only at night were we free to leave the house and stretch our legs. The best times during the days were during thunderstorms, when we could move about freely because we knew no unexpected visitors would be dropping by.

We were allowed to go into the town from time to time, in small groups or singly; we posed as travelers. The old man wanted us to become familiar with the area, especially since our raid would be at night.

The Harpers Ferry area is rivers and steep mountains, with the town occupying what little flat land there is. The northward-flowing Shenandoah River, which drains Virginia's Shenandoah Valley, flows into the eastward-flowing Potomac at this point. As everywhere along its length, the Potomac here divides Maryland from Virginia. The steep hills on almost all sides are part of the Blue Ridge Mountains. A covered railroad bridge spans the Potomac at the junction of the rivers, while a smaller bridge spans the Shenandoah a mile upstream. Westward from Harpers Ferry, the Baltimore and Ohio Railroad extends along the Virginia side of the Potomac; it crosses to the Maryland side on the covered bridge, then goes eastward to Baltimore, Washington, and Philadelphia. The town of

Harpers Ferry lies on the Virginia side of the Potomac, on a projection of land lying just to the west of the junction of the two rivers.

The military installations at Harpers Ferry constitute more than an arsenal, a place where weapons are stored; it is also an armory, where firearms—especially rifles—are manufactured. The various government buildings line the banks of both rivers, since water power is extensively used to operate the machinery. Almost all the employees of the facility are civilians who live in the town, which lies between the government buildings on the banks of the rivers.

I had several reservations about the plan. Although Harpers Ferry was located in Virginia, it did not belong to the state; it belonged to the national government. Exactly how did attacking a federal complex, no matter where located, advance the antislavery movement? President Buchanan, though widely regarded as something of a mugwump when it came to national policies, was a Pennsylvanian; there wasn't a proslavery bone in his body. Yet wouldn't he be forced to call out U.S. Army troops to counter an attack on federal property?

That brought up another problem. There were thousands of slaves within a thirty-mile radius of Harpers Ferry. How were they supposed to learn about the raid? And once they learned about it after it happened, how could they know that John Brown meant it as a signal that they were to rise up, escape from their masters, and join us? The tight secrecy that we maintained meant that no one had spread the word to the plantations.

My feeling was that we could take over as much of the facility as we desired, but not for long. We had to wait for the slaves. But suppose the Virginia militia got there first? Or the U.S. Army? Suppose the slaves never rose up at all?

I never spoke these thoughts to Brown himself or anyone else except one person, but the old man may have had people like me in mind when he reassured us about the projected slave uprising. "They rose up in 1831 for Nat Turner," he reminded us several times. "And that was also in Virginia. They were so desperate for freedom that they killed 59 people. Remember that Turner was just a slave; he really had nobody behind him. We are far better organized, far better armed, and far better known that Turner ever was. They will come."

I did not remind him that Nat Turner was caught and hanged, and that eventually all his followers were either shot or hanged.

What of the town people? There were three thousand of them living in Harpers Ferry, and every one of them depended on the government work in one way or another. Would they stand idly by while we raided the source of their livelihood? There were only twenty-two of us.

Of one thing I was certain: we could not wait long. If runaway slaves did not arrive quickly, we should grab whatever we felt we needed and get out while we could. Otherwise we would be in a mountain-ringed trap.

The only person to whom I confided these thoughts was Ben Tilton, whom everyone called "Sandy" because of his wheat-colored hair. Tilton had not been with us in Kansas; he had joined several months ago, brought in by another of our group who recommended him highly. He was tall and powerfully built, had an easygoing manner, a good sense of humor, and an attitude toward slavery that seemed more like an aesthetic distaste than a visceral hatred. He also seemed just a bit slow on the uptake, a notion exaggerated by a deliberate speaking habit. Best of all, he had money; his family was in the shipping business in Boston, where he first heard one of John Brown's sulfurous speeches. He had no nautical skills for ships and didn't want to be a clerk; he wanted adventure, which Brown could certainly give him. So he quietly joined us, without telling his family exactly where he was or what he was doing. It was his money we used to buy many of the supplies in town.

Sandy Tilton and I hit it off right away. I'm not sure exactly why; perhaps he was attracted to my rapid speaking and intensity, while I was attracted to his easy manner and slow smile. Opposites.

The first time I mentioned my reservations to him was in the middle of a driving rainstorm, as we sat on chairs on the porch, enjoying the strong weather. Low masses of dark sullen clouds, flat-bottomed but topped with towering gray cotton fantasies among which unicorns and centaurs might gambol, came tumbling in slowly from the west, turgid with heavy moisture. The bulk of the Blue Ridge

Mountains funneled the wind and clouds into the river valley, drenching the area with an autumnal deluge which reduced visibility to a dozen yards and turned the dirt roads into mud morasses in an instant. The billowing cool wet wind was blowing in from Ohio, Illinois, and the lands beyond the Mississippi, the vast and trackless western plains upon which untrodden thigh-high prairie grass grew from horizon to horizon—from Kansas itself, the place of that starry and bloody night three years ago. The thundering din on the porch roof was so loud that a person five feet away could not have heard us.

"I don't think we'll have too much trouble getting into the armory yard or the arsenal grounds, Sandy."

"I agree," Tilton said placidly. He was smoking a pipe, which I considered an affectation only of the very rich or the very poor; he was definitely not one of the latter. John Brown frowned upon it, as he did all uses of tobacco, but the old man didn't thunder at Tilton because he could use Tilton's money. "We will have the advantages of darkness, surprise, and planning. We also have the presence of the notorious Osawatomie Brown. Whom do they have?"

"How do you think we're going to get out?"

"Across the railroad bridge, Cutter." He liked my Kansas moniker. "We'll have guards posted there. Then we're back into Maryland, and we go north into the mountains. You know the plan."

"How long do you think those guards will last if the Virginia militia comes? Or the U.S. Army? Or even a gang of railroad agents from Baltimore, once the B&O brass learns about the seizure of one of its railroad bridges?"

Tilton gently let a wisp of smoke curl from his mouth. "You were with Brown in Kansas," he said quietly. "Don't you trust his plans?"

"I trust John Brown. Sometimes I just think he trusts the Lord too much."

We spoke guardedly a few other times, with the same result; Tilton placated my doubts, trusting in the formidable presence of John Brown and his oft-repeated direct communication with the Lord.

I wasn't sure I believed in God any more. How could an all-just Being allow such an abomination as slavery to exist?

A light drizzle was falling as we set out at 8 o'clock on the night of October 16. Three were left as a rearguard for the farmhouse; the two women had already departed. The old man drove a wagon which had some of the pikes, extra guns, and a number of tools we would use; if all went well, it would be loaded with rifles on the way back. The rest of us walked behind, our Sharps carbines hidden under large coats.

A group of six went on a special mission. They were to capture two nearby slave-owning farmers, one of them related to the family of George Washington, and bring them and their slaves into the building Brown had chosen to be his headquarters once we were in the complex. The slaves would be freed; the owners we would keep as hostages.

We reached the Maryland side of the railroad bridge and quickly overpowered the lone guard, who would become another hostage. No shots were fired, no alarm raised. Leaving two men to guard the bridge—they would be joined later by a third—we crossed over into Virginia.

Most of the armory buildings on the bank of the Potomac were behind a stone wall, ten feet high. Just inside the gate was a brick building, a 3-bay engine house for the fire protection equipment. It was this engine house that Brown chose for his headquarters, as it controlled the entrance to the armory grounds. It was also the post for the armory's night watchman. When he came out to investigate us at the gate, we covered him with our guns, broke the lock on the gate, and took him prisoner. It was not yet 11 o'clock, and we had control of the armory.

Brown sent several men down to occupy a rifle factory on the Shenandoah side of the complex. There was another guard there, whom they captured and brought back to the engine house.

Other men cut all the telegraph lines out of Harpers Ferry.

Across a broad street from the armory grounds was a smaller walled enclosure for two arsenal buildings where finished firearms were kept; it was called Arsenal Square. Surprisingly, it was unguarded. Ben Tilton and I were assigned to occupy it; we chose the larger building, easily breaking the lock on its main door. We settled down in the darkness to await developments, which I devoutly but unoptimistically wished would be the great slave uprising Brown predicted.

No alarm was raised until midnight, when the bridge guard we had captured was due to be relieved. Our men captured him, but he broke away and started running across the bridge. One of our men fired, but in the darkness only grazed the guard, who made it across the bridge to the Virginia side and into a nearby hotel.

It was the first shot of the raid. The word was now out.

At about 1:30 AM an eastbound B&O train arrived at Harpers Ferry. While at the depot on the Virginia side, its crew was informed of our presence. Two crew members were sent out to investigate the bridge. They were turned back at gunpoint by our guards on the Maryland side, and the train stayed where it was. Unfortunately it was not a freight train; it was a passenger train, full of disturbed, frightened, and outraged people who gabbled among themselves and further spread the alarm.

Later in the morning, still dark, the party with the slave-owners and slaves arrived, and joined the other captives in the engine house. The slaves were offered their freedom if they joined our group. They refused, which astonished the old man. They were therefore kept under guard with the other hostages.

At dawn a loud bell began to ring somewhere in the town.

"Think that's the town bell telling everybody that there's a thousand black slaves who are here ready to join us?" I asked sardonically in the dim light.

There was no reply at first. "Do not ask for whom the bell tolls," Tilton finally said quietly. "It tolls for thee."

"What?"

"An English poet." Tilton was an educated man, which could sometimes be exasperating. "The bell is telling everyone that we are here."

"Hmph," I said. "Got that right."

Shortly afterward the old man let the passenger train proceed east. I thought that was a mistake. As long as the train remained at Harpers Ferry, nobody on it could raise the alarm beyond the town limits because we had cut the telegraph wires. If we let it go, it would stop at the next town and telegraph the railroad headquarters in

Baltimore, and then the world would know. It did that, and more. John Brown had a talk with the conductor before the train left. He wanted *the conductor to telegraph his superiors, and told him to add that we had come to free the slaves, and would do whatever it took to accomplish that. Brown even instructed the conductor to advise his superiors to notify the Secretary of War.*

I thought that was really strange. The Secretary of War was John B. Floyd, a proslavery Virginian who would fly into a rage when he learned that an armed group of abolitionists had invaded his home state. Brown knew that. Why didn't he instruct that President Buchanan, a mild-mannered Pennsylvanian, be the first one notified? Brown wanted publicity, and now he was certainly going to get it. Unfortunately his action now guaranteed the last thing we wanted: the appearance, now sooner rather than later, of the U.S. Army.

Ten o'clock. There has been some shooting, and some townspeople have been wounded, perhaps killed. Virginia and Maryland militia must soon be here. Not a single slave has arrived.

Sandy and I have noticed that nobody from the town has even attempted to come into Arsenal Square. Everybody seems to think that the raiders are all in the engine house, except for the bridge guards. Tilton and I are unmolested. We further this illusion by not shooting at anybody, not even showing our faces or guns.

Eleven o'clock. We raiders could still shoot our way out, cross over the bridge, and escape north. It cannot last much longer, and it is now obvious to everyone that there will be no slave rebellion, regardless of—perhaps because of—the memory of Nat Turner. Why doesn't Brown give the order to evacuate?

Then comes disastrous news: a group of Virginia militia has arrived. Worse, they have seized the Maryland side of the bridge. One of our guards was killed, and the other two were forced back to the engine house, under fire all the way.

All of us are now in a trap, our escape route blocked. And still Brown does nothing.

Ben Tilton stood up. "The time has come," he said.

"The time for what?"

"To leave this place, Cutter. You were right. The slaves aren't coming, but the militia has. There will soon be other militia groups coming. After them may well come the army. Time to go."

"Great. Go where, Sandy?"

"Across the bridge."

Had Tilton lost his mind? "Sandy, the militia controls the bridge now."

"Leave that to me," Tilton said, bold as brass. "Now—the first thing to do is get rid of our weapons. That includes your saber, Cutter. There are more than a thousand guns in this building. We can hide ours almost anywhere. It may take weeks to find them, and when they are found, they may not necessarily be connected to the raid at all."

While he was talking, Tilton had walked around the large room to a place where a number of Sharps carbines were stacked vertically, barrels up, in a large rack; he simply added his Sharps to the group. "Bring your carbine over here. In the next room there's a place where a lot of swords of different kinds are kept, along with knives and bayonets. Leave your saber there. And the scabbard."

I stood still, scarcely believing what I was hearing. "Sandy, what are you doing? How can we fight our way out of here without weapons?"

Tilton walked back to me, his manner calm and resolute. He slowly took off his heavy coat, and his whole appearance instantly changed. He was wearing fine clothes, even a cravat and a waistcoat. He must have had them all the time we were at the farm—or possibly bought them in the town—and put them on in the darkness before we left. His black boots were polished. I remembered that one of the things he had done during the long hours of the night was to clean his boots, carefully wiping away the mud caused by the light night rain. I had wondered why in the world he was doing that. Clean boots, dirty boots, what did it matter to the success of the raid? Now they gleamed like ebony.

The transformation was complete when Tilton put on his hat. I had not noticed anything about it in the darkness of the night, merely that he was wearing one as we trudged behind the wagon. Now I could see that it was a fine hat of black felt, carefully contoured in a shape that looked western.

Before me was no bedraggled ruffian of a raider, but the very personification of a prosperous gentleman.

"You see, Cutter?" Tilton smiled at me, his voice measured and quietly authoritative. "We're not going to fight our way across that bridge. We're going to talk our way across. Now hide those weapons and come back here."

I obeyed, in something of a state of shock. This was an entirely new side of Benjamin Tilton.

He had a paper-wrapped package for me when I returned; he had hidden it under his coat. It was a brand-new business shirt. White. And a black cravat. "Had a tailor in town make the shirt," he said laconically. "Guessed at your measurements."

It fit perfectly.

Tilton looped the cravat around my neck and expertly tied the knot. "There, now you look halfway decent. When's the last time you wore one of these?"

My mind was a blank. "I honestly don't remember."

"Well, try to make it look like you do it all the time. Here, you will need these." Tilton passed me a number of small white cards.

TILTON SHIPPING COMPANY
Boston
JOSHUA CUTLER
Accountant

"You are good with numbers, Cutter. Now you are officially an accountant. Enjoy your promotion?"

I was nearly speechless.

"Had them printed in town. These, however, I did not." Tilton produced another card and handed it to me.

TILTON SHIPPING COMPANY
Boston
BENJAMIN X. TILTON
Assistant Vice-President

This was a real carte de visite; it even had the small photograph typical of such cards. The photograph was of Tilton, looking even more the gentleman than he did now. "Used these a number of times," he remarked. "Can't tell you how useful they can be."

"I thought you said you weren't in your family business." This very professional-looking card was cream-colored, not white, and the lettering was raised. It even had gold edging.

"I'm not in the day-to-day operations. Sort of an ambassador-at-large. If I find business the company can use, I try to obtain it."

"So you're not really an assistant vice-president?"

Tilton took back the card, tucked it into a waistcoat pocket, and cupped my cheeks. "Cutter, you are so persnickety. Do you think anybody cares? If anyone really wanted to investigate and telegraphed our home office in Boston, they would acknowledge me. My father is the executive vice-president, and my grandfather is the president and chairman of the board. But we don't even have to worry about that here. Somebody seems to have cut all the telegraph wires."

I grinned. Maybe this would work.

"Now listen. We carry our coats under our arms, so they can see we are unarmed. Let me do the talking. They will expect that after they see our cards. You speak only if you absolutely have to. Don't volunteer anything. Got that?"

I nodded.

"One more thing, Cutter," Tilton grinned. "Clean up your boots."

I found an oily rag and got right to it. We left a few minutes later.

Arsenal Square was not totally enclosed by the wall; the western side was open. We left that way. Once outside the square, we walked between the wall and the railroad tracks. We stopped at the

B&O depot, which was past the end of the wall. "Wait here," Tilton commanded as he went inside. There were a lot of people milling around, all talking excitedly. I said nothing, and nobody paid any attention to me.

Tilton emerged five minutes later. He volunteered no information, and I did not ask for any.

The covered railroad bridge was not far from the depot. We could see a line of militia across the entrance on the Virginia side as we approached. We could not see through the bridge to the Maryland side, but it surely was also well-guarded.

"Good morning, gentlemen," Tilton said breezily. "Thank God you're here." Several of the militia smiled and muttered incomprehensible replies. "I wonder if we might have a word with your commanding officer."

"And who might you be, sir?" asked an older member of the militia, none too friendly.

Tilton produced his carte de visite and handed it to the questioner. "Benjamin Tilton of the Tilton Shipping Company, Sergeant," he replied easily. "I would appreciate it if you would give that to your commanding officer. Please tell him I wish to see him on a matter of some urgency."

The sergeant and several other militia members stared at the card as though they had never before seen a gold-edged carte de visite with a photograph on it. They probably hadn't.

The sergeant eventually walked over to another man, clearly an officer, who was standing at a corner of the bridge talking to several civilians. He saluted the officer, showed Tilton's card, pointed us out, and said something. The officer nodded to the group and came over to us.

I was getting very nervous.

"Captain Rowan of the Jefferson Guards, part of the Charles Town militia." He glanced at the carte de visite, then at Tilton. "You are Mr. Tilton?"

"I am indeed, Captain. And this is my associate, Mr. Cutler."

I handed the captain one of my cards. He looked at it briefly, then at me, then back to Tilton. He was a man in his forties, possibly a veteran of the Mexican War. He had a neatly trimmed black beard *and a brusque no-nonsense manner. "What exactly is the problem, Mr. Tilton?"*

"The train, Captain. Mr. Cutler and I are supposed to be in our Baltimore office today for an important meeting. We arrived in town about 9 o'clock this morning to find all this commotion. We bought tickets at the depot, but no one there or anywhere else seems to have any idea when the next train will arrive." Tilton reached into a waistcoat pocket and produced two tickets, which he handed to the captain. "I can't even telegraph my office to let them know where I am, for the telegraph wires have apparently been cut."

Were my ears deceiving me, or did Tilton's voice have a more pronounced New England twang than usual?

Captain Rowan examined the tickets, then handed them back to Tilton. "Where are you coming from, Mr. Tilton?"

Tilton did not hesitate. "Charles Town, as it happens, Captain."

"Charles Town?" The captain raised his eyebrows. Charles Town was in Virginia, about eight miles from Harpers Ferry; it was the seat of Jefferson County. "That's where we're from. Not many ships there."

Tilton smiled. "We don't do all our shipping by sea. We also use rail. And rivers."

Rowan nodded. "Well, gentlemen, you two are not the only ones inconvenienced by the disruption of the train schedule. What do you expect me to do about it? I have no control over the trains. Surely you do not expect any, however, until this business of the raiders is settled, do you?"

"We don't, Captain," Tilton replied earnestly, "and that's our problem. Nobody knows how long it will last. Let us cross over the bridge. On the Maryland side we can follow the tracks, perhaps hire a wagon. The next town east is Monocacy. We may be able to get a train there. At least I could telegraph my office, for the wires are intact there."

Rowan fingered Tilton's card. "Boston," he mused. "I've been there several times. Faneuil Hall, the Old North Church, the Common. Where exactly is your company located, Mr. Tilton? Your card doesn't say."

"It's at 1723 Logan Street." Seeing the captain's blank look, Tilton added, "A large three-story brick building. Near the docks."

"Hmm. What about you, Mr. Cutler? Are you from Boston, too?"

I knew nothing about Boston. "Philadelphia," I said, seeing Tilton wince almost imperceptibly. "I joined the company at its Philadelphia office."

Rowan looked at us carefully. "Sergeant!"

"Sir?"

"Please escort these gentlemen across the bridge."

"Yes, sir."

Captain Rowan smiled for the first time as he handed us back our cards. "Have a safe trip, gentlemen."

It was dim inside the covered bridge, but I could clearly see Tilton's face as, halfway across, he winked at me. That is how we got out of Harpers Ferry.

We did find a train and eventually reached Baltimore. "What does the X stand for?" I inquired during the train ride.

"Pardon?"

"Your middle initial. X. What does it stand for?"

"Xavier." Tilton pronounced it Zav-yer. "Francis Xavier. Ever hear of him?"

I shook my head.

"He was a Catholic priest. A missionary to the Orient. Several hundred years ago."

"So you're a Catholic?"

Tilton sighed. "My parents are. I was raised as one. Haven't been to church for a little while."

"I'm not sure I ever met a Catholic."

Tilton chuckled. "Should come to Boston. Lots of them there. Maybe that's why I dislike slavery so much," he mused. "Catholics hate slavery."

"Well, then, I guess I'm for Catholics, even if you're the only one I know."

"How about you? What religion were you raised in?"

I shrugged. "My dad was gone a lot. When my mother went to church, it was to a nearby Presbyterian church. I haven't been to church much lately, either."

"You seem to have a very strong moral position for someone who did not have much of a moral upbringing."

I shrugged again. "It's just plain wrong for someone to be owned by somebody else, and it's gone on for far too long." I changed the subject; I never did like talking about myself. "That was pretty clever what you did back there. You must have been thinking about it for a time."

Tilton laughed quietly. "I covered my options, as we say in business. You know, Francis Xavier was a Jesuit; one of the first Jesuits, in fact. The Jesuits were famous for their bold action and clever but unorthodox thinking." He shifted his position in the railway carriage, crossing one elegant shiny-booted leg over the other, and favored me with a beaming smile. "Sometimes, Cutter, it helps to think like a Jesuit. By the way, you did well with that officer back there at the bridge. I was afraid there might be trouble when you said you weren't from Boston, after I had gone to such pains to convince him that was where the company was."

"I don't know anything about Boston," I said. "Never been there, and he said he had. If he had asked me some simple question about Boston, and I had muffed it, we could have been in serious trouble. So I said I was from Philadelphia, a city I know. He didn't know you don't have an office there."

Tilton laughed. "Know what, Cutter? It so happens we do have an office there. You did even better than you knew. I think you'd have made a very good Jesuit."

That felt good, even if I wasn't exactly sure what a Jesuit was.

We parted in Baltimore. Tilton returned to Boston; I never expected to see him again. I decided to go to Washington. If John Brown could not arrest slavery, then no private citizen could. It would have to be done by some sort of government action, and Washington was the seat of the national government. I wanted to be close to it. Finding a modest job was not difficult. I had no fear of pursuit, since none of the surviving raiders knew my real name except Tilton, to whom I had revealed it on the train.

I followed the aftermath of the Harpers Ferry raid in the newspapers, which couldn't print enough of it. More militia arrived during the afternoon of Monday, October 17, after Tilton and I left. Late that night the very eventuality I had feared happened: official U.S. military forces arrived, in the form of 90 Marines. They were commanded by an Army officer, Col. Robert E. Lee.

On the morning of the 18th, these Marines charged and captured the engine house. A number of the raiders were killed including two of John Brown's sons, Oliver and Watson. All of the hostages were released unharmed.

That was the end of the raid. Of the 22 of us, ten were killed outright during the raid; another five were captured, arrested, tried, and eventually executed by hanging. Seven escaped, but two of those were later captured, taken to Charles Town, tried, sentenced, and executed. Only five escaped and remained free.

John Brown was one of the five captured alive at Harpers Ferry. He was so badly wounded that he had to lie on a cot, unable to stand, in the courtroom at Charles Town. He was quite lucid, however, justifying his extreme actions by affirming they were necessary because of the extreme evil of slavery. He refused to plead insanity, despite the urgings of his defense lawyers because of several instances of certifiable insanity in his family. He also refused to name the raiders who escaped.

John Brown was hanged in Charles Town at 11:30 AM on December 2, only six weeks after the raid.

After his death, the newspapers published a note he had given to one of the jailers on the day of his execution.

> I, John Brown, am now quite certain that the crimes of this guilty land will never be purged away but with blood. I had, as I now think, flattered myself that, without very much bloodshed, it might be done.

No more prophetic words have ever been written.

The raid on Harpers Ferry was the most sensational thing that had happened in the country in years. It further split the nation, being universally condemned in the South and almost universally admired in the North. If bloodshed there would be, the raid hastened its onset. But as Brown himself might have said, if it takes a war to destroy slavery, then let there be war.

In my opinion, John Brown was the greatest man in the country. I felt humbled and honored to have served with him, even if I didn't always agree exactly with everything he did.

My attention began to focus on the man who had led the Marines, Col. Lee. Some newspapers made much of him. From their standpoint, his actions were exemplary and perfectly successful. The raid was terminated, the hostages were freed unharmed, all but a handful of the raiders were killed or captured, and peace was restored. Perhaps most satisfying of all to the newspapers—especially Southern ones—was the fact that the notorious John Brown was not killed in the raid, but captured. He therefore could be put on trial, mocked, derided, his ideals trashed, and then be publicly hanged.

Lee happened to have been the highest-ranking field officer in the Washington area at the time of the raid, so the War Department ordered him to go to Harpers Ferry; he did not volunteer. He was a Virginian, one of the famous and aristocratic Lees of Virginia. He was available because he was at home, on leave from the army. His home happened to be in the Virginia Heights above the Potomac, just across the river from Washington. It was a large estate. Its name was Arlington.

It may have been an accident of circumstances that Lee was the one ordered to take charge of the military situation at Harpers Ferry, but a black suspicion began to form in my mind when I learned that he owned a large estate in Virginia. More than one, in fact. Virginia was the most prominent of all the slave states. Would not a large estate in Virginia necessarily involve slaves? Perhaps a lot of them?

I eventually learned that Lee did own many slaves—dozens of them. The bitter irony, the full horror, the unbearable shame of what had happened then swept over me like a monstrous wave: John Brown, the most ardent abolitionist and the best white friend black slaves ever had, had been captured and sent to his doom by a major slave-holder, the precise sort of person Brown himself called "abominations of the earth."

I will never forget that name, that hateful name: Robert E. Lee.

* * * * *

Rufus Sloan awoke shivering. Harpers Ferry! He had known he would dream of Harpers Ferry again, and he had. The dreams of Kansas and Harpers Ferry were recurrent, but he could never predict the night they would happen.

He always woke up shivering from these dreams, no matter how warm the weather. As always, he used his mind in a powerful effort to control his body, pulling the blankets up close around his neck. Slowly, gradually, the shivering grew less and finally stopped. His mind, however, remained active, and would not let him sleep.

Harpers Ferry! Although the raid had failed, it was the ultimate experience of his life. John Brown had given his life, and that of two of his sons, in the spectacular effort to really do something about slavery. No private person could have done more. Now, however, a year and a half later, it looked as if the government was finally being pushed into an antislavery position. President Linclon could talk all the conciliatory words he wanted to the South, but everyone knew he hated slavery. By firing on Fort Sumter, the slavers had finally overstepped their bounds, and given the new president the opening he was looking for. On Monday the president had asked for 75,000 volunteers for the Army, which surely had only one purpose: it would invade the South, freeing slaves as it went. The die was cast, the Rubicon crossed. This was it, the beginning of the battle of Armageddon to rid the world of slavery once and for all.

Sloan realized he would have to see about signing up.

CHAPTER 26

Thursday
Washington
8:58 AM

Robert E. Lee reined in his horse in front of 1651 Pennsylvania Avenue. He was in uniform, since he intended to meet with General Scott after his meeting with Francis P. Blair. Dismounting, he tied the reins to a post and surveyed the house. Three stories high with a multitude of windows, it was one of a series of connected townhouses that occupied much of the block. Painted an attractive cream color with trim in white and dark gray shutters, it was as elegant as its exclusive address suggested. At the end of the block, on the northeast corner of 17th Street and Pennsylvania Avenue, stood the brand-new art gallery of banker W.W. Corcoran, an imposing pile of red brick done in the flamboyant architectural style of the French Third Empire of Louis Napoleon and the Empress Eugenie.

Lee was aware of Blair's reputation. Blair had been a member of President Jackson's famed "Kitchen Cabinet," the public esteem of which was at least partially responsible for Andrew Jackson being the last two-term president. Many of the informal meetings of that Kitchen Cabinet had taken place in Blair's home. Blair was now a newspaper publisher. His two sons were both influential; one was a congressman, the other was in President Lincoln's Cabinet. Although Jackson had been a Democrat, the elder Blair had powerfully supported Lincoln, a Republican, in the recent election.

Certainly helpful to Blair's influence was the fact that he lived only a stone's throw from the President's House. Although Blair now held no official government position, Lee did not doubt that the new president privately consulted Blair, perhaps often. From what Lee had heard, many presidents had done the same thing.

Lee turned and gazed at the brilliant white expanse of the Executive Mansion, less than two hundred yards away. He ruminated on the fact that he had served in the United States Army more than thirty years, and lived in a house only a few miles away from the President's House, but had never met a president during that time. When he had graduated from West Point in 1829 Jackson had been president, as he was two years later when Lee married. While he was stationed in St. Louis making improvements in the flow of the Mississippi River, Martin Van Buren was president. He was an engineer in the Washington area during the brief term of William Henry Harrison, who had died after a few months in office. He spent several years improving the defences of Fort Hamilton in New York Harbor while John Tyler was president. While he was in Mexico during the war, James Polk was president. While he was fortifying Baltimore, Zachary Taylor and then Millard Fillmore were the presidents. When he was Superintendant of the United States Military Academy at West Point, Fillmore and then Franklin Pierce were the presidents. He had been sent to Harpers Ferry while James Buchanan was the president. Now Abraham Lincoln was president, the first Republican to occupy the Executive Mansion. Lee had been in the U.S. Army under ten presidents—*ten*—and not met a single one of them.

Most of the time during those thirty years he could not have done any such thing, as he had been stationed somewhere far away. Now he was not; he was home. And at this very instant, he was merely across the street from the official residence of all those men whose bidding he had done for more than three decades. Should his mere notation of the fact that he had never personally met a president become an insatiable thirst, he had no doubt that right now, this very moment, he could simply walk across Pennsylvania Avenue, ask to meet with President Lincoln, and be accommodated. Swarms of mere office-seekers often were.

The oversized north portico of the mansion, with its gleaming white pillars two stories high, seemed to beckon seductively.

Ah, well, perhaps another time. Maybe after his retirement…

Lee opened the black wrought-iron gate, climbed the eight stone steps to the white front door, and operated the brass knocker. While waiting for the response, he admired the semicircular window above the door, which had individual panes of glass shaped somewhat like the panels of an opened umbrella.

The door was opened by Blair himself. "Come in, Colonel. I'm Francis Blair."

"Good morning, Mr. Blair," Lee said, stepping through the door and doffing his hat.

"Thank you for acceding to my request on such short notice. You are very punctual," Blair observed, shaking the hand of his guest. "Given your reputation, sir, I would have expected no less."

"Thank you, Mr. Blair."

Francis Blair was a short-statured man, 71 years old, frail in appearance. He was wearing a black waistcoat, black cravat, white shirt, and black trousers. His face was sallow, but traces of light brown hair remained on his otherwise-gray head.

The former Cabinet member did not waste any time showing Lee around the house. He ushered Lee into a small sitting room to the right of the entrance hallway. A small fire was burning in the fireplace at the far end of the room.

"May I get you something, Colonel?"

"Thank you, Mr. Blair, but I recently had breakfast. I have no needs."

Blair seated himself, inviting his guest to do likewise. "You have an outstanding military record, Colonel," he smiled. "Even I, a non-military man, have heard of it."

"Thank you, Mr. Blair. I have also heard many things of you."

"Have you? I am pleased. You therefore know that I am privileged to enjoy the confidence of a number of highly placed persons. *Very* highly placed, I might add."

"I am aware of your long and distinguished political service, sir."

"Good. Then I will come directly to the point, Colonel. My time is valuable, and yours certainly is." Blair cleared his throat. "You are aware of the president's call last Monday for 75,000 volunteers. Even now, young men from all over the nation are answering that call. And you may rest assured there will be future calls for more men." Blair stopped and eyed Lee.

"Yes," Lee replied calmly. "I read the president's speech in the newspapers."

"Well, then, as a long-time army officer you know what this means for the army. It will increase in size many times over. Virtually explode in size, one might say."

"Indeed it will."

"Colonel," Blair said, pronouncing the words carefully, "I have been authorized by both President Lincoln and Secretary Cameron to personally ask you if you would be interested in commanding that army." He keenly eyed Lee and folded his hands.

So this is how it is, thought Lee. General Scott had hinted such an offer might be made to him. Because of his long relationship with Scott, he assumed that any such offer would officially be made by Scott, his superior officer. But it wasn't; it was informally coming from a private individual, albeit one with enormous influence. Blair could not appoint him to anything, but he had the ear of someone who could. Someone who, in fact, had obviously requested Blair to ascertain his intentions. Blair was right; this offer was unmistakably coming from the man across the street, President Abraham Lincoln. Blair would never say any such thing on his own. And Scott, long familiar with Lee's record, must be the one who had recommended him to the president, for Lee himself had never met Lincoln.

Lee had already considered the immense ramifications of this offer, should it come. Now it had. He responded the way he had planned, the only way he felt he could respond.

"Mr. Blair, I have been in the United States Army for more than thirty years; thirty-five years, counting my years as a cadet at West Point. I could have asked for no more satisfying life. An offer like this could be looked upon as the culmination of my career. I think a great many officers would certainly consider it so."

"Then you accept?" Blair asked guardedly.

Lee hesitated. "Under ordinary circumstances, I would consider it the highest of honors. However"—he looked directly at Blair—"these are the most extraordinary circumstances."

Blair remined silent, but made a small motion with his right hand that Lee interpreted as an invitation to continue.

"There can be only one purpose for such an army, Mr. Blair. It will invade the South. It will attempt to force all the seceded states back into the Union by naked military force. I do not think I can be a party to such an action. I am certain that I cannot lead it. If the people of the Confederacy choose to resist such an army—and I am sure they will—we will be engaged in a huge civil war. American against American. Family against family. Brother against brother. I cannot imagine a sadder prospect. No, sir," Lee repeated, "I cannot lead it."

Blair steepled his fingers and thought a moment. "Do you think a state has a right to secede from the Union, Colonel?" he asked softly.

Lee frowned slightly. "With all due respect, sir, that is a political question. I am not a politician. I am, however, familiar with the secessionist argument: the Constitution does not specifically mention secession, and the Tenth Amendment specifically leaves to the states matters not covered in the body of the Constitution. Therefore, they say, secession is constitutionally a matter for the individual states to decide."

"And you agree with that?"

Lee smiled thinly. "I did not say that, Mr. Blair. I merely said I knew the legalistic argument for secession. Whether I agree with it, or how I feel about it, are different matters."

"How *do* you feel about it?"

Lee shook his head slowly. "Since you ask, Mr. Blair, I will tell you that I do not have an opinion about the legality of secession. I think that is a matter for lawyers to decide; a Supreme Court decision would be helpful. I *feel*, however, that secession is wrong. It has already caused a great rift in our country. Seven states have already invoked it and formed what they claim to be a new country. I think that is a tragedy."

Blair murmured an assent. "We are agreed on that, at least, Colonel. I, too, think it is a tragedy. A great one. Yet if I hear you correctly, you are unwilling to help put an end to this tragedy."

"Ending it by invading the Confederacy as if it were an enemy country would be a greater tragedy, Mr. Blair. What would be even worse for me personally is that my own state, Virginia, may also secede. In that case I would be invading my own state, making war on my own neighbors and friends, all in the name of unity at the point of a sword. What kind of unity is that? And how can I possibly be the commander of an army that would do such a thing? I simply could not draw my sword against my native state."

"So even though you disagree with secession, you would not fight to end it."

"Mr. Blair, please understand me. I am not a politician. My opinion about secession doesn't really matter to anyone involved with it. No one in the states of the Confederacy consulted me before voting for secession. No one in Richmond is consulting me now about Virginia's course of action, nor will they. It has all been done by politicians, all of whom were elected by the people. If Virginia secedes, by the action of its politicians I will be a resident of a seceded state, regardless of my feelings about secession. Although I am in the United States Army, I simply do not see myself as leading it on an invasion to crush secession. And that, even if successful, would not be a final answer. Secession is a legal issue, not a military one. If it is to be permanently ended, there must be a legal solution devised by politicians, acceptable to everyone. That is not my field."

There was a small silence before Blair responded. "Well, you have put your position fairly to me, Colonel, even if I do not agree with it. Now let me ask you about a different matter, although a related one. You have a number of slaves on your estate, I understand. You know that an army invading the South is going to liberate slaves wherever it goes. Virginia is the first state south of here, just across the Potomac. And your estate is one of the closest places in Virginia to the river. In other words, if Virginia secedes, your own estate is going to be one of the very first places invaded. If you were commanding the army, would you liberate your own slaves? And if the army were commanded by someone else, wouldn't you rue the day it liberated them? Might it not be that your declination of command is due to an overfondness for the comforts that slavery has given you, and which you know will soon be taken away?"

Blair spoke in a calm manner in a voice tinged with dryness, yet his words had a galvanizing effect upon his guest.

"Mr. Blair, I am simply at a loss to comprehend a view like that." Lee's dark eyes snapped. "Why are abolitionists in the North so bent upon rooting out slavery in every cranny in the South? And *right now*, or else? The people in the northern states are not accountable for slavery in the southern states. We do not threaten them with war if they do not accept our view. Why do they threaten us with war if we do not accept theirs?"

"Because they feel slavery is a moral evil no matter where it is," Blair stated quietly.

"I *know* they believe that, sir. And I have no problem with someone feeling that way. But for them to say that disunion of this great nation is preferable to living with slavery somewhere in the country, no matter how far away, until it dies a natural death—which I believe it will—is a very different matter. It is not only ridiculous, it is pernicious. I myself have already agreed to the manumission of my own servants sometime next year. I tell you truthfully, if I personally owned all the four millions of slaves in the South, I would free every one of them if it would save the Union."

Blair thought of the plan he had proposed to the president concerning Lee's slaves. However, that plan was contingent upon Lee accepting the command first. If Lee refused the command, regardless of the disposition of his slaves, there was no point in pursuing the matter further. He forced himself to smile.

"So, Colonel, is there nothing my once-vaunted powers of persuasion can do to induce you to accept field command of the United States Army? Assuming, of course, it were to be formally offered to you?"

"I regret to say that there is not," Lee replied. He stood up. "That is not due to your lack of persuasion, I assure you. It is my own decision, from which I cannot be dissuaded." He extended his hand, firmly grasping that of his elderly host. "Mr. Blair, it has been an honor to meet you. Thank you for your time amd your courtesy. Please extend my thanks to the man who could have made the offer. Tell him that I sincerely appreciate his consideration, but that I cannot oblige him."

"I will, Colonel. Thank you for stopping by."

A blackness seemed to descend upon Blair as he shut the door behind his guest. This was a man who could certainly command an army. He even *looked* the part of an army commander better than any officer Blair had ever met. Although Lee's decision was obviously his to make, Blair still felt that he had failed. He was not used to failing, and he did not enjoy the sensation.

Black feeling or not, President Lincoln would have to be informed at once.

CHAPTER 27

Thursday
Washington
9:47 AM

Standing outside Blair's house next to his horse, Robert E. Lee knew what he must do next. He did not look forward to it. In his mind, he had repeatedly turned over in his mind various scenarios of how the matter might be handled, if it ever had to be handled. Now it was here, brutal and inescapable. The more he thought about it, the more he realized that it would be the hardest thing he ever had to do in his life, much harder than any mere military action.

He was going to have to tell General Winfield Scott. Perhaps General Scott had foreknowledge of Blair's offer, and requested the meeting with Lee in order to know Lee's response as soon as possible; he did not know.

The War Department was on the southeast corner of 17th Street and Pennsylvania Avenue, across from the new Corcoran Art Gallery. A large white building three and a half stories high, it had a large white-pillared portico resembling that of the Executive Mansion, from which it was separated by landscaped grounds. It was less than a block from Blair's house. Lee thought briefly of leaving his horse tied up in front of Blair's house and simply walking to the War Department, but then thought the better of it. He mounted his horse and rode it slowly up Pennsylvania Avenue.

At the War Department he dismounted, tied up his horse, and went inside. General Scott's office—actually several rooms—was on the second floor at the front of the building. An office with several aides connected with Scott's private office. Lee presented himself to one of the aides.

"Colonel Lee to see General Scott. I have an appointment."

"Yes, sir." The aide, a lieutenant, rose, walked across the room, opened the door to Scott's private office, and disappeared inside. Fifteen seconds later he reappeared, left the door open, and walked over to Lee. "The general will see you now, Colonel. Please follow me."

Lee followed the aide across the room and through the door. "Colonel Lee, General." The aide left the room, closing the door behind him.

Lee had been in this office several times before; its layout was familiar to him. Unusually, General Scott had a large round table near the center of the room; most men would have had a rectangular table placed near the windows. The room was bright, the sun streaming in the windows and illuminating the general and his table almost like a stage light. There were a number of papers neatly arranged on the table.

"Please come in, Colonel." Scott did not attempt to rise. Not only did his age and girth mitigate against movement, but he was the most senior officer in the entire United States Army. He rose only for high-ranking political figures such as the president, vice-president, members of the Cabinet, and a handful of members of Congress. He probably would not have risen for the governor of any state. "Thank you for responding to my letter. Please be seated."

Lee saluted and seated himself. As he did so, he noticed another person in the room. A secretary was seated at a modest-sized rectangular desk in a corner, almost in shadows compared to the bright center of the room. The secretary did not rise or introduce himself, and made no effort to leave.

"So, Colonel, you are still, in effect, on a leave of absence, are you not?"

"Yes, sir, that is correct. I am staying with my family at Arlington. You will recall that I am here in response to your direct order, which I received in Texas in February."

"I remember indeed. You arrived in early March, was it not? About the time the president was inaugurated?"

"Yes, sir."

"So you have been home now about six weeks."

"Yes, sir, that is so."

"Well, Colonel, let me come to the point. You know that since the self-proclaimed secession of several Southern states, and the formation of the Confederacy, many officers from those states have been resigning their commissions and returning to their native states. At the same time, our army will soon be expanding greatly, increasing our need for good officers at precisely the time when so many are leaving. In my half-century of service to this country, I have never seen anything like it."

The old general stopped briefly, then continued in a softer tone of voice. "You also know, Colonel, the high regard I have for you personally. These are times when every officer in service to the United States should fully determine what course he will pursue and frankly declare it. No one should be in government employ without being actively employed. I have not issued recent orders to you because I thought you could use the time to ascertain your feelings. Now I can use you, Colonel. The army is expanding. How do you stand, sir?"

Lee shifted in his seat and cleared his throat. "General, you should know that I have just come from the home of Francis P. Blair, just a block from here. He is a confidant of the president, as he has been for several presidents." He hesitated.

"Yes, yes, I know Mr. Blair," Scott said, waving a hand. "We have met a number of times. Any president's trust in him is not misplaced. What did he say?"

"He said that he had been empowered by President Lincoln, with the knowledge and assent of Secretary Cameron, to ascertain if I would accept field command of the new army being formed for the invasion of the South, should it be formally offered to me." Lee paused.

"And your reply?" Scott leaned forward slightly. His usual mask of gruff inscrutability was slightly softened by the combination of keen interest and a touch of pleasure.

"I told him that I was deeply honored to be considered for such a position. I also detected your hand in the matter, General, for which I am both honored and grateful."

Scott waved his hand again. "Yes, yes, of course. But what of your decision about such an offer? Have you reached it yet? If so, did you tell Mr. Blair?"

"Yes, I have reached a decision," Lee said gravely. "I told Mr. Blair that I could not accept. This army is going to invade the South and attempt to force the seceding states back into the Union at the point of a sword. In my opinion, the Confederacy is not our enemy, and will not become one unless we invade it. I regret that I cannot be a party to such an invasion." Scott was silent for a time, as the hint of a smile vanished from his face. "I feared as much," he finally sighed, "although I had hoped it would not be so. I am very sorry to hear this." He paused again. "Well, Colonel, you have turned down a supreme offer from the Secretary of War and even the President of the United States. Do you think you can stay in the army in some lesser capacity? If you feel you could not carry out certain commands because of sectional sympathies, do you think your superior officers can trust you? I would think not, sir. And I am the most superior of all those officers."

"I put it to you this way, Colonel. If you propose to resign, I suggest you do so immediately; your present position is an equivocal one."

Lee had kept silent during Scott's reaction to the news of the offer. "The property belonging to my children, all they possess, lies in Virginia," he finally said slowly. "They will be ruined if they do not go with their state. I cannot raise my hand against my children."

"I might remind you that I am also a Virginian, Colonel," Scott responded curtly. "Yet I do not elevate my duty to my state above my duty to my country. Yes, Arlington and your other properties do lie in Virginia. However, I might point out that they lie in the northern part of the state; Arlington lies just across the river, very close to where we are sitting this very moment. If Virginia secedes, and war comes, do you think Virginia can protect your property from Union forces which will be massing right here in the capital? Do you imagine the entire *Confederacy* could protect it? I tell you, Colonel, that if you truly want to protect your property from seizure, and if you truly love your children as I am sure you do, I would mightily recommend that you stay in service to the United States and lead this future army. No one in the world would then be in a better position to protect those properties. You would, in effect, be invading your own properties, and their integrity would be guaranteed by the United States Army, of which you have been a conspicuous part for thirty years. For what better guarantor could you ask?"

The general looked at his favorite subordinate officer, his seamed and craggy face a mask of sternness tinged with sadness. "You know the esteem in which I hold you, Colonel. It is with great sorrow that I am now learning of your refusal. I must tell you that I believe it to be the greatest mistake of your career. The contest may be long and severe, but eventually the issue must be in favor of the Union."

Lee sat thoughtfully, not answering. Finally he rose. "Thank you for your time, General. And thank you for the trust you have extended to me on numerous occasions in the past. I also hold you in great esteem. You have given me much to think upon. I will contact you." He saluted. "May we meet again in happier times, General." He walked slowly over to the door, opened it, and walked out. He did not look back.

General Scott looked over at the secretary, E.D. Townsend. "You heard, Mr. Townsend?"

"Yes, sir, I did."

"I don't suppose you made any notes."

"As a matter of fact, I did so, General."

"Destroy them."

"Sir?"

"Destroy them, Mr. Townsend. I do not wish any official record of the conversation of this meeting."

"As you wish, General."

"Some time in the future, after I am gone, you may relate the conversation from memory, if you wish. But not now. This may be the most bitter disappointment of my career. I considered Colonel Lee to be the finest officer in the army, the man who might some day take my place in this very office. I do not want our actual words committed to paper. Just record that Lee came here, as requested, and that he informed me that he had decided to decline the offer of the president."

"Yes, sir. If I may offer an opinion, General, it almost sounded to me as if the Colonel's decision may not yet be absolutely final. He said nothing about signing any piece of paper with Mr. Blair, and he did not sign anything with you. Perhaps your words touched something within him. Perhaps he will yet change his mind."

Scott rubbed his forehead. "I doubt it. Colonel Lee can be a very single-minded man, as I know from long experience with him. Besides, Mr. Blair is probably on his way this very minute to see President Lincoln with the news. However, you have a point. If Colonel Lee really intends to resign his commission, he will have to inform me, or the Secretary of War, in writing. I will take no further action until I receive such a communication, or Mr. Cameron informs me he has received it. Mr. Blair is informing the president about Lee's refusal of the command, and the president will undoubtedly inform the secretary. Nothing more, therefore, is needed from me for the time being."

"Yes, sir."

Mr. Townsend returned to his work, and the general busied himself with papers in his desk. To himself, under his breath, so softly Townsend did not hear, he uttered one word, accompanied by a monstrous scowl. "Bah."

CHAPTER 28

Thursday
Washington
12:16 PM

"Hello, Cutter."

Rufus Sloan whirled around. The slow-paced mellifluous voice was coming from a tall handsome well-dressed man with wheat-colored hair and an easy smile.

"Sandy! Sandy Tilton!" Sloan grabbed Tilton's outstretched hand. "What in blue blazes are you doing here?"

"About the same thing you are, Cutter. Signing up."

The two of them were in one of the several recruitment centers which had sprung up in the city since Monday. This one had been hastily set up in the open field south of the Executive Mansion, near Constitution Avenue. The army felt that having the President's House in plain view would stimulate recruitment.

The army was right. There were more than a hundred men milling around the several tents, many talking in loud voices. Sloan had been standing in line. Tilton had seen him and came over to stand behind him.

"Well, I'm happy to have you join up with me, Sandy. But what are you doing in Washington? The last time I saw you, we were in Baltimore. You were on your way back to Boston."

"I did go to Boston. The family was pleased to see me safe and sound. Spent some time there in our home office. Also spent some time at our New York and Philadelphia offices. As the war loomed closer and closer, I was finally able to convince my family that Washington itself was going to become the nerve center for massive amounts of shipping, especially military shipments. Our company ought to get some of these government contracts. If we don't, our competitors will. So we opened a Washington office." Tilton produced a card and handed it to Sloan.

"Oho! Another fancy card!"

"They work well, remember?"

The gilt-edged *carte de visite* had a photograph of Tilton and identified him as a vice-president of the Tilton Shipping Comapny and the assistant manager of its Washington office.

"Your photograph looks a little different."

"What a sharp memory you have, Cutter. It is different. My previous card was made in Boston. When we opened our office here I had a new card made by Mathew Brady over at his studio on lower Pennsylvania Avenue near 6th Street. He seemed as blind as a bat to me, but everyone said he was the best photographer around. His studio was certainly a photo palace."

"This says you are the assistant manager. Why aren't you the manager?"

"Not quite old enough for that august position, Cutter. The manager is my cousin Seth. Older and wiser. Well, older, anyway." Tilton winked.

The line moved forward. "I think we should talk, Sandy," Sloan said in a lowered voice.

"I agree," Tilton replied. "But not here. And from the looks of things, we might not have much of a chance later."

They were close enough to the front of the line to hear much of what was said between the recruiting officers and the recruits. Three months service. Pay and service to begin immediately upon taking the oath. "I didn't realize it would begin immediately," Sloan whispered. "That means I can't go back to work."

"Do you *want* to go back to work?" Tilton whispered sardonically.

"Well, not really. I do want to join up. I guess I just wanted a little time to settle my own affairs."

"Cutter," Tilton whispered urgently, "come with me." He grasped Sloan's elbow, took him out of line, and together they walked outside the tent. "Look," he continued, once they were safely out of earshot of everybody else, "I didn't know you would be here. I knew you were probably somewhere in the Washington area, because that's where you said you wanted to go when we parted company a year and a half ago. After I moved to Washington I didn't try very hard to find you, because I had absolutely no idea where to look. And you, of course, had no idea I was here. All right, now we found each other. I think we should talk, lay some plans, settle our affairs, and especially see if we could arrange it so that we serve together. Don't worry about missing any opportunity today. The army is not going to strike that tent tomorrow. We can always join up."

"Thanks, Sandy. You're right. I'd like to serve with you, if I could. I hadn't thought about that."

"Tell you what. I've got to get back to work now. I guess you do, too. Do you like oysters?"

"Oysters?"

"Yes. Oysters. Do you like to eat them?"

"I don't often eat oysters, Sandy. I'm not sure I ever have. I don't know what they taste like."

"High time you learned. If you join up, you won't find out soon. They don't serve oysters in the army. Not to the enlisted men, anyway. On C Street, between 10th and 11th Streets, there's a place called Harvey's Oyster Salon. Best oysters in the city, maybe the world. Meet me there at seven o'clock tomorrow evening. We can talk, and you can have all the oysters you want. My treat."

Sloan shook his head in amused bemusement. *Oysters!* Sandy Tilton surely lived in a world different from his own. "I'll be there, Sandy. Thanks."

"Good. By the way, have you heard the latest about Harpers Ferry? Our place of sacred memory?"

A rush of images flooded Sloan's mind. "Harpers Ferry? No. What happened?"

"A friend of mine in a news service told me about it just before I came here. It's not in the newspapers yet. There's fighting going on there."

"Fighting?"

"The Virginians are trying to take it."

CHAPTER 29

Friday, April 19
Washington
8:08 AM

Rose Greenhow had walked briskly from her home to be at the Central Market early. Most of the best food was brought in before dawn, and she liked to be there before the selection had been picked over by later crowds.

She did not bother looking for Mr. Thomas. She knew he would find her.

He came alongside while she was examining vegetables. "Good morning, Mrs. Greenhow." His voice was very low, although there was no one near them.

"Good morning, Mr. Thomas." She did not look at him, which was an effort. She liked looking at men. "You may call me Rose," she added in an inviting tone.

"I prefer Mrs. Greenhow," he said evenly, all business. "I have something of extreme importance. Please listen carefully. On Wednesday afternoon the Virginia Convention in Richmond voted for secession. It is not common knowledge yet because the convention also voted to keep its proceedings secret. However, news of such a nature cannot remain a secret indefinitely. It will become public knowledge soon."

Greenhow turned slightly toward Thomas and started to speak, but he raised a hand and cut her off. "The reason for the secrecy," he continued, "was to enable the governor to quietly mobilize the militia and seize all Federal installations in the state. They have already seized the arsenal at Harpers Ferry. They will seize everything else in the state soon, perhaps today." He paused briefly. "You understand this is explosive news, Mrs. Greenhow. You must not say a word of it to anyone. Repeat, to *anyone.* The timing is delicate. Premature exposure will compromise the plan, perhaps defeat it. Even after it happens and everyone knows about it, I would caution you not to say anything which would reveal you had prior knowledge of it. That would compromise *you*, and you are very important to us." He paused again. "I am telling you this so that you will know, without question, that I am who I say I am and that you can have complete confidence in me. I hardly need to tell you of the enormous significance Virginia's secession has for the Confederacy."

Greenhow picked up a bunch of carrots and examined them carefully. "I do indeed have every confidence in you, Mr. Thomas. Thank you for the information, and thank you for the confidence in me. I assure you I shall not tell a soul."

"Good." Thomas also picked up some carrots. "There is another matter, not nearly so explosive but still important. Do you personally know Colonel Robert E. Lee, a career officer in the U.S. Army? Lives in the Virginia Heights across the Potomac from Washington? On an estate named Arlington?"

"I have heard of him in a social way, Mr. Thomas, but no, I do not personally know him."

Thomas paused briefly. "Do you happen to know anyone who *does* know him personally?"

Greenhow thought a moment. "No, I regret to say I do not."

"Hmm. I ask you because the Virginia Convention also voted to establish a military post to command all the military and naval forces of the state. It is to be filled by gubernatorial appointment. Lee was recommended for the position. Although I do not know for sure, I believe the governor is attempting to contact him right now. If you knew a close friend of his, who was also a friend of ours, I could bring that information to the attention of the governor, who might make the approach to Lee through his friend. However, since you don't know a good friend of Lee's—I don't either—we'll have to leave the mechanics of the offer to the governor."

Greenhow took the bunch of carrots with her and moved over to the radishes. Thomas followed her. "Is Col. Lee still with the U.S. Army?" she asked quietly.

"Yes," Thomas replied. "And he may stay with it. However, when he learns his state has seceded, he may not. No one knows. The governor will do his best, I'm sure. I would also keep this information quiet. Nothing may come of it, but something may. If it does, it would not be wise to appear to have known too much of it."

"Thank you, Mr. Thomas. I shall keep that in mind. Now I am pleased to tell you that I have already started a group of people to gather information. I should have some results by next week."

"Very good. Let's meet here again next Friday, same time. I will have a code for you. After that I suggest we hold our meetings to a minimum and stay in contact through intermediaries. It would not do for us to be seen together."

"As you wish, sir, although I must say I shall regret not seeing you." Greenhow gave him a dazzling smile.

Thomas smiled back. "All in our glorious cause, madam." He picked up a bunch of radishes and left.

CHAPTER 30

Friday
Washington
12:06 PM

Meagan O'Connor came into Grinell's Goods with her curls bouncing, smiling like a self-satisfied cat. Rufus Sloan was busy with a customer, so she sat in one of the several chairs usually reserved for special customers and unwrapped her lunch.

Finished with the customer, Sloan brought his own small lunch over and joined O'Connor. Unlike the three other clerks at Grinell's, Sloan didn't eat much; he simply was not very hungry. Meagan O'Connor usually ate more than Sloan did.

"What do you think of Harpers Ferry?" she began.

Sloan knew she was referring to the capture of the arsenal by the Virginia militia yesterday—it was in all the newspapers—but it still unnerved him. It almost seemed as if she knew his deepest secret. "An act of incredible treachery," he replied. "Virginia's still in the Union. At least I thought it was."

"Harpers Ferry must not be very well defended," Meagan volunteered. "Isn't that the place those John Brown raiders captured two years ago? And they weren't even militia."

"Yes, that's the place," Sloan replied carefully. "And you're right; I guess it wasn't defended very well."

"So now what?"

"I really don't know, Miss Meagan. However, if I were the president, I would triple the guards on everything else the government owns in Virginia. I can't believe the Virginians would seize that arsenal at Harpers Ferry and then do nothing about all the other Federal property in the state. The biggest prize would be that huge naval base near Norfolk. I hope the navy is doing something about it right now."

"I hope so, too," Meagan smiled between bites. "Rufus, I simply have to tell you the latest gossip. I'm not sure exactly what it means, but I thought you might. You know so much," she added brightly.

"Well, I don't think I'm much for gossip," Sloan replied with a slow smile. "What sort of gossip?"

"It's about the army. And you know a lot about the army."

Sloan had already decided not to tell O'Connor about planning to join the army. Not yet. "What about the army?"

"Well, have you ever heard of a colonel named Lee? Robert E. Lee?"

Sloan caught his breath and froze. His heart seemed to stop beating momentarily, then started to race. He stared at O'Connor, but she was glancing down, looking for her apple, and did not see his startled eyes.

"Lee?" Sloan finally forced himself to say the name he had once hated with a consuming passion, but had almost come to forget in the year and a half since Harpers Ferry. O'Connor looked up. "Yes, I have heard of him," he said steadily, meeting her eyes while willing his heart to slow its racing. "Not much, though. I certainly don't know him."

"See? I *knew* you would know something!"

"Do you know him?"

"Me? Of course not, silly. I don't think I even know anybody who's in the army at all. Certainly not a colonel. Goodness!"

"Is this gossip about him?"

"Yes." Meagan grinned widely, now knowing that what she had to say would interest him.

"All right. So what is it?"

"Well, Amanda Fletcher—she's one of our seamstresses, although she only works part time—is married to an army officer. Last night he told her that this Colonel Lee was offered command of the army! And he turned it down! Can you imagine that?"

A giant vise seemed to grip Sloan's chest. He couldn't seem to speak. Meagan O'Connor looked at him with concern, seeing a strain on his face. "Rufus! Are you all right?"

"Fine," Sloan managed to say. "Just a little indigestion, I guess." He smiled wanly. "This seamstress—her husband—where did he get this information?"

"Well, that's the best part of the story," Meagan said with relish, happy to be back on the gossip track. "He got it from another officer, who got it from another officer, and so on. She said her husband told her the whole army is buzzing with it. It supposedly started with General Scott's private secretary, who overheard Scott and Lee talking about it."

"The two of them talking about it? With a secretary present? You mean it took place in General Scott's office in the War Department?"

"Yes, his office," Meagan beamed. "That's right. That's where it was."

Rufus Sloan thought furiously, all the while attempting to keep his face impassive. Colonel Robert E. Lee was the man who had captured John Brown at Harpers Ferry. This had to be the same officer Meagan was talking about. Could it actually be possible that this colonel had now been offered command of the United States Army? If so, it had to be the field command, for there had been no mention of Scott retiring yet from his post as the highest-ranking army officer. Yet given Scott's age, that retirement could not be far in the future. Was Lee even being groomed to succeed Scott as General-in-Chief when the legendary hero retired?

Such a promotion seemed so implausible as to be quite suspect. The story had passed from person to person, and Meagan O'Connor herself was hardly someone to bother her pretty golden head with strict accuracy in details. Yet it *had* to be true, if the details of this rumor were accurate. Lee had been seen—no, seen and *overheard*—talking with Scott about it. By Scott's own secretary. Why in the world would the secretary fabricate such a story, since it reflected poorly upon General Scott?

So Lee had turned down an offer from the great general. A mere colonel had turned down a grand and surprising offer from the greatest general in the country! Wait; wouldn't the *president* have to know about such an offer? Grand and imperious as he was, Scott could not make any such offer without the knowledge and permission of the Commander-in-Chief, could he?

"Meagan, did you hear who made this offer? Was it General Scott himself?"

"No." O'Connor swallowed a bit of apple. "I heard that the secretary said that the offer was made by a man who lives near the White House. A Mr. Blair, I think. Yes, that's it. Mr. Blair. I never heard of him. Have you?" She took another bite of the apple.

"No, I don't think so."

"The secretary supposedly said that both Scott and Lee knew that Mr. Blair was an intermediary, and that the offer was really coming from the president."

The president! Lee, an officer in the United States Army, turned down an offer from President Lincoln? The Commander-in-Chief himself? How could this be true?

"Meagan, are you sure about this? That Colonel Lee turned down an offer to command the army that he knew was coming from President Lincoln?"

"That's what I heard." O'Connor took another bite of the apple.

Sloan knew that Meagan, totally unknowledgeable about military protocol, did not realize that great insult Lee had given to the President of the United States by refusing the greatest military offer that it was possible for the president to bestow. Why would he do that?

"Meagan, one last question, and then you had better be getting back. Did you hear any reason why Colonel Lee refused the offer?"

"Yes. He said he couldn't invade the South."

The *South*! *That* was why! Of course! Lee was a *Virginian*! And a *slaveowner*! He couldn't make war on people like himself, genteel highborn Southern gentlemen with *slaves*! How very high-minded of him to turn down a specific request from the president and his famous general to help the United States in its hour of need, just so the precious institution of *slavery* would not be disturbed! Lee's presence at Harpers Ferry may have been an historical accident, but *this* was no accident!

Sloan could feel the once-passionate hatred he had felt for Lee rekindle.

"Thank you for your information, Meagan. You'd better be getting back now. However, if you hear any more about this Lee business, I would very much like to hear it."

O'Connor stood up. "You will, Rufus." She smiled as she left.

All that afternoon Sloan worked perfunctorily. He was polite to all customers, but his mind was elsewhere. His inner rage grew as the day lengthened. He considered Robert E. Lee, captor of John Brown, prominent slave-owner and presidential insulter, to be the most traitorous person in the entire United States.

Lee deserved death.

Sloan would be the executioner.

All he needed was a plan.

CHAPTER 31

Friday
Washington
7:03 PM

Sloan met Tilton outside the entrance to Harvey's Oyster Salon, which was not an easy thing to do. Although Harvey's was not a small place—its main oyster bar was a hundred feet long—it was packed with a boisterous crowd. Friday evening was the busiest night of the week.

Catholic religious practices forbade the eating of meat on Fridays, but fish was allowed—and oysters counted as fish. Although Catholics were not a large percentage of the population of Washington, a great many of them swelled the usual large Friday evening crowd at Harvey's, preferring to eat oysters rather than fish.

Harvey's did not have the usual restaurant arrangement of tables with waiters, although there were some tables. All patrons ordered at the huge oyster bar, which could serve fifty customers at a time. After getting in line, Tilton instructed Sloan on some of the finer points about oysters. "You can eat oysters raw or steamed," he declared, raising his voice to be heard above the happy din. "Opening an oyster is called 'shucking,' and requires a special knife. Oysters served on the half shell are raw; they open them up for you. You can take the oyster out of the half shell and dip it into a number of sauces, such as tartar, mustard, and horseradish. You can squeeze a lemon on it, as with fish. Many people prefer steamed oysters, in which the oysters are immersed in boiling water for a short time. This cooks the oyster inside the shell, and also opens the shell. Then there's oyster stew, in which cut-up pieces of oyster are cooked with potatoes and vegetables. All of them are delicious, especially here. The Harvey brothers know their business. You might want to start with some steamed oysters."

"Sounds like you come here often."

"I do indeed," Tilton agreed with a lazy grin. "Boston is a seaside city, but oysters are not as common there as here. They like warmer waters, and the Chesapeake Bay is just right for them. I've been places where you can't get any oysters at all, so I enjoy them here."

Sloan did as Tilton suggested, and ordered a dozen steamed oysters; Tilton ordered a dozen on the half shell. Tilton ate his oysters with relish, dipping them into various sauces, while Sloan tentatively bit into one. The consistency was a bit rubbery, the taste delicate and delicious. Sloan ate with increasing gusto, washing the oysters down with a mug of draft beer.

"Tell me, Sandy," Sloan said after eating half his oysters, "why do you want to join the army? You have a new office here in Washington, you're the assistant manager, I'm sure you're busy, and I'm sure you're going to become busier now that the war has started. You live well. Your family trusts you with a responsible position. Why risk it?"

Tilton squeezed a lemon over an oyster. "Suppose you were in my position, Cutter. Would you risk it?"

"I'll never be rich like you, Sandy. I'll never know what it feels like to be rich. I won't be giving up much when I join. I don't even have a family. You would be giving up a lot."

"All right, Cutter. Just pretend you were rich. You're good at pretending, aren't you? So make believe you have a family and money. Would you leave them, if just for a time, to fight slavery? Just how much does that mean to you?"

Sloan considered, slowly chewing. "You're right," he finally said. "I would give it up."

"There. You see? Now you know how I feel. But cheer up. It's only for three months. Then you can come back and do whatever you do. By the way, what *is* it you do?"

Sloan told Tilton about his job as a clerk at Grinell's Goods. The pay was fair, and the work was interesting with its steady influx of customers. Some of the customers were political; he often hear Amos Grinell discussing politics with them. He said nothing about Meagan O'Connor.

"But you don't say anything, do you?" Tilton grinned. "Quiet as a little church mouse, our Cutter."

"I have to be," Sloan said defensively. "Mr. Grinell can spout off all he wants, but he's the owner. I'm a clerk. I'm not supposed to have any opinions. And even if I did, I am expected to keep them to myself. So I do. It's an effort, but I do it."

"Don't be offended, Cutter. I admire your invisibility, and your determination to keep it that way. You're starting a new life. You're keeping your nose clean, building up a reputation as a steady dependable person. Keep it that way. It will serve you well later. I have a highly visible position in a highly visible company. There are many times I wish *I* could be invisible. The closest I ever came to it was when I was with the Old Man you know where. That was tragic, but it was the most exciting thing I've ever done in my life."

"You know, Cutter," Tilton went on earnestly, "out there we were lonely. There was just a handful of us daring to fight the good fight. Now look where we are. Less than two years later, the whole United States government is behind us! We're *winning*! When we go out to fight this time, there will be *tens of thousands* of us! We *cannot* lose! Doesn't that make you feel proud? Aren't you glad you were a part of it? All was not in vain!"

"Yes. Yes, I am," Sloan averred, downing another mouthful of beer. "I'm ready to fight again. Do you really think the war will last only three months?"

"That what all the military experts seem to say. We far outnumber the South. We have a much bigger economy, with lots of coal, steel, and ships. We will win, even if it takes longer than three months. And if it does, so what? You and I will be signing up for only three months. We can leave after that. Or stay on, if we like. It will be another grand adventure."

"I'll drink to that." Sloan finished his mug of beer with a flourish.

"Careful there, my friend. That was your second mug. It can hit you later. The whole idea coming here was to eat oysters, not get sloshed on beer. Besides, I have something to show you."

"So show me."

"Not here. It's in my room. Let's finish up and we can go there. Like oysters now?"

"Love them."

"For a minute there I thought you liked the beer more."

"Love beer now, too. Don't get to drink much of it."

"I can tell. Let's go."

Tilton led the way outside, through a crowd that was still milling to enter Harvey's. They turned east on C Street and followed it four blocks to its oblique intersection with Pennsylvania Avenue, which was also its intersection with 7th Street. Going north on 7th Street, it was a short distance to Tilton's boarding house. This was a larger and finer boarding house than the one in which Sloan resided on 4th Street, almost a small hotel.

"Not bad," Sloan observed.

"It's even better inside," Tilton replied.

It was. A modest but ornate sitting room was to the right of the entrance, with a fine carpet and leather chairs. A small chandelier hung in the entrance hall. The polished brass of several lamps gleamed like California gold. Carpeting that matched that of the entrance hall flowed up a wide staircase with a well-waxed mahogany balustrade.

Tilton's room was on the second floor at the front. It was actually a suite, with a separate bedroom. As with all boarding houses, there was no kitchen; breakfasts and dinners were served in a common room on the first floor. Windows in the parlor and the bedroom, framed by drapes, looked out on the bustle of 7th Street.

Sloan sat down in a comfortable chair as Tilton lit two lamps. "Why not move your company office here, Sandy? It can't be any better than this."

Tilton laughed. "Yes, I like it." He went into the bedroom and returned a few moments later with a medium-size box, which he placed in Sloan's lap. "Open it."

Sloan opened the box. Inside it was a pistol. It was brand new and quite big.

"It's one of the new Remington Army model revolvers," Tilton said proudly. "I bought it yesterday. This is what army officers are issued. Privates are issued muskets. However, I thought if I bought one of these myself, the army would let me keep it. Go ahead, pick it up."

Sloan took it out of the box. "It's heavy."

"That's because it fires a big bullet—a .44 caliber. The weight of the gun helps to minimize the recoil. I haven't fired it yet, but I'm told it has a healthy kick. You have to hold it firmly, and let it ride upwards a bit after each shot. If you try to fire it too rapidly, the shots will go all over the place. There's a smaller, lighter version, a .36 caliber, used by the navy; it's called the Navy model."

Sloan examined the pistol carefully. "Is it loaded?"

"No. I probably won't load it until after I'm in the army." Tilton paused. "We had muskets and Sharps rifles at Harpers Ferry. Have you ever handled a pistol?"

"No. I wasn't much for guns when I was growing up. I went out hunting a few times with my father. He had an old gun that I shot several times. A flintlock."

"Ah. Well, the new caplock technology has really transformed guns. Especially pistols. It's next to impossible to make a multiple-shot gun with flintlock ignition. As far as I know, nobody ever figured out how to do it. But with caplocks, you can. See, you have a rotating barrel with a number of chambers in it—this gun has six—each of which can contain a bullet and the powder. On the back of each chamber is a little nipple, where you push on a firing cap."

"Like a Sharps," Sloan interrupted.

"Exactly, Cutter. Like a Sharps rifle. Only instead of a single shot, here you have six shots. All you have to do is pull the trigger.

The secret is in the advancing mechanism, which automatically and precisely rotates the barrel to the next chamber when you pull the trigger. You can understand how precise that mechanism has to be. In fact, how precise *everything* has to be. If each chamber is not perfectly aligned with the barrel when it fires, then the bullet will jam and the gun will blow up in your hand. But it *is* aligned perfectly. So now you have six shots just by pulling the trigger. Amazing, isn't it?"

Sloan looked at the pistol with interest and respect. "So how is it actually loaded?"

"Here, I'll show you." Tilton went back into the bedroom and returned with two smaller boxes, which he placed on a table. "This box contains cartridges," he said, taking off the lid of one. He took one out and showed it to Sloan; it was a paper container with a round metal ball, about the size of a marble, attached to it. "One of the problems with older guns was knowing exactly how much powder to put into them. Two little and the bullet would not go far enough; too much and the gun might explode. Here the manufacturer provides you with exactly the right amount of powder. You just tear open this little paper container and pour in the powder. Then you ram it tight. Then you put in the bullet, the round lead ball, and ram it in also." Tilton did not actually open a cartridge and insert either powder or bullet, but demonstrated how it would be done, using the gun's self-contained ramrod. "Now you would have loaded one chamber. Do it to all six chambers and the gun is fully loaded. To actually make it fire you have to install a firing cap for each chamber." He opened the other box and took out a firing cap. It was a circular silver-colored disc, resembling a small silver coin. Pressing a small lever, he opened up the left side of the gun, revealing the back side of several of the chambers. "You take one of these caps and press it on that nipple on the back of the chamber. When the hammer strikes the cap, which contains fulminate of mercury, it detonates. The force of the detonation goes through that small hole in the center of the nipple, which sets off the powder, which pushes out the bullet. Using your hand, you rotate the barrel until you have placed a cap on each of the nipples. The gun is now ready to fire. When you reload, you remove a used cap and throw it away. That's it."

"Oh, there is one precaution they warned me about," Tilton added. "If you're going to carry a loaded gun for a while, it is advisable not to put a firing cap on the chamber directly under the hammer. This prevents the gun from accidentally firing if it receives a sudden shock, such as being dropped."

Sloan was fascinated. "Looks simple enough, once you get used to it."

"Is is simple. Takes a little time to reload, but then you're a shootin' fool. It's also weatherproof. Ever try to shoot a flintlock in the rain? If the powder in the pan gets wet, you're done."

"I don't remember."

"Well, I just thought you would like to see it." Tilton gathered up the gun, cartridge, and firing cap, and put them back into their respective boxes. He then took them back into the bedroom. Sloan casually followed him, and saw Tilton put them away into the top of an armoire.

"Thanks, Sandy. I'd better be going now."

"I would offer you a drink, my friend, but I think it's the last thing you need. Are you sure you will be all right?"

"Yes. It's only three blocks. I live on 4th Street."

"Think about when you would want to enlist, so we can do it together. I think we should do it some time next week."

"I will, Sandy. Thanks again for the oysters. I would like to do that soon again."

"We will." Tilton opened the door. "Good night."

"Good night."

CHAPTER 32

Friday
Arlington House
7:38 PM

"There, that's better."

Robert E. Lee had just finished igniting the kindling to a fire in the family parlor. He sat down, and all three men in the parlor gazed silently at the slowly growing fire, each busy with his own thoughts. The rest of the Lee family was scattered throughout the house, busy with their after-dinner activities, some in the white parlor across the entrance hall.

"I asked the two of you here," Lee slowly began, "to help me with some difficult decisions. Custis, you are my eldest son. You will inherit this property. My decisions may very well affect the destiny of this property, so you should not only have a knowledge of them, but a say in them. Mr. Cosby, you are a representative of the governor, even if in a nonpolitical matter as agriculture. You were a companion in arms in the Mexican War, even if we did not know each other then. In your short time here you have had a great and favorable impact on our family, especially Annie; she is ecstatic about your suggestion to build a vineyard and winery here. Even though you are not a member of the family, you are a distinguished guest whose advice I would value."

"I am honored, Colonel."

"Yesterday morning," Lee continued, "I met with Mr. Francis P. Blair at his home on Pennsylvania Avenue; it is very close to the Executive Mansion. Mr. Blair, as you may know, holds no position in the government. However, he has been a valued advisor to many presidents, including Mr. Lincoln, our new president; one of his sons is the Postmaster General in Lincoln's cabinet. Mr. Blair, clearly acting at the behest of the president, offered me the command of the huge new army the government is raising."

"What!" Custis Lee exclaimed. "Father, you have not mentioned this before!"

"No, I have not. The reason is that I have had to do a great deal of thinking, not only about that offer but also many things related to it."

"What did you reply to Mr. Blair?" Custis pursued.

"I refused, as politely as I could."

Silence. "May I ask why, Colonel?" Cosby finally asked.

"I took an oath to defend the United States against all enemies, Carter. I think secession is foolish and divisive; I am against it. However, I do not see the people in seceded states as enemies. To me they are still Americans, a point of view which I believe even President Lincoln still espouses. A war in which the North invades the South will be a disaster; for me to be the leader of that army of invasion is unthinkable. And let us not forget that this state of Virginia, where I and so many of my forebears have been born, may be one of the states invaded. For me to lead the army that may very well invade the state where I and my children live is not only unthinkable, it is beyond imagination. I simply cannot do it."

"And you said all this to Mr. Blair?" Cosby asked after a moment.

"I did. Quite explicitly."

Custis Lee stood up and walked over to his parent, taking his hand. "For whatever it is worth, father, I think you did the right thing," he said huskily. "I support you completely. And I have never been prouder of you than I am at this moment. Even prouder than the day I graduated from West Point, with you in attendance as the Superintendant." He kissed his father lightly on the top of the head.

"Thank you, son." Lee gripped his son's hand tightly for a moment. "What about you, Carter?" he asked as Custis resumed his seat.

"It is obviously your decision to make, Colonel. If you believe that strongly about it—and you undoubtedly do—then you made the right choice."

"Thank you both. That settles the matter to my complete satisfaction. I feel very much better about it. However, it immediately raises several other points. I next must tell you that after leaving Mr. Blair, I went to the War Department to meet with General Scott, at his order."

"What happened there?" Custis inquired.

"I related what had just happened at Blair's house. It is clear that the general recommended me to the president, for which I am very grateful. However, it seems the president did not then order General Scott to offer me the position; the offer was made as a request, rather than an order, and it was made privately. General Scott obviously knew the offer would be made, but did not know how or when. I told him."

"What was his response?"

"He was upset, son. From his point of view, I understand." Lee was silent a moment. "General Scott and I have been together a long time," he continued reflectively. "Do you know that he was born in 1786? That's only a decade after the Declaration of Independence. It's only three years after the Treaty of Paris. It's a year *before* the Constitution was written. He was three years old the year that George Washington was inaugurated as the first President of the United States. In a real sense, he is as old as the country."

"He has been in the army for more than half a century. He has fought along the Canadian border and in Mexico. He fought against the British in the War of 1812 and was awarded a gold medal by Congress. He has fought against Indians many times. He was the officer in charge of the relocation of the Cherokees from their homeland across the Mississippi to the Indian Territory, a tragic event. He was the commanding officer of U.S. Army troops in

Charleston Harbor during the Nullification Crisis in 1832, when South Carolina's actions almost ignited a civil war. He was the commanding officer of the army in Mexico, for which he was awarded another gold medal by Congress and which opened up the new lands to the West. And he has been the highest-ranking officer in the army for twenty years. He was even a candidate for president. Perhaps more than any other person—certainly more than any person alive—General Scott has shaped the United States into what it is today. He is truly a great man. That such a man would consider me worthy of commanding the largest army in American history is an indescribable honor. Still," Lee lowered and shook his head, "I cannot do it."

"Your appreciation of General Scott only makes your own decision more admirable," Custis commented.

"Thank you, Custis. I only meant to point out that the general sees things differently than we do. He was born in Virginia—in Petersburg, south of Richmond—but he does not think of himself as a Virginian. To him, Virginia just happens to be the state in which he was born. He does not live here, and has not for a very long time. Right now he lives in a house in Washington. He is naturally an advocate of the national government. He also tends to see people as either enemies or friends. To him the seceded states are rebels, enemies which must be militarily crushed. Period. I simply do not see things that way. I am gratified that you don't, either."

There was silence again. The fire in the grate was going well now, hissing and crackling. None of the lamps had been lit, and the light of the fire was the only illumination in the darkened room.

"I have told you that General Scott was disappointed," Lee continued, his face partly in shadow. "He said several things to me which have struck me deeply."

"What sort of things, father?"

"For one thing, he said my position was equivocal. I took that to mean that he disapproved of my desire to remain in the army after turning down a presidential offer. He also questioned my trustworthiness. If I turned down the offer to command the army because I disapproved the invasion of the South, how could any officer trust me to obey orders completely if I remained in the army while it *was* invading the South?"

"Sounds like the general was suggesting that you resign," Cosby commented quietly.

"That was also my interpretation, Carter."

"Did you resign?"

"No. I replied that I would think about what he said."

"Resign?" Custis exclaimed. "Why should you have to resign, father? You have not disobeyed an order. Nobody *ordered* you to accept that position. It was a *request*, an *offer*. It is not insubordination to decline an offer. Even General Scott could not cashier you for insubordination."

"You are right, Custis," Cosby said. "It was not insubordination. Not officially, anyway. However, if I follow your father correctly, he is considering resigning not because of what General Scott thinks, but because of what *he* thinks. Is that right, Colonel?"

"Thank you, Carter. It is clear that this army will be used to invade the South. I cannot lead it, and I have already refused that position. The question for me now is this: if this army is indeed going to invade the South, but with someone else in command, can I be a party to it in *any* position? How can I morally be a follower in something which I have said that it would be immoral to lead? If something is wrong, it is wrong. If I claim that it would be morally wrong for me to give the orders in such an enterprise, how can it become morally right for me by following the orders of someone else? I cannot evade the moral responsibility simply by shifting the burden of command."

"You are right, father. It would still be wrong, regardless of your position."

"Therefore there is no role for you in this army of invasion. But if there is no role for you there, the question then becomes: is there any role for you in the army at all?" Cosby finished.

"Precisely, Carter. Is there any role for me at all? I cannot think of any position in the army which would not be connected, in some manner, to the invasion. Even if I were placed in charge of some supply depot in California, three thousand miles away, I could not escape; California was admitted to the Union officially as a free state, and would be sending supplies and troops in support of the invasion. Therefore to remain in the army at all, in any position, would mean that I am a party to the very thing I refused to command. I do not see how I can do that."

"Father, how can you resign? You have given your entire adult life to the army! Moreover, you love the army. It has taken you many places. Some of them I remember, because you took us there. Do you know what my earliest memory of any trip is?"

"No, son, I don't," Lee said kindly. "What is is?"

"It is the trip we took to St. Louis in the spring of '38. I didn't really know the date then. You had been stationed there the previous year, doing some work on the Mississippi. Then you came back home for Christmas and stayed in Washington for several months. When it came time to return to St. Louis, you and mother decided that we should all go: the two of you, myself, and even Rooney, although he was less than a year old. Even our nurse, Kitty, went with us. Mary stayed here with grandfather and grandmother. Rooney doesn't remember any of it, but I do. I was five years old. We went to Baltimore, then Philadelphia, Pittsburgh, Cincinnati, Louisville, then up the Mississippi to St. Louis. I had never even heard of steamboats before we boarded one in Pittsburgh to go down the Ohio River. I remember that all that summer several boys and myself, including little Rooney, played steamboat; we dressed up in special clothes, wore bells, and made steam noises."

"Since then I have thought about that trip many times, and realized how lucky I was. How many other five-year-old boys have had a chance to see what I saw? It was the finest time of my youth. I owe it to you—and the army."

Lee smiled. "I remember that trip also," he said quietly. "It was a great adventure. I can't tell you how proud I was of your mother that she would agree to take such a trip with two small boys, one less than a year old. But do you know what I remember most about that trip?" He gestured toward the two large portraits that hung in the room, one of himself and the other of Mrs. Lee. "These portraits. They were painted on that trip, in Baltimore. I had made previous arrangements for mine, and initially your mother was resistant to the notion of having one done of her. However, as my portrait neared completion, she liked it so much that she agreed to have her portrait painted, but only if it were done by the same artist. That unexpected development meant that our trip was delayed for a week. I fretted that I was going to have to explain to my superior officer and the War Department that my delay in reporting for duty was caused by having our portraits painted! Most unmilitary. As it turned out, the subject never came up." Lee smiled at the recollection. "Such travel was subject to many delays in those days. Everyone was simply happy that we had made it safely."

The three men again stared at the fire.

"You are right, son," Lee finally sighed. "I have been with the army all my adult life. All that I am, I owe to the army. I do love it so." He paused. "I will have to consider the matter a bit more." He turned toward Cosby. "What are your thoughts, Carter?"

"Well, Colonel, it seems to me that there are three issues here, all intertwined." Cosby opened his right hand and started ticking off the issues with his fingers. "The first is the question of command. That has already been decided; you have declined a specific offer to do it. The second is the question of your resignation, since the army certainly seems destined to do the very thing which caused you to decline the offer of command. You will ponder that matter further. The third matter is the question of Virginia's secession. We do not yet know what will happen in that regard. However, it seems to me that the seizure of the Harpers Ferry arsenal by the state militia yesterday is a strong indication. Even more tellingly, you will note that the state government in Richmond has not disavowed that action, such as claiming it to be some sort of mistake by the militia; it has simply kept silent on the matter. That hints very strongly that the seizure was deliberate, and that the state militia may very well soon seize other Federal installations in Virginia. It may well be that the state convention in Richmond has already voted for secession, and that we here simply do not know about it yet."

"Let us postulate some scenarios, Colonel. Suppose you resign from the army, and Virginia does not secede. I think that would be the best possible situation. You would be a private citizen of the United States, working on your estate here. You are already doing that successfully, although you are still in the army. It would be peaceful. I think it is safe to say that no Confederate army could penetrate this far north, right to the outskirts of Washington itself, across a loyal Virginia."

"I would agree," Lee commented.

"Second scenario: you resign, and Virginia secedes. If it does, it would naturally soon join the Confederacy. That means the very land where we are now sitting would be claimed by the Confederacy. But could it enforce that claim? Could a Confederate army occupy this very land, or nearby land, overlooking the Union capital and dare a Federal army to come force it out? I would like your professional military opinion on that precise point."

Lee thought silently a few moments. "If Virginia seceded," he finally said, "and I were in charge of the defense of Washington, one of the very first things I would do is to seize the entire Virginia heights above the Potomac. Strategically, it is simply too valuable to allow the Confederacy to even think of controlling it. All of Washington would then be open to artillery bombardment. That alone, even the threat of it, would probably be enough to end the war in a Confederate victory."

"I could hardly disagree with the chief of artillery in the Mexican War when it comes to artillery bombardments," Cosby said with a smile. "But you know where that leads, don't you, Colonel? It means that all the Virginia heights, including Arlington—probably *especially* Arlington—will be seized by the Union, sooner rather than later, if Virginia secedes. And it may already have seceded," he added softly.

"Yes, I know," Lee said glumly. "Have you any other scenarios, Carter? Perhaps a happier one?"

"There is this, Colonel. Suppose you resign, Virginia secedes and then joins the Confederacy, the United States Army invades, and there is a devastating civil war—but the Confederacy wins. Victory for the Confederacy would consist not in conquering the United States, but in proving that the United States cannot conquer the Confederacy, and must therefore politically recognize it as a separate country. In the peace treaty the territorial integrity of Virginia would be assured, and therefore your ownership of your lands would be confirmed. You would still be here, but you would be living in a new country."

"To enjoy the fruits of thousands of dead men who fought in my stead?" Lee exclaimed with heat. "While I, a military officer with thirty years experience, sat out the war as a civilian, depending on others to save me? That would be the basest of cowardice," he asserted strongly. "It is humiliating to contemplate. Besides, during all the time of the war, I would be a tenant farmer on my own property, subject to the whims of a military overseer. And, of course, the Confederacy might not win at all, meaning the confiscation of my property would stand and it would be lost forever."

"I merely pointed out the possibility," Cosby shrugged. "Let me ask you the key question, as I see it. If the Lord Almighty stood before you this very moment, and revealed to you that Virginia would indeed secede and join the Confederacy, and knowing that if you resigned from the United States Army that it would mean the loss of Arlington and your other estates, would you still resign?"

Lee was silent for a time. The fire, now slowly dying, snapped in the grate. "If the Lord Almighty Himself appeared before me this moment," Lee finally said in a slow voice, "I hope He would not consider me sacrilegious if I asked that this cup could be taken from me. Failing that, I would ask for wisdom. When Solomon asked God for wisdom, God was so pleased that He granted wisdom to Solomon as well as many other things." He paused for a moment, then looked at Cosby. "You have indeed posed the key question, Carter. I cannot answer now. I must ponder still."

"Whatever your decision, father, remember that I support you. Despite the possible calamities which Mr. Cosby has so clearly pointed out, I trust you to make the right decision. Whatever it will be, I fully support you. And I cannot imagine any member of this household doing otherwise."

"Thank you, Custis," Lee said with feeling. "You cannot imagine how comforted I am by that thought."

The three were silent again. The flickering flames threw dancing shadows on the walls. The dying fire seemed a too-real symbol of all the decades of happy life at Arlington, a portent of the coming calamity that not even the comforting walls of the great mansion could hold back.

"The hour grows late, gentlemen," Lee finally said. "We must bid each other good night. However, I do not think that mine will be a good one."

Custis Lee and Carter Cosby arose, shook hands with Lee, and left. After a while Lee walked over to the remains of the fire, took a poker, and silently scattered the embers.

* * * * *

Carter Cosby lay awake in bed in the first-floor guest room, thinking about the events of the past few days and marveling at the prescience of Jefferson Davis. The Confederate president had correctly predicted Lincoln's massive call for army volunteers, and also the offer to Lee to command that huge new army. It also appeared that Davis would be right on another point, the most important of all: Virginia's secession. If Virginia, the "Mother of Presidents," and with a land area as large as all of New England, actually did secede, then other border states would surely follow. Davis' dream of a 13-state Confederacy no longer looked like a fevered imagining, but an oncoming reality about to be born. Such a large Confederacy might very well prove to be unconquerable, which would mean that the United States would be forced to recognize it as an independent nation, precisely the fondest hope of Jefferson Davis.

The fate of Robert E. Lee was very small compared to the fate of Virginia. However, it was not unimportant. Cosby's assignment from Davis had been to nudge Lee against accepting the offer of command, and also nudge him in the direction of resignation from the army. As far as the command offer was concerned, Lee had decided that for himself; Cosby had not even known about it until Lee revealed it a few hours ago. Now the question of resignation was at the door, and it was clear Lee would also decide that for himself. Cosby realized that any words of his could not persuade Lee to do anything; despite his aristocratic charm, Lee had a forceful personality. It turned out that it was General Scott who was doing the nudging, if not outright prodding, despite his long friendship with Lee.

Cosby felt certain that Lee would resign. Lee's sense of honor would force him into the decision he personally felt so wrenching. His reluctance to resign could not overcome his revulsion to invading the South and waging bloody war against fellow Americans, even fellow Virginians. Although Lee had never expressed his position in precisely this manner, Cosby felt he could summarize it this way: although Lee opposed secession, he would rather see a successful Confederacy emerge without a war than to see the Confederacy invaded, beaten, and crushed in a massive bloody civil war. And to lead that invasion, even to take part in it, was, in his own word, "unthinkable." So resignation it would be.

The last part of the mission he had agreed to undertake consisted of assisting Lee to accept an offer of command from his own state. When Virginia later joined the Confederacy, Lee would become a high-ranking Confederate officer. This was one scenario that he had not mentioned in the discussion in the parlor several hours ago. Suppose Lee resigned, Virginia seceded, and then the state asked for hs military services to help protect it against the forthcoming invasion. Would Lee accept?

Cosby felt it was premature to raise that question. There were too many suppositions piled on top of each other. Let Lee's resignation proceed at its own pace, then let Virginia's secession—if it actually came to pass—proceed at *its* own pace. He could not really influence either one. After both were accomplished facts, *then* the question of a Virginia command could legitimately be raised. But such an offer would have to come from the Virginia government; he, Cosby, could certainly not make any such offer. It would be inappropriate to even mention the possibility of it before it actually happened.

How would it happen? And when? Perhaps it would not even happen at all. Governor Letcher had not mentioned it. Perhaps what would happen is that Virginia would secede, then join the Confederacy, and then an offer of command would come directly from the Confederacy itself—perhaps even from Jefferson Davis personally—with no intervening Virginia command. That could take weeks. Cosby could be gone from Arlington by then.

Cosby tried to examine his own feelings in the matter. When he first accepted the assignment in Montgomery, Robert E. Lee was only a name to him, dimly remembered. Now he had met that magnetic man, and liked him very much. It seems everybody did. He was lying in a comfortable guest bed in Lee's grand house, in which family history hung so heavily. The family was charming and delightful, the estate magnificent, the spectacular view without equal. And all of it was in jeopardy.

Cosby felt a mild sense of shame that he was part of the reason that the Lee family and its grand estate was in jeopardy. Although it was true that Lee was the one making the decisions, Cosby felt sadness that he was even supportive of those decisions. Yet what could he do? Tell the Lee family to start packing right now and leave their home to escape the future Federal onslaught?

And what about Annie? Cosby realized he was becoming very attracted to her. She reminded him so much of Letitia, although she was a bit younger. He also felt some guilt about raising her hopes with talk of a vineyard and winery, as if merely discussing them implied an assurance that the land would remain peaceful and secure enough to allow such an enterprise. If war came, her dreams would be shattered. But then, so would everyone else's. Even his own.

He knew that if he could have his own way, there would be no war, and he could pursue and court Annie, perhaps marry her. He could help her build the vineyard and winery here at Arlington. He could take her back to Cymru, and perhaps every six months they could alternate their place of residence. Of course, if he could have had his own way, Letitia would never have died.

Enough of fantasies. Cosby turned over and tried to sleep.

Later he awakened with an urge to go to the bathroom. There was one at the end of the hall just outside the guest room door. He opened the door, turned right, and found the water closet. Finished, he wandered silently through the first floor of the house. There was so much beauty here, so much graciousneess, so much history. He noted details that he would like to incorporate into his own house at Cymru. Was it really possible that the horrors of war might soon deprive this wonderful family of this home, simply because it was situated so close to the capital city of what might soon become an enemy country?

On an impulse, Cosby quietly opened the rear door of the house and stepped out. He walked around the house and then across part of the front lawn, his slippers insulating him from the cold wetness of the dewy grass.

The grand view of the city of Washington was even more enchanting and magical by night and moonlight than by day and sunlight. The major thoroughfares were outlined by the soft yellow glow of street lamps, which by their regular spacing and uniform height imparted a greater sense of orderliness and purpose than the streets exhibited during the bustling day. The great flood of silver-white moonlight highlighted the moon-facing sides of buildings in bright relief, casting the other sides into deep shadow. The bulk of the domeless capitol building and the stump of the Washington Monument were clearly discernible, while the distant pale gleam of the Executive Mansion was certainly congruent with its sobriquet, the White House. The ghostly shimmering ribbon of the Potomac seemed like part of an heroic moat that should encircle the metropolis and complete the illusion that it was a fairyland, happily isolated from the cares and storms of a hostile world. Erroneous though such an illusion might be, it was almost a sensory overload to take in this sweeping compelling vista.

Cosby turned and walked back to the rear of the house. All was dark except for a dim glow from one of the second-story windows. He knew that the room behind that window was the master bedroom of Mr. and Mrs. Lee. A low-set lamp, or a candle, was lit in that room, in the middle of the night. The Lees were sleepless. It was indeed not a good night for Robert E. Lee.

CHAPTER 33

Saturday, April 20
Arlington House
8:04 AM

Mildred, the youngest of the Lee children, was the last to arrive for breakfast, seating herself after her sisters. As soon as the entire family was at the table, Robert E. Lee stood up. Normally the picture of vigor and vitality in the morning, full of enthusiasm for the day's projects, this morning he looked drawn and haggard. Nevertheless, he forced a smile.

"My children," he began, "your mother and I have been up most of the night, considering our position. I must reveal to you all that last Thursday I was offered field command of the large new army that the government is raising." A buzz went around the table, as none there had heard about it except Mrs. Lee, Custis, and Carter Cosby. Lee held up his hand. "Please. Let me finish. I declined the position, because this army will be used to invade the South, and I cannot be a party to such a thing. My good friend General Scott was very upset with me. That is understandable, as he was the one who recommended me for the position to the president. Therefore, after a great deal of thought and prayer, I have reached a decision, although it is not one which makes me the least bit happy." He picked up two letters from the table and held them up. "One of these is to Simon Cameron, the Secretary of War. It is a short note, informing him that I am resigning my commission as an officer in the United States Army." Lee held up his hand again as another buzz started. "The other is a letter to General Scott, informing him of the same thing. However, I have included a brief explanation stating why I have felt compelled to take the action I did. I think that is the least I could do, given the long and respectful relationship between us. I considered General Scott to be a good friend as well as my superior officer, and I genuinely regret that the path dictated by my conscience runs counter to the path dictated by his." Lee paused and looked around the table. "It seems as though I have become a gentleman farmer. Since that is much of what I have been doing for the last several years, perhaps there will be little change in our status here."

After the expected questions, the table talk was desultory. There was not the slightest attempt on the part of anyone to talk Lee out of his decision, but the knowledge of what he had done weighed heavily on everyone. Lee had been in the army for the entire lives of all of his children. They all knew a major chapter in their lives was being closed, and no one knew what the next chapter would bring.

Later in the morning a courier arrived from Alexandria. He carried a letter from a John Robertson, who was staying at a hotel in Alexandria and who wished to meet personally with Lee on a matter of private business. Since Lee did not know Robertson, and since the matter of the meeting was not specified nor was there any indication of urgency, Lee replied by the same courier that he would meet with Robertson the following day after Sunday worship services at Christ Church in Alexandria, where the Lee family habitually worshipped. The meeting would take place in the churchyard.

CHAPTER 34

Saturday
Washington
11:56 AM

The luncheon was not due to start officially until noon, but everyone was so excited they all arrived early. All except Phoebe MacPherson, of course. Phee was always late.

The eleven of them sat around a large table in the dining room of the National Hotel, situated on the northeast corner of 6th Street and Pennsylvania Avenue. The National was the natural gathering place for people in Washington who held Southern views, a counterweight to Willard's Hotel eight blocks farther up Pennsylvania Avenue at 14th. Though not quite so grand as Willard's, the five floors of the National held spacious accommodations—fifty double rooms, eight single rooms, and ten parlors. With its pillared portico and understated gracious charm, it had exactly the elegant ambiance that appealed to Southern gentry and others who had a romantic view of Southern life.

The loose but elite social group of which Rose O'Neal Greenhow was a part met here for lunch at irregular intervals. All were Southern sympathizers, from tepid to rabid, so Greenhow felt right at home. She knew all these people well, and had entertained them often in her home. She listened to the buzzing table talk as the group waited for Phee MacPherson.

"Virginia has *done* it!" Dr. Anton Ashby exclaimed. He was a tall thin man with the disconcerting habit of blinking rapidly when excited. "I really thought Virginia might stay in the Union. When I heard about its secession last night, I couldn't *believe* it!" He blinked four times in quick succession. "This is the best possible news!"

"Wasn't it *clever* of the Virginians to vote for secession and then keep it a secret?" Myrtle Evans chimed in. "Nobody knew about it until the state militia was ready to pounce. All the Federal properties in the state were caught by surprise." That wasn't quite true, as news of the secession had become known last night, but everyone forgave Myrtle in their enthusiasm. Besides, even though most Federal officials in Virginia had learned about the secession, they put up no resistance when the properties were seized this morning.

"The Federals are putting up a real battle at Norfolk, I hear," said Oliver Miller, sipping a glass of water as a waiter brought a silver pot of coffee to the table.

"And no wonder," added Asa Whitlock. He was the most distinguished-looking man at the table, with a square clean-shaven jaw and a carefully-combed head of silver-gray hair. He would have made a perfect-looking politician, but was a speculator in western lands. "That is perhaps the greatest naval base in the Union. *Was* in the Union, I should say. Losing it would be almost as great a disaster for the Union as losing the whole state of Virginia. Mark my word, they'll fight to hold onto it."

"Then they'll have to fight plenty hard," observed Donnell Moncure, the lawyer. "They can't get any reinforcements. It's almost like Fort Sumter, except this time the Federals are in a harbor surrounded by land, instead of a fort surrounded by water. I don't think they can last."

As if on cue, Phoebe MacPherson appeared, waving a newspaper. "The latest edition," she cried, accepting the assistance of two of the men as she seated herself. She had the most unusual occupation of the group. She owned a company in Baltimore which made, of all things, steam engines. It had been started by her late husband, a Scottish-born engineer, and was left to her upon his death. Since she knew nothing of steam engines, she was content to let managers run it while she lived in Washington, which she much preferred to the industrial grittiness of Baltimore. She did not sell it and invest the proceeds in an enterprise she knew something about because she enjoyed occasional trips to the shops in Baltimore, where she could watch, fascinated, as "her" sweaty men hammered sheet iron and riveted boilers, and experience the giant reptilian hiss of live steam, malodorously mixed with oil, venting from steam valves. She loved the clangor of great enterprises, equating noise with importance. Phee MacPherson *adored* being important.

The newspaper was full of the secret secession vote of the Virginia Convention last Wednesday, but everyone already knew about that; the National had subscriptions to several newspapers, if they hadn't already read their own. What it did have of immediate interest was late news of the fighting in Norfolk.

"Fierce Fighting," the headline screamed as MacPherson animatedly read it to the table. "Union Forces Holding Their Own."

"Ha! I'll bet they are," Ashby chortled, blinking twice.

"Anything about the ships there?" Whitlock asked.

"Wait—yes, here's something. 'Several ships deliberately set on fire. The most important of these is the U.S.S. *Merrimac*, the latest and fastest steam frigate in the Navy.'" MacPherson looked up, puzzled. "Why would they do that?"

"That means the Federals are *losing*, Phee," Jesse Dabney exclaimed gleefully. "They're setting fire to their own ships to prevent the militia from getting them. They even set fire to their most important one. The Virginians would never set those ships afire—they *want* them. So the bluecoats are *losing.*"

"Aha! I *knew* it!" Moncure grinned knowingly.

Everyone ordered their meals, and the table talk continued. Greenhow contributed little, content to listen to the others excitedly talk. She had an enormous feeling of satisfaction. Not only were events unfolding in favor of the Confederacy, but the information of Mr. Thomas about Virginia's secession had proven to be absolutely correct. He could therefore be trusted, and she looked forward with no little anticipation to providing valuable information to him and to the Confederacy.

The meals arrived, but the conversation barely slowed even as the group ate. Greenhow had ordered an omelet containing a favorite delicacy, one of Virginia's greatest contributions to world cuisine—Smithfield ham. Its distinctive tang was so strong it could be eaten only in tiny portions. There were flakes of it in her omelet, along with sliced scallions, green peppers, and cheddar cheese. Greenhow took a bite of it, and let its palette of complementary flavors sensuously explode on her palate. It was the purest ambrosia.

"Oh, my, I almost forgot," Phee rattled on. "Have you all heard about Colonel Robert E. Lee? He was offered field command of the Federal army, but turned it down. A *Virginian*! Isn't that simply *grand*?"

Greenhow's second forkful of ambrosia abruptly stopped in midair. *Lee!* She considered herself perhaps the best-informed private citizen in Washington, yet she had not heard anything about any such offer. Neither had any of the others at the table.

"Who is this Colonel Lee?" Whitlock asked of MacPherson. "I never heard of him."

"I didn't either," Phee admitted. "I just heard he was the one who was offered the position, and turned it down."

"I know who he is," Miller volunteered. "He's one of the Lees of Virginia, perhaps the most distinguished family in the state. Been in the army for years. Engineers, I believe. Lives on a great estate in the Potomac Heights. Can't remember its name."

"Arlington," Rose Greenhow said quietly. "Its name is Arlington."

Miller turned to Greenhow, snapping his fingers. "That's right, Rose. Arlington. Have you ever been there?"

"No. Have you?"

"No. And I never met Lee."

"I haven't either. But I've heard of him, too. How was the offer made?" Greenhow asked MacPherson, keeping her tone conversational with an effort.

"Well, I heard it this morning from Louise Phillips, who heard it from her husband, who heard it from a saddler, who heard it from an army officer," Phee gushed, delighted to be the center of attention. "The officer said the news was going all around the army. It happened Thursday morning. Colonel Lee talked with General Scott at the War Department, and explained why he could not accept the command. Scott was *mad.* A secretary in Scott's office heard it all, and spread the story." She grinned from ear to ear. "Isn't it *wonderful*?"

"Why couldn't Lee accept?" Moncure asked quickly.

"Because he would be invading the South," Phee replied. "Maybe even his own state. He couldn't do that."

"Sounds accurate enough to me," Whitlock opined, joining in MacPherson's grin.

"Ho, ho," Dabney chortled. "So our Virginia colonel not only snubbed Old Abe, he even turned down Scott. *That* must have *really* ruffled the feathers of Old Fuss and Feathers."

"Can you imagine Abe Lincoln having to ask a *colonel* to lead the army?" Agatha Philpott asked rhetorically.

"He has to," Moncure gloated, between bites of roast turkey. "He's scraping the bottom of the barrel. All the other officers have gone South." Everyone laughed.

Rose Greenhow joined in the general merriment, but behind her smiling face she began to think. Everyone at the table was treating this surprising information about Lee as so much delicious gossip, painfully embarrassing to the awkward new abolitionist-leaning president and the haughty old general, and therefore grist for the scandal mills feeding Southern pride. But there was much more, as she knew from Thomas. Greenhow noted that Phee MacPherson had not really answered her question: *how* had Lee been offered the command? Could Lincoln have offered it to him in person? That didn't seem likely, or the meeting itself would have been an item of frantic gossip. Perhaps he had done it in a letter. Perhaps he had used an intermediary, or perhaps Scott himself had made the offer. Yet Lee had come to Scott's office to explain why he couldn't accept. That sounded like Scott knew about the offer before it was made, yet hadn't been the one to make it. However it was done, Greenhow was certain of one thing: Scott was heavily involved. Either he had made the offer directly himself, or he had recommended Lee to President Lincoln, who had made the offer in some manner. Unlike his

Confederate counterpart, Jeff Davis, Lincoln had no military experience and would never have offered such a military position to anyone without Scott's prior recommendation.

Why hadn't Mr. Thomas mentioned anything about this offer? He probably hadn't known at the time, Greenhow realized. The two of them had met less than a day after the incident had happened. She knew nothing of the movements of Thomas, or where he lived. He may not have even been in Washington when it happened. He surely knew now. The Virginia governor's attempt to reach Lee, whatever it was, must be getting frantic.

Greenhow's mind distanced from the gloating chatter around her, even the savor of the omelet forgotten as she continued to eat mechanically. Howevermuch people might poke fun at the rough-edged *persona* of the haughty old general, no one whom she knew—absolutely *no one*—had anything but the highest respect for the military acumen of Winfield Scott. He was a legend in his own time, and deservedly so. Greenhow did not know Lee's military record, but she didn't need to—Scott did, better than anyone. Since Scott was behind the offer to Lee, that must therefore mean that Lee, though only a colonel, must be very, very good.

Greenhow's mind raced on. Phee MacPherson had said that the meeting between Scott and Lee had taken place Thursday morning. According to her story, Lee had declined because he could not "invade the South." Virginia's vote for secession was taken on Wednesday in Richmond, but the vote was secret; Greenhow herself had not learned of it until Friday morning, yesterday, and then only because a professional Confederate spy had told her. It had not become public knowledge until last evening. Could Lee, living on his estate a hundred miles north of Richmond, have learned of his state's secret vote for secession as early as Thursday morning, only half a day after it had happened? Greenhow thought that was highly unlikely, almost impossible. Therefore Lee *could not have known of Virginia's secession when he refused the offer.*

To Greenhow this fact seemed to be of extreme significance. Lee refused the offer of field command of the huge new Federal Army of invasion *even before he knew his own state had seceded.* He may very well have suspected that Virginia would secede, and that he couldn't bring himself to invade his own state, but he didn't know for a fact at the time that it already *had* seceded. That's how much the South, and especially Virginia, meant to him.

Now what? Colonel Lee had turned down General Scott, the highest-ranking military officer in the country, and also the president, the Commander-in-Chief. Could an officer who did that remain the the army? Greenhow was no military expert, but she knew enough about military people and military affairs to greatly suspect that it would not be possible. This conclusion was reinforced by what MacPherson had said about Scott being "mad." Old Fuss and Feathers certainly would have been mightily miffed if he had recommended Lee to Lincoln, and then Lee turned down a presidential offer; that made Scott look bad, his advice questionable.

So, despite his long and honorable military career, Lee would probably have to resign his commission as an officer in the United States Army. Maybe he had already done so.

And then? Did Col. Lee think he would stay on his comfortable estate and sit out a huge civil war while somebody else led the invasion of the South? While somebody else invaded *Virginia*? According to Thomas, wasn't the governor of Virginia trying to reach him, even now, to ask for his military services to help defend his native state? Would he refuse? *Could* he refuse?

Even more: would not Virginia, now seceded, soon join the Confederacy? Of course it would. Then suppose the *Confederacy* asked for his services? Would he accept, since his state would then be a part of the new nation? *Why wouldn't he?*

Greenhow's mind reeled at the huge implication to which her thought processes had inexorably drawn her. *Could not this officer, hand-picked by no less than President Lincoln and General Scott to invade the Confederacy, soon be forced by circumstances to become the defender of the Confederacy?*

This glittering prize so dazzled Greenhow that she caught her breath. She controlled herself with an effort, and looked around the table at her friends, all still blathering on. Didn't any of them see this staggering possibility? Of course not—they didn't have the information of Thomas. She said nothing to anyone, yet her mind refused to rest. Was there anything she could do to help bring it about?

CHAPTER 35

Saturday
Arlington
2:35 PM

Annie Lee quietly entered the guest room. She and Cosby had been out riding earlier that afternoon, just after lunch, during which the family had learned the stunning news that Virginia had seceded. The family had naturally talked about nothing else at lunch. Afterwards she had felt the urgent need to get away, and had invited Cosby to go out riding with her. They had gone to her sacred spot, the spring. There Annie had poured out her heart, voicing all her fears and frustrations. She felt like a leaf in a current, being swept along at a rapid pace but totally unable to do anything about it. She had even ventured the subject that she was feeling a tinge of romantic interest in him. He gave advice, and responded to her tenuous advances by admitting that he was developing similar feelings about her. That was the one bright spot, although a very big one indeed, in a day otherwise filled with cosmically calamitous events. She had returned home in a far better frame of mind.

While riding together near the spring, Annie had seen a tree branch make a small tear in Cosby's jacket. He had been saying something to her at the time, and she did not think he had noticed.

She could repair that tear. Sewing was something she knew how to do. It gave her the tiniest feeling of control in a day of uncontrollable events. It also made her feel closer to the man with whom she wanted a closer feeling.

Cosby was in the family parlor, talking with Custis. Passing by, Annie had noticed that Cosby was not wearing his jacket; it must be in this room. She found it hanging in an armoire. Taking it, she left the room, closing the door behind her.

Annie thought of doing her repair work in the morning room, where her grandfather had done his painting. However, that was on the first floor, where anybody could come in, and she preferred more privacy. So she took the jacket upstairs to the dressing room, which adjoined the bedroom she shared with Agnes and Mildred. No one would come in here except her sisters, and they were busy elsewhere.

Retrieving her sewing equipment, Annie sat on a chair and held up the jacket for inspection. This was an article of clothing worn by the man to whom she was warming. She admired the cut of it, then held it close and felt the tinge of a rich sexual thrill at the sheer manliness of it. There were no personal possessions in the pockets, as Cosby had removed them before hanging it up. The tear was on the right side, near the outside pocket. It was small, less than an inch long. Almost invisible, and easily repairable.

As she flexed the fabric near the tear, Annie heard a faint crinkling sound. Surprised, she flexed the fabric again, and again heard the faint sound. Holding the jacket up to her ear, she repeated the process with the same result. Puzzled, Annie flexed the fabric on the corresponding opposite side of the jacket; there was no noise, no matter how or where she bent the cloth. Could it be a loose piece of lining or insulation? But the lining of clothing was also made of cloth; it should not make any such noise.

Annie opened the jacket, and examined the inner lining on the lower right side. The dark gray-flecked lining material had been cut in a horizontal slit about six inches long, then loosely and rather crudely sewn back together in a stitch with several wide-spaced loops. It was clearly not original; not only was the workmanship unworthy of a clothing manufacturer, but there was nothing like it on the other side of the jacket. It was, in effect, an inside pocket which had been cut into the lining, then sewn closed again. And there was something inside it. Something made of paper.

Annie decided it must be money. That would make sense. Cosby traveled quite a bit. Hiding money on his person would make him less vulnerable to highwaymen and thieves. Even as she examined that thought, however, she rejected it. Cosby had been at Arlington now for six days, and would remain for some indefinite period. Who would, or even *could*, rob him here? He was safer here than even in a big hotel in the city.

She hesitated to invade the privacy of a man for whom she had such burgeoning hopes, but those very hopes afforded her the luxury of feeling a shared imtimacy which would allow such an invasion. Besides, she had her sewing kit right here; she could quickly sew up the slit again.

Annie took a pair of scissors and cut the loops.

Inside were several bills. So there *was* money. There was something else, a sheet of heavy white stationery paper folded into quarters. She slowly unfolded it.

It was a short note. The first thing that caught her eyes was the signature; it was that of Jefferson Davis, the president of the Confederacy.

Annie gasped. There could be no mistake. The printed letterhead read, blackly and crisply, "Office of the President, Confederate States of America."

The body of the short note identified Carter Cosby as "a friend of the Confederacy."

Annie put down the note and stared across the room, her mind reeling. *A friend of the Confederacy? A note signed by Jefferson Davis himself?*

She sat unmoving for several minutes, her mind attempting to come to grips with the enormity of what she held in her hands.

With trembling fingers, she refolded the note and slipped it back into the crude pocket, along with the money. She resewed the lining shut again, duplicating the previous sewing as best she could.

She sat still for several more minutes before realizing that she had to decide whether or not to repair the tear. She decided against it.

Annie walked back down the stairs to the first floor. Rather than walk through the central hallway, which passed by the dining room, the family parlor and the white parlor where people mught see her holding the jacket, she walked through the back of the house and then down the side hallway to the door of the guest room. She knocked timidly. There was no answer. Slowly opening the door, she saw that the room was empty. She replaced the jacket in the armoire, left the room, closed the door, and followed the circuitous route back upstairs to the dressing room.

She needed to think.

A short while later Annie walked downstairs. As she passed the family parlor, she glanced inside; her brother and Cosby were still there. Cosby glanced up and saw her; she quickly averted her eyes, not meeting his gaze. She continued walking down the main hallway, finally reaching the front door. Instinctively she opened the door and walked outside.

Weekend afternoons were often the time when a number of family members would sit on chairs on the portico, enjoying the shade, the breezes, and the magnificent view. Relatives from both the Lee and Custis sides of the family were regular visitors, and Annie's mother was fond of chatting with her women kinfolk while all were gathered on the spacious portico.

There was no one on the portico now. Annie crossed it, walked down the stone steps, crossed the front lawn, and sat down a few yards from the edge of the hill. She felt so miserable she thought that if she fell down the hill and died, it would be no great loss. She drew her knees up, buried her head on them, and cried.

After a few minutes she gradually stopped crying, rested her head on her knees, and gazed unseeingly at the grand vista before her.

Footsteps sounded behind her. Carter Cosby wordlessly sat down beside her.

For a minute neither of them spoke. "I'm sorry we did not get all your fears and frustrations out earlier, Annie," Cosby finally said kindly. "I had hoped you would feel better."

"I did," she answered in a flat tone. "That was before I found out that you are a Confederate spy, Mr. Cosby." She did not look at him.

Silence. "How did you find out, Annie?" he finally asked quietly.

She turned to him quickly. "Are you going to deny it?" she asked bitterly.

"No," he replied calmly. "I just wondered how you found out."

"What does it matter?" she exclaimed. "If you must know, I found the note from Jefferson Davis inside your jacket. A twig made a small tear in it while we were out riding earlier. I didn't think you noticed. I was going to repair that tear."

"So you went into my room, took the jacket, and were going to mend it?"

"Yes. I'm sorry I invaded your privacy. A woman shouldn't do that to a man. I apologize. I was simply trying to help you. I was thankful that you had done so much to help us, and I wanted to do a tiny bit to show my appreciation."

"You did. I thank you. You are right. I was not aware of the tear."

"I didn't actually mend it. I stopped when I found the note inside the lining. It was very close to the tear."

"Ah, well. It's the thought that counts."

"Carter, please. What have you to say for yourself?"

"Well, I can say one thing. I'm glad we're back to 'Carter.' 'Mr. Cosby' now sounds so dreadfully remote."

Annie's eyes started to well up. "How can you say such things? This is no light matter. You came here under false pretenses. To *spy* on us! I thought the world of you. How could you engage in such deception?"

Silence. "Not so false, Annie," Cosby finally said gently. "I am a published agriculturalist, I do own a plantation, and I am the governor's appointee. I am a native Virginian, and I did attend the University of Virginia. The suggestion I made about this property was a real one; I genuinely do believe that a vineyard and winery would do well here." With his hand Cosby gestured toward the sweeping slopes before them. "And it is certainly true that I am becoming increasingly attracted to you personally," he added.

"What about your…your wife," Annie asked after a few moments. "Was all that true?"

"Yes. Letitia. She died of consumption two years ago."

"And she lived with you on this plantation you own?"

"Of course. She helped run it. She was very knowledgable. She was actually the one who inherited it from her parents; she was an only child. It was somewhat the same situation that you have here. Arlington was really left to your mother, who was your grandfather's only child."

"That plantation's not in Virginia, is it."

"No. It's in Alabama. It's called Cymru, which is a Welsh word. Letitia's father was of Welsh ancestry."

"*Alabama!* That's where *Montgomery* is! The capital of the Confederacy!" Annie glanced at him sharply. "You really *are* from the Confederacy!"

Cosby sighed. "Agriculture is universal, Annie."

She looked back at the city. "I appreciate your…your candor, Carter," she said in a softer tone. "And I am genuinely sorry about your wife. However, I still don't understand this business with Jefferson Davis. Why are you carrying around a note from him?"

Cosby also gazed out over the city. "Your father is a remarkable man, Annie. He is obviously a gifted military officer. Everyone seems to agree on that, including General Scott and President Lincoln. He has an enormous sense of family history, both from his own side and your mother's side. That has resulted in a sense of duty which goes far beyond merely obeying orders.

He has declined a great command and then resigned. He has, in effect, been forced out of the army because of his beliefs. Because of his sense of duty to something beyond mere orders, one might say."

"I know all that. I'm very proud of him. What has all that to do with you?"

"It was felt in certain quarters that it might be possible that your father could be induced to join the Confederacy. I was sent to advise him and help him, if I could."

"*Join the Confederacy?*" Annie glared in astonishment at Cosby. "Mr. Cosby, how in the world could he do that? It would be a...a *betrayal* of all he has worked for all his life! It's impossible!"

"Is it?" Cosby responded quietly. "There was a time, Annie, when I would have agreed with you. Now look what has happened. Today we learned that the Virginia Convention voted for secession several days ago. The state legislature will soon make it official. Several other southern states will surely follow. If they then join the Confederacy—and it would seem a certainty that they will—then the Confederacy would have expanded northward hundreds of miles to reach the Potomac River itself. *That* river," Cosby emphasized, pointing at the shimmering ribbon less than a mile away. "Not some river out West or down South somewhere. *That river right there*, Annie. This very land where we are sitting right now will be part of the Confederacy, or at least claimed by it. And when that happens, you will be a citizen of the Confederacy. So will your father. So will the rest of your family. So will several million other people not now in it. How will you feel about the Confederacy then? Will you leave Virginia and move to Michigan or New York or Ohio to avoid being a part of it?"

Annie crossed her arms on her knees, rested her head on her arms, and started sobbing softly.

"And when that happens, Annie, will you still think of me as a spy?"

She sobbed harder.

"I do not mean to criticize you, Annie. I merely show you the times."

Cosby was silent for a few minutes, as Annie's sobs slowly subsided into deep breathing. "Earlier today, Annie," he finally said, "you told me that you felt like a leaf in a current, being rapidly carried along but with no control of your direction. That's not an uncommon feeling these days. I feel it. So do millions of people. Events seem to be outrunning our ability to understand them, let alone control them."

"When I first heard of your father, he was only a name to me, dimly remembered from the Mexican War. Now that I have met him and understand his position, and have met you and the rest of your wonderful family, and have seen this beautiful place, I conceive of my mission differently. I could not influence your father, even if I wanted to. He has made all his own decisions. I now believe that the best thing I can do is help protect him. And that is something you could do, too."

Annie looked up. "Me? How?"

"By supporting him the best way that you can. He has just made two of the hardest decisions he has ever made in his life. He may have to make more. When he was a young man he could afford to think primarily of himself. Now he has to think first of you, his family, all of whom except Rooney live at home. He cannot wish to do something if he feels that his family will rebel against him if he does it. Let him be in no doubt that you fully support him, even if it means personal hardship for you. Even if you disagree with him. That sounds easy to say, but it may prove to be difficult. Do you think you can do that?"

"Yes, I think so." Annie paused. "What decisions might they be?"

"The slaves, for one. He might be forced to free them."

"He *is* going to free the servants," Annie replied quickly. "It was in grandfather's will."

"Yes, but he might be forced to free them sooner than he would like. If the army of invasion marches south, it will come right here on the first day. It might declare that everywhere that army marches will be considered free territory. You have more than sixty slaves here at Arlington, with more on your other properties. If they are all freed at once, it could create hardship. Some of them might leave, which means you would be short-handed. Those that stay would have to be paid a wage. Your lands will somehow have to grow more food. However, you should be able to sell that food at higher prices. Armies have to be fed, and wars bring shortages. If somehow your family can keep your properties intact and productive, I think you could weather the storm. And don't forget that there may not be a war. If the Confederacy grows so much larger, Lincoln may call off the invasion and negotiate. I'm sure Jefferson Davis would welcome that. We just don't know."

"It is all so very sad and very confusing." Annie rested her head on her arms again. "What about us, Carter?" she asked in a small voice.

"Lord, I wish I knew, Annie. If I had my way, there would be no war, I would stay here and help you plant your vineyard, build your winery, and watch you become the business manager of an enterprise that would provide the embassies in Washington with America's finest wine. I care for you more every minute that I know you. Yet I do not see how we can make any further plans until we know something more of the future. We are witnessing the birth of a new nation, or at least an assemblage of states which claims to be one. You live right at the dividing line. The Potomac could become an international border. And we live hundreds of miles apart." Cosby looked down at his hands. "I really don't know how much more I can say."

Annie looked over at him, her head still on her arms. "Say it, Carter," she said softly.

He looked at her. "I believe I'm falling in love with you."

Annie moved closer and took his hand. "That's enough," she said quickly, her eyes glistening. She lightly and fleetingly put her finger on his lips. "You need make no further commitment now. You are right. There are many problems. Let us see how events work out and proceed from there."

"Thank you. Yes, I think that is what we should do."

They were silent a while. "You didn't ask this, Carter," Annie finally said, "but there is something I could do. I will keep quiet about all this. My family does not need to know it. I also want to do it to show that you can trust me. Trust must be a part of love, and I want you to know that I am falling in love with you." She looked at him brightly, the sobbing gone. "Are we agreed?"

"*Oui, madamoiselle*. We are agreed."

CHAPTER 36

Saturday
Washington
7:28 PM

"There. What do you thnk of *that*?"

Meagan O'Connor had taken her first tentative bite of a steamed oyster at Harvey's Oyster Salon; Rufus Sloan had already wolfed down two oysters. At their little lunch today Sloan had described his experiences the night before at the oyster house, and O'Connor revealed that she had never eaten an oyster. Sloan then invited her to accompany him on a return trip to Harvey's this evening, and she accepted.

"It's very…*good*," O'Connor ventured.

"See? I told you," Sloan reminded her. He swallowed another oyster, washed down with a generous slug of beer. He was enjoying his one-day role reversal, from being the oysterdom neophyte last night to the shellfish connoisseur tonight. While waiting for seats at the crowded bar he had grandly expounded on all the salient points about oysters he had recently learned from Tilton without mentioning his name, and implying he had known such things for years. She was impressed, which made him feel powerful.

Sloan ate another oyster and drank some more beer. He had encouraged O'Connor to order a mug of beer—he had seen several other women do it here—or even a glass of white wine, but she had politely declined. She wanted to try her new experiences one at a time.

By the time O'Connor had finished half a dozen oysters, Sloan had eaten a dozen. He had also drunk two mugs of beer. Beer seemed to go so well with oysters.

Much to her surprise, O'Connor still felt hungry after her half-dozen oysters. "Do you know what, Rufus?"

"What?"

"I think I would like some of that oyster soup. It looks delicious. May I?"

"Oyster *stew*, ma'am," Sloan remarked with a smile, mentally thankful for Tilton's indoctrination. "Of course."

"You know so much." Impulsively she reached out a hand and took Sloan's arm just above the wrist. "Want to know something else?"

"What?"

"I'm having fun." She gave his arm a squeeze. Her smile was dazzling.

Sloan felt so happy and proud he thought he might burst his buttons. He wished this young night might never end, and that tomorrow would never come. His first evening engagement with Meagan O'Connor was even more delightful than he had imagined it could be.

He ordered another half-dozen oysters. And another mug of beer.

O'Connor dawdled over her stew, reveling in its delicious taste and also in the appreciative glances she received from a number of men in the crowded restaurant. By the time she had finished the stew and leaned back with a satisfied sigh, Sloan had eaten two dozen oysters, a small loaf of bread, and drunk four mugs of beer. They both felt so full that neither one wanted to walk around sight-seeing at night, but simply wanted to go home.

At about half-past eight, Sloan and O'Connor started their trek to Swampoodle. Sloan was feeling no pain, and his walk was unsteady. O'Connor found she actually had to help him walk from time to time. She started to feel a bit frightened and repelled. The area of town in which she lived could be dangerous. Especially at night, and most especially on a Saturday night. She herself had never been personally accosted, but she had heard plenty of stories.

Sloan started muttering to himself. His words were incomprehensible to O'Connor.

"Rufus, you're drunk," she said bluntly as he stumbled again.

Sloan grinned vacantly at her. "Mish Meagan, how imp…how impo…how *crude* of you. The word is sn…schno…*snockered.* Thash it. I'm *schnockered.*" He stumbled again.

"Well, whatever it is, I wish you weren't." They were approaching 7th Street. "This is Saturday night, Rufus. Suppose somebody should attack us. I would need your protection. Right now it seems I'm protecting *you.*"

"Protecshun? Is *that* all yoo want?" Sloan grinned again at O'Connor. "Wal, then yoo *got* it, Miz Meagan. Yure safer wi' me than…than *annyone*." He stumbled again, then burped longly, wetly, and loudly.

"Rufus, that's disgusting."

"Thass me. Disgussin'. But yure safe wi' me. I'm a *killer*, Miz Meagan. A *killer*."

"A killer." O'Connor chuckled. "You may be many things, Rufus, but one thing I'm sure you're not is a *killer*."

Sloan stopped and swayed slightly, his dark eyes suddenly snapping. "Thass right, *laff. Laff* at me. But yoo don' *know* me. *Nobody* knows me. *Nobody*. I *am* a killer. An' I'm gonna kill *again.* Yoo hear me? *Again*! Then *ever'body* will know me!"

They were now on E Street between 7th and 6th, about halfway to O'Connor's home. She had no wish to be stranded in the dark, with only the flickering street lights for illumination. She now wished they had taken a hack cab to her home, even if she had to pay for it herself. There had been a number of them in the street outside Harvey's. She looked around; there were none in sight. She walked back to Sloan.

"Come on, Rufus," she said. "Let's go. You can lean on me if you have to."

"Don' have to," Sloan said, standing still and swaying slightly. "Yoo b'lieve I'm a *killer*?"

"If you say so," O'Connor replied with a sigh, taking his hand and leading him forward. "Let's go. Why don't you tell me about it?"

"Thass better." Sloan looked around him as he allowed himself to be led, almost losing his balance. "Can yoo keep a secret, Miz Meagan?" His voice was almost a whisper.

"Of course." They were almost to 6th Street.

"I *kilt* people. In Kansas. Thass what I did there. Wi' a sword. A *saber*. Ran 'em through. Heh heh. Served 'em right. Dirty proslavers. Thass why they called me *Cutter*."

A thrill of secrecy and discovery ran through O'Connor. "Cutter? Who called you Cutter?"

"*They* did."

"Who's *they*?"

Sloan looked around again. "John Brown did. An' his gang. *They* called me Cutter." His voice was even lower. He was grinning in stuporous satisfaction.

O'Connor could scarcely believe what she was hearing, but she did not stop. "You were called that by *John Brown*? Cutter Sloan?"

"No, no. Not Cutter *Sloan*. Nobody there knew my name. Cutter *Cutler*."

"Cutter *Cutler*?"

"O' course. Thass th' name I used there. Cutler. Joshua Cutler."

"Rufus, do you know what you are saying? You used the name Joshua Cutler when you were with John Brown's gang in Kansas? And you killed people there?"

"Thass right."

"How many people did you kill?"

"A cupple. We kilt five altogether."

O'Connor shuddered.

"*Now* do yoo b'lieve I'm a *killer*?"

"Rufus, this is all so…*strange*. How long ago was this?"

Sloan visibly tried to think as he was being led along. "I dunno 'zactly. 'Bout five years."

O'Connor tried to remember some history. She knew there had been a great deal of violence in Kansas several years ago, and she vaguely remembered the name of John Brown as having been involved in it in some way, but she could not recall any details. All she remembered clearly about Brown was his notorious raid on the Harpers Ferry arsenal.

"Still don' b'lieve, ha? Awright, tell yoo more. I was wi' Ol' Man Brown at Harp'rs Ferry, too. How 'bout *that*?"

This rocked O'Connor. "*Harpers Ferry*? Rufus, you couldn't have been there. All those raiders were either killed or captured. John Brown was tried and hanged."

Sloan stopped again. By the light of a nearby street lamp, O'Connor could see that his eyes were blazing. "Who tole yoo that?" he snapped at O'Connor. "*Who tole yoo that?* We were *not* all capchured! Some ovus got *away*! I was *one* ovum! *Me! Cutter Cutler!*"

O'Connor tried to get Sloan moving again, gently pulling him. "That was very clever of you, Rufus. How have you managed to stay free?"

Sloan started moving. "I *tole* yoo, Miz Meagan. *Nobody knows me! Nobody knows who I am! Thass* how!" He looked at O'Connor. "'Cept yoo, now. Good thing yoo can keep a secret."

"Of course I can." They were now across 4th Street. "How smart of you, Rufus. What did you mean when you said you were going to kill again? How will everybody know you?"

"Lee," Sloan said.

O'Connor waited a few moments, but Sloan said nothing. "Lee?" she prodded.

"Yesh. Lee."

"Do you mean *Colonel* Lee? The man I told you about yesterday?"

"Yesh. Him. Thass the one."

"You want to kill Colonel Lee?"

"Yesh."

"Rufus, I don't understand. Yesterday you said you didn't know him. Why do you want to *kill* him?"

"'Member John Brown?"

"Yes. He was hanged."

"That was 'cause of Lee."

"Because of Lee? John Brown was hanged because of Lee?"

"Yesh. Lee capchured 'im."

"*Captured* him? You mean at Harpers Ferry? Lee was in charge of the soldiers who captured Brown at Harpers Ferry?"

"Zactly."

"Oh."

"Greates' man in th' cuntree—greates' man *ever*—an' Lee got 'im. *Kilt* 'im."

"Well, I'm sorry, Rufus, but—"

"Ain't all."

"It isn't? Well, what—"

"Lee won't lead th' army. Turned down th' presydunt. Th' *presydunt*. That *scum*. That *traitor*! That *slaver! I hate 'im! I'll kill 'im!"* Sloan almost shouted the last words.

O'Connor did not reply. They had just crossed over 3rd Street. She had been watching two roughly-dressed men on the other side of E Street, walking the opposite way she and Sloan were walking. Looking over her shoulder after they passed, she saw them quickly cross E Street, scurrying shadows in the dimly-lit darkness; they reversed direction and were now walking behind Sloan and herself. Only they were not walking; they were half-running, and rapidly closing the distance. She thought she saw cudgels.

"Oh, Rufus, run!" She tugged him forward violently.

"Wassamatta?"

"Robbers!"

Sloan turned around and saw the approaching men. With surprising speed, he put out his right arm and backed O'Connor up against a board fence that was near the sidewalk, then stood beside her.

The two men came up to them and stopped. They indeed had cudgels. One man was the size of Sloan, the other considerably bigger. "Well, well, what 'ave we 'ere," the smaller man said sneeringly. "A purty little missy an' her *gennulman*." He spat the last word out. "No screamin', Missy, or Bert here'll have to bash th' brains out of yore purty head." The bigger man took a step closer to

O'Connor. He held his cudgel in his right hand, and tapped the shaft of it into the palm of his left hand. The big cudgel looked like an axe handle. "Yeh," he leered, "An' then we'd see what's in yore panties. A right nice little blonde pussy. So sweet it purrs, I betcha. We already know what's in his," he said, pointing at Sloan with the club. "Nothin'."

Beside him, Sloan could feel O'Connor tremble. "Look 'ere," he said, "I'm drunk. If you don' b'lieve me, ask her." The eyes of both men shifted to O'Connor, who nodded, then hung her head in shame and fear. "Please let us go," she sobbed.

"See? I don' wan' no trubble. Yoo wan' money? Yoo got it. I got twenny dollars. If I had more, I'd giv' it to yuh. Ain't, though. She ate too much t'night. Here's muh wallet." Sloan reached inside his coat, withdrew a small leather billfold, and flipped it on the ground between the two men.

What happened next was so fast O'Connor had trouble remembering it clearly later. As the two men turned to look at the billfold and the shorter man started to bend to retrieve it, Sloan leaped forward, grasped the smaller man's club with his left hand, and pulled the man toward him. His right hand went back inside his coat and emerged instantly with a shockingly huge knife. The knife flashed dimly in the lamplight as Sloan slashed it across the man's throat. The man fell backwards as Sloan released the club; he lay writhing on the gravel sidewalk, his only noise a ghastly gasping gurgling sound.

In the same fluid motion Sloan quickly grabbed the bigger man's club and made the same slashing sweep toward the man's throat. The man quickly raised his left hand to ward off the deadly arc and succeeded in knocking Sloan's hand slightly upwards, causing the knife to slice open his cheek to the bone and go through his nose. Sloan completed his arc and then made another one, this one catching the opened palm of the man's left hand and almost slicing his hand in half. The man was still holding onto the club with his right hand, vainly trying to pull it out of Sloan's grasp, not realizing that his retention of the club was keeping him with the range of the huge knife that was moving so quickly it was almost invisible.

The next slash of the knife was downwards onto the man's right wrist, almost severing the hand holding the club. Screaming in agony and bleeding profusely, he stumbled backward and tumbled into an open sewage ditch. Sloan jumped right in after him. O'Connor did not see what happened, but in a few moments the man had stopped screaming. She heard some ripping noises, then Sloan muttering. She could not hear him clearly, but he seemed to say something like, "Now whose pants have nothin' in them."

Sloan emerged from the ditch with the bloody knife. He wiped off the blade on the clothing of the man on the sidewalk, who was dead in a pool of blood. He then opened his coat and put the big knife back in its sheath, which was attached to the inside of the coat. "Let's go, Meagan." After picking up his billfold, he escorted the terrified and sickened girl just a block to 2nd Street, then a bit north to her home.

"Get inside and stay there," Sloan ordered as she fumbled with her key. "You saw nothin'. You heard nothin'. You know nothin'. *Nothin'*. You talk to nobody! Do you understand? *Nobody!*" His inebriation seemed to have left him.

O'Connor was so overwhelmed by all that had happened in the last half hour that she could barely speak. "Yes. Yes, of course. Nothing. Nobody." She opened the door and stepped inside, thinking she might be violently sick at any moment. "Good night, Rufus." She closed the door without looking at him.

Sloan waited until he heard the deadbolt click into place. Then he walked to his boarding house by a different route than the one they had come. "I *am* a killer," he said to himself as he walked along. It made him feel very good. Very good indeed.

CHAPTER 37

Sunday, April 21
Washington
8:16 AM

Rose Greenhow, wrapped in a dressing gown, answered the persistent sound of the brass knocker on her front door. It was early on a Sunday morning, and she could not possibly imagine who in the world would be knocking on her front door at such an hour.

When she opened the door, it was Meagan O'Connor. She looked pale and drawn, with a reddened face, and as if she had been crying for some time.

"Meagan! What on earth—"

"Oh, ma'am, I'm so sorry to have bothered you, but I've just *got* to talk to someone, and you're the best person I could think of. I hope you don't mind."

"Of course not, my dear. Do come in." Greenhow led O'Connor to a sofa, helped her off with her cloak, then sat down beside her. "Now—I presume you are not going to tell me that you are simply a little early for our appointment this afternoon," she smiled. "So what is it?"

"Oh, ma'am, something terrible has happened. But it does have something to do with what you wanted me to do, so I thought you should know about it." Meagan sniffed.

"There, there. Calm yourself, Meagan. You've walked a long way to see me, so I know it must be important. Relax." Greenhow stopped, then held up a finger. "I have an idea. Wait here a moment."

Greenhow arose, then went up the stairs. O'Connor could hear a low murmur of voices. Greenhow soon reappeared, followed by a young girl. "Meagan, this is my youngest daughter, also named Rose. You met her briefly when you were here a week ago. Although she is only eight years old, she is a very responsible young lady. I have asked her to make some tea for us. Does that meet with your approval?"

"I would be happy to do so, ma'am," little Rose said with a smile and a curtsey toward O'Connor.

"Oh, that would be so nice, Rose," O'Connor said with a great sigh of relief. "I cannot think of anything I would enjoy right now more than a nice hot cup of tea. Thank you so very much."

Little Rose disappeared into the kitchen. "Now, then," Greenhow began again, "suppose you tell me everything."

O'Connor started with the oyster dinner with Rufus Sloan, the man she had mentioned last week and the one to whom Greenhow had encouraged her to become closer. She had been out walking with him twice during the previous week, but last night had been their first evening engagement. All had gone well, except that Sloan had become drunk on beer.

"My dear, men often become drunk," Greenhow interposed. "That's when they reveal much about themselves."

"That's exactly what happened," O'Connor said quickly. "And what Rufus revealed was very strange. I already knew he was an abolitionist. He told me that last Sunday, when we were out walking. Last night he claimed he had been with John Brown in Kansas five years ago. He said he had killed two men there."

"What?" Greenhow exclaimed. "*John Brown*? There *was* an enormous amount of violence in Kansas five years ago, and John Brown *was* involved. Meagan, do you really think your young man was there?"

"I didn't at first, ma'am. I thought it was just the beer bragging. Then he said something else. He said he had also been with John Brown at Harpers Ferry."

"What?" Greenhow exclaimed again. "*Harpers Ferry?* Meagan, such a thing is not possible! That raid was a failure. Brown himself was captured, tried, convicted, and hanged."

"Yes, ma'am, I know. That's what I told him. He became very angry. He yelled at me. He said some of the raiders had escaped, and that he was one of them. I didn't know what to think. Is that true? Did some of the Harpers Ferry raiders escape?"

"My stars! Do you know, Meagan, I think that some of them *did* escape. But I thought that even they were eventually found and captured. Perhaps that was not so. But how could this be possible? As I recall, you told me that this Mr. Sloan works in a general store near Apperson's Apparel, where you work." O'Connor nodded. "In other words, he is right out in the open, and right in the capital city of the country. Why has he not been arrested? Did this Mr. Sloan tell you how he has evaded justice for so long?"

"Yes, he did. He said that he used an assumed name with John Brown's group: Joshua Cutler. He said they even nicknamed him Cutter Cutler because of his work with a saber. Even if the authorities were still looking for him, they would never find him under that name."

Rose Greenhow leaned back on the sofa and regarded her visitor keenly. "This is something of an incredible story, Meagan. A John Brown raider, both in Kansas and Harpers Ferry, still at large? Right here in Washington? Unfortunately, it seems to me that it would be quite difficult to ascertain the truth of it. You know this man; you have spoken to him many times, even been out on social occasions with him. What is your best estimation of his veracity? Do you think he is telling the truth? Or do you think, as you so nicely put it, that it was simply the beer bragging?"

Before O'Connor could answer, little Rose brought in a silver tea set; it was the same one Mrs. Greenhow had used a week earlier with O'Connor. Greenhow changed the subject and poured two cups of tea. "Have you had any breakfast yet, Meagan? It is still rather early for a Sunday morning."

"I had a little something, ma'am. I wanted to get here as soon as I could. I told my parents I was visiting a friend."

"And so you are, my dear." Greenhow glanced at her daughter and slightly nodded her head. The girl disappeared again into the kitchen. "Any milk or sugar?"

"A little sugar, ma'am." When the sugar had been stirred in, O'Connor sipped the tea eagerly. Its sweet heat spread slowly throughout her body, calming her. As she finished her second long sip, little Rose reappeared bearing a plate on which there was a partial loaf of bread. She set it down on the mahogany coffee table next to the tea set.

"Thank you, Rose," Greenhow said. "You have been most helpful, darling. I will call you again if we need you." The girl curtsied again and then went up the stairs.

"This is bishop's bread, Meagan. We made a loaf yesterday. It keeps very well, so we did not have to eat it all. Please have some. It is a bit like fruit cake, with chopped walnuts, dates, and candied cherries. It goes extremely well with tea or coffee."

O'Connor took a bite, and her face lit up. "Oh, ma'am, it *does*! It's *wonderful*! You always have such wonderful foods here when I visit!"

"And we always shall," Greenhow said with a smile. "Feeling better?" she asked after O'Connor had eaten a few more pieces of the bishop's bread and taken a few more sips of tea.

"Oh, yes, ma'am. Much better, thank you."

"Good. Now perhaps you can tell me what you think of the truthfulness of those claims of your Mr. Sloan."

"I still wasn't sure, ma'am. Then something happened. Something horrible."

"What was it, child?"

"Oh, ma'am, I don't know what to do! He warned me not to tell anyone!"

"He? You mean Sloan? He told you not to tell anyone?"

"Yes, ma'am. 'You saw nothing. You heard nothing. You know nothing. You tell *nobody*.' That's what he said."

"Are you afraid of him, Meagan? I thought he cared for you."

"Yes, ma'am, I am afraid of him." O'Connor's voice started to tremble. "After what I saw last night, I am very much afraid."

"Meagan, you are certainly safe now. Why, we are only a block from the President's House itself. No one can reach you here. No one even knows you are here, not even your parents." Greenhow reached over and took the young woman's hand. "It would help both of us if you unburdened yourself. Is it perhaps a police matter?"

"Yes, ma'am, I think it is." O'Connor started crying softly.

"Heavens, my dear. What could it be?"

O'Connor related the meeting with the two ruffians with clubs. "They threatened to kill me if I screamed. Rufus was drunk; I thought he would be absolutely useless. Besides, what could he do? One of them was a big man. I have never been more terrified in my life."

"I am sure you were, my dear. It was indeed a terrifying situation." Greenhow sympathetically squeezed O'Connor's hand. "But you were not beaten, were you? I see no bruises. So they robbed the two of you and then let you go? How fortunate that you were not really harmed. Yes, I agree with you; this is a police matter. You should report it to the police as soon as possible, regardless of what Mr. Sloan says. Did they injure him?"

O'Connor shook her head. "No, he was not harmed."

"Thank goodness for that. Even so, it was brazen robbery. You should report it at once. If you wish, I will accompany you to the nearest police station." Greenhow stood up. "Just let me get dressed—"

"Ma'am," O'Connor said through tear-filled eyes, "I don't think you understand. It wasn't what they did to us, it was what he did to them."

Greenhow stared at her visitor. "What *he* did to *them*? Meagan, I don't understand. *What* did he do to them?"

"He killed them."

Greenhow gasped and gaped. She seemed to sway slightly, then sat back down quickly. "*Killed* them?" she finally asked.

"Yes, ma'am."

"*Both* of them?"

"Yes, ma'am."

"Meagan, are you *sure* they were dead?"

"Yes, ma'am. At least I think so. We didn't stay around. Rufus took me home right away. Told me to stay there and keep quiet."

"How did he do it?"

O'Connor described the sudden slashing knife and how quickly and expertly Sloan had used it. "It was a big knife. The biggest I've ever seen. Its sheath was sewn on the inside of his coat. I had never seen it before. I had no idea he had it. But you see what I mean, ma'am. About starting to believe him, I mean. If he was that expert and deadly with a knife, then I think he may very well be telling the truth about being with John Brown and being called Cutter Cutler."

Greenhow considered. "I see. What time did this happen, Meagan?"

"About nine o'clock, ma'am.

"And where did it happen?"

"On E Street, between 3rd and 2nd Streets. I remember that because we were almost to my house."

"This morning, when you walked over here, did you come down E Street? Did you pass the spot where it happened?"

O'Connor shuddered. "Oh, no, ma'am. I used a different route. I couldn't go by there again. Not so soon, anyway." She shuddered again.

"And you're sure both men were dead? They couldn't have been badly wounded, and then later got up and left?"

O'Connor shook her head. "I don't see how, ma'am. There was blood *everywhere*. The first man—I saw the knife slash his throat. I saw him lying in a pool of blood. The second man, the bigger one—he fell backward into a ditch. I didn't see exactly what happened, but he stopped screaming. Rufus came up out of the ditch; I don't think he would have left that man alive."

"Mmm. I ask because if they were merely wounded, and later left, then there would almost certainly be no police report about it; after all, neither you nor Mr. Sloan have said anything about it to the police, and the robbers certainly wouldn't. On the other hand, if they were dead, then their bodies would certainly have been found by now, and the police would be investigating. There might even be some mention of it in the newspapers, although there are already a depressingly large number of murders in this city. That way we could check on it."

"Ma'am, I'm so frightened. What do you think I should do?"

"For you personally, Meagan, I see no problem," Greenhow said decisively. "You were accosted by the men, you were threatened, you feared for your life, and you had nothing to do with their deaths. You have not reported it because you were warned not to by a man you personally saw kill two men, and who claims to have killed others. I am no lawyer, but I certainly think you are legally safe. No, the real question concerns Mr. Sloan. Perhaps I could report it to the police without mentioning your name, at least at first. If Mr. Sloan is picked up for questioning and mentions your name, then you would have to make a statement. However, he may not mention your name, since he would want to protect you. Yes, that is what I think I will do. I will go to the nearest police station and offer some information about the incident without involving you."

"Oh, would you, ma'am? I would be eternally grateful."

"Yes, my dear. I will be happy to do it. Now," said Greenhow as she stood up again, "It is time to get dressed."

"Um, there is one more thing, ma'am. If you are going to the police, there's something else they should know."

"Oh? What is that?"

"Rufus. He said several times that he is going to kill again. And he has the victim already picked out."

"And just who might that be?"

"An army officer named Colonel Robert E. Lee."

Greenhow put her hand to her throat and stared in stupefaction. She sat quickly back down again. "Colonel Robert E. Lee. You're absolutely sure that's the man?"

"Yes, ma'am."

"Do you know happen to know Colonel Lee?"

"No, ma'am."

"Does Mr. Sloan know him?"

"No, ma'am. I asked him that when I first told him about Lee. He said he didn't know Lee."

Greenhow shook her head in bewilderment. “Meagan, I am really all at sea here. Please help me. You just said that you don’t know Colonel Lee. Then what do you mean when you say that you first told him about Lee?”

“That was on Friday, ma’am. We had our regular lunch together, at his store. I told him the latest gossip about Lee, which I heard from one of our seamstresses at Apperson’s. She’s married to an army officer. The story was that Lee had turned down an offer to command the new Union army that’s building up. The offer supposedly came from President Lincoln himself, through an intermediary—I forget his name. Lee refused.”

Greenhow realized that this young woman, beautiful but unsophisticated, had actually learned about Lee and his refusal to command the army earlier than she herself had. “I see. I happened to hear the same story myself, so I would certainly find it credible. So what was Mr. Sloan’s reaction when you told him this gossip?”

“Not much, ma’am. He asked some questions, but that’s all. It was nothing like last night, when he screamed out that he hated Lee and wants to kll him.”

“Then you must have been as perplexed as I am now. Why does he want to kill Lee, of all people?”

“Because of John Brown, ma’am. It was Lee who was in command of the troops that captured Brown at Harpers Ferry. Sloan was a follower of Brown. Last night I heard him say that Brown was the greatest man in the country. Brown was hanged. Sloan blames Lee for Brown’s death. He wants revenge.”

“I see. I had forgotten that about Lee.”

“Lee also has slaves. And then Rufus found out about Lee’s refusal to lead the army. So Lee stands for everything Sloan hates: slavery, Brown’s death, and now something he considers a traitorous act. Ma’am, I think he *is* going to try and kill Colonel Lee.”

“And so do I. Meagan, if even half of what you told me is true, the colonel’s life is in danger. And I believe every word. Now—I think the best thing we could do is to have the police arrest Mr. Sloan on a suspicion of murder. Leave that to me. Where does he live?”

O’Connor’s hand flew to her lips. “Oh, ma’am, I don’t *know*. I’m so sorry. I never thought of that.”

"You've never been to his house?"

"No, ma'am. Every time we went out, he always picked me up at my house. Then he returned me there. We never went to his house. And he never talked of it."

"Well, never mind. Where does he work again?"

"Grinell's Goods. It's a general store on 11th Street, between F and G. Nearer G Street. It's in the same block where I work, but on the opposite side of 11th Street."

"Good. Now here is what we will do. I normally go to church with the children, but not today. I can think of several places to go and several people to meet, but not with any children. Please stay here. You will be safe here, and you can mind the house and its occupants. Help yourself to any food. I will try to return here more than once to let you know what I have been able to accomplish. Then later this afternoon you can return home. How does that sound?"

"Oh, ma'am, it sounds wonderful. Thank you so much."

"Good," Greenhow said again with a smile. "Now I really do think it is about time I got dressed."

CHAPTER 38

Sunday
Arlington and Alexandria
8:45 AM

Due to her arthritic condition, Mrs. Lee decided to do what was increasingly common for her to do: stay at home on Sunday and have a worship service there. Most of the Lee family decided to stay with her.

Robert E. Lee decided to attend the Sunday worship service at Christ Church in Alexandria, where he habitually worshipped when he was at home. Besides, he had already informed John Robertson that he would meet Robertson there.

Lee invited Cosby to accompany him, and Cosby accepted. When Annie Lee learned that Cosby was going to Alexandria she invited herself, and her father agreed with a tolerant smile. Since the three of them were going Lee decided to use the family carriage; Daniel, the family coachman, would be their driver.

Alexandria was approximately six miles south of Arlington. The group inside the carriage was quiet as it retraced the route by which Cosby had come to Arlington almost a week before. He enjoyed the ride on this beautiful day, catching grand views of the

Potomac on his left and the gently rising hills of the Virginia Heights on his right. Annie had seated herself next to him, rather than her father, and the sweet closeness of this woman brought back sharp memories of Letitia while simultaneously hinting powerfully of a magnificent future.

After six miles the carriage entered Alexandria from the north side of the city, and proceeded south on Washington Street. At Cameron Street Daniel turned the carriage right, and proceeded one block to Columbus Street. Christ Church was situated at the southeast corner of the intersection of Columbus and Cameron Streets, facing Columbus. A brick arch marked the entrance to the church grounds. Daniel pulled to the curb and the three passengers stepped out.

Lee helped his daughter out, and then mentioned a few facts about the church to Cosby, who had never been here before. "This church was built in 1773," he stated, pointing toward that date set into the top of the brick arch. "The bell tower was not part of it then; that was added in 1818."

The brick bell tower was an impressive affair, rising more than fifty feet into the air. The large rectangular brick base of the tower was itself almost as high as the top of the hipped roof of the two-story brick church. Above the base the tower rose in several octagonal stories, terminating in a belfry topped by a cupola. The whole tower, although architecturally pleasing and impressive, seemed to Cosby almost a bit too large for the church.

Entering beneath the arch, Cosby found himself on a wide brick walkway. The church property, he noticed, extended completely across the block to Washington Street, for this walkway ran beside the church straight across to that street, where there was another brick-arch entranceway.

"I love this church," Lee mused. "I grew up here in Alexandria, and this was our parish church. I have lived many years in many other places, but I still consider this my home church. Every Sunday when I attend services somewhere else I think of this church and wish I were here. I am sure George Washington felt the same way. This was his church too, you know." Turning left, the group went into a covered entranceway and then through the front door into the church.

The interior was a symphony of white-painted wood, a masterpiece of American colonial design. It was not overornamented, but it was an Episcopal church, and therefore did not have the spartan austerity characteristic of certain denominations such as Shakers or Congregationalists. Two aisles divided the pews into three areas. The raised pulpit was supported by a single slender rod. Glancing over his shoulder as he walked down the right-hand aisle, Cosby beheld a magnificent organ in the second-floor loft.

Perhaps the most unusual feature was that all the pews had white-painted swinging doors on them. When closed and latched, these doors were then flush with the ends of the pews and prevented anyone from sitting in the pews. They had varnished rails on their tops, which allowed anyone sitting at the end of the pew to rest his or her arm on top of the door.

On the outside of each pew door was a small black-painted number. Lee stopped at number 46, opened the pew door, and allowed his daughter and guest to enter first. When they were all seated, Cosby quietly inquired about the doors and numbers.

"Virginia was originally founded as a crown colony, Mr. Cosby," Lee replied in a near whisper. "It did not develop from a large tract of land granted by the English sovereign to a private person, such as Pennsylvania or Maryland. It was owned outright by the English crown and run directly by it." Lee leaned forward and picked a bible from the rack mounted on the back of the pew in front of him. "That is why the first settlement in Virginia—the first permanent English settlement anywhere in the New World—was named Jamestown. It was in honor of the King of England at the time, James I. He was also the same person responsible for this English translation of the bible, the King James Bible." He replaced the bible.

"In Williamsburg, the capital of the colony after Jamestown, the colonial governor—who was directly appointed by the king—resided in a palace, while the elected representatives met at the House of Burgesses. So we had there an exact miniature version of the king and parliament in England."

"Since Virginia was a crown colony, its official religion was the Church of England, the Anglican Church, just as it was in England itself. Each church was supported by a pew tax, an annual assessment paid by each family in the congregation. In return, the church guaranteed a pew that fit the family's needs, and was reserved exclusively for that family. Numbering the pews was the easiest way to denote them. This church was built during the late colonial period, belonged to the Church of England, and used the customary pew tax to support itself. After the Revolution, the Constitution forbade any government-supported official religion. The Episcopal Church sprang up as sort of an American cousin of the Church of England, although it is independent and there is no official connection. The former Anglican churches became Episcopal churches, and simply retained the pew tax. This pew is our family pew. Everyone here has one."

As Lee and Cosby were quietly talking, the church was filling up. Finally the service started as the crucifer led the way down one of the aisles, leading the celebrant and acolytes from the back of the church to the front. The great opening hymn of Episcopal services swelled from the congregation and the organ, and Cosby was conscious of Lee's fine baritone voice among the leaders.

Holy, Holy, Holy,
Lord God Almighty,
Early in the morning
Our song shall rise to Thee.
Holy, Holy, Holy,
Merciful and Mighty,
God in Three Persons,
Blessed Trinity.

The service took approximately an hour. Although Cosby was not an Episcopalian, he took communion with the rest of the congregation, and did not feel out of place doing so.

At the end of the service was the traditional closing hymn of Episcopalian worship.

Praise God from Whom all blessings flow,
Praise Him, all creatures here below,
Praise Him above, ye heavenly host,
Praise Father, Son, and Holy Ghost.

After the "Great Amen" the service was concluded, and the congregation began filing out.

There was no obvious place for people to gather and fellowship together outside the church. Nevertheless people did so, creating groups in the confined space between the front of the church and the Columbus Street entrance. Many wanted to talk to Lee, including the rector, the Reverend Cornelius B. Walker, to whom Lee introduced Cosby.

As the people slowly began to disperse, Lee looked around, his eyes examining the remaining people. He finally came over to Cosby. "Carter, I would be most appreciatve if you would escort Annie to the carriage. I know many of the people here, and I do not see anyone who could be Mr. Robertson, who wanted to meet with me. Perhaps there are too many people around to suit him. Annie will be safe in the carriage with Daniel there. When you are finished, please come back here."

Cosby did so. When he returned, Lee had still not found the elusive Mr. Robertson. "Perhaps he does not know Alexandria," Cosby suggested. "Could he have become lost?"

Lee smiled. "This is the most well-known church in the city, Carter. And it has been here for almost ninety years. Everybody in Alexandria knows where it is. He could stop anybody on the street and they could have told him exactly where to go."

"How about the other entrance to the church yard?" Cosby gestured down the brick walkway toward the entrance on Washington Street, where there were a few people. "Maybe he is waiting to meet you there, where a conversation with you could be much more private."

"Good idea. Thank you, Carter. I'll go down there. Please be so kind as to wait for me here. If anyone asks you about me, tell them I will return shortly."

Several people introduced themselves to Cosby in the next few minutes, but none of them was a man named Robertson. Cosby finally saw Lee returning on the walkway, briefly showing empty hands. Only a few people were left in front of the church.

"We had best leave," Lee said. "I do not believe the gentleman will appear."

As the carriage started out, Lee informed Daniel that he would like to stop at the Lloyd house. Daniel knew where it was, as Lee had stopped there many times before. John Lloyd's wife, Anne Harriot Lee, was a first cousin to Robert E. Lee, and the families visited often. It was a handsome three-story brick house at 220 N. Washington Street, near the intersection of Washington and Queen Streets.

Inside the house Lee and Annie were greeted warmly, and Lee introduced Cosby to the Lloyds. Scarcely had the greetings been made than Anne Lloyd burst out, "Oh, Robert, you must be so proud! *We* certainly are!"

"Yes," her husband beamed. "When we heard the news we could scarcely believe it. But, then, of course, we really shouldn't have been surprised. We know you so well as a relative that we sometimes forget how splendid your military record is. From all of us here, we extend our sincerest congratulations, and I am sure we are joined by all your relatives everywhere."

Lee's face showed his puzzlement. He had resigned from the army only yesterday morning, and had not told anyone about it. Had word of his resignation reached Alexandria in less than a day? Is that what the Lloyds were talking about? Or had they somehow learned of his refusal last Thursday to accept command of the recently-announced huge Union army now building for an invasion of the South?

"My dearest cousins, I am always willing to accept your warmest wishes, but I must confess that I do not exactly know what they are for. Could you enlighten me?"

John and Anne Lloyd stared at Lee, then at each other, then back at Lee. "Robert, do you mean to tell us you haven't heard?" asked Anne. "Hasn't the governor been in communication with you?"

"No, he has not," Lee responded. "Has he with you?"

"No, not at all," Anne said, showing a touch of consternation. "It's just that we heard…" She stopped and looked at her husband.

"Robert, yesterday we spoke with friends who had just arrived from Richmond," John Lloyd explained. "They told us the word is all over the city that Governor Letcher wants to appoint you as the head of all the military and naval forces of Virginia. On Wednesday the Virginia Convention, besides voting to recommend secession to the state legislature, also voted to create such a post, to be filled by gubernatorial appointment. The governor apparently wants you for it. All this was supposed to be kept secret for a time, but you know how such things leak out. Naturally we thought you knew."

"No, I didn't." Lee sat down. "Well, this is certainly an interesting turn of events. I suppose I shall soon receive a letter from the governor. Thank you for giving me some advance notice."

"It's because you live in such splendid isolation over there at Arlington," Anne remarked. "Perhaps you should consider installing your own telegraph office there." She smiled at her own joke.

John Lloyd was eyeing Lee speculatively. "Would it be an intrusion, Robert, to ask if you will accept?" he asked quietly.

Lee made a dismissive gesture with his hand. "No, John, of course it would not be an intrusion. I just don't know yet. I will have to digest this information. And, of course, if it be true, I have to wait for some sort of official request from the governor."

The group was silent for a few moments. "This is a very big decision for you, Robert," Lloyd said sympathetically. "If you accept, that would mean that you would have to resign from the United States Army. You have been in the army your whole adult life. You were a cadet at West Point, and later even the superintendant there. I'm glad I don't have to make such a decision. I am quite sure I couldn't do it."

Lee smiled wanly. "Well, then, cousins, I have some news for you. That is a decision I have already made. I resigned from the army yesterday. Only my immediate family knows. There is no point in not telling you. It will be common news soon enough."

"What?" John and Anne Lloyd exclaimed in unision. They glanced at Annie, who nodded glumly. "Robert, I don't understand," Anne pursued. "If you have not yet heard from the governor, why would you resign from the army?"

Lee rubbed his forehead. “It seems that I have displeased my superiors so severely that I cannot, in good conscience, or even reasonably, remain in the army.”

The Lloyds were thunderstruck “What?” John Lloyd exclaimed again. “*You* displeased your superiors? Robert, I thought you were considered a model officer! What in the world are you talking about?”

Lee sighed. “You might as well know this, too. Last Thursday I was offered field command of the new army that is being raised. The offer was made indirectly, but unquestionably, by President Lincoln. The president made the offer because General Scott recommended me for the position. I declined. That army is clearly going to be used to invade the Confederacy, and I felt I could not be a party to that. My decision did not sit well with General Scott. Later that day I had a personal interview with him, and he implied that I could not honorably remain in the army after declining the president’s offer of the highest command he could give. I completely understand the general’s point of view. Intellectually, I even agree with it, even though emotionally it rends my soul. So, yesterday I resigned my commission. You therefore see before you today not an army officer, model or otherwise, but a private citizen.”

“I must sit down,” John Lloyd muttered, and promptly did so.

His wife’s reaction was quite different; she burst into tears. “Oh, Robert,” she sobbed, walking over to him and throwing her arms around him. “You gave up your career in the army just so you wouldn’t have to invade us.” She disengaged from him and held him at arm’s length. “This land where you and so many others were born—you cannot make it into a battlefield. And you gave up everything for that. I cannot tell you how much I admire you.” She kissed him on the cheek.

“Many other officers in the deeper South have resigned their commissions when their states seceded,” Lee commented, a bit embarrassed. “It is nothing unusual these days.”

“Yes, but they were not offered the supreme command,” Anne said, wiping her cheeks. She looked over at Annie, who had silently started to cry. “You were. That makes you something of a saint, in my opinion.”

"Oh, Anne, please," Lee scoffed. "If there's anything in the world I'm not, it's a saint. Ask my wife. I'm afraid you make the Almighty cringe by using a word like that."

"Well, we're probably going to need a saint, or something very much like one, in the very near future, I daresay. And I certainly don't see one in that Mr. Lincoln or in the gang around him across the river. So there." Anne walked over to comfort her young cousin.

"If only my wife had strong opinions." John Lloyd shook his head. "Perhaps, Robert, this new position will enable you to stay in the military. That is where you clearly belong."

"Perhaps so, John," Lee agreed. "There is much to consider. Well, we had best be getting along. Thank you for your usual warm hospitality, and thank you again for this unexpected information."

Lee spoke briefly to Daniel before entering the carriage. "Now we know who this mysterious Mr. Robertson may be," Cosby remarked as the carriage started to move. "He's probably an emissary from the governor. The governor wanted to make his offer to you more official and more personal than merely sending you a letter."

"Yes, it would certainly seem so," Lee agreed. "Well, we will wait and see what develops. If he is a personal representative of the governor, I certainly think he will try to reach me again." The carriage moved slowly north on Washington Street. "I have asked Daniel to stop at a certain house, Carter. I thought you might like to see it. It is the dearest house in the city to me."

The carriage turned right on Oronoco Street, only two blocks north of the Lloyd house. It stopped in front of a house numbered 607, on the north side of the street. It was a brick house of two and a half stories with a handsome pedimented entrance, and joined to the house next to it.

"This is my boyhood home, Carter. When I was three years old our family had to leave Stratford Hall, where I was born. It is farther down the Potomac, below Mount Vernon. We came to Alexandria and stayed first in a house on Cameron Street, then moved here."

"Although I did not know it at the time we moved here, this house would become doubly important to me later when I married, for it is a part of the Fitzhugh and Custis family history. It was originally owned by the Fitzhugh family, and in 1804 Mary Lee Fitzhugh married George Washington Parke Custis here; they later became my mother-in-law and father-in-law."

Cosby grinned. "Mr. Lee, it does seem that you are related to about half the people in Virginia."

"Maybe more than half," Lee grinned back. "Now you know why I cannot invade this state. Most of the people fighting against me would be my own relatives."

"There were some momentous times then, Carter. The War of 1812 was fought while we lived here. My father was very restless during that war. He thought the army would call him back into action, and he looked forward to a command again, although he was philosophically against the war. The army pay would also ease his financial condition. However, the army did not recall him. In July of 1812 he went to the aid of a friend who was a newspaper publisher in Baltimore. A mob assaulted the house of the friend, which my father was helping to defend. He was badly wounded in that riot, so badly that he was reported in Washington as having died. He did not die, but lingered in a Baltimore hospital for several weeks before returning home. He never fully recovered, and was never offered an army command."

"While he was still in that Baltimore hospital, President Madison very graciously came to this house to express his condolences to my mother for how my father had been mistreated. That was the only time I have ever met a president. I remember him as short and intense, but very well-spoken and very much in command."

"Two years later, when I was seven, I was one of many who stood on the docks and watched the burning of Washington by the British. My boyhood friends and I were too young to realize the full horrors of war, and simply thought it was tremendously exciting. Many adults, I remember, were panic-stricken. 'If the British can burn our capital city," they asked one another, 'what hope is there for us in this war?' Even the Executive Mansion was burned after President Madison, Dolley Madison, and the entire cabinet had fled. It was a tragic thing, but we did finally win that war."

"My father died in 1818 while returning from a trip to the West Indies. I had the responsibility of reading to my mother, in that house, the letter which informed us of his death. I was eleven years old. She took it very hard, and she was already a partial invalid."

"It was also in that house that the Marquis de Lafayette came to visit us in October of 1824. He had never met any of us, but he wished to pay his respects to the family of my father, whom he remembered well. My two older brothers were away, but my two sisters and I were there to help our mother. That was quite an occasion."

"Annie has shared with me the fact that Lafayette also came to Arlington at that time," Cosby remarked.

"Yes, he did," Lee agreed. "He visited many places on his 1824 trip. He was almost 70 years old at that time, and wanted to revisit the great places of his youth. He wanted to meet Mr. Custis as a man, since he remembered him as a small boy. He was very impressed with Arlington, so I'm told. My wife remembers him well; she was a 16-year-old girl at the time, and rather overwhelmed by such a distinguished visitor. I must admit that I was, too, when he visited us right here."

"What became of your mother?" Cosby asked.

"Shortly after I left for West Point in 1825," Lee replied, "she left here and went to live with my oldest brother, Carter, in Georgetown. We call him "Carter," like you," he explained, "even though that is his middle name. He is a successful lawyer. I was granted a furlough for the summer of '27 and came there to be with her. She was becoming very ill. I would carry her into the carriage for Sunday rides."

"That was the year I began to visit Miss Custis," Lee continued. "We had met a few times at family functions, but I remember the summer of that year as the time that I began to have thoughts and hopes that perhaps someday we might be married."

"I was not able to return home again until after I had graduated in '29. Mother was so ill that she was no longer living with my brother, but was at the estate of a relative where she could have constant care. She died in July of that year; I was at her bedside when the end came."

Lee was silent for a time. “I think she just gave it up to God, Carter. She fought her illness as long as she could. She raised us all on her scant family income; because it was her own, from her family, it was protected from my father’s creditors. She lived to see all three of her sons safely embarked in their chosen professions, her oldest daughter was married, and her youngest daughter with friends. She had fought the good fight, and won. She died peacefully.”

Lee gazed out the window of the carriage at his boyhood home. “I do not think a greater woman has drawn breath,” he said quietly. “Ah, well.” He leaned out the window. “Daniel, let’s go home.”

CHAPTER 39

Sunday
Washington
11:17 AM

"Good morning, Mr. Secretary."

Simon Cameron had been chatting casually with a friend outside St. John's Church after the ten o'clock service. He turned around at the sound of a pleasant female voice.

The woman he beheld was even more pleasing to look at than listen to. She had a full but not buxom figure, dark lustrous hair, a faintly olive tint to her clear skin, and dark eyes that glowed with intelligence. Although not tall, she had a commanding presence. She was dressed in church finery of simple but elegant cut. Cameron thought she may have been the most dazzlingly attractive woman he had ever seen.

The striking woman extended her hand. "So pleased to finally meet you, Mr. Secretary. I'm Rose Greenhow."

Cameron grasped the outstretched hand almost too eagerly. He had a strong impulse to bend over and kiss her hand, but knew that would be inappropriate for someone he had just met. Being interested in the social affairs of the city, he had heard Greenhow's name mentioned several times, and also knew that she was a member of the congregation at St. John's, but had never met her. He had been in Washington only a month, arriving later than the other Cabinet secretaries. "Mrs. Greenhow! I have heard of you, but never had the opportunity to meet you. It is indeed a pleasure."

"And a great pleasure for me." Greenhow appraised him appreciatively, letting her hand rest in his. "I am now quite convinced that you are even handsomer than ladies' gossip has maintained."

Cameron laughed. "That is gossip I would like to hear. And please—do call me Simon."

Greenhow smiled, showing perfect teeth. "Thank you. I shall. And I hope you call me Rose."

"I would be honored." Cameron started to disengage his hand, but Greenhow held on.

"Simon, I know you are one of the busiest people in Washington, but I wonder if I might have a private word with you."

Cameron looked around at all the people in front of Washington's most fashionable church. "You mean—right now?"

Greenhow nodded. "I have recently received information which I believe to be important, but you would know better than I. It involves something which may be of national significance. And it is military in nature, so I naturally thought you should be the person I should approach."

All this sounded a bit presumptuous coming from a woman standing in front of a church on a pleasant Sunday morning, but Cameron had heard of Greenhow's great interest in politics. "All right, Rose. I would be happy to listen. What is it?"

"Do you know of an army officer named Colonel Robert E. Lee? Recently stationed in Texas, now at home in Virginia? On an estate named Arlington, just across the river?"

Cameron withdrew his hand and narrowed his eyes. "As a matter of fact, I do. Why? Do you know him?"

"Unfortunately I do not. If I did, perhaps I could personally warn him."

"*Warn* him? Of what?"

"I have information that indicates an attempt may soon be made on his life."

"*What?*" Cameron looked around again, then lowered his voice. "Someone may try to *kill* him?"

"That is my information, yes."

"I cannot believe such a thing. Why are you telling me?"

"Because you are the Secretary of War. Colonel Lee is a distinguished officer. You are, in effect, his superior. I thought there might be some way you could protect him."

"*Protect* him? A *Virginian?* The Virginians are doing precious little to merit anything at all, let alone protection, from the government of the United States. That state has *seceded*, Rose. The Virginia militia has seized the Harpers Ferry arsenal and the Gosport navy yard. I wouldn't lift my little finger to do anything to help a Virginian right now. Besides, there's a bigger reason why I should now have nothing to do with Colonel Lee."

"A bigger reason?"

"Yes. Yesterday a courier delivered to me a brief note from Lee; he has resigned his commission. I am informed that General Scott received a similar note. Mr. Lee is therefore no longer in the United States Army. By his own choice, he is now a private citizen. And living in a state which, also by its own choice, has seceded. Both he and his state have turned their backs on the United States of America. I most certainly do not see it as my duty to provide protection for a private citizen residing in a seceded state."

"But—"

"Good *day*, Mrs. Greenhow."

CHAPTER 40

Sunday
The Executive Mansion
1:21 PM

Ward Hill Lamon approached the Executive Mansion from its east side. He was not on duty on Sunday, but there were a few things he wanted to do before Monday, when the usual crowd of shameless office-seekers would be milling about. Besides, he would be here later this evening, as he had started the practice of sleeping on a couch just outside the presidential bedroom on the second floor. There had been threats against Lincoln's life even before he had reached Washington. No one would reach the president and first lady in the Executive Mansion at night if he, the Marshal of Washington, could do anything to prevent it.

There was no guard at the gate. People were expected to respect the privacy of the president, especially on Sundays. As he approached the north entrance under the high white portico, however, he could see that an army officer was on guard duty outside the front door, as he should be. The officer was talking to a woman. That in itself was unusual, as women visitors to the President's House were unusual, unless they were invited for some social function. Lamon knew there were no social gatherings scheduled for today. As he drew closer, he could see that this was no ordinary woman. She was quite well dressed and very attractive—a lady. And she was alone. What was an unescorted lady doing here on a Sunday? Was she perhaps a friend or relative of Mrs. Lincoln? The officer seemed to be gently remonstrating with her.

"Hello, Lieutenant," Lamon greeted the officer. White House guards were picked from the ranks of commissioned officers in the army. "Is there some trouble?"

"No trouble, Mr. Lamon," the officer responded. "This lady wishes to personally see the president. I told her she cannot possibly do that today. If she comes back tomorrow, perhaps he might see her."

"He's right, ma'am," Lamon addressed the woman, whom he could not help but notice was strikingly attractive. "The president does not receive visitors on Sunday. He usually does that on Mondays. There will be many people here tomorrow, and he will certainly see some of them. If you wish, I could make an appointment for you."

The woman looked steadily at Lamon for a few moments. "Are you Mr. Ward Lamon? The Marshal of Washington?"

"Yes, ma'am, I am."

The woman held out her right hand, palm down, and smiled warmly. "Good afternoon, Mr. Lamon. I'm Mrs. Rose Greenhow."

The name meant nothing to Lamon. "Well, Mrs. Greenhow, I'm pleased to meet you," he said, briefly taking her hand. "As I was saying, perhaps tomorrow—"

"Mr. Lamon, I am not an office-seeker," Greenhow said crisply. "I live only a short distance from here, on 16th Street, just across Lafayette Square. I have come here because I have recently learned some information which I believe to be of extreme importance to the government. I considered it my duty to inform a high-ranking government official. Mr. Cameron didn't seem all that interested, so I thought I should go directly to the president."

"Mr. Cameron? *Simon* Cameron? The Secretary of War?"

"Yes. I spoke with him two hours ago."

Lamon considered this woman. She was authoritative, knowledgeable, educated, and decisive. Somehow she knew a prominent member of the president's cabinet, and had recently spoken with him. She had even recognized who *he* was, once the officer had spoken his name. She also said that she lived on 16th Street, where no paupers lived. Although he had never met her or heard of her—he had been in Washington less than two months—she was clearly a person of some influence.

"Come with me, Mrs. Greenhow." He opened the door. "I'll be responsible for her, Lieutenant."

"Thank you, sir," the officer replied with obvious relief.

Lamon and Greenhow entered the door, and walked through the vestibule to the central hallway. Ignoring the state rooms on the first floor, Lamon turned left, then used a stairway known to the staff as the "back stairs" to reach the second floor. He walked down the central corridor to the east end of the building, stopping before a door which led to an office in the northeastern corner. He opened the door for Greenhow to enter, but she had stopped and turned around, facing the other side of the hallway. She pointed to a door diagonally across the hall.

"That is the president's office, isn't it, Mr. Lamon."

"Why, yes, ma'am, it is. How did you know that?"

"I have been here before. I am a friend of former President Buchanan."

Greenhow entered the room, leaving Lamon to ponder her again. Could she possibly have been a mistress of Old Buck? He had not been known as a loose type with women, but he had been a bachelor, the only bachelor president in American history; his niece, Harriet Lane, had been the official White House hostess at social events. If he had an appreciative eye for women, Mrs. Greenhow would certainly have caught that eye.

Lamon left the office door ajar a few inches. He had never had a private conference with a woman in the White House, let alone with one who knew her way around it and was a friend, possibly an intimate one, with a former president. It would not be a happy circumstance if someone were to open a closed door and find him in close private conversation with such a woman.

After they were seated, Lamon reached for a pen and paper. "Now, then, Mrs. Greenhow, the first thing I would like to do is to record your name. How do you spell it?"

Greenhow told him.

"And your first name?"

"Rose."

"Your address?"

"398 16th Street. It is near the corner of 16th and H Streets, across from St. John's Church."

"How about your husband, ma'am?"

"I am a widow, Mr. Lamon. My late husband, Robert, was a lawyer and linguist for the government. He negotiated several treaties with Indian tribes in the West. He died in San Francisco several years ago."

"I'm sorry about that, ma'am. I didn't know. It seems as if the government lost a dedicated and valuable public servant at the death of your husband. We thank him, and you."

"It did. Thank you."

"Well, now. What is this information which is so compelling?"

"It concerns a high-ranking officer in the army. That is why I first approached the Secretary of War. For various reasons he declined to act. However, I still believe this matter to be quite important."

"Who is this army officer?"

"Colonel Robert E. Lee, Mr. Lamon. He—"

"Just a moment," Lamon interrupted quickly. "What was that name again?"

"Colonel Robert E. Lee," Greenhow said more slowly and distinctly. She stopped. Lamon was eyeing her sharply. He was not writing that name down on the sheet of paper in front of him.

"Do you know him?"

"Not personally, no," Lamon replied. "However, I do know *of* him. Do you know him?"

"No, sir, I do not. If I did, I would go to him directly."

"Why? What has he done?"

"It is not something he has done, Mr. Lamon. It is something which is about to happen *to* him. His life is in danger. Someone is planning to kill him."

In the hallway, eight-year-old Tad Lincoln was playing with a toy train made of wooden blocks. "Choo-choo-choo," he said softly to himself as he guided it down the hallway floor from the residential rooms on the west side of the building toward the offices on the east side. Besides its tender, the little locomotive was pulling three passenger cars, all connected by hook-and-eye couplers. All the wheels actually turned, which delighted the boy since he didn't have to slide the train and pretend the wheels were turning. Even more delightful was the absence of his obnoxious older brother, Willie, who often took his toys and played with them himself. Under Tad's skilfull guidance, the little train even successfully navigated the short flight of steps in the hallway. Approaching the end of the hallway, glowingly illuminated by a large fan window, the boy heard low voices. They seemed to be coming from the last door on the left side of the hallway. He noticed that the door was slightly ajar. He guided the train to the door, then stopped and listened. There were only two different voices. One of them was a woman's. The man's voice was definitely that of Uncle Hill, but he did not recognize the woman's voice. Lying flat on the hallway floor, he slowly peeked into the room. He could not see Uncle Hill, but he saw a pretty lady with dark hair and nice clothes. He had never seen her before. After a few moments he slowly withdrew from the edge of the door and sat against the wall, listening.

"What?" Lamon exclaimed. "Mrs. Greenhow, did you say someone is planning to kill Colonel Lee? You mean *assassinate* him?"

"Yes, that is indeed what I mean."

"This is very hard to believe, ma'am. Who in the world would want to do such a thing?"

"It is a young man who lives in the city. His name is Rufus Sloan. He works as a clerk at Grinell's Goods, a general store on 11th Street."

"A clerk? In a general store?" Lamon regarded the visitor dubiously. "Mrs. Greenhow, Colonel Lee is an exemplary officer. He is a member of the Lees of Virginia, perhaps the most distinguished family in the entire state. Although I have never met him, I know that he has a long history of service to his country in the army. Why does this clerk want to assassinate him?"

"I am pleased, Mr. Lamon, that you know so much about Colonel Lee. You must know, therefore, that although he lives in Virgina, his estate is just across the river." Lamon nodded. "The fact that he lives in that state was one reason Mr. Cameron cited for minimizing my concern and refusing to help."

"How did you want him to help you?"

"By protecting Colonel Lee."

Out in the hallway, a few minutes of listening convinced Tad Lincoln that Uncle Hill and the lady were not going to talk about anything really interesting, so he turned the train around and began its journey back to his room.

"What exactly did the secretary say?" Lamon pursued.

"He said that he would not lift his little finger to help a Virginian, now that the state has seceded. He also said that yesterday he had received a note from Lee in which Lee resigned his commission. That would technically make Lee a private citizen. Mr. Cameron stated emphatically that it was not his duty to protect private citizens residing in seceded states."

"Ahum," Lamon commented. This was the first he had heard of Lee's resignation. If Cameron had received such a note, then surely he would have notified the president, wouldn't he? "Well, that seems reasonable from the secretary's point of view. It also seems to me to be reasonable from the president's point of view. Is that why you wanted to see the president? To convince him to protect Lee?"

Greenhow nodded. "Yes."

"And even if the president agreed with you, how would you propose to have him do that?"

"By arresting Sloan."

Lamon sighed. "Mrs. Greenhow, the president was a practicing lawyer for a long time. So was I. We both could assure you that we cannot go around arresting people on the mere suspicion that they might be planning some illegal act, even one as serious as murder. We need proof. If not proof of action, then at least proof of intention. What sort of proof do you have of this allegation?"

"Thank you for pointing that out, Mr. Lamon. Mr. Cameron dismissed me curtly because, from his point of view, he was interested only in the military and political aspects of this information. You, however, are the Marshal of Washington. Any illegal activity in the city is of interest to you. Here, then, is your proof: this man Sloan is a fugitive from justice. He is already wanted for major crimes."

"Really? We could do something about that. What crimes?"

"He was one of John Brown's raiders at Harpers Ferry."

"*What?*" Lamon almost stood up. "*Harpers Ferry?* Mrs. Greenhow, are you sure of this information?"

"Yes, sir, I am. There is more. He was also with Brown five years ago, when Brown's group murdered several people in Kansas. He used the name Joshua Cutler there. That murderous group nicknamed him Cutter Cutler because of his handiness with a saber."

This time Lamon did stand up. He had to think. He wordlessly walked slowly over to a window in the north side of the building, and gazed out over the White House grounds with the statue of Jefferson that President Polk had erected, Pennsylvania Avenue, Lafayette Square, and St. John's Church, which stood at the northeast corner of 16th Street and H Street, just across H Street from Lafayette Square. His eye automatically traveled across 16th Street from the church to a three-story house near the opposite corner; he realized with a start that he was looking right at his visitor's house. He also realized that of all the residents of Washington, Mrs. Greenhow was one of the very closest to the Executive Mansion, only a block away.

Kansas! Lamon knew that there had been a great deal of sectional violence there in the middle of the previous decade, all because of contentious provisions of the Kansas-Nebraska Act. The worst had been the sack of the town of Lawrence by proslavers; *cannon* had been used there. But there had been a lot more violence, and John Brown had been heavily involved in it. He had reputedly led a group of abolitionists which killed a number of proslavers—four, five?—along one of those creeks named for an Indian tribe. Newspaper reports had called it a massacre. Yes, that was it: the "Pottawatomie Massacre."

Brown's involvement in that bloody event had never been a secret. The problem of bringing him to justice, or anyone else there, had been a lack of law enforcement. Kansas had been a territory at the time, not a state. In fact, it had been finally admitted as the 34th state only three months ago, in late January of this year. It was the newest state in the Union. In the mid-'50's it had been on the frontier. U.S. laws and the law enforcement personnel to back them up had been practically nonexistent. An additional complication had been the rival claims of two towns, one proslavery and one antislavery, each claiming to be the capital of the whole territory, and each promulgating laws which were ignored outside its sphere of influence. In such a fractious and volatile environment John Brown could wreak his violence almost unopposed.

Now Mrs. Greenhow was telling him that someone who had been with Brown in his two most notorious raids was at large right here in Washington. Moreover, he was supposedly planning to kill the very man President Lincoln had asked him to investigate, because the president had been considering Lee for the field command of the army. No matter that Lee had declined that command, and had now apparently resigned his commission. He, Ward Hill Lamon, was the Marshal of Washington. He could not ignore this information.

Lamon turned around, still standing by the window. "Mrs. Greenhow, I am prepared to act, but I must be absolutely assured of the accuracy of these claims, which are rather startling. What is your source for this information? Do you know this Sloan person?"

"No, sir. I have never met him."

"Then how do you know so much about him, including his nickname?"

"I am sorry, Mr. Lamon." Greenhow smiled. "I would like to accommodate you, but I must protect the confidentiality of my sources. I can assure you, however, that I am positively convinced that everything I have told you is true. My particular source *does* know him personally." She paused. "I realize that this association with John Brown was several years ago. Although the crimes were spectacular, they occurred in places far from here, and therefore there may be some difficulty in connecting this Mr. Sloan with Brown and his raiders. However, there is something more immediate. I am informed that there was a double murder committed last night right here in Washington. Two men, killed by knife wounds. The incident took place on E Street, between 2nd and 3rd Streets. About nine o'clock. I am sorry that I have no way of verifying this information. There has been no mention of it in the morning papers; perhaps there will be some in the afternoon papers. It was Sloan who killed those men."

Lamon stared at Greenhow. "This Sloan killed *two men*? *Last night*?

"That is my information," Greenhow asserted. "With the powers you have under your command as marshal," she added, "I would presume that you have ways of verifying all this information."

Lamon considered this as he seated himself again. He indeed had extensive powers, probably exceeding those of the chief of the Metropolitan Police. "All right, ma'am," he said. "If you won't tell me the name of your source, at least tell me how long you have known this information about this Rufus Sloan."

"I found it out shortly before I talked with Mr. Cameron this morning. I have known it only six hours."

"Ahum. That is very prompt. You are to be commended, ma'am."

"Thank you."

Lamon checked his notes. "And you say this Sloan works at a general store called Grinell's Goods? On 11th Street?"

"That is so."

"Where on 11th?"

"Between F and G Streets. I do not know the exact address. I have never been there."

Lamon scribbled something on the paper. "Do you happen to know where he lives?"

"Unfortunately, no, except that it is somewhere in the city. A boarding house, I would assume."

More scribbling. "How about his age and general description?"

Greenhow repeated the description that O'Connor had given her.

"Do you know when this Sloan intends to attack Lee?"

"No. It could be soon. That is why I felt that someone in authority should know about this as soon as possible."

"Do you know where? Or how?"

"No. I am sorry."

"Does this Sloan have any associates in this plan? Is he part of a group?"

"My source did not mention any others. There may be."

Lamon wrote on the sheet of paper, then was silent for a while. "There is stll something which I believe has not been answered, ma'am. Exactly why does this Sloan want to kill Lee?"

"Sloan was a rabid follower of John Brown, Mr. Lamon. Robert E. Lee was the officer in charge of the soldiers who captured Brown at Harpers Ferry. My source states that Sloan hates Lee for capturing Brown, and blames him for Brown's subsequent execution. He wants revenge. A life for a life. He is also an abolitionist, and obviously violent. Lee has slaves. So he also hates Lee for being a slave-owner."

"Mrs. Greenhow, Harpers Ferry was a year and a half ago. Why now? Why didn't this Sloan try to exact his revenge earlier?"

"As I understand it, Colonel Lee was often away. Now he is at home. Sloan just learned of it."

Lamon was silent for almost a minute, examining his notes. "Is there anything else you would like to add, Mrs. Greenhow?" he finally asked.

"No. If there is anything you can do about Mr. Sloan, I would be most gratified."

"There are indeed some things we can do. Now, then, allow me to escort you out of the building."

The two were silent as they retraced their steps down to the first floor and out the front door. Lamon thanked Greenhow again and watched her as she exited the mansion grounds.

Back in the second-floor office, Lamon planned his next move. Although he knew that most of the Harpers Ferry raiders had either been killed at the arsenal or captured, and then tried and executed, he knew that several of them had escaped. Although the raid had generated an enormous amount of newspaper coverage, he could not recall any of the names of the raiders except that of John

Brown himself. Question: was this Sloan/Cutler person really one of the escapees, as Greenhow alleged? The best person Lamon could think of to answer that question was Edward Bates, the Attorney General.

Bates could also help with a legal question. Lamon recalled that Brown and the other captured raiders had been tried in a Virginia court for crimes against the state of Virginia; they had not been tried in a federal court for crimes against the government of the United States, despite the fact that Harpers Ferry was a federal arsenal. If this Rufus Sloan were arrested, could he be tried on *federal* charges arising from the raid? Virginia had now seceded from the Union, and the government of the United States was not about to do the state of Virginia any favors by turning over a Harpers Ferry raider to be prosecuted by the state.

And what about Kansas? That had been a territory at the time of Brown's activities, not a state, but it was still subject to territorial laws of the United States. John Brown was now dead, and no possible witnesses need fear any retributive violence from his followers. Were there any witnesses still there who could testify against Sloan? Or would everyone there be so caught up in the monstrous gathering storm of civil war that they couldn't care less about a few murders in Bleeding Kansas of half a decade ago?

Bates would have to be contacted. Lamon wrote out several papers for him, asked him to reply as soon as possible, and arranged for a courier to take them to the Attorney General's private residence.

The murders could be handled more quickly. Had they actually occurred? This was a matter for the Metropolitan Police. He himself had not heard about them, but surely the police were already investigating them—if they had really happened. Mrs. Greenhow seemed to be one of the most incisive and level-headed women he had ever met, but he really know nothing about her except information she had provided about herself, and that was scant. He wrote a note to the police department, asking for details about about a double killing which had supposedly happened on E Street last night. He did not provide any information about Sloan; that could wait until he learned more about the alleged crimes. He would not make a fool of himself with the police department by providing details about the perpetrator only to learn that the crimes were the figments of a woman's hyperactive imagination.

Now, then—what about Sloan himself? Greenhow had known where he worked, but not where he lived. Could he, Lamon, afford to wait until tomorrow morning and have agents pick up Sloan at the general store? Greenhow also had not known where, when, or how Sloan would strike, or whether he had accomplices. Several of the Harpers Ferry raiders had escaped; Lamon could not remember how many. Could it be that *all* of the escapees shared Sloan's hatred of Lee, and that *all* of them were now in the city conspiring together to kill him?

That thought gave Lamon the chills. Sloan would have to be located, detained, and questioned as soon as possible. But where was he?

Lamon thought of Allan Pinkerton. The former railroad detective, charged with the safety of President-elect Lincoln on his trip from Springfield to Washington for the inauguration, had uncovered a plot in Baltimore and foiled it by changing the train schedule. As a reward, Lincoln had created an army rank for him under the ficticious name of "Major E. J. Allen," and placed him in charge of all counterespionage activities in and around the city of Washington. In effect, this made Pinkerton a presidential private detective with a military rank, operating outside the Metropolitan Police.

Lamon was not exactly sure whether his own powers included those of Pinkerton, or whether Pinkerton would insist that he reported exclusively to the president. However, he felt that this information was something the Scottish-born detective should know. If anybody could locate Sloan before tomorrow morning, Pinkerton could.

As insurance, Lamon also decided to send two of his own men to locate Sloan and arrest him. He would instruct them to defer to Pinkerton and cooperate with him if they encountered him, but they would report back to him, the marshal. He also decided that the president did not need to know about this. Not yet, anyway.

CHAPTER 41

Sunday
Arlington House
3:10 PM

A civilian courier rode up to Arlington House with a letter for Robert E. Lee. It was from John Robertson, who was staying at a hotel in Alexandria, apologizing for missing the church appointment. In it Robertson revealed that he was an emissary from Gov. Letcher of Virginia, and that the governor wished to personally see Lee in Richmond as soon as possible. The letter did not state why the governor wished to see him, but Lee already knew the reason why.

After Lee read the letter, he instructed the courier to wait, then wrote a letter in reply. In his letter he stated that he would meet Robertson at the depot of the Orange and Alexandria Railroad the next morning, and they would travel to Richmond together.

After the courier went on his way, Lee invited Carter Cosby to accompany him to Richmond. Cosby was the governor's appointee, and he could take this opportunity to report to the governor in person. Depending on how Lee's own arrangements with the governor proceeded, Cosby could return to Arlington if necessary. Cosby agreed.

CHAPTER 42

Sunday
Washington
3:51 PM

Rufus Sloan had lain on his bed for more than an hour, turning thought after thought over in his mind. The hangover he had nursed for most of the day was now gone. He finally sat up, swung his legs over the side of the bed, and stood up. *Now*, he thought, *it has to be now*.

He had always been a man of few possessions. There was really nothing of sentimental value in this boarding-house room that he wished to take with him. Although he read a lot, he actually owned few books; most of the books he read were from the public library. He owned no furniture, no mirrors, no lamps. One of the principal reasons he had chosen this particular boarding house was that its owner, Mrs. Sturdevant, had agreed to provide modest furnishings for a small additional rental fee. He did, however, own a pocket watch. This was not an affectation, but a device of necessity; he did not want to ever be late for work, which would call undue attention to himself.

The watch was small. He would take it with him, for it could certainly come in useful where he intended to go. Into a small valise he packed a change of clothing, some underwear, and toiletry articles. He also included some field camping equipment and eating utensils.

Ever since he had seen Sandy Tilton's new Army-model revolver, a plan to kill the traitorous Col. Lee had gradually solidified in his mind. He knew that any such plan would have to involve a firearm of some sort. Lee was ensconced in his big mansion up on the Virginia heights overlooking the Potomac, and rarely left it; he could not be waylaid at night in some dark alley in Washington.

Sloan knew from the conversations at the recruiting center, and with Tilton, that Lee was rarely at home; he was usually stationed at some army post, often a great distance away from Virginia, and surrounded by soldiers. Untouchable.

Sloan knew he was good with a saber, but he had none; he had to leave his at Harpers Ferry in order to escape. He had not bought another because that would have called attention to himself. Besides, a saber called for close quarters and—if used for a sudden attack—concealment. A saber was almost impossible to conceal. His knife was much better for close quarters, as he had proved last night. But how could he get close enough to Lee?

A rifle? Sloan had dismissed that idea almost as soon as he had thought of it. Even if he had a rifle, how could he shoot Lee? Somehow hang around the Arlington estate, as obvious as a spider on a wedding cake to the dozens of people—including the slaves—who lived there, and wait for some chance when Lee would come out of the house and present himself as a target? Even if that happened, Sloan had scant experience with rifles; he would almost certainly miss. Due to the cumbersome procedure for reloading a rifle, Lee would be long gone before he could get off a second shot. Even a Sharps had to be reloaded one cartridge at a time. And rifles were as hard to conceal as sabers.

A pistol would be best. Easy to conceal, multiple shots as fast as you could pull the trigger, infallible at close range. But how could he get Lee within that range? Since it could not be done in Washington, it would have to be done at Arlington.

The answer had finally come to him as he contemplated the isolation of Lee's mansion on its great estate, the very thing which made Lee so unapproachable. How did the army get information to

Lee? For ordinary information there was the mail. But suppose the army wanted to reach Lee with urgent information, or with sensitive information that it didn't want exposed to possible prying eyes in the mail service, or wanted absolute proof of delivery? Then it must use a *military courier.* That made sense, especially since the War Department was only a few miles from Lee's estate; it would be a quick and easy horseback ride for a mounted courier. In fact, a commercial courier must be the way urgent non-military information was brought to the estate. Since Lee was a prominent person as well as a high-ranking military officer, couriers must be a common sight on the estate when Lee was in residence. Sloan could therefore gain direct access to Lee at Arlington by *posing as a courier.*

To pose as a courier Sloan would need a horse; one could easily be rented. To kill Lee he would need a pistol; Tilton had shown him the very pistol he would need just two days ago. He could borrow that pistol. All right, *steal* it. He could even return it to Tilton by mail when he had reached someplace safe.

Sloan had experienced a warm glow of pleasure and the anticipatory thrill of danger as he lay in bed two nights ago, when all the pieces of his plan had come together in his mind. He had even figured out a way to steal the gun.

Time was of the essence. Lee had turned down the field command of the army and the general's rank that would undoubtedly have accompanied it. He was therefore still a colonel. The army could assign him to a post at any time. From what Sloan had learned of Lee's past history, that post could be anywhere. If Sloan were going to strike Lee at the estate, he wanted it to be tomorrow.

That meant he would have to move *tonight. Now.*

Yesterday at Grinell's he had put the first part of his plan into action, the way to steal the gun. He had taken a 4-ounce glass bottle, of which the store had many in stock; it was similar to the type used by apothecary shops. He filled the bottle three-quarters full with ordinary water, adding a little blue food coloring. He then attached what looked like a label from an apothecary. He had labored long over this bogus label in his room at Sturdevant's, writing and rewriting versions of it until it had the proper degree of casual illegibility so typical of apothecary labels. This bottle he now set conspicuously on top of the dresser.

The last thing he did was to withdraw the money he had hidden in a box on the shelf at the top of the closet. He had not put it in a bank. It was $347.55, some of which he had before being hired at Grinell's. Living frugally, he had added to it during the year and a half he had clerked at the store. It was the most money he had ever had in his life.

Putting on his hat and picking up the valise, he took a last quick look around the room. He did not expect to be back.

Walking briskly, he covered the distance to Seventh Street in ten minutes, checking the time by glancing at his pocket watch. He turned down Seventh Strret until he reached the boarding house where Tilton stayed. The front door had not yet been locked for the night, so he did not need a night key. He put his valise and hat next to a sofa in the unoccupied small front parlor, then went up the staircase to Tilton's room. Knocking softly, he was gratified to hear a noise inside the room; Tilton could have been absent, which would have spoiled his plan.

"Hello, Sandy," he said quietly when Tilton opened the door.

"Hi, Cutter," Tilton replied in a surprised voice. "Come on in. What brings you here?"

Sloan entered the room and seated himself. He came right to the point. "Sandy, I really enjoyed our supper together the other night. I'd like to do it again, if it's all right with you. And I've got a special deal." He paused. "This time, I'll treat," he smiled.

"This evening?"

"Sure. Why not?"

"Want to go back to Harvey's again? Sure looked like you were getting to fancy oysters."

"No, I thought I'd like to try something as special as I could make it. Let's go to Willard's."

"Willard's?"

"That's right. Willard's."

Tilton sat down on the edge of his bed and smiled his cat-like smile. "Cutter, that's the most expensive hotel in the entire city. I've been there a few times, but not often. Only swells eat there. Only swells even *go* there."

"So for once in my life I'd like to be a swell."

"You're really serious about this?"

"Sure am."

"Some rich aunt just die and leave you a bundle?"

"Something like that."

"Well, *all right*. Got a hat, I'm *ready*. Tell you what. Willard's is such a dandified place that it's a treat just to walk around the lobby, dawdle over some drinks at the bar, and take a gander at everything. If you promise not to drink too much, I'll stand you to a drink or two. Then we can have a nice leisurely supper of the best food in the city, with waiters bowing and scraping, and pretty women giving you the eye."

"That's exactly what I want."

Sloan did not even glance inside the front parlor when they left the boarding house.

They walked through the fine spring late afternoon, chatting casually. Finally they came to Willard's Hotel, the famous five-story hotel on the northwest corner of 14th Street and Pennsylvania Avenue. Situated on the busiest avenue in the city and only two blocks from the Executive Mansion, Willard's was also close to the State Department, the Treasury building, the War Department, and the Navy Department. It was the largest and grandest hotel in the city and *the* gathering place for businessmen, politicians, military officers, reporters, distinguished visitors from other nations, movers and shakers of all kinds, and even pretenders who wanted to see and be seen. President Lincoln had stayed there before his inauguration. There was one overriding provision, unspoken but understood by all: voices expressing sympathy for the South were not tolerated. Southern sympathizers tended to frequent the National Hotel, eight blocks farther down Pennsylvania Avenue at Sixth Street.

Tilton and Sloan entered the hotel by its Pennsylvania Avenue entrance. While Sloan tried not to gape at the opulent surroundings, Tilton led the way to the Gentlemen's Parlor, which was really an elaborate bar. "Two mint juleps," he ordered from the nattily-attired bartender. "The mint julep is the signature drink of Willard's," he explained. "The story goes that the first mint julep in Washington was prepared by Henry Clay, the famous Kentuckian, right here, about ten years ago. It quickly grew in popularity, and now a Willard's mint julep is *the* drink of Washington."

"What's in it?"

"Bourbon, sugar, water, crushed mint leaves, and ice. Down the hatch, my man. You're drinking history. If it was good enough for Henry Clay, it's good enough for you."

From Tilton and especially the bartender Sloan learned that a series of hotels had occupied this site since 1818, not long after the end of the War of 1812. The name of the current hotel had come from Henry Willard, who had taken over operations in 1847. Aided by his brothers Edwin and Joseph, Willard greatly expanded and improved the hotel to its present magnificence.

The Gentlemen's Parlor was full on this Sunday evening. Many of the men wore military uniforms, and those uniforms were not shy of gold braid. At any time, there would be more colonels, even generals, than privates in this male retreat of fine liquor and heavy conversation.

Finally it was time for dinner. The two men walked to a dining room, were seated, and handed large menus. Tilton, who had been here before, examined the extensive listing of food with nonchalance, but Sloan was astounded. The appetizers were oysters, oyster stew, and a variety of soups. There were three kinds of fish available: black bass, rock fish, and Potomac herring. In a separate category of boiled dishes were turkey, chicken, corned beef, ham, tongue, and beef *a la mode*. Roasts included beef, pig, chicken, and lamb. In another category called side dishes were filet of beef, sweetbreads with peas, veal chops, lamb chops, *fricandeau* of veal, rabbits, *aspec de huntres*, *pate de foie gras*, and quail with croutons. For those desiring wild game, there was yet another listing of entrees: wild turkey, pheasant, canvasback duck, partridge, goose, wild pigeon. For desserts there were cabinet pudding, *blancmange*, *charlotte russe*, four kinds of pie, and a variety of fruits and ice cream.

Sloan was overwhelmed. "I never knew that such a variety of foods even existed, let alone that they would all be available at one place," he whispered over the white linen tablecloth and the heavy silverware.

"Feeling like a swell yet?" Tilton grinned.

"I could get used to it. You've been here before. What do you recommend?"

"Lord, I would have to order something different every night for two years just to sample every combination available here. You can start with oysters. You like them. That's what I'm going to have."

Sloan did not reveal that he had stuffed himself with oysters just the night before. Nor would he reveal anything else that happened last night. "No, I think I'll just have some chicken soup."

"Really? Well, suit yourself. If you're going to have chicken soup, then you don't want a chicken entree. Do you like fish?"

"Not really."

"Cutter, I know you well enough to know you've hardly ever eaten fish in your entire life. As you can see from this menu, eating well is more than just corn pone with some occasional burnt mutton. You might want to consider fish. Bass is mighty tasty. As for herring—there's a delicacy."

"I don't think I want a delicacy. I want something substantial."

"Then you would be well advised to skip all those wild game dishes. Also all dishes with a French name. How about good old roast beef? That will stick to your ribs."

"Sounds better."

"Good. Now, when the waiter asks you how you would like it, don't say, 'I'd like it a lot. Just bring it.' He's asking how long you would like it cooked. Whatever you do, don't say 'well done.'" He would probably pour a pitcher of water over your head. Just say 'rare' or 'medium rare.' Got that?"

"Got it. What about dessert? What's this thing?" Sloan leaned over the table and pointed out something in the dessert portion of the menu.

"*Charlotte russe*. A special chilled custard dish. Do you like custards? Never mind, I know. You've hardly ever eaten any."

"How about that thing right next to it? Looks like a disease."

"*Blancmange*. Don't even ask. Look, Cutter, just order some sliced peaches and vanilla ice cream for dessert. Everybody likes those. I think they serve them in chilled crystal goblets here."

"All right."

"Good. You're all set. I'll signal the waiter."

"What about these?" Sloan leaned over the table again, pointing out names under the "Wines" portion of the menu.

"Veuve-Clicquot, Mumm's, Piper-Heidsieck, Moet & Chandon, Krug. Those aren't just wines, Cutter, those are *champagnes. French* champagnes. The best in the world. And very expensive. Stick to beer. I don't think you would want those."

"Why not?"

"Well, for one thing, they are expensive. For another, they have about three times the alcohol content of beer. For another…oh, hang it. If you've never tasted bass, I guess you've never tasted champagne. Everyone should taste champagne at least once in their lives. Go ahead, order a bottle. I'll help you drink it."

"Which one?"

"Moet & Chandon. Waiter!"

The meals were served, the champagne was brought and drunk. Sloan was fascinated by the tiny bubbles which spontaneously and endlessly generated themselves out of the amber liquid. He professed himself so fascinated that twice he visited the nearest men's room carrying his glass of champagne. Once inside, he emptied the glass into the sink, then returned to the table claiming he had drunk it. Sloan noted that Tilton had no trouble drinking more than his share of the champagne. The end of the best meal that Sloan had ever had in his life, and the end of the bottle of the best and most expensive liquid he had ever drunk in his life, ended on a high note indeed.

Sloan and Tilton walked a bit unsteadily back to Tilton's boarding house, Sloan occasionally bursting into snatches of song. At the front door Tilton thanked his friend. "Thanks for a great night, Cutter. You did yourself proud." Sloan sagged against him. "Listen, are you all right?"

"Shure, Sandy. Shure." Sloan gagged and made a retching noise.

"Cutter, you're drunk as a skunk." Tilton looked around. They were directly under the porch lamp; anyone on the street could see them.

"Worsh than that, old man. Gotta piss. Gotta *poop*, too."

"I'll walk you home. It's only three blocks."

"Nope. Gotta poop *bad. Major* poop. *Big-time* poop. *Poop-poop*!"

"All right, let's go in. Let's get you emptied, then I'll walk you home."

Tilton produced his night key and managed to open the front door, Sloan still sagging against him. He then helped his friend up the flight of stairs to the second floor. Like most boarding houses, this one did not have a private bathroom for each of the rooms; there was a common bathroom at the end of the hallway. Tilton half guided, half dragged Sloan to it, opened the door, and took him inside.

"Here you are, Cutter."

"Thanksh, Sandy."

"Think you'll be all right?"

"Jus' leave me be."

"Remember, I'm just down the hall. Drop by when you're finished."

Five minutes later, Tilton heard a weak knock on the door. He opened it to find Sloan leaning against the doorpost. "You done already?"

"Well, I'm pooped," Sloan said, entering the room. "But I don't feel so good, Sandy." He sat down on the edge of the bed.

"You shouldn't have eaten so much. Or drunk that champagne."

"It isn't just that. It's the cramps."

"Cramps?"

"I get cramps, Sandy. Real bad." He leaned over, seemingly gasping for air. "I take medicine for them. Real prescription medicine."

"Glad you do."

"They're gettin' worse." Sloan slid off the bed, crumpling to the floor. He lay on his side, holding his stomach. "Oh, *geez*—"

"Oh, God, Cutter. Look, I'll drag you back to the bathroom."

"No," Sloan gasped between clenched teeth. "Sandy, you've got to get me my medicine." He drew up his knees and curled into a fetal position.

"So where is it?"

"At my boarding house. Sturdevant's. At 651 Fourth Street. *Oohhh!* Room 202."

"Well, I—"

"Sandy, I feel like I'm *dyin.*' It's in a small bottle on the dresser. Blue stuff. It works quick."

"How do I get in?"

"My jacket," Sloan replied, indicating the jacket which Tilton had hung on the back of the chair. "In one of the pockets. Night key and my room key. *Nnhhh*!"

"All right." Tilton found the keys and grabbed his hat. "Be right back. If you get any worse, you know where the bathroom is."

"You're a true friend, Sandy."

Sloan arose quietly when he heard Tilton go down the stairs, his feigned malaise gone. Putting his ear to the room door, he heard the front door close. Going to the closet, he removed the items on top of the box containing the pistol. He took everything—gun, balls, powder, caps. From his pants pocket he then withdrew the note he had written in his own room earlier, and left it on top of Tilton's dresser. He put on his jacket, walked quietly down the stairs, retrieved his valise and coat from the dimly-lit parlor and put the pistol and its ancillary items into the valise, picked up his hat and left. Less than three minutes after Tilton had left by the same door, Sloan was walking south on 7th Street.

He was not afraid of running into Tilton, who was headed east. Nor was he afraid of meeting any ruffians who might lurk about the gas-lit city. He had a serious knife inside his coat and a big pistol in the valise, just inches away from his fingertips. Even unloaded, the gun would be intimidating in the evening darkness. Striding purposefully, keenly aware of his his surroundings almost as if he had a supernatural sense of perception, he felt so full of fierce energy it seemed as if he must glow in the dark. He was armed, determined, focused, *dangerous*, a man on a mission from God and for God—if

God there be—to smite the iniquitous betrayers of the United States and to help slay the monstrous abomination of slavery.

He was Cutter Cutler again, the scourge of slavery, an avenging angel of John Brown. He was ready to do to others what he had done last night.

He strode across Pennsylvania Avenue, across Constitution Avenue a block farther, then another three blocks to Independence Avenue, where he paid no attention to the seductively crude invitations of an evening courtesan. Angling to the southwest, he approached the bank of the Potomac at 14th Street, where the wooden Long Bridge spanned the river.

There were no sentries.

Sloan calmly walked across. In half a mile, he was in Virginia. He had met no one else crossing the bridge in either direction.

He breathed deeply when he stepped onto Virginia soil. Tilton would have returned to his boarding house by now and, because of the note, discovered the pistol missing. Yet Tilton could have no idea where Sloan had gone, since he was obviously not at his own boarding house. The brief note Sloan had left mentioned no destination. The last place Tilton would think of—or suggest to authorities, if he should report the missing gun—was across the river in a seceded state. A *slave* state, and Tilton knew how much Sloan hated slavery. Though he was technically in enemy territory, paradoxically Sloan felt safer. Besides, he was closer to his objective.

The Potomac flowed almost due south at this point. Sloan knew that Alexandria was several miles to his left, farther south along the Virginia shore. Going inland a short distance, he found a road, which he took towards Alexandria. He did not know exactly where Lee's estate was, nor did anyone of whom he had made discreet inquiries. However, it had to be somewhere close by. Someone in Alexandria would surely know.

The night was cool but not cold, a fine night for brisk walking. In little more than an hour Sloan reached Alexandria, where he checked into the first hotel he found. He boldly signed "Joshua Cutler" in the hotel registry. A few minutes later he was stretched out on a bed on the third floor. His pocket watch showed a little past 10:30.

Although he had done a great deal of walking this evening, Sloan did not feel tired; he felt exhilarated. After eighteen months of lying low, keeping his nose clean, saying, "yes, sir," and "no, ma'am," to everyone in sight, he was ready. He had watched, listened, and learned in the nation's capital, and knew the way to strike a massive blow. Hard, clean, fast, and alone.

Tomorrow he would rent a horse, buy some supplies, ride out to Lee's estate, and shoot him. He would then ride northwest to Harpers Ferry, about 45 miles from Washington—a day's ride. He could cross the Potomac into Maryland there. Unless the army sent a telegraph signal to Harpers Ferry, he would be there before the news of Lee's shooting even reached there. To make sure, he could even cut the telegraph wires somewhere along the way. And the army couldn't possibly know who had done it. From Harpers Ferry northward it was 30 miles to the Pennsylvania border. If there were some problem at Harpers Ferry, he would continue northwest; Maryland was even narrower there. Once in Pennsylvania, he would be safe.

Pennsylvania! The very thought of it gladdened his heart, even if he hadn't been there in years. Great stone houses, fertile fields of rich earth, gently rolling hills. Forsythia, lilacs, and daffodils in spring, crisp snow in winter, spectacular trees in autumn, the greenest of grass in summer. The occasional sleet storm in winter which transformed everything into a dazzling crystal fairyland. Philadelphia with Independence Hall, the Liberty Bell, the busy Delaware, the lazy Schuylkill, and roasted chestnuts for sale on every street corner at Christmastime.

Home.

The tiniest part of Sloan's mind regretted leaving Meagan O'Connor just as a relationship seemed to have begun. Perhaps he could write to her from Pennsylvania…

Sloan fell into a troubled sleep, his dreams an incongruous mixture of peaceful green fields, violent death, and sparkling golden corn-silk curls dancing in a spring breeze.

CHAPTER 43

Sunday
The Executive Mansion
9:16 PM

"Father, come to bed."

Abraham Lincoln stopped pacing the bedroom floor, lowered the sheaf of papers in his hand, and kindly regarded his wife. She was in bed, reading a book, the lamp on the bedstead beside her turned low. "Is that a direct order, Mother?"

"Indeed it is," Mary Lincoln smiled. "I'm the only person in the world who *can* give you orders, so I might as well." Her face and tone became serious. "You've only been president for six weeks, and already I see changes in you. You cannot ruin your health, Father. You will be no good to anyone, especially the country, if you do. It is after nine o'clock. Can't those reports wait until tomorrow?"

Lincoln sighed. "I suppose they could. They are estimates from the War Department of troop strength available from the various states. They even include estimates of troops available to the Confederacy from the southern states. I really need to know this information for the Cabinet meeting tomorrow."

"I'm sure you do. But why pace the floor? Just get in bed and read them here."

The president gave in. "You're right, my love." Mary could be pleading, petulant, snobbish, and even imperious at times, and Lincoln did not want to set off any of her moods. He turned up the lamp on his side of the bed and climbed in. The sheets were cool but not cold. He wriggled his toes in contentment. "Winter's over, and spring is here. Isn't it pleasant to lie in a bed without frozen sheets? It makes such a difference."

"Yes, it does," Mary agreed. "We had best enjoy it while we can. In a few months it will be summer. You know how beastly the summer heat is in Washington. I'm sure I will find it frightful."

"Not like Illinois, is it?" Lincoln ruminated. "Wonderful summers there, but colder winters. Actually, the winters here are not so bad, so I'm told." He had been a one-term congressman a decade earlier, but had never actually spent a winter in Washington. "You're right about the summers here. Too hot. Perhaps we should have two national capitals; Boston for the summer, and some place in Florida for the winter. How would you like that?"

"Father, really. Be serious. Besides, Florida's in the Confederacy now."

"So it is," Lincoln agreed ruefully. "I wonder if there's any place in this country—or even the world—with an ideal year-around climate. Perhaps some tropical island in the Pacific. Or California. I've heard some interesting things about California from several people who have been there."

"California? You would actually want to go to *California*?"

"Of course. A strange land that now belongs to us. I would love to visit it. The farthest west I have ever been is the Missouri River. That's hardly even half way." Lincoln folded his hands behind his head, resting them on the pillow. "Perhaps some day we could build a railroad to California. Then you and I could travel there in civilized comfort, and in just a few days. Wouldn't you like to do that?"

"California? Humph!" Mary Lincoln gave a noise which would have been considered a snort in a person less concerned with the appearances of gentility. "A ragamuffin land that even the

Mexicans had no use for. Now it has the dregs of the earth, all scrabbling after gold. You have to cross a thousand miles of desert just to reach it. Why would you want to go *there*?"

"Oh, I don't know." Lincoln gazed unseeingly up at the ceiling. "Travel. Adventure. Something new, a place I've never been. The Pacific Ocean. The call of the great unknown."

Mary put down her book and turned to face her husband. "Father, you simply must put such romantic notions out of your head. Do be serious. You're the president now. You simply cannot go gallivanting off on a trip that would take months."

"Of course not," the president replied easily. "That's why I'd like to build a railroad there."

"Oh, Father." Tears of frustration welled up in Mary's eyes.

"There, there, Mary." Lincoln held her hands. "I've been teasing you. You know me. Big dreams. I've always had them. So have you. Now look at us. We're in the Executive Mansion. Haven't our dreams come true? Isn't this what we wanted? Hasn't the Almighty been good to us?"

"Yes. Yes, He has." Mary wiped away her tears. "Except for Eddie." Eddie was their second-oldest son, who had died ten years ago. Mary still grieved for him.

Lincoln held her close. "Hush, hush, Mother," he said, gently rocking her. "We have been blessed with three more sons. Three *wonderful* boys. You are a wonderful mother. And I love you very much."

Mary's tears became ones of relief. "Oh, Father, I know you better than anyone, yet often I cannot tell when you are serious and when you are not. We have been married for more than fifteen years, but sometimes you seem like a stranger to me. I cannot follow you. Especially when you dream your dreams and tell your jokes."

"Yes, I know. Sometimes I have trouble following them myself." He stroked her dark hair. "Now I find I need them more than ever. They help to blunt the harsh reality, the staggering situation which seems to grow worse every day. The Confederacy was formed before I became president; I could do nothing about it. After I became president and had some control—or so I thought—my worst fear was that Virginia and the Upper South would secede and then join the

Confederacy, doubling its size. If only I could have kept the Confederacy its original size! I would have done anything to have kept the Upper South in the Union! And now my worst fears have been realized. The most important job I had was to keep the Union together as best I could. I couldn't. I feel like a failure. That's why I dream dreams of the West, and California, and a railroad to reach it—anything that smacks of a great peacetime vision, something unifying, something worthwhile. Not the horrors of war staring us in the face."

"You couldn't help it, Father. It was not your doing. You didn't fire on Fort Sumter. And you could't give it up. You didn't want war with the South. They did it. You cannot blame yourself for everything just because it didn't turn out the way you wanted it."

"Yes, Mother, I know." Lincoln patted her hand comfortingly. "Thank you. But I still *feel* it. Now we will face a much larger Confederacy. I think even Maryland might have seceded if we did not have a strong military presence there. You know what happened in Baltimore on Friday. Nine civilians and four soldiers killed when rioters attacked a Massachusetts regiment on its way here. Thank God they're here now. Think of it! We might have been an isolated speck of the Union here in Washington, surrounded by a sea of Confederacy."

"Father, you must be so very careful. Nothing so stirs up passion like this business of states' rights and secession. I fear for you so. You have very little protection here. Why, this very afternoon Tad heard the word 'assassination.' He even asked me about it."

"What? *Assassination*? Where did Tad hear such a word as that?"

"He was playing outside Lamon's office; he said 'Uncle Hill' used the word several times talking with someone."

Lincoln's dark eyes expressed his concern. "Who was this someone? Did Tad see him?"

"It wasn't a man, it was a woman. Tad says she was a pretty lady."

"A *lady*?" Female visitors were rare in the Executive Mansion. "Does this lady have a name?"

"I don't know who she was. Tad didn't hear her name. He said she had dark hair. The important thing, Father, is that they weren't talking about you."

"Oh? That's a relief. How do you know that?"

"Tad says they were talking about somebody named 'Kernaly.' I never heard of any such person. Perhaps he heard it wrongly. At any rate, that couldn't possibly be you. For that I am profoundly grateful." Mary glanced at her husband, whose face was drawing into a frown. "Does that name mean anything to you?"

Lincoln pushed himself away from his wife and stared at her, his mind working furiously. *Kernaly?* He knew of no one with such a name, and he knew everybody Lamon knew. But—the thought jangled like a berserk bell—*could that possibly be "Col. Lee?"* So far as he knew, Mary did not know of the meetings he had with Frank Blair, and certainly did not know anything they had said in their discussion of Lee. Blair could be implicity trusted to maintain silence about the matter, and he himself had not said a word about it to anyone. However, he knew that somehow the word had gotten out about his indirect offer of command of the army to Lee; both Scott and Cameron had mentioned it to him. So far, he had not had to issue a public disclaimer about the offer, and wouldn't if he could avoid it. Had that knowledge, however imperfectly understood, somehow have triggered an assassination plot? Or was it all a mistake? Even the mischievous invention of an imaginative small boy? But surely not even Tad would have invented a story about a pretty dark-haired woman privately visiting Lamon in the mansion itself, would he? If it had been someone the boy was familiar with, he would have said so, perhaps even known her name. She must, therefore, have been someone he had never seen before. Who could she have been?

There was a quick way to find out.

Without a word, Lincoln rolled back his covers, leapt out of bed, picked up the lamp on his nightstand, walked over to the bedroom door and opened it, ignoring the cry of "Father!" from Mary. Ward Hill Lamon was asleep on a sofa just outside the door. He had begun this practice a little less than a week ago, shortly after the presidential call for 75,000 volunteers, saying that the president needed additional security, particularly at night, and that he, Lamon, would personally provide it. Lincoln mildly discouraged his old friend, but was secretly pleased that the tall and husky Virginian was so concerned for his personal safety.

Lamon was stetched out on the sofa, almost fully clothed, a pillow under his head and an afghan over his body. Lincoln gently touched his shoulder. "Hill! Wake up, Hill!" he said softly.

Lamon awoke to find the president of the United States in his nightshirt, leaning over him. "Mr. President! What is it?" He glanced quickly around the hallway. "Is something wrong?"

"Calm yourself, my friend. There is no danger. However, there may indeed be something wrong." He looked keenly at Lamon's face. "Hill, I need you to be fully awake. I want to ask you some questions. Are you up to it?"

Lamon sat up and threw aside the afghan. "Of course," he replied, rubbing his eyes and stifling a yawn.

Lincoln went over to a wall-mounted gas lamp, which had been set very low, and turned it up, brightening the hallway. He dragged a chair in front of the sofa and sat down in it. His shapeless nightshirt, with his long legs sticking out from under it, made him look more gangly than ever. "Hill, listen carefully. Did you have a visitor here today? A pretty woman with dark hair?"

"Yes, Mr. President." *How did Abe find out about that*, Lamon wondered.

"Who was she?"

Lamon thought for a moment. "Greenhow. A Mrs. Greenhow. I made a note of the spelling of her name, because it was unusual."

Mary Lincoln emerged from the bedroom, decently wrapped in a bathrobe and wearing slippers. She carried another bathrobe, which she proceeded to wrap around her husband's shoulders, and handed him a pair of slippers. "Thank you, Mother," Lincoln murmured, glancing up from the chair. "Had you ever met this Mrs. Greenhow before?" he asked, turning back to Lamon and putting on the slippers.

"No, never. I had no idea who she was. Do you know her, Mr. President?"

Lincoln shook his head.

"Mrs. *Rose* Greenhow?" Mary Lincoln asked quietly.

"Why, yes, ma'am," Lamon said, surprised. "Rose Greenhow. Is she a friend of yours? She didn't mention you."

"No, she's not a friend," the first lady replied slowly. "I have never met her. But I have heard of her." She turned toward her husband. "Mrs. Greenhow is a prominent socialite. She was a younger member of Dolley Madison's social set, and she is related by marriage to Senator Douglas. She is the widow of a Dr. Greenhow, a government linguist and lawyer. She hosts wonderful parties, I'm told. She is also a well-known Southern sympathizer, and was a great friend of the late Senator Calhoun."

Lincoln grinned broadly. "Bravo, Mother! I knew your fascination with society would pay dividends one day. You have certainly earned our government pay today."

"I also understand she is quite beautiful," Mary added with a touch of impishness. "Did you find her so, Mr. Lamon?"

"Yes, ma'am. She is attractive," Lamon admitted. For years Mrs. Lincoln had affectionately called him "Hill," as the president still did, but ever since the inauguration she had socially distanced herself from him—and everybody else—by using formal names. Mary's social pretensions annoyed Lamon, but he tried not to show it. He responded by calling her "ma'am" instead of "Mary," a distinction which she seemed to consider appropriate. "Quite attractive."

"All right, so we have a Southron socialite who comes to visit you on a Sunday, Hill," the president said. "A person you've never met, never even heard of, yet she wanted to visit you here, and on a Sunday. Most unusual. So what did she want?"

"She wanted to see *you*, Mr. President. She said she had something very important to tell you. Well, that's what everyone says who wants to see you. We can't let everyone in to see you just because that's what they want to do. When I finally got her to talk to me, she had some story about an army officer whom she said was going to be killed. 'Assassinated,' she said."

"What army officer?"

"Colonel Robert E. Lee, sir." Lamon glanced at the first lady, not sure of what she knew or was allowed to know. "The same man I investigated for you," he added in a lowered tone.

Lee! It was Lee! Lincoln stood up and slowly began pacing the hallway. "What did this lady tell you about Colonel Lee?"

Lamon seemed relieved. "She said many of the same things I already knew from the report. Lee has had a very distinguished career, and been in the army for a long time. The most interesting thing she said about him was that he was the officer in charge of the troops who captured John Brown at Harpers Ferry a year and a half ago. I didn't know that. I suppose I must have read something about it at the time, but I had forgotten it."

Lincoln stopped and faced Lamon. "*That* was the most interesting thing she said about Lee? Hill, are you sure? Did she say anything else about him?"

"Well, the man who was going to kill him—*supposedly* kill him—"

Lincoln held up his hand. "We'll come to that, Hill. Just a moment. Right now I want to be clear about exactly what this woman said about Lee himself. Can you think of anything else she said about him? Anything at all? Why, for example, she is so concerned about him? They are not related, are they?" He glanced at his wife, who shook her head and shrugged.

"I don't think they are related, either, Mr. President," Lamon said, taking his cue from the first lady. "I don't know that for certain, but she said nothing about any relationship. I don't know exactly why she is so concerned. And, no, I can't think of anything else she said specifically about him."

Lincoln resumed his pacing. *So Hill doesn't seem to know about the offer, and I know Mary doesn't. Question: does this Mrs. Greenhow know? Is that why she came here? To save the man who might lead the army? But she is a prominent Southern sympathizer. Why would she want to do that? What's the connection?* Aloud he said, "All right, Hill. So who did she say wants to kill Lee?"

Lamon rose from the sofa. He had removed his boots, vest, and tie, and his shirt was open at the collar. He had intended to arise later and change into proper night clothes. "Somebody named Rufus Sloan, sir. Works as a clerk in a general store here in town."

"A *store clerk*? Hill, why would a *clerk* want to kill a distinguished army officer?"

"Yes, sir, that's what I thought. It sounds a little crazy. Mrs. Greenhow said it was because this Sloan had been at Harpers Ferry. He was one of John Brown's gang, but somehow escaped. The raid was a failure, and Brown was hanged. Since it was Lee who captured Brown, this Sloan blames Lee for Brown's death, and wants to avenge Brown by killing Lee." The words tumbled out of Lamon, as if he were anxious to be rid of them, almost embarrassed that he lent any credence to them.

Lincoln stopped pacing and faced Lamon. "Hill, that's even crazier. Harpers Ferry was a year and a half ago. Even if this clerk were there, and even if he hated Lee, why would he wait to kill him *now*? Why not a year or more ago?"

Lamon blew on his fingers to warm them. "I asked Mrs. Greenhow that same question, sir. She said it was because Lee was on duty far away most of the time. Only recently has he been home, and Sloan just found out about it."

Lincoln started pacing again. "Well, that part's true enough. Lee was stationed in Texas recently. He returned when that state seceded. And that was only two months ago. He's been home less time than that."

"Mrs. Greenhow said some more things, Mr. President. She said this Sloan was not only with John Brown at Harpers Ferry, he was also with Brown in Kansas in 1856, when that gang killed five people. He used a different name with Brown: Joshua Cutler."

"So which one is his real name?" the president asked in exasperation.

"She thinks Sloan is, sir."

Lincoln shook his head. "Hill, did this woman say how in the world she knows all this information about this supposed raider? Does she know him personally? If so, why didn't she reveal him earlier?"

"She said she does not know him personally, Mr. President. She got the information from a friend, who does know him personally. And she only just learned it. She said she had known this information only six hours when I talked to her this afternoon."

The president stopped pacing and slowly rubbed the back of his neck. "I've heard some tall stories in my time, as you well know, Hill. This one, however, takes the cake."

"Yes, sir. That's why I didn't tell you about it right away. I wanted to do some checking. The Attorney General says he has no record of a Harpers Ferry raider named Joshua Cutler. Or Rufus Sloan, for that matter. Even if this story is true, you are not the one threatened, so I didn't think you needed to know. At least not right away."

"So Bates hasn't heard of him, either," Lincoln muttered. "Mother," he said suddenly, "I know you never met this Greenhow woman, but what have you heard about her? Her personality, I mean. Is she someone likely to invent such a story? Does she have a reputation for flightiness?"

"Not at all," Mary Lincoln answered firmly. "Just the opposite. Everyone who knows her says the same thing: she is shrewd and highly intelligent. Even cold and calculating, some say." She turned to Lamon. "Mr. Lamon, you say she came to see the president. What did she want to see him for? What did she want my husband to do?"

"Good question," Lincoln put in, back to pacing. "What did she expect me to do, Hill?"

"Arrest Sloan," Lamon replied simply. "And protect Lee. She seems to think there may be more than one person involved, though she's not sure. She was very disappointed that she couldn't get the Secretary of War to protect him."

"What?" Lincoln stopped again. "She's been to see Cameron?"

"Yes, sir. Saw him earlier today, before she came here. Told him the same story. He said he couldn't protect Lee, because Lee resigned his commission just yesterday. Moreover, Lee lives in Virginia, even if it is only a few miles from here. Cameron told her it was not part of his duty to protect private citizens in seceded states."

"So then she came here?"

"Yes, sir."

"Let me completely understand you, Hill. She came here, trying to save Lee from this John Brown raider, *after* Cameron told her Lee had resigned from the army?"

"That's what she said," Lamon nodded.

Lincoln put both hands to his head as he continued pacing. *Now what? Why would a calculating Southern-leaning socialite go to such great lengths to save Lee—even if she somehow knew about the offer—and then continue with her efforts even after she learned he was* <u>*not*</u> *going to lead the army? In fact, had left the army altogether?* He knew he could not let anything happen to Lee, even if he was no longer in the army, now that the news of the offer had somehow leaked out—people would assume the presidency had something to do with it. Then, in order to deny it, he would *really* have to go public about the offer. He hated that thought.

"I'm trying to figure out this woman's motives, Hill. Not having any luck. Mary says she's not stupid, not flighty, but she's obviously very determined. She's a Southern sympathizer, which means the likes of you and me must be poison to her. Yet she comes here, right into the lion's den, talking to any important person she can find—including me, if she could have reached me—all because she wants to save a relatively obscure officer. And from someone we never heard of, and who may not even exist. Why? I cannot help but feel I'm missing something important here, and it bothers me."

"Could they be friends?" Mary volunteered. "They are both socially prominent. Maybe they know each other from social functions. Perhaps she's doing it simply to protect someone she knows and admires."

"She say anything like that, Hill?"

"No, Mr. President. Nothing."

The president scratched his chin. "I suppose something like that is possible, Mother. However, I happen to be familiar with Lee's record, as I had the opportunity to review it recently. He's rarely been home. And when he is home, he has a big estate to maintain. He's also happily married, with a number of children, so there isn't a romantic liaison. I think it's much more likely that he and Mrs. Greenhow have never even met. Which, of course, only deepens the mystery."

"There's more, sir. Mrs. Greenhow said that she had been informed that two men had been killed last night on E Street. Knife wounds. She said that this Sloan was the one who had killed them."

"*What?* He killed two men *last night*?"

"That's what she said, sir. She apologized for not being able to confirm it, as nothing had appeared in the papers at the time she talked to me. I hadn't heard any such thing, either. So I contacted the police. Sure enough, two men *had* been killed last night. Their bodies were found on E Street, between 2nd and 3rd, right where Greenhow stated it had happened. And they had died from slashed throats. One of them had been mutilated."

"Mutilated?"

Lamon glanced at the first lady. He then walked over to the president and whispered in his ear.

"Good God!" Lincoln exclaimed. After a moment he asked, "Did the police identify them?"

"Yes. They were local ruffians. They both had been in and out of jail a number of times. The police had no suspects, so I gave them Sloan's name and what information I had about him. So now the police are looking for him, too."

"Hill, we simply cannot afford to ignore this situation. If I've learned anything in life, it's that true stories are often stranger than fictional ones. And it does happen to be important to me. I cannot tell you everything right now, but I can reveal this much: I don't want anything to happen to Lee. I *really* don't. Now, then—tell me what you've done so far."

Lamon related the sending of two men to find Sloan and bring him in for questioning, using his authority as the Marshal of Washington and the information that Sloan was reportedly a Harpers Ferry raider and a fugitive from justice. He also said that he had sent a courier to notify Allan Pinkerton. "I hope that was all right, sir."

"Yes, yes, of course. Good thinking. How long ago was that?"

"Several hours, sir."

"Any reports yet?"

"None." Lamon did not volunteer the information that no one seemed to know Sloan's address, and that the agents would have to find that out on their own.

"Mr. Lamon," the first lady interjected, "did Mrs. Greenhow say when this raider was planning to strike?"

"Not exactly, ma'am, but she thought it might be soon. That's why she wanted to let us know as soon as she found out."

"Did she say *how* he planned to attack Lee, Hill?" the president asked.

"No, sir. Nothing."

"Hmm. Well, then, he might be planning to strike at this very moment, mightn't he?" Lamon nodded.

The president clapped his hands and then rubbed them together nervously. "All right, Hill, here's what we'll do. Until we have this person in custody and get the full story from him, we will operate as if he is already attempting to carry out his plan, whatever it is. Lee lives in Virginia. I would assume this fellow plans to attack him there somehow, as I am not aware of any plans Lee has to come to the city. Unless this Sloan knows more about Lee's movements than we do, I don't think he can plan on attacking Lee in Washington. Therefore he must cross the river to get to Lee. There are only two ways he can do that: by the bridges or by a boat. I want the bridges guarded. Not tomorrow morning, Hill; now. *Tonight*. Everyone—and I mean *everyone*, including women—who crosses the bridges will be questioned. Do we have a description of this fellow?"

"A general one, sir. Mrs. Greenhow provided it."

"Good. Make sure the bridge guards get it. I want the patrols around the Navy Yard doubled. Have them particularly look for anyone trying to steal a small boat, even a rowboat. I doubt he'd try to steal a boat from the Navy, but I don't want to overlook anything. Make sure the patrols have this man's description. And let's get some river patrols out. He may steal a private boat somewhere. He may even own one." Lincoln held up a warning finger. "However, these people are *not* to be told *why* they are to be looking for this person, unless you want to make up some reason. No word about the real reason."

"Yes, sir. I'll get on it right away."

Lincoln regarded his old friend warmly. "This looks like a long night for you, Hill. I'm sorry." He gestured to a room off the hallway. "You can use this room as your office, at least temporarily. Tomorrow's Monday. The usual crowd of office-seekers will be around, so an office on this floor will give you more privacy. Besides," he grinned, "you can still keep an eye on me from here."

Lamon grinned back. “Thank you, sir. By the way, do you want Col. Lee warned?”

The president hesitated a moment. “Good thought. I think not, Hill. We need to know more about this Sloan first. All we have so far to show that he is a former John Brown raider and a killer of two men last night is a Confederate sympathizer’s word. And that currency’s a little cheap these days. Now,” he added, “Mrs. Lincoln and I are going to retire, and I leave all this excitement in your capable hands.” The president and the first lady returned to the bedroom. At the door Lincoln paused, waited until his wife had entered, then closed the door and turned around. “Hill, when you catch this fellow, I want to know about it right away,” he said quietly. “The time doesn’t matter. Just knock on the door. Softly, my friend. We don’t want to upset Mother any further. She’s upset enough already.” With a final wink, he went inside.

CHAPTER 44

Sunday
Washington
9:31 PM

Allan Pinkerton waited patiently in the darkness, sitting at the foot of a tree in the front yard of Sturdevant's Boarding House on upper Fourth Street. Two agents from the Marshal's office were also here; one named McNeill was hiding in some bushes and the other, Howard, was boldly sitting in a chair on the porch.

This case had intrigued Pinkerton immediately when Ward Lamon had described it to him. He decided to handle it himself, rather than delegate it to one of his agents. It reminded him of the assassination plot against President-elect Lincoln he had uncovered on the train journey from Springfield to Washington less than two months ago, which he had foiled by changing the train's schedule through Baltimore.

Lamon had told him of the two plainsclothesmen had had assigned to stake out Sloan's residence. He surprised Pinkerton by revealing that he didn't know where the residence was, which meant the two agents didn't, either. They did, however, know the name of his employer, so they spent time in city postal records looking up

Amos Grinell; Rufus Sloan was, as they had expected, not in the records. They then went to Grinell's house and questioned him.

Pinkerton was more direct. He went straight to Grinell's Goods, used his comprehensive set of skeleton keys to let himself in, lit a lantern, rifled the files in the office, and found Sloan's address. He was not in the least afraid that a policeman might investigate and question him, for he had immense powers. As a reward for thwarting the Baltimore assassination plot (and to thwart others), Lincoln had arranged an Army commission for him under the fictitious name "Major E. J. Allen"; he reported directly to the War Department, from which his reports went directly to the president. His duties: he was in charge of all counterespionage activity in the District of Columbia and the immediate area. Since Lamon was the Marshal of the District, the two of them sometimes worked together.

At the boarding house Pinkerton talked to Mrs. Sturdevant, a widow, and confirmed the fact that a Rufus Sloan was indeed a boarder there. However, he was not home at present, a fact which Pinkerton had Mrs. Sturdevant confirm by opening his room and letting it be examined. She numbered her rooms, like a hotel; Sloan rented room 202. Mrs. Sturdevant's description of Sloan matched Lamon's. Pinkerton also learned that there were six other boarders, two of them women; in his meticulous way, he made notes of their names and descriptions. He had a keen eye and a razor-sharp memory, yet he still made notes. He was thus quite prepared when Howard and McNeill eventually showed up. The three men had talked quietly and briefly; Pinkerton informed them that Sloan was not there. They would wait for him.

The Scottish-born detective shifted his position. He had been under the tree for two hours. Dozens of people had passed on the street in that time, but only two had entered the boardinghouse; neither was Sloan. Pinkerton pulled out his pocket watch. By the light of a pale moon filtered through the tree branches, he could see that it had been fifteen minutes since the last person had passed on the street.

Pinkerton did not doubt that Sloan would arrive, sooner or later. This was where the suspect lived. Tomorrow was a Monday, and Sloan had to be at work. That meant he soon had to be home to get a good night's sleep. It would be only a matter of time. It always was. Pinkerton yawned. He shook his head to clear it, then stopped and listened intently. He heard footsteps, sounding unnaturally loud in the stillness of the night.

Someone—almost certainly a man—was walking north on Fourth Street. Pinkerton could hear him before he saw him. The footsteps were hesitant. An old man? As the person stepped into the flickering glow of a street lamp, the detective could see that he was a man, but not an old one. He also wasn't Sloan—too tall, too broad of face, light hair. He was looking at the buildings on this side of the street—slowing down, peering, speeding up. There were many boarding houses in this part of the city, all just a bit seedy. This person seemed to be looking for a particular one.

The man stopped right in front of Sturdevant's. After examining the building a few moments, he walked up the brick pathway to the front door, illuminated by a small gaslight, and nodded wordlessly to the agent in the porch chair. He opened the door with a night key, stepped inside, and closed the door.

None of the agents made any move toward him, for he obviously wasn't their quarry. Pinkerton, however, noticed that this man did not fit the description of any of the boarders. Yet he had opened the door with a key, so he couldn't be a mere visitor. Besides, it was too late for visiting. Who was he?

A few minutes later the same man came out the front door, carrying a small object in his right hand. This was too much. Pinkerton confronted him on the brick walkway.

"Good evening, sir. Might I ask who you are?"

The startled man was taken aback. "I could ask you the same question, friend. Who are you?"

"Major E.J. Allen, United States Army," Pinkerton answered easily. "Special operations. These men are my associates." He gestured to the two agents approaching them. "We are investigating a series of robberies that have taken place in this area recently."

"Army?" the man said dubiously. "You're not in uniform."

"I'll be happy to show you my authority, sir, if you wish. Now, then—what's your name?"

"Tilton," the man said reluctantly. "Benjamin Tilton."

"Well, Mr. Tilton, you're not a boarder here, are you?" It was a flat declaration, not a question.

"No."

"Then may I ask what you're doing here?"

"Picking up some medicine for a friend." Tilton displayed the object in his hand, which was a small bottle.

"This is not an apothecary shop," Pinkerton said crisply. "How did you know there would be medicine here?"

"It's for my friend. It's his. He lives here. He's sick."

"And he gave you his key?"

Tilton nodded.

"How do we know you're telling us the truth, Mr. Tilton? How do we know you didn't murder this man, rob him, find his key, and come here to loot his room?" Pinkerton put asperity into his voice.

"Really, Major," Tilton smiled easily. He held up the small bottle again. "Does this look like loot? I tell you I have a friend who is sick. He gave me his key and told me to come here to pick up this bottle of medicine. I've never been here before. It took time to find this place."

"Who is this person?"

"Rufus Sloan," Tilton answered quickly. Out of the corner of his eye Pinkerton saw the two agents exchange significant glances. "He really does live here. Room 202. Look, he gave me the key to his room, too." He reached into a pocket.

Pinkerton instantly pulled out his two-shot derringer and covered Tilton. "Hands up!" he shouted. "Search him!"

One of the agents searched Tilton from behind. "No weapons." He looked at the objects in his hand. "A lot of keys."

"Explain the keys," Pinkerton demanded.

"The ones on the ring are mine," Tilton said. "The other two are the ones Rufus gave me. One is the night key, and the other is his door key." One of the two loose keys was clearly stamped "202." "I'm not a robber. I'm just trying to help a friend."

"Where is this Rufus Sloan now?"

"He's at my place. He really is. He's sick. He needs this medicine."

"So you've told us. Now you need to show us. I warn you, it will go very hard on you if you're lying. We have a low tolerance of robbers. Where do you live?"

"A boarding house. At 426 Seventh Street."

"Good. Then that's where we'll go."

It took twelve minutes for the four men to walk to Tilton's boarding house. The trip was almost completely in silence. Pinkerton did not want to start a gabfest with someone who could be a suspect in a serious crime. Tilton could be an innocent friend of Sloan's, but he could also be an accomplice. Pinkerton knew he would arrest Tilton and thoroughly question him, but he didn't want to tell him that now. He was the avenue to Sloan.

"Where is your room, Mr. Tilton?" Pinkerton asked briskly as they approached the boarding house.

"Second floor." Tilton replied. "Front room on the north side of the hallway."

"All right, here's what we'll do. You will precede us. You will open the door to your room. If it is locked, we will use your key. You will not say anything unless you are spoken to. We will follow you into your room. Where was Sloan when you left?"

"On my bed. He was in pain."

"You may give him a dose of the medicine. Then we will take care of him. No talking."

Using a key from Tilton's ring, McNeill opened the front door. The four men wordlessly went up a stairway to the second floor, and stood behind Tilton as he tried his door. It was unlocked. He opened it and went inside, and the three agents rushed in after him.

A quick search revealed that Sloan was not there. McNeill went down the hallway to the bathroom; it was unoccupied.

Tilton sat on the bed, the three agents around him. "Where is he?" Pinkerton asked peremptorily.

"I don't know, Major. Really I don't. He was right here when I left him half an hour ago."

"Maybe he's visiting someone else in the building," Howard suggested. "Maybe he got so sick he went to the manager's apartment. We can quickly find out."

"How many times has Sloan been here before today?" Pinkerton asked Tilton.

"Only once. Last Friday."

"Did he meet anyone else here?"

"No. It was just the two of us."

"Then I don't think he would be visiting anyone else here," Pinkerton said to the agents. "If he really isn't here, I'd rather not alert the manager that we're looking for him. Search this room."

Howard and McNeill had scarcely started the search when Howard handed Pinkerton a scrawled note. "You'd better read this, Major. It was lying on top of the bureau."

Sandy,

Thanks for the loan of your equipment. I'll return it when I'm finished.

Cutter

Pinkerton showed Tilton the note. "Who's Sandy?"

"That's me." Tilton pointed to his tawny hair. "It's always been my nickname."

"Who's Cutter?"

"That's Sloan, sir. That's what we called him—" Tilton stopped short.

"Yes? Who's 'we?'"

Tilton lowered his head and did not answer.

"Why did you call him 'Cutter,' Tilton?" Pinkerton pursued. Still no answer. "Is it because his name was *Cutler*? *Answer* me!"

Tilton's head snapped up, his eyes a mixture of fear and fury. "What is this equipment you loaned him?" Pinkerton shouted.

"I didn't loan him *anything*," Tilton shouted back. "And I don't know—wait!" He suddenly stood up, went over to the closet, and looked under the hats and gloves piled on the top shelf. "It's *gone*! He *took* it!"

"*What's* gone?"

"My *gun*!"

"Your *gun*? You had a *gun* here? What kind of gun?"

"A *pistol.* I bought it last week. I plan to join the army volunteers. I knew the army would provide me with a musket, but not a sidearm unless I was an officer. I thought a sidearm would be nice. So I bought one at my own expense. A new Remington revolver."

"Are you saying that Sloan took your pistol?"

"Yes. He must have. It was right here in the closet. The supply of balls, powder, and caps are gone, too."

"Did he know it was there?"

"Yes. I showed it to him when he was here on Friday. *Damn.*"

Pinkerton did not know that Tilton was planning on joining the army—if it were true. That would help his case, but he would still be arrested.

"How big is this pistol, Mr. Tilton?"

"A .44 caliber. What they call the Army Model."

"Six shots?"

Tilton nodded glumly.

Pinkerton inwardly winced. A new pistol big enough to blow a hole in a man. There was no time to lose. Lamon must be informed immediately. Sloan had a half-hour head start. And now he was armed.

CHAPTER 45

Monday, April 21
Arlington House
8:17 AM

Robert E. Lee gathered his family together in the family parlor, adjacent to the dining room. Breakfast had been served a bit earlier today, for Lee and Cosby had to leave for Alexandria. Cosby waited in the white parlor, across the central hallway, as he did not wish to intrude on this family gathering.

"My dearest family," Lee began, "you all know why we are here. The governor has requested to see me in Richmond. Mr. Cosby and I will leave shortly. Mr. Robertson, the governnor's emissary, will meet us at the Alexandria depot and accompany us to Richmond. Thanks to our cousin John Lloyd and his wife, I know why the governor wants to see me: he will offer me command of all the military forces of the state. And I must tell you all this now: if he does, I have decided to accept. I really do not see how I could do otherwise."

Silence initially greeted this revelation. All present were aware, to one degree or another, of the huge price their family might well have to pay for this decision.

"You know we all support you, father," Custis said strongly. "You need never fear on that account."

"Yes," echoed Mary assertively, as if she were the appointed spokesperson for her three younger sisters. Agnes and Mildred were starting to cry silently. "And we're more than supportive of you, father. We're very proud of you. And we always will be."

"Thank you, my children," Lee said with misty eyes. "I need that approval for the long road ahead, which may be very hard. And I am very proud of every one of you."

"I wanted us to say our farewells in this room," he continued, "because this is my favorite room in the entire world. As you know, your mother and I were married in this room. A few months from now—June 30—will mark the 30th anniversay of that occasion. I pray that there will be a way that we can all be here again on that date. For I have known for 30 years a simple truth: that was the best day of my life. I have made some wrong decisions in my life, but the best decision I ever made—the best decision of my life, no matter how long that may be—was the one to seek the hand of Mary Anna Randolph Custis in marriage. And the greatest honor ever bestowed upon me was her decision to accept."

All eyes in the room converged upon Mrs. Lee, sitting in a chair with her walking sticks leaning against it. Custis was the first to stand and start clapping, followed immediately by the rest of the family.

Lee came over and sat beside his wife, taking her hand. "Do you remember that day, Mary? All that rain?"

"How could I forget?" Mrs. Lee replied in a voice with a slight quaver. "It rained so hard that we couldn't see the river at times. And it kept up." She looked lovingly at her husband. "I confess, Robert, that there were times that day that I briefly entertained the notion that the Almighty might be displaying His displeasure at our union by sending so much rain."

Lee laughed. "But of course you quickly banished such thoughts from your head."

"Of course. I wasn't about to let a little thing like a flood ruin our wedding day, especially since it had taken so long to convince father that you were really the man I wanted to marry. He didn't cotton to that notion right away, did he?"

"No, he certainly didn't," Lee laughed again. "His only daughter, the grandest belle in Virginia, marrying a man with no land or money? And an army officer at that? He was afraid that I would never be home, would care more about military rank and promotion than you, and might get shot in action or even scalped at some frontier outpost." He patted his wife's hand. "You must have been a persuasive talker, my love."

"I was," Mrs. Lee agreed with a smile," but it was worth it."

Lee turned to his children. "The funniest part of our wedding was what happened to the clergyman. What was his name again, Mary?"

"Keith," she answered, smiling. "Reverend Mr. Ruel Keith."

"Yes, that was it. The Reverend Keith. Since the ceremony took place here, and not in a church, and since he did not have a carriage, he arrived here by riding a horse. In that torrential rain he was soaked to the skin. Naturally he had to have a complete change of clothes. Mr. Custis loaned him some clothes, but the two men were quite different in size, and the tall Reverend Keith had to conduct the ceremony with his limbs sticking out in a most undignified manner. He was a bit embarrassed, but we all took it in excellent humor."

None of the Lee children were crying now. They were listening with rapt attention to the recount of their parents' wedding in this very room, although they had heard it before.

"And all those guests!" Lee continued. "Most of them stayed here an entire week."

"That was the custom for grand weddings in those days," Mrs. Lee said. "And that wedding was nothing if not grand. There were parties every night. As I recall, the punchbowl was in heavy use that week."

"Ah, the punchbowl. The one with the painting of a ship on its inside." Lee chuckled. "Your father never tired of telling everyone that it came from Mount Vernon, and was the same punchbowl George Washington used to entertain his guests. Yes, it did see heavy use that week. Fortunately it survived, and we still have it." Lee looked around at his six children. "It is my fondest wish that some day it will see heavy use here again when you are married. Rooney was married at Shirley, which was certainly no bad choice. However, I like to think that some of you might wish to be married here."

There was a chorused murmer of agreement.

"Ah, well, I forgot why we are here." Lee rubbed his forehead. "We cannot dwell too long in the past, pleasant though it may be, when we have such an uncertain future facing us. We must ask God's blessing and protection upon all of us. I have given a little thought to the best prayer, and I can think of nothing more appropriate than the 91st Psalm. I will read it."

Lee walked over to a nearby table, picked up a copy of a bible, and opened it to the proper place. Several of the girls knelt.

Ye who dwell in the shelter of the Most High,
Who abide in the shadow of the Almighty,
Say to the Lord, "My refuge and my fortress,
My God, in Him will I trust."

For He will rescue thee from the snare of the fowler,
From the perilous pestilence.
With His pinions He will cover thee,
And under His wings thou shall take refuge;
His faithfulness is a buckler and a shield.
Ye shall not fear the terror by night,
Nor the arrow that flies by day:
Nor the pestilence that roams by darkness,
Nor the destruction that lays waste at noon.

Though a thousand fall at thy side,
Ten thousand at thy right side,
Near thee it shall not come.
Rather with thine eyes shall you behold and see
The requital of the wicked.

Because ye have the Lord for your refuge,
Ye have made the Most High your stronghold,
No evil shall befall thee,
Nor shall affliction come near thy tent;
For He has given His angels charge over thee,
That they guard thee in all thy ways.
Upon their hands they shall bear thee up,
Lest ye dash thy foot against a stone.
Ye shall tread upon the asp and the viper,
Ye shall trample down the lion and the dragon.

Because he clings to Me, I will deliver him;
I will set him on high because he acknowledges My name.
He shall call upon Me, and I will answer him;
I will be with him in distress;
I will deliver him and honor him;
With a long life will I gratify him,
And show him My salvation.

"Thanks be to God. Amen." Lee closed the bible and set it aside. "And now, my children, come to me for my blessing, for I do not know when we shall meet again." He placed his hands on the heads of each of his children individually and prayed a simple personalized benediction for each of them. His hands rested longest of all on the head of his wife and his benediction lingered. At its end he bent over and lifted her up into a long and deep embrace; she kissed him on his cheek.

"Goodbye, my family. I will write to you with instructions from Richmond." Lee turned and walked out of the parlor and out of the front door. Daniel was waiting with a trap, which he had already loaded.

Annie flew across the hallway and into the arms of Cosby in the white parlor. They kissed passionately, and did not care who saw it. "I'll write you," they both murmured at the same time.

Cosby then said goodbye to each of the members of the family. He joined Lee in the trap, Daniel flicked the reins, hands everywhere waved farewell, and the vehicle slowly rolled away from Arlington.

CHAPTER 46

Monday
Alexandria, Virginia
8:20 AM

Rising early, Rufus Sloan carefully loaded the pistol the way Tilton had showed him. He was careful not to put a firing cap on the nipple of the cylinder under the hammer so that an accidental jolt would not cause the gun to fire. Pulling the trigger would cause the barrel to rotate to the next cylinder, which would fire.

He then took a blank sheet of stationery paper provided by the inn, folded it, and placed it in an envelope, also provided by the inn. After sealing the envelope, he wrote "Col. Lee" on the outside. Careful to preserve the envelope from wrinkling, he placed it inside a pocket of his coat.

He ate a good breakfast at the inn, knowing he might not have a chance to eat again for some time.

Sloan then rented a horse from a livery stable in Alexandria. He insisted on, and got, a Western saddle. He stated that he would need it for only one day, and signed a paper that he would return it by 10 AM the following day. Since he was unknown in the area, the stable required payment in advance. He did not mind; he had no intention of returning the horse. Riding a short distance to a general store, he bought some essential equipment and just enough food for two days.

The stable manager knew the way to the Arlington estate. Just to make sure, Sloan also asked at the general store; the directions agreed. It was approximately six miles north of Alexandria, near the bank of the river; there were no other houses near it. Sloan realized that he had actually been much closer to the estate when he crossed the bridge last night than he was now, but didn't know it at the time.

Sloan rode slowly out of the town. The road north was clearly marked; it was the same road by which he had come into Alexandria last night. There was very little traffic.

Approximately two miles outside of Alexandria a trap approached from the opposite direction. It was driven by a black man, obviously a servant. Seated behind the driver were two white men. One was an older distinguished-looking man with grayish-white hair; the other was a younger man with dark brown hair. As they passed, the older man smiled slightly and raised his hand in a little wave. The other man did not wave, but studied Sloan distantly. Sloan gave the trap only a passing glance.

Shortly afterward, making sure there was no traffic on the road in either direction, Sloan rode off the road into the shade of a thicket of trees. He took a small canvas bag he had bought at the general store, looped its cord around the saddle horn, and put the revolver into the bag. Next to the revolver he placed the envelope. This allowed him to take off the long coat he was wearing, and in the pocket of which he had carried the gun. He did not think couriers wore long coats. He rolled the coat up and fastened it behind the saddle. He then practiced what he intended to do when Lee approached him: hold out the envelope, and then, when Lee took it, quickly draw the pistol from the bag and shoot him at point-blank range. Lee would be facing him with his arm out. He could not miss from a distance of a few feet. One .44-caliber bullet in the chest would kill Lee, or any man. He would then gallop away, his identity unknown.

Ten minutes later he rode up to the impressive front portico of Arlington House. As soon as he saw it, he knew this must be the Lee mansion; there was nothing else like it anywhere near it.

The raised floor of the portico gave him pause. He could not actually ride up the several steps onto it; no courier, or anybody else, would do that. Yet to knock on the front door he would have to dismount. How could he pose as a courier while carrying a canvas bag? Unless he brought the bag, he would not have the gun.

The front door opened, and a well-dressed black man came out. “May I help you, suh?”

“Good morning. Is this the residence of Colonel Lee?”

“Yes, suh, it is.”

“I’m a private courier with an urgent message for him. Could I see him, please?”

“I could take it, suh. I’m the butler.”

“Thank you, but I was told to make sure I delivered it personally into his hand. I was also told it is extremely urgent. I must insist.”

The butler appeared uncertain. “Will you wait here a moment, suh?”

Sloan nodded. The butler disappeared inside, swinging the door behind him but leaving it slightly ajar. A minute passed. Sloan’s heart was thumping so loudly in his chest he imagined everyone in the house could hear it. His right hand, resting lightly on the saddle horn, was only inches away from the opening of the small canvas bag. He fidgeted, trying to ignore the majesty and wealth of this great house, steeling himself to do this act against the great slave-owning traitor.

The front door opened. Sloan’s hand moved closer to the bag opening. A handsome well-dressed young man of about thirty years of age, clean-shaven and with close-cut rich brown hair, moved towards him. He stopped several feet from Sloan.

“May I help you?”

Sloan stared. Surely this person could not be Colonel Robert E. Lee? Lee was in his fifties.

“A private courier, sir. I have an urgent message for Colonel Lee. I was ordered to deliver it to him personally.”

“You may leave it with me. I’m Custis Lee, the Colonel’s eldest son. I am in charge of the estate while my father is away.”

“The Colonel is not here?”

"No, he is not. However, if the message is that urgent, I can arrange to have it sent to him."

Sloan's heart sank. "Where is he? Perhaps I could reach him."

Custis smiled tolerantly. "I doubt it. He is on his way to meet with the governor in Richmond. He left some time ago to catch a train in Alexandria."

The trap!

"Mr. Lee, was your father riding in a trap? With another man? Driven by a servant?"

"Why, yes, he was."

Sloan spun the horse around and sped off.

"What about the message?" Custis called out.

Sloan didn't hear. His horse was already at full gallop.

CHAPTER 47

Monday
The Executive Mansion
8:42 AM

"Any luck, Hill?"

Abraham Lincoln had seated himself in a chair in front of Lamon's desk, far enough from it so that he could stretch out his long legs. He briefly noted the sensation, now unusual for him, of sitting in front of someone else's desk, rather than having people sit in front of his.

"Some, sir. Not as much as we'd like. Sloan has not returned to his boarding house. It's on 4th Street. Last night we arrested a friend of his who approached the boarding house with some story that he wanted to enter Sloan's room to get some medicine. The friend's name is Tilton—Benjamin Tilton. He claimed Sloan was sick over at his own residence, and had sent him over to Sloan's residence to pick up the medicine."

"Was there actually such medicine?"

"Yes, sir. A bottle of it in Sloan's room. We're now checking through lists of doctors and apothecary shops. When we find the right ones, maybe we can learn more information about Sloan."

"I see. What about this friend? I presume you searched his residence."

"Yes, sir, we did. Last night Allan Pinkerton and two of my men accompanied him there. It's a boarding house on 7th Street. A nice one, so my men say. He appears to be financially comfortable. Sloan was not there, but a note from him to Tilton was."

"So this Sloan fellow has slipped away?"

"So far, sir. However, there's more to Tilton's story. He claimed he recently bought a new pistol—a big one, a .44-caliber Remington Army Model revolver. He showed it to Sloan last Friday night. Now it's gone, along with caps, powder, and balls. He says Sloan stole it."

"*Stole* it? Mmm. What do you think of that story, Hill? Sounds just a little too pat. Why, for example, would he have bought such a gun in the first place? And if he did, how do we know he didn't buy it specifically *for* Sloan? Maybe he's part of a conspiracy."

"Yes, sir, that's what we're thinking. Tilton says he bought the gun because he wants to join the army, and knew the army would not issue him a pistol unless he were an officer. Being a man of means, he simply bought one for himself." Lamon caught Lincoln's sideways glance. "Yes, sir," he continued ruefully, "I know it's a fishy story. We checked on the army angle. There's no record of anyone named Benjamin Tilton having recently signed up. But Tilton did not say that he *had* signed up, only that he *intended* to. I know, I know—how do you prove or disprove an *intention?* Tilton emphatically states that he did not buy the gun for Sloan or loan it to him, and has no idea why Sloan stole it. Maybe he's telling the truth. Yet the note we found at his residence indicates that perhaps he *had* loaned it to Sloan. His story is full of holes. We're holding him indefinitely until we can sort it out."

"Good. Now what about this Sloan fellow himself? He hasn't shown up at his own residence, and he wasn't at his friend's residence, either. That means he's been out somewhere else all night. It is now nine o'clock in the morning. Since you are sitting here looking so glum, that must mean that he also hasn't shown up at the place where he works, for you surely have one or more men there. He should have reported for work an hour or so ago. Is that right?"

"Unfortunately it is, sir. We have two men at the general store where he works. Nothing yet."

"Any activity on the river? Any boats reported stolen?"

"None, sir."

"How about the bridges? Are they guarded?"

"Since 10:30 last night, Mr. President. Double patrols, all bridges, both ends. I should mention that since the action of the Virginia Convention in Richmond became widely known on Saturday, the bridges have had little traffic. Very few Virginians seem to want to come to Washington, and few Washingtonians want to go there."

"Regrettable, but understandable, Hill. However, that means that if this Sloan person tried to cross a bridge, he would be easily spotted."

"Exactly, sir."

"Has he any other friends?"

"The owner of the general store was quick to say that a certain young woman ate lunch in the store with Sloan almost every day."

"Aha! Now we're getting somewhere. A girl friend?"

"We think so. Her name is Meagan O'Connor. She is a seamstress at a custom apparel shop half a block away from the general store. We questioned her little more than an hour ago, when she showed up for work. She had dinner with Sloan on Saturday evening. Our biggest concern was that perhaps Sloan spent last night with her, and that was why he did not appear at his own residence. She emphatically denied that, said she has not seen him since Saturday evening, and has no idea where he is now. We checked on that; sent an agent to her house. She lives at home with her parents on 2nd Street. She has no brothers or sisters. Her father wasn't there; he was at work in his leather business, down near the Navy Yard. We have an agent talking to him now. Her mother confirms that O'Connor was home all last night, and Sloan was not there. The mother met him only once, when he came calling to take her daughter out for an afternoon stroll Sunday a week ago. She doesn't know where he could be, either."

"Well, this store clerk seems to have turned into a rather elusive character. Are the police also looking for him?"

"Yes, sir, they are. They're concentrating on hotels, inns, and hospitals, the latter in case Sloan was wounded and entered for treatment. Nothing yet. Their manhunt is becoming intensified because we were able to verify, just this morning, that Sloan was indeed the killer of the two men Saturday night. This O'Connor woman was with him at the time; she is an eyewitness. She was the source of Mrs. Greenhow's information; she stated that she told Greenhow about it yesterday morning."

"All right, that little information gap is now cleared up. Good work. If we didn't know it before, we surely know it now—this man is extremely dangerous. And now he's got a new Army Model pistol, as if his knife weren't enough." Lincoln paused. "I've been thinking, Hill. You, Pinkerton, and the police seem to have the city covered like a wet blanket, yet Sloan is still at large. He seems to have vanished. I find the fact that he did not report for work today to be highly significant. Perhaps he is not in the city at all. We know his target is Lee. Do you think it is possible that he is *already* across the Potomac and that his plan of attack is *already* in operation?"

"I hate to admit it, Mr. President, but I do think that is possible."

"Then I suggest we ought to do something about protecting Lee directly."

"Sir, how can we do that? Virginia has seceded. We can't send anybody over there. And how could we induce Lee to come here?"

"Not so fast, my friend. You and I are both lawyers. Let's take a lawyerly view here. The Virginia Convention voted for secession last Wednesday. Technically, that vote was an *advisory* vote. It will not actually become official until the Virginia legislature ratifies it, or a statewide vote of the people ratifies it. No one doubts that the convention vote *will* eventually be ratified, but until it is, Virginia exists in some sort of legalistic and constitutional gray area. Let us take advantage of that temporary confusion in statecraft to send over a group of soldiers to guard Lee's house until this Sloan fellow is arrested. If they find Sloan there, the soldiers can arrest him themselves."

"Soldiers, sir? That sounds like real trouble to me. Suppose they end up clashing with the Virginia militia? A great many people would interpret the presence of even a small number of U.S. soldiers in Virginia as the start of a great invasion."

"Courage, my friend. We wouldn't be sending many, we wouldn't be sending them far, and we wouldn't be sending them for a long time. You do expect to catch this Sloan fellow soon, don't you?" Lamon grimaced slightly and shrugged. "Well, *I* think you will. Now, imagine what will happen if this fellow, who is successfully eluding us at the moment, does manage to get to Lee and succeeds in killing him. Can you imagine the uproar that would ensue? A violent *abolitionist*, a *John Brown raider*, kills the very man to whom I offered command of the army?"

Lincoln looked sharply at Lamon. "You do know I did that, don't you?" Lamon nodded. "Don't worry about it, Hill. I don't mind you knowing, but it seems too many people already know about it. *Everything* would come out if Lee is harmed! He is a prominent Virginian who declined that offer; that alone will make him a hero in the South. Many people would say that we deliberately put this Sloan up to the killing of Lee. And if we didn't do that, how come we were unable to stop him? How could a John Brown raider have lived right under the government's nose for a year and a half and *we didn't even know about him*? If Lee is killed now by this Sloan, he will become a Southern hero of mythic proportions. His death could conceivably become the single greatest rallying point for the Southern cause, and unify them more than anything else imaginable. It would not matter what happened to Sloan afterward. It would be the martyrdom of Lee that people would remember, not the fate of a store clerk. *This must not be allowed to happen*, Hill. I cannot emphasize that enough. Sending a few soldiers over to his house for a day or two seems to me to be infinitely preferable to having him die because we did not take sufficient precautions."

"All right, sir. We'll do it."

"Good. Now prepare a brief order to General Scott. I would suggest no more than a platoon. I would also suggest that they be cavalry. Sloan's plan of attack might involve a horse, and I would not want him to get away because he had one and our soldiers didn't."

"Very good, sir."

"And don't forget to include a description of Sloan."

"No, sir, I won't."

"When you're finished, bring it to me and I'll sign it. Then you can rush it right down to the War Department. I'll be in my office, talking to people who want to feed at the public trough. *They* never seem to be hard to find."

Lamon grinned widely. "Yes, sir."

CHAPTER 48

Monday
Alexandria
9:07 AM

Robert E. Lee and Carter Cosby got out of the trap, took some of their luggage, and walked into the depot of the Orange & Alexandria Railroad. Daniel followed with the rest of their luggage.

At the ticket booth Lee and Cosby bought through tickets to Richmond. This would necessitate a change of trains at Gordonsville, as the Orange & Alexandria Railroad, the route of which ran into Virginia to the southwest of Alexandria, did not go to Richmond; at Gordonsville they would change to the Virginia Central Railroad.

Their tickets purchased, Lee and Cosby stood in the depot, with Daniel and their luggage nearby. Since Alexandria was a terminus of the Orange & Alexandria Railroad, outbound trains did not arrive from another station; they were made up in Alexandria's extensive rail yards, which also served several other railroads. Their train had not yet arrived from the yards.

A man approached. He introduced himself as John Robertson, the governor's emissary. Lee introduced Cosby, and the three chatted together for several minutes.

With a hissing of steam and a soft chuffing, the outbound train rolled into the depot and stopped. Daniel turned over the luggage to the porter, received the claim checks, and gave them to Lee and Cosby. Robertson and Cosby stood respectfully aside as Lee and Daniel made their farewells.

The three passengers then boarded the train. Lee and Robertson automatically sat together, talking about affairs in Richmond. Since the seats could only fit two abreast, Cosby was content to sit several rows back, on the opposite side of the aisle.

A lathered horse arrived at the depot. The rider leaped off, quickly threw several loops of the reins around a hitching post, and raced to the ticket booth.

"Does this train go to Richmond?" he asked, panting and pointing.

"Actually, it does not," the ticket agent replied with a smile. "Is that where you want to go?"

"Don't play games with me, man!" Rufus Sloan practically shouted. The ticket agent's smile vanished. "Yes, I want to go to Richmond," Sloan said, keeping his voice down with an effort. "What train do I take? I know there are several railroads around here."

"Sir, this is the Orange and Alexandria Railroad," the agent explained patiently. "It does not go directly to Richmond. None of the railroads in Alexandria go directly there. But if you want to go there, then this is the train you want. You will have to change trains at Gordonsville, to the Virginia Central Railroad. You can buy a through ticket here."

"Then that is what I want to do. Wait—have there been any other trains which left here recently?"

"All abooaard!" came the call from a conductor standing on the platform near one of the entrances to the coaches.

"This is the first train in an hour, sir."

"Good. How much?"

"Round trip or one way?"

"One way."

"One way through to Richmond, that'd be $4.85."

Sloan shoved a five-dollar bill at the agent. “Keep the change. And hold the train a moment—I have to get a few things from my horse.”

As Sloan vanished around a corner of the building, the agent slowly walked over to the conductor. “Hold the train a moment, Al. We got another *late* customer.”

“Well, tell ‘im to move ‘is butt,” the conductor replied acidly. “This ain’t no baby carriage out for a stroll. This is a *train*. We got a dam’ *schedule* to keep.”

CHAPTER 49

Monday
Arlington
9:18 AM

Lt. Andrew Kirby pulled his platoon of cavalry up in front of Arlington House and gave the order to dismount. After crossing the Long Bridge, his group of 24 horsemen had turned right and then inland. It did not take long; from the Virginia end of the bridge to Arlington House was only two miles.

They had encountered few people after crossing the bridge. Some had expressed surprise, even shock, at seeing them; other had smiled and surreptitiously waved their hands. Kirby was relieved that his orders did not include passing through any towns, just this open farmland.

A young man opened the front door of the mansion and walked out, over the floor of the portico, down the few steps to the lawn, and over to Kirby, who was obviously the officer in charge.

"Lieutenant, what is the meaning of this?"

The officer saluted. "First Lieutenant Andrew Kirby, Seventh Cavalry, sir. Whom do I have the honor of addressing?"

"Custis Lee, Lieutenant. I am the eldest son of Robert E. Lee. I am myself an officer in the United States Army, as was my father, until his recent resignation."

"Yes, sir, we know. You are a first lieutenant, as I am. Your distinguished father was Superintendant at West Point and a colonel until his resignation. It is because of him that we are here."

"What do you mean?"

"Sir, I have an order signed by General Scott himself that we are to throw a protective cordon around this residence in order to intercept a man who is trying to assassinate your father."

"*What*? Kill my *father*?"

"Those are my orders, Lieutenant Lee. It is only temporary, until this man is caught. Government agents are looking for him right now. So are the police, because he is suspected of killing two men in the city Saturday night. He is armed and dangerous. We have information that he wants to kill your father. There may even be several others involved."

"But why in the world—"

"Sir, I do not know. I have my orders. Now I know that your father has resigned his commission, and is no longer in the army. It would surprise no one if you yourself soon did the same thing. However, at the moment you are still in the United States Army. Besides my own orders, I have orders for you from General Scott: you are to cooperate with us. The general—and, I was made to understand privately, even the president himself—are concerned about your father's safety." Kirby held out several papers to Lee. "Here. You may examine them yourself, if you wish."

Custis Lee took the papers, quickly read through them, and handed them back. "Well, this is certainly an unexpected development, Lieutenant. When you first described a cordon, it sounded suspiciously to me like a house arrest."

"I assure you that is not the case, sir."

"I believe you, and I thank you. I will be happy to cooperate. However, I must inform you that my father is not here."

"Not here?"

"No. He is not. You have my permission to search the house and the grounds, if you like."

"That will not be necessary, Lieutenant Lee. You are a fellow officer from a distinguished family. I trust you. Where is your father? I have orders to protect him."

"He left earlier this morning for Alexandria. He will catch a train for Richmond, where he will meet with the governor."

"Richmond?" said Kirby. "That's a hundred miles away. Well, that would certainly seem to put him beyond the reach of this fugitive. It would also seem to satisfy my mission. If you would be so kind, Lieutenant Lee, to put that information in a brief note, and then sign it and date it, I will take it back to the War Department so that everyone will be assured that your father is safe."

"I would be happy to do so. Just give me a moment."

Custis went back inside the house. The dismounted cavalry men quietly looked over this great house and the spectacular view, all of them wishing they could call such a place as this their home. "Don't bother electing me president, boys," one of them said. "Just make me a Lee. I'd rather live here than the White House." He was greeted by jeers and scoffing.

Custis Lee returned and handed a folded piece of paper to Kirby. "That should do it, Lieutenant. I have added an expression of thanks to the War Department."

Kirby saluted. "Thank you, sir."

Custis Lee returned the salute. "Oh, there is one more thing, Lieutenant," he added as Kirby mounted his horse. "My father has departed and is safe enough now, but this assailant you mentioned does not know this. If he is as dangerous and determined as everyone seems to fear, he may show up here after you and your men have gone. Perhaps you could give me his name and description so that I could recognize him if he does appear."

"A wise precaution, sir." Kirby gave Sloan's name, nickname, and general description. He noted that Lee's expression started to change as Lee heard the description.

"Long dark hair? Dark eyes? Thin build? Mid-twenties in age? By any chance, Lieutenant, does this man work as a courier? A mounted civilian courier?"

"A courier? No, sir. My information is that he works as a store clerk in the city. Hasn't shown up for work today. Why do...my God! Sir, has a courier fitting that description been here?"

"Not more than an hour ago," Lee exclaimed. "He asked for my father. Said he had an urgent message for him that had to be delivered personally. I told him the same thing I told you—that my father had left for the train station in Alexandria to go to Richmond. He immediately galloped off in the direction of Alexandria."

"Did you see this urgent message?"

"No."

"Did he give his name or offer any identification?"

"*No*. Good Lord, Lieutenant, it had to be him! He's going after my father at the *train station*!"

"I agree. Men! Mount up! We're going to Alexandria!" Kirby turned to Lee. "What station, sir?"

"The Orange and Alexandria Railroad. Its depot is near the intersection of Duke and North Fayette Streets. *Get him*, Lieutenant!"

Kirby gave a flying salute as the horsemen thundered off.

CHAPTER 50

Monday
Northern Virginia
9:31 AM

Rufus Sloan tried to make himself as comfortable as he could in the passenger car, but he was fidgety. He had managed to bring his rolled-up coat and the all-important canvas bag from the horse, which he had left tied up at the hitching post at the Alexandria depot. Somebody would eventually notify somebody else, and the horse would probably end up being returned to the livery stable from which he had rented it. He didn't care. He had something infinitely more important to think about. He was finally—*finally*—close enough to strike at Robert E. Lee.

The ticket agent had said this was the only train to have left the station in more than an hour. Presuming that this was the right railroad, then this *had* to be the train Lee had taken. Where, however, *was* he? Sloan did not know what Lee looked like. He had never seen a photograph of Lee, and certainly never met him in person. He had never met anyone who *had* met Lee. In all the times Sloan had thought about Lee he had mentally visualized him, but had no idea whether his mental picture of Lee was anything close to reality. The only description he had was the vaguest of generalities: a distinguished-looking man in his fifties. That could be almost anyone who was obviously not a young man.

Actually, Sloan had *seen* Lee. He had caught a glimpse of Lee in the trap he had passed on his way to Arlington. He had paid only the merest attention at the time because he had not known it was Lee, and his attention was focused on what he planned to do at Arlington. If only he had known! He could have shot Lee then and there, and been done with it! He would have had to shoot the other two men, too. The black man was obviously a servant—Lee's coachman—while Sloan had no idea who the other person had been, and could not remember anything about him except that he was not as old as Lee. It would not have mattered. He would have killed all of them. No witnesses, no clues. He would have been in Maryland before the day was old, and in Pennsylvania the next day.

Well, no use crying over spilled milk. The only detail he could remember from that inattentive glimpse he had of Lee in the trap was that Lee was a man in his fifties. He already knew that.

Sloan also knew that Lee was a colonel in the United States Army. That, in fact, was the way he had always visualized Lee: in uniform. Was it possible that Lee was in uniform on this train? If so, he would be instantly recognizable. However, the Virginia Convention had voted for secession; Sloan did not think a U.S. Army officer would wear his uniform while traveling in a seceded state. Moreover, he did not remember Lee wearing a uniform in the trap; that would have caught his attention.

That brought up another question, which Sloan had not much time to ponder during his mad dash from Arlington to Alexandria. Why was Lee going to Richmond? To see the governor, his son had said. Was this a meeting *requested* by the governor? Or was meeting with the governor Lee's idea? Either way, it raised a huge dark suspicion. Was Lee going to *switch sides* and offer his military services to his state, as so many other Southern-born officers had done? This suspicion, added to Lee's other crimes, sent Sloan into a black rage. He *had* to find Lee. And kill him.

Sloan decided to walk through the train. In addition to the baggage car there were four passenger cars, and they were nearly full.

The darkling specter of war had the effect of increasing the rail traffic, especially to and from the state's capital city; it was as if people wanted to get in a last bit of personal business before the huge storm burst, bringing about massive changes that no one could foresee.

Carefully folding his coat over the canvas bag so that the bag was hidden, Sloan left them on his seat. He walked to the very front of the first passenger car, turned around, and then slowly walked back through the train. He examined the face of every passenger, while trying not to be obvious about it.

When he reached the end of the last car, he stood looking out the window of the rear door at the receding train tracks. He had kept count of every face he had seen. Discounting the 12 women, there were 67 men on board. Absolutely not one of them was wearing a military uniform of any kind. He thought that possibly ten of them could be Lee.

Now what? He could think of nothing better to do than to rewalk the train again, this time paying particular attention to the suspects.

Returning to the front, he started again. He was halfway through the third car, and beginning to despair, when he heard a distinct voice behind him. "Pardon me, suh, but aren't you Colonel Lee?"

Sloan whirled around. A dozen feet from him, the head of a man on the right side of the train was leaning across the aisle. The man sitting across the aisle turned and said, "I am, sir."

The two men started talking, but Sloan didn't hear a word. He stood transfixed, his eyes glued trance-like to the face of the man whose indistinct visage had filled his dreams so many times. He felt as if he were in a dream right now. *Robert E. Lee was sitting only a dozen feet from him this very moment!* It did not seem possible—yet it was.

Sloan forced himself to tear his eyes away from Lee and look around. The aisle seat right next to him on the right-hand side of the train was vacant; the window seat was occupied by a well-dressed man dreamily gazing out the window at the passing scenery.

"Your pardon, sir. Is this seat occupied?"

The man turned. He was a well-formed man in his thirties, with short-cropped curly brown hair and blue eyes. "No, it is not," Carter Cosby smiled. "Please take it. I would be happy for your company."

"Thank you. There are a few items I have to get from my previous seat. I will be right back."

When he returned, Cosby noticed the canvas bag and the long outer coat, which the passenger folded several times before placing it over the bag, both of which he carried in his lap. During the folding Cosby caught a glimpse of the sheath of a large knife on the inside lining of the coat. Once settled, the passenger seemed intent on looking down the aisle of the railroad car.

"I'm Carter Cosby," Cosby said affably.

The passenger glanced at Cosby. "Cutler. Joshua Cutler," he said laconically. He then returned to staring down the aisle.

"Going far?"

"Richmond."

"Why, so am I," Cosby smiled. "Do you live there?"

"No."

"Ever been there?"

"No."

"Beautiful place. Interesting architecture. They—"

"Sir, I have never been there," Sloan said with a rasp of irritation, still looking down the aisle. "I am sure I will enjoy it." He paused. "Do I understand that in order to reach Richmond, passengers have to get off this train and then get on another one at some place called Gordonsville?"

"Yes, that is correct."

"How long does such a change of trains take?"

"Well, that depends. Sometimes the other train is not there yet. You have to wait for it. Other times—"

"How long does it *take*?"

"Fifteen minutes."

"Thank you."

Sloan pulled out the schedule he had obtained at the Alexandria station. It showed that the scheduled time for arrival at Gordonsville was 12:35. He then pulled out his pocket watch: it showed 9:44. So it was somewhat less than three hours to this Gordonsville. From a scheduling point of view, that seemed like the best place to strike. There would be lots of bustle, with people moving around and baggage being transferred. Best of all, Lee would be on the ground. He could walk right up to Lee, shoot him, and run away. Steal a horse, cut telegraph lines. It could be done.

There was one problem, a big one: he would be deep in Virginia. He would prefer to shoot Lee as soon as possible. He could not do it on the moving train. He would then be forced to make his way to the end of the rail car through a group of disturbed and outraged people—some of whom might be armed—open the car door, move down the steps to the edge of the car, and jump. He did not want to be slammed into a tree, rock, or telegraph pole at 40 or 50 miles per hour.

No, it would have to be at a station. Perhaps Lee would get out to walk around or visit a water closet. If Lee remained on the train while it was stopped, maybe he could shoot him and then run out of the stationary car. He decided the best thing to do would be to take advantage of any opportunity that presented itself at any station, with Gordonsville as the ultimate plan if nothing happened between here and there.

With the plan settled, Sloan leaned back with a degree of satisfaction, still keeping an eye on Lee.

"May I make a suggestion?"

It was that idiotic window-gazer again. Didn't the man have anything better to do? "Yes?"

"You don't have to carry that coat and bag in your lap all the way to Richmond. You can put them under the seat."

"I prefer to carry them."

"Just trying to help."

"Thank you."

Sloan looked at the schedule again to see what the next stop would be.

It was a place called Manasses Junction.

CHAPTER 51

Monday
Alexandria
9:48 AM

The Union cavalry detachment drew up at the Orange & Alexandria station with a great clatter, scattering scores of pigeons into the soft spring sky. The ride through Alexandria had made the horsemen nervous. Virginia was not part of the Confederacy—yet—but every one of the troopers was aware what the state militia had done at Harpers Ferry and Gosport recently, and did not relish a possible encounter with them.

Lt. Andrew Kirby dismounted and strode purposefully into the depot, accompanied by his second-in-command. They ignored the glances and stares from people in the building and walked up to the ticket agent. "Lieutenant Andrew Kirby, United States Cavalry," he announced briskly. "We are seeking an armed and dangerous man. He is a fugitive from justice. We believe he came to this station less than an hour ago. We would appreciate any information you can give us. Then we will leave."

The agent, an older balding man, regarded the officers skeptically. "The United States Army is seeking someone? A runaway soldier, perhaps? What concern is that of ours? Why should we help you?"

"He killed two men in Washington Saturday night."

The agent shrugged. "If that's true, go to the police. It's not our business."

Kirby knew that he could not go to the Alexandria police. Even if he did, the local police would refuse to cooperate and would notify the nearest Virginia militia post as soon as possible that there was a detachment of U.S. Army soldiers in Virginia. He also knew that the ticket agent knew this.

"May I ask your name, sir?

"Wilson. Donnie Wilson," the agent said reluctantly.

"Well, Mr. Wilson, let me ask you a question. Do you know of Colonel Robert E. Lee?" Kirby did not mention that Lee had resigned his commission two days ago. He did not think that was common knowledge yet.

"Colonel Lee? Yes, I do," the balding agent said defensively. "Everybody in Alexandria does. We're proud of him. He's our neighbor, and comes into town regularly when he is home. He is one of the finest men who ever walked the earth."

"My sentiments exactly, sir." The agent blinked in surprise. "Have you ever met him personally?"

"Why, yes. Several times. Right here."

"Good. Then you know that he must have been here less than an hour ago. He was going to Richmond. Was he here?"

"Well…" The ticket agent looked about himself nervously. Everybody in the station was looking at him.

"Thank you, Mister Wilson. He was. Now listen carefully. The man we are seeking was going to attack Colonel Lee. He is very dangerous. So I have to ask you: was there any kind of an altercation here in the station? Was Colonel Lee attacked in any way by a young thin-faced man with dark hair?"

"No," Wilson said emphatically. "There was no commotion."

"So Colonel Lee boarded the train safely?"

"Yes. Yes, he did," the agent admitted. "He boarded with two other men, but he had been talking quietly with them, right here inside the station, for some time before the train arrived. No one attacked him."

"Good." Kirby sighed with relief. "So the train departed on schedule with Lee safely on board. That's what we wanted to know."

"Yes." The balding agent smiled for the first time with these officers. "Well, not *quite* on schedule. We had to hold it up a minute or two for some late passenger. Came galloping in here on a horse—wait a minute! What did you say this man looks like?"

"Young, thin-faced, dark hair, dark eyes," Kirby said quickly.

"Why, that's him! It musta been! His horse is still here! What kinda man would leave a perfectly good horse tied up while he takes a train to Richmond?"

"Someone who doesn't need it any more," Kirby snapped. "To *Richmond*, you say?"

"Yes. Through ticket."

"My God!" Kirby slapped his forehead. *"He's on the train with Lee!"*

"What's going on here?" a stentorian voice called out. A big man with a florid face and a curly crop of reddish-brown hair was striding across the floor, pushing past groups of waiting passengers.

"Lester Ebert," Wilson whispered quickly and quietly to Kirby. "Station master. Hard-ass."

Station master Ebert came up to Kirby. "Who are you?' he demanded belligerently.

"Lieutenant Andrew Kirby, United States Cavalry," Kirby answered calmly. "I understand you are the station master."

"That's right. And I don't want the likes of you in here."

Kirby ignored the hostility. "Good. You can help us."

"I don't want to help you. Clear out."

"Do you want to help Colonel Robert E. Lee?"

"Colonel Lee? What's he got to do with this?"

"We understand the colonel boarded a train here less than an hour ago. We are pursuing a known killer who is attempting to kill him. We just came from Arlington. The colonel's son confirmed that this man had been there, then came here. Just this minute we learned that he is on the train with the colonel."

The station master glanced over at the ticket agent. "That right, Donnie?" Wilson nodded.

"I might add," said Kirby, "that this man is one of the John Brown raiders who escaped from Harpers Ferry."

These words had an electrifying effect upon the listeners; the name of John Brown was anathema in Virginia.

"John Brown?" Ebert's exclamation was a mixture of awe and hate. "One of his gang is on the train with Colonel Lee?"

Kirby and Wilson both nodded.

"Gawd A'mighty! What can we do?"

"What time did that train leave?" Kirby asked quickly.

"'Bout 9: 20," Wilson said.

"And what time is it due in Richmond?"

"Lieutenant, there seems to be some confusion about our trains," Wilson commented. "The Orange and Alexandria Railroad does not go to Richmond, which is almost due south of here. It was originally built between here and Orange, which is to the southwest. Later it was extended to Gordonsville, which is the next stop after Orange. To reach Richmond you must change trains at Gordonsville to the Virginia Central Railroad. I had to explain this to that man you're chasing, too."

"Gordonsville," said Kirby. "How far away is that?"

"About 75 miles as the crow flies. Eighty-four miles on our tracks," said Eberts, now becoming animatedly involved.

"And what is the scheduled travel time between here and there?"

"Three hours and ten minutes."

Kirby looked at the large wall clock that was a standard fixture in all railroad stations. "It is now shortly after ten o'clock. The train has therefore been on its way more than 40 minutes. That means it is about a quarter of the way to Gordonsville, maybe a little less. How many stops are there between here and Gordonsville?"

"Eight, Lieutenant." Ebert started to name them, but Kirby held up his hand. "That's all right. I don't need to know their names. I just wanted to know how often the train will come to a stop. We believe that this man will strike at Lee, otherwise he would not have made such an effort to get on that train. The question now is: where will he do it? I don't think he will try it between stations, because then he would be trapped on a moving train with no means of escape."

"That would mean one of the stations," Wilson interjected.

"I think so," Kirby said, "but which one? Mr. Wilson, are you sure that you explained to him that Richmond-bound passengers must change trains at Gordonsville?"

"Indeed I did, sir. I distinctly remember because he was quite rude about it."

"All right. He knows Colonel Lee is going to Richmond because Custis Lee told him so at Arlington. From you he knows all Richmond-bound passengers must physically change trains at Gordonsville. Therefore there is going to be some confusion at that station. Passengers will be changing to go to Richmond and other points on the Virginia Central Railroad. Passengers from Richmond and those other points will be changing to come here. Baggage will be loaded and unloaded. It will also be the only time during Lee's entire trip to Richmond that we know for sure—and the killer knows—that Lee will be on the ground. Yes," Kirby said with finality, smacking a fist into his other hand, "that's where I think he's planning to strike." He glanced at the wall clock again. "That gives us some time. We don't want to wait until the train reaches Gordonsville before taking action—that's too long a time. He might strike earlier. Lee might get off the train at an earlier station just to stretch his legs for a few minutes, and the killer might take the opportunity to strike then. Mr. Ebert, exactly where do you estimate the train is right now?"

All the men looked at the clock. "Between Fairfax and Manasses Junction," Ebert said after a moment. Wilson nodded.

"Manasses Junction. Does the train stop there?"

"Yes," Ebert replied. "There's a junction with the Manasses Gap Railroad there."

"And how far away from Manasses Junction would the train be now? In time?"

Ebert squinted. "Twenty minutes or so. That about right, Donnie?" Wilson nodded again. "All right. That means it should arrive at about 10:25. Do you have a telegraph here, Mr. Ebert?"

"Yes. Of course."

"Good. Then here's what I think we should do. Telegraph the station master at Manasses Junction. Inform him that Colonel Lee and an assassin are both on the same train that's due to arrive there at 10:25. Include the assassin's description; Mr. Wilson has it. Have the station master notify the police to be there at the station and intercept this man before he can harm Lee."

"Sounds good to me," Ebert said. "We'll get right on it. Donnie—"

"Um, pardon me, Lieutenant," Wilson said slowly. "I hate to be a spoilsport, but do you really think that anybody near Manasses Junction is going to arrest this man just because we send a telegram from here? He may be wanted for some crime in the city of Washington, but that won't cut any ice in Virginia. Even if the police down there or anywhere else catch him, they won't send him back up here and turn him over to the Washington police. Not now. As far as threatening the colonel, all anybody there will have is our telegram, and all *we* have is your word. A *Yankee's* word, beggin' your pardon. I ain't no lawyer, but that don't seem like much proof to me, even if it's true. They may just turn him scot-free."

"Thank you, Mr. Wilson, for pointing that out," Kirby responded calmly. "They will *not* turn him free if you include in the telegram the information that he is a John Brown raider. Remember that the surviving raiders were tried in a Virginia court for crimes against the state of Virginia. He is therefore already wanted by the state. For good measure, you can advise the station master there to notify the nearest post of the state militia. They would certainly want him, regardless of what the police do."

"That'll help," Ebert said eagerly. "Manasses Junction's a purty small place. Not much police around. But the militia—they'll get 'im. I'll get that telegram sent off right now. C'mon, Donnie. I'll need that description." He stalked off.

Wilson said quietly to Kirby, "I do b'lieve you could charm the birds right outta the trees, Lieutenant." He winked. "Leave it to us. We'll take it from here."

CHAPTER 52

Monday
Manasses Junction, Virginia
10:26 AM

The Manasses Gap Railroad was an important part of Virginia's railroad system. From its western terminus at Harrisonburg in the magnificent Shenandoah Valley, the railroad went 50 miles northeast to Strasburg, them turned east through a gap in the Blue Ridge Mountains. Near Front Royal it crossed the fabled Shenandoah River, flowing north to join the Potomac at Harpers Ferry, forty miles away. The railroad continued almost due east through Warren County and then Fauquier County, passing through small towns such as Linden and Markham, and near to such delightfully-named prominences as High Knob and Big Cobbler. It then entered fertile level country—the plains of Manasses, a name derived from a local Indian tongue—and Prince William County before joining and terminating at the Orange & Alexandria Railroad at Manasses Junction, 60 miles east of Strasburg.

The Manasses Gap Railroad was the only railroad in an east-west direction across northern Virginia. Perhaps even more important than the flexibility it afforded passengers was the fact that it was the way that the agricultural products of the lush and lovely Shenandoah Valley reached markets outside the valley. From Manasses Junction passengers and produce, after changing to the Orange & Alexandria Railroad, could proceed northeast to Alexandria and Washington, or southwest to Gordonsville. After another change there to the Virginia Central Railroad, they could proceed further southwest to Charlottesville and Staunton, or southeast to Richmond. If they wished to go farther south, both Richmond and Petersburg, 25 miles south of Richmond, had extensive rail facilities which connected them with the entire South.

There was only a small town near Manasses Junction, although it was rich farming country and there were plenty of farmhouses. When the station master at Manasses Junction received the telegram from the Orange & Alexandria depot in Alexandria, he could not summon local police because there were none. However, because Manasses Junction was such a key point in the state railroad system, the Virginia militia had established a post not far from it. The militia had even equipped this post with a telegraph receiver, since the telegraph lines adjoining the railroads could easily be tapped and expanded to the post. Therefore the station master could, and did, send a telegram to the post. Since every farm in the South had one or more horses, there were nine members of the militia at the station when the train came into view. The commander of the unit, and several of his men, had uniforms; most of them did not, having been called rapidly from fields.

All the militia men stood with their muskets, lined up along the station's platform. There were no passengers mingled with them, as they had ordered all the passengers back inside the station building.

Many passengers noted the line of militia as the train slowed and pulled into the station. "Those look like militia!" a passenger cried. "What are they doing here?" Similar cries were heard from a number of other passengers.

Rufus Sloan heard the exclamations in his passenger car. Could it be that the militia was looking for *him*? How could that be possible? No one knew of his connections to John Brown, or involvement with what had happened in Washington the night before last—except Meagan O'Connor. He remembered only imperfectly what he had revealed to her, since he had been half-drunk at the time, but he knew he had told her to keep her mouth shut. Had she talked? To whom? The police? But why would militia in Virginia, a state which had just seceded, pay any attention to Washington police?

Sloan could not figure out how he had been discovered—*if* he had been discovered. Maybe the militia were here for a totally different reason. Maybe they were simply boarding the train to go somewhere else. However, if they *were* here for him, he knew this would be the last time in his life he could settle accounts, one and for all, with the man he hated most.

Sloan's hand moved under the folded coat on his lap and closed on the canvas bag.

Out of the corner of his eye, Carter Cosby was watching his neighbor with heightening interest. When this thin-faced young man had first seated himself, Cosby had tried to draw him out in conversation, for the man seemed rather ill at ease; he had been coldly rebuffed. He had seen this man walk slowly through the train several times after it had left Alexandria, seemingly scrutinizing every passenger, including Cosby himself. He had also seen him whirl around at the sound of some conversation behind him, stare fixedly at something or someone in the forward part of the car, and then seat himself in the nearest possible vacant seat, which happened to be the one next to Cosby. Most interesting of all, this Cutler had moved his possessions from a previous seat to this seat. That meant that he had originally taken another seat, then left his precious possessions in that seat while he walked through the train, apparently looking for someone. Those possessions, a coat and a small canvas bag, were so important to him that he was now holding them in his lap, and indicated he would do so all the way to Richmond. If they were that important, why would he have left them unattended in another seat while he walked through the train? More than once, in fact? And why change seats at all? It certainly had not been for a desire for conversation.

Ever since taking the seat next to Cosby, this man had stared straight ahead. Well, not *quite* straight ahead. Rather regularly he leaned his head out in the aisle, and always looked ahead. It was as if he wanted to constantly reassure himself that something—or someone—ahead of him in the car was still there. In a word, Cosby thought him "jumpy."

The last interesting fact Cosby noted was that this man was armed. He had caught a fleeting glimpse of a large knife in a sheath sewn on the inside of the coat when the man had folded his coat when first sitting in his seat—his *new* seat.

All in all, Cosby had concluded, this was a man who would bear watching.

As the train glided to a stop, Sloan cast aside the coat, stepped out into the aisle, and brought up the bag with his left hand while reaching inside it with his right. *"Colonel Lee! Do you remember John Brown?"* he screamed at the top of his voice. He withdrew the big .44-caliber Army Model revolver from the bag and pointed it down the aisle.

Carter Cosby launched himself from the train seat. His left hand closed over Sloan's right hand holding the gun, knocking it upwards. The gun went off, firing a bullet into the roof of the rail car. As the two men fought for control of the gun, cries, exclamations, and oaths erupted from the passengers, some of whom ducked down and others of whom stood up to see what was going on.

Using his left hand to aid his right hand, Sloan tried to pull the gun away from Cosby, a bigger and more powerful man. He succeeded in pulling the gun slightly to the left. The gun fired again, sending a bullet crashing through a window. Cosby's left hand was now firmly grasping the barrel of the revolver, preventing it from turning and therefore preventing it from firing.

A militia soldier appeared in the rear of the car. He raised his musket to shoot, but did not know whom to shoot; all he could see was two men struggling in the center of the aisle.

With his right hand Cosby reached back to the coat lying on the seat behind him. He reached inside it and found the haft of the knife.

Lee stood up and faced the struggling pair. "*I am Robert E. Lee*," he roared out over the tumult of the passengers. "Everyone get down now!" He pointed to the two men. "The one with his back to you tried to kill me with a pistol," he shouted to the militia man. "The other man is my friend. Be careful whom you shoot!"

The knife in Cosby's hand penetrated Sloan's bowels at the same time as the Minie ball from the musket penetrated Sloan's back and entered his heart. He collapsed on the floor as his life blood ebbed away and his heart stopped beating. His lips moved in some final words.

No one heard them in the general tumult and commotion.

"Who was he?" everyone asked.

No one knew. Neither the militia nor even the station master knew his name, for the telegram from Alexandria had not included that information. By the time the Alexandria station master and ticket agent had thought to ask, the Union cavalry group had left.

His name was not known for several days. By that time he had been buried in a potter's field. Even after his name became known, no one was sure it was the correct name. No relative or friend ever appeared to claim the body. No one attended the interment, no one mourned him. Only a few people ever claimed to have known him at all.

It was almost as if he had never existed.

CHAPTER 53

Monday
Richmond
5:42 PM

Robert E. Lee stepped out onto a balcony at the Spotswood Hotel. He waved to the large crowd below him, which cheered lustily. News of his arrival in the city, and then at the Spotswood, had spread like wildfire. Everyone, it seemed, had heard of his refusal to lead the Union army of invasion, followed by his resignation from the United States Army, and now his appointment to lead the military and naval forces of Virginia. A son of the finest family in the state, the very man picked by Abraham Lincoln to invade Virginia, would now defend Virginia! Surely this could be nothing less than a sign from God, many marveled. The huge crowd raised a cheer that could be heard at the Capitol building, up the hill at the top of Capitol Square, and they kept cheering long after Lee had disappeared back into the hotel. Richmonders slept more easily, more justified, and prouder that night than they had in a long time.

That evening Lee met with Governor Letcher where he was formally offered, and accepted, command of the military and naval forces of Virginia. His rank would be major general. The next morning he went right to work, opening a temporary office where he drafted his first order, announcing he had assumed command. He assumed that the private session with the governor was all that would be necessary in order to begin his new job, and was therefore a bit surprised when the Virgina Convention insisted on some more ceremony. Accompanied by four members of the convention, he entered the capitol building at noon on Tuesday, April 23. He insisted on stopping briefly before the famous marble statue of George Washington in the rotunda. He was then escorted into the Senate chamber, which was packed with convention delegates and other official dignitaries including the gnome-like Alexander H. Stephens, the vice-president of the Confederacy, who had come from Montgomery to, as he expressed it, "negotiate concerning all matters interesting to both republics." The mission of Stephens was crowned with success; that same day, April 23, the state government of Virginia entered into a pact with the Confederate States of America which approved its constitution and provided for a temporary union with it.

After a long and fulsome introduction by the president of the convention, Lee was formally presented to the massed represntatives of Virginia. Dressed in civilian clothes as there was no uniform yet ready for him, and not mounting to the speaker's platform but remaining standing the the aisle, he uttered a three-sentence speech so brief that many people there did not hear all of it.

"Mr. President and Gentlemen of the Convention,—Profoundly impressed with the solemnity of the occasion, for which I must say I was not prepared, I accept the position assigned me by your partiality. I would have much preferred had your choice fallen on an abler man. Trusting in Almighty God, an approving conscience, and the aid of my fellow citizens, I devote myself to the service of my native state, in whose behalf alone will I ever again draw my sword."

Carter Cosby was one of the people who heard every word. He applauded politely, unlike some of the raucous cheering around him, and sat back with a feeling of mingled satisfaction. He still thought that the Confederacy was an illogical and slapdash contrivance, although it was now clearly destined to become a larger one. He feared the massive war which seemed to loom so frighteningly and inevitably. He did not know how his personal relationship with Annie Lee would turn out. Yet he took a certain pride in the successful completion of a mission which had seemed so utterly impossible at first. It had enabled him to become a friend of the most remarkable person he had ever met. He had given his word, and kept it.

It was time to return to the wide fields and soft nights of Cymru. He owed Jefferson Davis some money. He would have to return it.

EPILOGUE

On Thursday, May 23, 1861, the citizens of Virginia, in a statewide public referendum, formally ratified the Ordinance of Secession voted by the Virginia Convention and made official the secession of Virginia from the United States of America.

Very early on the following morning eleven regiments of Union troops poured out of Washington and occupied everything of importance on the Virginia shore of the Potomac River near Washington. Three regiments crossed the Aqueduct Bridge, a bridge with a wooden superstructure on stone piers crossing the Potomac near Georgetown, which carried a Chesapeake & Ohio canal and allowed canal boats to cross the Potomac. These troops controlled the bridge, the area near it, and the road which led northwest to Leesburg.

Two regiments occupied Alexandria. One crossed the Long Bridge and marched south, entering Alexandria from the north by Washington Street. The other, under the protecting guns of the Union warship *Pawnee*, disembarked at daybreak from three steamers onto the city's wharves at the foot of King Street. The occupation of Alexandria was complete by 5:30 AM.

The remaining six regiments all crossed the Long Bridge, secured the bridge itself, spread out along the Virginia shore, and seized the Alexandria road and the Columbia Pike. They also seized the Virginia Heights, which included the Arlington estate and its mansion, Arlington House.

When the soldiers reached the house, they were greeted only by silence. The Lee family had gone, never to return.

AUTHOR'S NOTES

A Silence At Arlington is an historical novel which includes many historical characters and historical places. An addendum of author's notes is considered appropriate in a book of true history, but not in a novel, even one based on actual history. However, the ending to this book, although historically accurate, might understandably strike many readers as too abrupt, and almost begs an explanation. Where were the Lees, if they were not at home when their estate and mansion were seized? I sympathize, for I am both an historian and a novelist. Therefore I will make an exception to accepted literary practice and mention a few subsequent facts.

There was no member of the Lee family at Arlington when Federal troops arrived because the family had moved to Ravensworth, the Fitzhugh family estate in Fairfax County, Virginia. Later they moved to several other family-related locations in Virginia. In early 1864 the Lees rented a brick house on Franklin Street in Richmond, which was their official residence for the duration of the war.

The death toll of the Civil War was staggering, far more than either side could have possibly imagined when hostilities commenced in April, 1861. The cemeteries in Washington ran out of room to bury the bodies of Union soldiers, so the government started burying them on the Arlington estate.

Robert E. Lee never saw Arlington again after he left on Monday, April 22, 1861. After the surrender at Appomattox Court House on April 9, 1865, he lived in the rented house in Richmond. In September of 1865 he was offered the presidency of Washington College in Lexington, Virginia, and accepted. He and Mrs. Lee lived in a house on the campus.

Lee died in 1870 and is buried in a sarcophagus in the Lee Memorial Chapel at that school. After his death his name was added to the name of the school; it is now Washington and Lee University. His son, Custis Lee, succeeded him as president of the college, and remained in that position until 1897.

Mrs. Lee died in November, 1873, and is also buried in the Lee Memorial Chapel at that school. She returned for a brief visit to Arlington in 1873, a few months before her death.

After his father's death Custis Lee sued the government of the United States for wrongful seizure of the Arlington estate, which he would have inherited. The case went all the way to the United States Supreme Court, which in 1883 decided that the government *had* acted wrongly. The government settled with Custis Lee for $150,000, and continued the wartime practice of burying military dead there. The former Custis-Lee estate is now, of course, Arlington National Cemetery.

The Custis-Lee mansion, Arlington House, sits in the middle of the national cemetery. It has been lovingly restored and is a National Historic Site, administered by the National Park Service. Visitors are welcome. Its front lawn, the view from which is described several times in this novel, is, in my opinion, the most moving spot in the entire United States of America.